MANSLAUGHTER UNITED

MANSLAUGHTER UNITED

A Season With a Prison
Football Team

CHRIS HULME

YELLOW JERSEY PRESS
LONDON

Published by Yellow Jersey Press 1999

2 4 6 8 10 9 7 5 3 1

First published in Great Britain in 1999 by
Yellow Jersey Press
Random House, 20 Vauxhall Bridge Road,
London SW1V 2SA

Random House Australia (Pty) Limited
20 Alfred Street, Milsons Point, Sydney,
New South Wales 2061, Australia

Random House New Zealand Limited
18 Poland Road, Glenfield,
Auckland 10, New Zealand

Random House South Africa (Pty) Limited
Endulini, 5A Jubilee Road, Parktown 2193, South Africa

Random House UK Limited Reg. No. 954009
A CIP catalogue record for this book
is available from the British Library

ISBN 0 224 05151 2

Papers used by Random House UK Limited are natural,
recyclable products made from wood grown in sustainable forests.
The manufacturing processes conform to the environmental
regulations of the country of origin

Typeset by Deltatype Ltd, Birkenhead, Merseyside
Printed and bound in Great Britain by
Mackays of Chatham PLC

'We do not wish to abet confusion . . . The oppressor remains what he is, and so does the victim. They are not interchangeable, the former is to be punished and execrated (but, if possible, understood), the latter is to be pitied and helped; but both, faced by the indecency of the act which has been irrevocably committed, need refuge and protection, and instinctively search for them.'

– Primo Levi, *The Drowned and the Saved*

CONTENTS

ACKNOWLEDGEMENTS

I'm indebted to many people who helped this book on its way. These include my agent Caroline Dawnay, Clare Sparks at the Prison Reform Trust, Terry Allison and Colin Macey of the Postsmouth North End League, Jenny Hulme and Angus Mackinnon.

The account of the M25 case is partly based on the work of the BBC *Rough Justice* team headed by Dinah Lord and Elizabeth Clough. Elsewhere, Patrick Barclay's coverage of the 1990 World Cup in the *Independent* was inspiring.

Manslaughter United owes much to the vision and commitment of Rachel Cugnoni, who commissioned it, and whose revisions improved the original drafts, but it would not have been possible without the staff and inmates of Kingston Prison, Portsmouth, who spoke frankly and bravely about their lives.

AUTHOR'S NOTE

My visits to HMP Kingston were made between August 1997 and March 1998. The prison's football team, Kingston Arrows, trained on Thursdays and played league matches on Saturdays. There were 23 inmates and two prison officers in the full squad. I got to know some of them very well. Others kept their distance. For a variety of reasons, I have changed several names and omitted certain geographical details.

THE TEAM

At the beginning of the season (4–4–2)
Zebedee
Eddie   Nigel   Jonah   Mick
Steve   Calvin   Bunny   Rizler
Carl   Paddy
Subs: Morgan, Shaggy, Scouse

At the end (3–4–3)
Zebedee
Teddy   Nigel   Bunny
Duffy   Raph   Calvin   Wayne
Carl   Paddy   Rizler
Subs: Morgan, John, Scouse

1

RUNNING

On match days Eddie forgot about everything. The ritual began at one p.m. Standing alone in his cell, he reached for the linoleum floor with his finger-tips, keeping his legs as straight as telegraph poles. This exercise was followed by others. Eddie stretched the muscles in his groin and thighs, and bounced on the spot a few times to flex his Achilles tendons. By the time the door unlocked at 1.30 p.m., he wore the team's all-red strip and had banished much of the lethargy from his body. The end of the cell block was a few paces away. There, boots in hand, he waited with the other footballers, eager for the outside doors and gates to be opened.

After each match the players hurried back inside the jail. At weekends they were locked up between four and five p.m. During this hour, one shift of prison officers left for the day and another returned from the free world. As league games finished at 3.40 p.m., this meant Eddie and the other members of the squad had just twenty minutes if they wanted to have a shower and make the canteen before bang up. If one thing had to be sacrificed, it was the trip to the bathhouse, which could wait until after five. Eating was another matter entirely. Missing the last serving of the day meant they were left with the choice of cooking at their own expense in the cell-block kitchen, open to all 110 inmates, or going hungry.

Before being banged up for the night at nine p.m., the players sometimes gathered to talk. These conversations only ever took place in small groups, each man wary of straying beyond his own circle of acquaintances. Having spent twelve years inside, Eddie trusted no one, not even his 'friends'. He believed sharing opinions was acceptable solely on the basis that you understood anything you said would become common knowledge. Now, it was bad enough if the latest calamity in whatever remained of your life on the outside was reduced to idle gossip, but talking about football could get you into trouble. It was all too easy for a remark to be taken the wrong way. An honest and reasonable judgement such as 'I thought he had a bad game' was capable of going schizoid on the grapevine.

'Did you call me a cunt?'

The perpetrator of such careless talk could not expect much sympathy.

'You cunt. You fucking wanker. I'll take you out!'

Of course, not everyone overreacted. Kingston Prison, in Portsmouth, specialised in the incarceration of men serving life sentences. Almost all of them had been convicted of murder. But Eddie said there were at least as many diplomats as tough guys in the cell block. That was the thing about murder. All sorts of people got banged up for it. In fact, Eddie thought Kingston was a monastery compared to some of the zoos where he had spent earlier parts of his sentence. Places where the landings were stacked on top of each other like the floors of a hotel from hell, where drugs and violence were part of the fabric of life. And there was no football, let alone with outsiders.

Still, Eddie's instincts told him to smother the urge to talk, at least in any critical sense, about the game. Instead, he took pleasure from replaying the highlights in his head. The occasions where he won and lost the ball. The passes, the runs, the headers, the things people said. He rewound everything, talking to himself without speaking, playing the game in his mind's eye, the place where long-term prisoners lived half their lives.

By Sunday nights, however, he'd exhausted the match. And when Eddie was tired of reading or listening to the radio he replayed other scenes in his head. Doing so required scavenging among the memories of his life before prison for something, anything, to conjure with. The most vivid recollections concerned his last days on the outside.

It is May 1993. Eddie has been allowed out of Swaleside Prison, on the Isle of Sheppey, to attend his uncle's funeral at Golders Green Crematorium in north-west London. By the time the prison van sweeps into the car park Eddie has long since decided to make a break for it. His focus is so intent, his body so poised for flight, that he barely acknowledges his relatives among the gathering of mourners. Later, Eddie can only hope that these smartly dressed people assumed his stupor was involuntary. Maybe Eddie was banned from talking.

The crematorium resembles a redbrick country house. It has a spacious atrium where drivers can unload coffins sheltered from the wind and rain. Flower pots and baskets of pink, white and yellow carnations are intended to bring some respite, but the organ music and the wisps of smoke rising from the chimney maintain a sombre grip on everyone's mood.

Except Eddie's.

There are three guards. When they escort him inside Eddie asks if they will remove his handcuffs for the duration of the service. They choose to act with humanity.

Within an instant Eddie is gone. He bursts through two sets of swing doors and finds himself in the open air, at the back of the building. The Garden of Rest stretches out before him. Eddie sprints up the green, sloping lawns, passing flower beds littered with tiny commemorative plaques – Eldridge, Holmes and Cooper, Taken From Us Suddenly; Holroyd, Dowson, Baker, Forever In Our Hearts; Kelly, Wick and Dhandsa, Much Missed – fathers, sons, mothers and daughters. Eddie is only a few strides from the boundary fence. He hits the mesh barely breaking his stride. In one movement his arms pivot his compact, muscular frame into the air and Eddie becomes a pole vaulter at the Nightmare Olympics. Failure to clear the bar will condemn him to many more years of wretched isolation, the carcass of his so-called life owned and controlled by Home Office civil servants.

Eddie soars over the fence.

He is pounding the residential streets of Finchley. At one point he stops to ask an elderly couple the directions to the nearest tube station. They point to the left. Eddie, already the paranoid fugitive, runs to the right. He finds an alley and briskly extracts a cling-film parcel from his rectum. It contains fifty pounds. A series of bus journeys carries him into the heart of the capital.

The police will issue a description of the escaped prisoner: 5ft 6in male, mid-twenties, Scots accent and closely cropped red hair. So Eddie goes into a pharmacy and buys black hair-dye. In the first public lavatory he finds there is no mirror. Eddie uses the chrome button on the hand dryer. The reflection is distorted. He makes a mess of the disguise.

Some hours later, when Eddie meets the friends he telephoned, they laugh at him. He's been wandering around London with a black stain on his cheek, where the dye ran. Eddie laughs without smiling. He is just grateful to have found the hide-out, and to be inside, away from the prying eyes of every prison guard, police officer, traffic warden and sharp-eyed lollipop man in London.

The large Victorian house is empty. None of the rooms has carpets. His friends have paid for a woman as a coming-out present. They leave, and Eddie listens to every step as she clunks up the stairs. The girl is on something, maybe cocaine. Still, for Eddie the encounter is a miracle of eroticism. The way she stumbles out of her clothes. Her washed-out cotton lingerie.

When she finally moves into position she laughs softly. 'I bet you're looking forward to this.'

Eddie is dumbfounded.

When it is over she slumps on to the mattress. In time his attention is drawn to a carrier bag, which she brought with her. He finds a bottle of vodka and some packets of crisps. Someone has also taken the trouble to include a Scottish newspaper. Eddie has not seen one for years and curiosity immediately guides him to the back pages. The English newspapers only touch upon Scottish 'fitba' in the most cursory fashion. Not so the *Daily Record*.

DURIE SIGNS FOR RANGERS

The headline captures his attention as surely as if a loudhailer had cracked into life and announced, 'Come outside with your hands up.' The report tells of how, after four unsuccessful attempts, Glasgow Rangers have finally signed Scottish international striker Gordon Durie. The club is paying Tottenham Hotspur £1 million for the twenty-six-year-old, who previously played for Chelsea, Hibernian and East Fife. Durie is pictured wearing the famous blue shirt of Rangers FC.

Eddie ravenously considers the ramifications. Durie would help Rangers cope with the long-term loss through injury of Ally McCoist, and ease the burden on fellow striker Mark Hateley. But there is no reason to get carried away. Durie has never done much in a Scotland shirt. And these days, what counts is not scoring at Motherwell or Dundee United, but performing against the top European sides.

Eddie falls asleep absorbed in the question of whether Durie, McCoist and Hateley could play together. A three-pronged attack employing Durie's pace to get in behind defenders, big Hateley's dominance in the air, and McCoist's ability to pick up the pieces would certainly be a bold and adventurous ploy. At the same time, accommodating an extra striker would mean losing something in defence or midfield.

That uncommon night Eddie dreams about being pursued by a police constable down the flanks at Ibrox Park. Before the copper can grab him, Eddie's right foot sends the ball towards the back post. Durie is up early, hanging in the air, ignoring the attentions of goalkeeper Pat Bonner and the Celtic defenders, who jump as though the ball contains the gift of eternal life. Durie prods his forehead into the white leather ball. It flies into the net, bulging the nylon mesh on its return to earth.

A deafening roar from the crowd.

Eddie replays the goal over and over. And when he wakes up in the morning, the girl is gone.

2
THE NINETY-MINUTE UNIVERSE

The first team sheet of the season was pinned to the cell-block noticeboard at two p.m. Nigel Wheeler, the thirty-six-year-old physical education instructor, performed the task without ceremony; it was just that everything that happened inside the jail drew comment.

'So that's the best you've got, is it?' teased one of the younger prison officers.

'Yep, first game of the season tomorrow.'

'Are you gonna win something this year?'

'We'll have to see, won't we?'

Nigel half-smiled, walking away in the direction of the gym office. He was not in the habit of making jokes at the expense of the prison's football team. The fact that he picked the side, and played in the centre of its defence, partly explained this. But it was also true that Nigel had no time for small-talking football with people who lacked feeling for what really happened on Saturdays.

And why bother explaining? His team, Kingston Arrows, played in Division One of the Portsmouth North End League, along with nine other amateur clubs. At the start of the season, each of the managers registered around twenty-five players with the county branch of the English Football Association. That meant 250 men taking part in 180 football matches staged between late summer and early spring. For Nigel and the players it did not matter that these events were of no consequence to anyone but themselves. The enjoyment came from committing mind and body to the contest. If you understood the love of that, of sapping every oxygenated cell in the interests of overcoming the opposition, then Nigel was your man and he would talk for hours. As he worked through the merits of a certain player, team, referee, the state of the pitch, you name it, Nigel maintained an open stance, inviting conversation. His hand sometimes swept through the air, pausing to allow time for his words to be absorbed, before returning to its starting position. There was also a kind of waltz, in which he stepped forward with one leg and then retreated.

In coaching mode, Nigel was captivating. At eleven a.m. on match days, he stood beneath the orange anti-dazzle lights in the prison's small sports hall. This was a live show: the Ninety-Minute Universe. Sat on wooden benches, the players listened as Nigel mapped out the task ahead, apportioning responsibility: 'You, Eddie, stand on the edge of the six-yard box at corners so that if the ball's knocked in low you can cut it out. Carl, come ball-side of your marker! Make it easy for us to pass to you.' The players enjoyed the talk because it was so full of promise. The script rarely contained any surprises, but it did galvanise anticipation of the struggle ahead, echoing each man's private concerns about doing himself justice.

At the very best of times, when the Kingston Arrows were flying, the team meeting became the catalyst for a day when the hardships of incarceration could be set aside. Normal cell-block relations, which were fraught with mistrust and suspicion, were adjourned. Had the lifers merely played against each other, this osmosis would not have taken place. Seeing free men file into the prison on match days was a stark reminder of the lives they might have led. Petty squabbles were all but forgotten. They were in this together.

And while the grace and skill of professionals may not have been on show, the guarantee of a contest was absolute. Bridging the gap between the Portsmouth North End League and top-flight football required a journey of fantastic proportions, with promotions through all the divisions of the Portsmouth and District League, the Hampshire League, the Wessex League, the Dr Martens League and the Ryman League – the point where regional competitions gave way to a national league, the Conference, which served as the gateway to the English professional game. Nonetheless, the park footballer understood his obligation to perform. If an amateur boxer asked his opponent to go easy because he did not, on the occasion of their contest, feel like Sugar Ray Leonard he would receive an unmerciful beating; it was the same with park footballers. They needed commitment. Anyone who fell below the desired standards invited scorn.

So on these grand and glorious days the huff and puff of an ordinary football match became a chance to commune with life. The rigour of competition allowed the inmates to slip into different personas, the dreadful identity each man assumed in crime revoked, temporarily. The menace to society became a defender, a midfielder, or a forward.

The consideration that the footballers showed each other, and their opponents, was part of this process: 'Well played, mate!' 'Nice ball, Calvin!' 'Let's keep it going, Eddie!' And in the past their civility had assumed grimly ironic proportions: Kingston Arrows once went an entire season without collecting a single booking for foul play.

That screws and cons were on the same side, disregarding a traditional loathing, also made a difference. Several inmates claimed to have been given 'a good kicking' by staff at other jails. The guards, for their part, all knew of colleagues who had suffered physical abuse carrying out duties. Yet here they were, team mates.

Nigel was too modest to claim that he was doing something important. He contented himself with the obser-vation that sport was 'a great leveller'. But it was obvious to outsiders that he had an unusual relationship with the lifers, one based on mutual respect. A shared love of sport fused a connection between them, creating a community of sorts. It was no small achievement considering that many of the inmates had been alienated by everything else within the penal justice system. Of course it was still Nigel's job to make sure they behaved themselves, but in the Ninety-Minute Universe it soon became apparent that the first question he asked himself when appraising a newcomer was simply: Can he play? And, if so, Will he be fit for Saturday?

In fact, there were times when it was Nigel who seemed to make the most of the release that sport brings. Some members of the squad, like Eddie, said little and remained almost expressionless as they sprinted and battled for the ball. Nigel was loud and animated. Teeth clenched, cheeks blowing, he entered tackles like a depth charge. Spectators flinched, imagining breaking bones, yet the other guy usually came away unscathed. Nigel had played to the standard of semi-professional football and his technique was good enough to allow him to go in hard without causing injury. And when Nigel won the ball, his back straightened, his arms spread like stabilisers, and his eyes rose to face the action. Sometimes he knocked it short, to one of the Kingston midfielders. But often he simply checked his stride and launched a long ball down the pitch for one of the strikers to chase. And whenever that ploy was reversed, a remarkable scene unfolded.

'Nigel's ball!'

On this shout the Kingston defence parted like extras in a

biblical epic. Even in the midst of the fray, when a moment's hesitation could prove decisive, they ignored the falling projectile, concentrating instead on the opposition forwards scampering into the Kingston penalty area. For Nigel would attack the ball, bracing himself underneath it, a step to the left, a correction to the right, with the urgency of a father trying to catch his baby thrown from a burning building. Once those clear blue eyes fixed on the target they stayed there as the ball loomed larger and larger. Until Nigel rose to meet it.

Boom!

The sound of Nigel's forehead impacting against the ten pounds per square inch of air, sealed inside a rubber bladder, encased in white leather, reverberated off the prison walls. And everyone on the green grass, the people lining the white touchlines, knew that they were in the company of a man who took his responsibilities seriously.

The clink of the cell-block gate shutting came with a little jolt. The sound carried no sense of the past, no echo of those people whose life or death struggles were silenced with violence. And the lighting was calm and sterile, a world away from the crime scene discotheque of red and blue. But standing there, staring into their world for the first time, a wave of revulsion swept over you. And then it was gone.

The smell of a closed community was quite distinct. Wet towels, baked dry for the umpteenth time. Bleach wiped across a floor somewhere. Tobacco smoke and cooking. It could have been much worse. All that body odour, all that farting, belching, shitting, pissing and wanking, all the dirty clothes and the bad feet, each and every paperback, newspaper and case file, yellowing like the skin of the white boy inmates. Perhaps the worst of it drifted upwards towards the high ceilings way above A, B, C, D and E wings. The prison was clean.

Like the spokes of a wheel, the five wings were spaced around a hub, known as 'the centre'. They resembled long, narrow barns, with speckled cream walls of smooth plaster. On each wing an iron staircase linked the ground floor with the landing above, which was ringed with metal railings and provided a vantage point to observe the routine below. A wing was completely sealed off, awaiting redevelopment. B wing was a corridor of storage cupboards that led to a sports hall the size of a badminton court, with lockable changing facilities for visiting teams. Most of the prisoners lived on C and D wings. E wing was barred off from the general population, reserved for the zimmer-framed lifers who would otherwise have been a soft touch for bullying. The C wing basement housed a segregation unit and the prison's drug-testing facility. The bathhouse was located beneath D wing.

If a building could speak, this one would whisper, 'I'm watching.' The wings were arranged so that it was easy for a guard standing at the hub to see what was going on in any direction on the ground floor. The upstairs landings were randomly patrolled. The lifers got used to the sense of constant surveillance, but it became a part of who they were in prison. Everyone was on guard.

At Kingston, if there was such a thing as the wrong side of the tracks it was C wing, where the cells were not equipped with electric power sockets. Prison wages averaged about seven pounds a week, so buying batteries for radios was no small inconvenience. It was money better spent on tobacco, phone cards or other comforts. But to be upgraded to a D wing cell, which had power, meant residents could no longer afford to be caught smoking cannabis or displaying any serious anti-social behaviour. They also needed to be around long enough to take advantage of a vacancy.

On Fridays the inmates were locked up between two and four p.m. to allow time for staff training. Their absence made it easier to get to know the building. Beyond C and D wings, though, the prison became a warren of corridors which looked the same, lacked windows, and were divided at regular intervals by bars and locked gates.

Nigel's office was upstairs in the gymnasium block. On entering you faced his desk at the far end of the rectangular room. To your left, a pane of reinforced glass occupied the centre of a wall, and overlooked the sports hall. A small refrigerator and a row of filing cabinets stood on either side of this observation point. Another desk was positioned beneath the window sill. On the opposite side of the room, beyond a metal wardrobe and above a couple of easy chairs, a window offered the only sight of the outside. Through white painted bars the hockey pitch came into view. A half-naked sink, its plumbing exposed, filled the far right-hand corner, next to Nigel's desk.

The gym office was the only place where an outsider was likely to feel comfortable. The pale green walls were dotted with old team photographs, fixture lists, first aid information, Home Office bulletins, and a map entitled 'Penal Establishments in England and Wales'. A notice advising IT IS BETTER TO KEEP YOUR MOUTH SHUT AND APPEAR STUPID THAN TO OPEN IT AND REMOVE ALL DOUBT was fixed to a space behind Nigel's chair. There was one other desk, adjacent to the doorway, but still enough floor space for two or three men to get changed for sport. Most of the furniture looked like it came from a second-hand shop. The filing cabinets, arranged in a row, suggested laudable standards of administration. In fact, the draws contained a steam iron and an extensive collection of towels and sportswear.

Nigel shared the office with Geordie Foster, Kingston's other physical education instructor. His Official Newcastle

United Mug sat on top of the fridge. The gym radio, tuned to Ocean FM, remained switched on whenever either man was on duty. Their stainless steel kettle was not equipped with a mechanism to turn itself off. Sometimes Nigel and Geordie forgot, and returned to the office to find it spewing out huge clouds of steam.

A lousy summer was drawing to a close. Working on the sports field much of the time, Nigel had still managed to acquire a healthy tan. Fresh-faced and modestly handsome, he had strong, wholesome features – much too honest-looking ever to have been picked out of a line-up. At 5ft 10in, Nigel was hardly a giant in the image of Charles Atlas, but he did possess a trim, muscular physique, which most men would envy. The lack of grey in his chestnut hair added to the impression of vitality and only the tired skin around his eyes hinted at the approach of his forties. As with most prison officers, there was something yeomanly about his manner. Nigel considered his work 'a service' and was required to call his boss 'Governor', 'Sir' or 'Mr McLean'.

'Our job is to provide an opportunity for sport, fitness and remedial work,' said Nigel, sitting at his desk and, for once, dropping into Home Office speak. 'It's a case of allowing the inmates to express themselves through sport. We want them to gain a greater insight into team games and, with success, to improve their self-esteem.'

The sports program featured basketball, badminton, bowls, hockey, running, volleyball and weight training. None of these rivalled football as a focal point for inmate life.

'I try to run the football as much as I would an outside team, but there are certain differences. On the out, if you can't get in a team, or if you fall out with someone, you can just walk away, join another side. Here, you can't do that, so there's a pressure on people. You get arguments and disagreements at all football clubs but these are normally forgotten about when you have a laugh in the pub after the game. Here, because the inmates are locked up, things get blown out of all proportion. It makes a difference, for example, if, when I drop a player, I let him know in advance. That way he can prepare himself for when other inmates come up to him and say, "Have you seen the team sheet? That cunt's dropped you."'

It had been ten years since Kingston won the championship. As optimism comes cheap in pre-season, the fact Nigel restricted his comments about the forthcoming campaign to declaring that his team worked hard and were 'difficult to break down' was telling. There was no hint of a title bid.

Terry Allison, a Portsmouth North End League official, and Kingston's one and only fan, confirmed the need for realistic ambitions. For fourteen years Terry had visited the prison on Saturday afternoons to watch the Arrows play. He thought the present squad would do well to finish in the top half of the table. 'It's hard for Nigel because he can't go out and sign another player. And he's very competitive, always wants to win. Some of the other club secretaries think Nige has got it easy because it's not like he has to get lads off a building site or something on match days. But let's face it, it's not a normal club. He's got his hands full organising everything. For security reasons, he has to write to every visiting team to get the names of people coming through the gates on match days. A lot of that gets done in his own time. Nigel also gets into trouble with his wife. She can't understand why he goes back into the prison on his day off. I mean, that's commitment.'

Terry, who was fifty, jowly and moustached, had his reasons for watching Kingston. 'One, I got a bench to sit on. Two, I gets a cup of tea and looked after. And three, I can do a newspaper report on every team in the division at least twice a year. If you go around local parks, you end up missing teams. And people moan. They can't moan if they have a bit in the *Football Mail*.' He laughed at his own good fortune. 'Plus it's near my home, so I don't have to spend ages on the bus.' A former electrical fitter at the naval dockyard, Terry was interested in crime. 'My missus always says, "You're morbid." You know *Murder Casebook*? I got every one of them – one hundred and forty five.' His eyes narrowed behind red-framed I'm-a-jolly-person spectacles. 'Since I been coming in here there's only one bloke who ever made me feel a bit cold down inside. Said he was with the Krays. He was cold. You could feel it.'

The first name on the team sheet was always Paddy, Kingston's captain. At twenty-eight, he was the youngest member of a squad that mostly consisted of men in their thirties. Even those inmates who loathed Paddy – and there were a few – recognised that he was an accomplished footballer. Paddy had what opposing managers called 'genuine pace', but it was his ability to keep the ball close to his body and make decisive moves in tiny spaces which made him good to watch.

The captain's face was open and unguarded. His high forehead gave him an expectant look. Paddy, six feet tall, said he shaved his head because the prison barber was hopeless when it came to Afro-Caribbean hair. The skinhead crop was popular among the players, and on Paddy added to the general impression of purposefulness. The captain also played hockey, volleyball and basketball, and spent hours in the weights room building muscle strength, but not excessively so, as football required agility almost as much as power. His long legs, for speed, completed what was, for the beautiful game, the perfect physique.

'Paddy's probably the best striker in the league,' said Terry Allison. 'He reminds me a bit of Chris Armstrong – and not just because he looks like him. He makes lots of runs, and tends to pull out wide, creating things for the others. He's not just a finisher.'

A volunteer 'listener', Paddy was occasionally summoned from his D wing cell to sit with an inmate whose despair was proving too much to be handled alone. Some of these men had psychiatric problems – they complained of 'hearing voices' – but, being prison, there were no psychologists available to provide professional help at short notice. Paddy did not have a prison job but spent his time in education. Having recently passed A-level English Literature, he was studying Psychology.

There were inmates for whom a life sentence was the culmination of a career in crime, for whom the prison gate would swing open as if it had been expecting them. Paddy was at pains to distance himself from these men. This irritated some of the guards. 'I'm not a con,' they would mock when he was out of earshot. On the pitch Paddy did not suffer fools gladly. Whether it was a glimpse of the peacocky athlete that formed part of his psyche, or something else – who could say? – his exasperation with the failings of his team mates only added to his unpopularity. Wayne, an ever-present the season before, dropped out of the squad protesting about Paddy's reappointment as captain.

Painfully thin, and with black spiky hair, Wayne was a soldier who gave up the army for marriage, only to regret it. He missed the direction, the crack and being fighting fit. A big, awkward nose protruded from his face. With sallow skin and drawn cheeks, Wayne looked like a starving prisoner of war. His large brown eyes were anything but shell-shocked, though, encountering the world in snatched glances, like a pick-pocket regards a busy shopping street, or as shyly as a man self-conscious about his own absence of beauty – it was hard to tell which. Wayne lived on C wing. A stark figure, he often went days without shaving and was disposed to underwear ill-suited to football. Y-fronts, briefs, or a proper jockstrap would have preserved his modesty, but no, Wayne wore boxer shorts which, in the course of a slide-tackle, rode up with no thought for the rest of us.

Wayne nudged ahead of Morgan, one of the reserves, for the title of Most Dishevelled Member of the Squad, but he became a different character, one at ease with himself, when he talked about painting. His work had been displayed at the Royal Academy of Art as part of a prison exhibition. There was a manic take on Munch's *Scream*. Another painting, full of spontaneous emotion, featured a skull tilted back with the jaws open, as though laughing. The wild, textured background was somehow revolting. Not long after the painting went on display in a prison classroom another inmate asked for it to be taken down because he found it disturbing. Wayne was complimented, and flashed a rare smile at the memory. The people who knew him before jail would have been amazed by the passion he had discovered for expressing himself with acrylics and canvas. 'They just thought I was a grumpy, ignorant bastard,' he said.

Only Nigel and Calvin, one of the midfielders, were more adept at winning the ball than Wayne. So it was some loss to the team when he told the manager in his flat, nasal North London accent that he no longer wanted to be considered. Paddy had shouted at him once too often; it was just intolerable, there was no way he was going to leave himself open to any more criticism. Wayne thought the captain a prima donna who stood with his hands on his hips when he lost the ball, rather than fighting to win it back, as Paddy himself demanded of others.

Nobody made any great effort to persuade Wayne to rejoin the fold; lifers often withdraw from situations to avoid any potential physical confrontation. Sure, they would fight if they had to, if they really wanted to, but the frustrations of being caged were overwhelming, and most had suffered them long enough to be wary of when and where they went to war. Besides, these things went down on report.

Over 100 metres Paddy was the fastest runner in the squad. Everyone knew this because the likely contenders had raced each other earlier in the summer. Carl, his striking partner, had even more snap over the shorter distances that are all-important in football, and twenty-yard bursts to get to the ball first. The trouble was, Carl lacked Paddy's anticipation; he merely reacted to situations.

Carl had street beauty. There never seemed to be anyone taller on the pitch. With his mane of dreadlocks and goatee, he might have been the muse for some futuristic designer, representing a coming age where we are all bigger and stronger. His lean, muscular legs imparted so much energy that they almost amounted to an unfair advantage. Carl read the game so poorly that he usually gave defenders a head start in a chase for the ball, but he always closed the gap. Legs a blur, his pace often got him away to face the goalkeeper alone. Carl never rushed, and often scored. Still, it was commonly said that he was 'not a natural footballer'. As Eddie put it, 'When it comes off for Carl he's just sensational, but at other times, forget it, man.'

Carl kept himself busy. He worked in the laundry, a menial prison job, but he took pride in being the television and video monitor, a position of real power. It was Carl alone who decided what got taped after they were all banged up for the night. If you wanted something unusual recorded, well, that was a favour, wasn't it, so how were you going to repay him?

Dreary prison chores were just fine with Rizler. The twenty-nine-year-old Welshman lived on C wing, where he worked as a cleaner, just as he had on the outside. Rizler cited his 'happy' nature to account for his easy-going demeanour. It was nothing to do with his interest in cannabis – although, yes, he had been fined 'six or seven times' for failing drugs tests, and was expelled from a previous institution after guards found instructions for tampering with urine samples hidden in his cell.

Rizler was not only the shortest player in the side, he was also the palest. His smiling blue eyes shone out from a complexion which properly belonged to a frozen chicken. Where there had once been a sandy thatch there was only a bald scalp, shaved by a Number One razor. In training, when Rizler came up against giants like Jonah, Kingston's biggest defender, he looked like a naughty little boy, squeezing through gaps and evading capture. His first touch was neat, and his ability to use different parts of his right foot to chip, curl or drive the ball wherever he wanted it to go could have been the subject of a coaching video. He was quick, too. Yet these qualities did nothing to protect Rizler from his detractors. To them, he had most of the technical attributes of a good footballer, but none of the mental ones. Riz delayed passes too long, made ill-considered solo charges towards packed defences, and tended to shoot from impossible angles. He shrugged off the carping. The very mention of criticism, however, wiped away the impish grin that was usually fixed on his face.

The centre of midfield was bossed by Calvin, the team's thirty-three-year-old vice-captain, who looked like a wealthy, out-of-condition boxer. Calvin smiled a lot, but rarely said much. Some people interpreted his reticence as arrogance, others saw reserve. Calvin had been a member of an ultra-violent South London gang. Stripped away from his old life, though, he was full of surprises, apparently quiet and bookish. His head, shaved years before at the first sign of a bald patch, was a glossy brown dome. In terms of taking pride in his appearance, Calvin was everything that Wayne and Morgan were not. He wore branded jeans, T-shirts and tracksuits. A gold rope chain hung around his neck.

Calvin had a talent for the big tackle, and often triggered attacks when the play was built through midfield. But by his own admission, he lacked confidence in what he could do with the ball. Calvin felt more comfortable anchoring the midfield. However, for the start of the season, he was required to take a play-making role.

His favoured position went to Bunny, who, at forty-two, was considered too old to be supporting the attack. As a schoolboy Bunny trained with Queens Park Rangers. His mother kept a photograph of him standing side-by-side with Terry Venables during the twilight days of the former England manager's playing career. Bunny, upstairs, and Calvin, on the ground floor, were both D wing residents and worked together in the visitors' block, sweeping the floors and washing up the Home Office cups and saucers. They were friends.

Bunny shuffled about in his own time, tall but stooping, as though weighed down by the implacable monotony. His square shoulders and long arms lent themselves to lifting heavy objects. And that partly explained why, in his former life, Bunny spent years working as a roadie.

His features were as square as Calvin's were rounded. The rectangle of his forehead and the stub of his chin framed small, friendly eyes and puckered lips. In the squad no one had darker skin. Bunny claimed to have been beaten up by officers at another jail over his refusal to cut off his dreadlocks. Now they had gone of his own volition. All that remained was a short carpet of frizzy hair. Like most of the older inmates, Bunny seemed better able to cope with prison, a different presence to Calvin, Paddy and Wayne, who were always watching their backs. Maybe it was just that the years

21

working unsociable hours, travelling on coaches and staying in cheap hotels had seasoned him in the matter of being good company. Bunny let people have their place in a conversation.

Nigel aside, the best defender was Jonah, a 6ft 2in East Londoner. Jonah was notoriously injury prone, but the ground did shake when he came running, giving the opposition something to think about. At least that's how it seemed. A little of the working-class ruffian charm that had undoubtedly been his on the outside remained. It was easy to imagine Jonah on a vegetable stall, outselling everyone else as he entertained the old ladies with his cockney patter. For all that, his face folded into a grimace if he thought he was not making himself clear. Jonah wanted to be understood. He, like Carl, was in for what the cons called a 'dodgy crime'. So he kept himself to himself. Jonah lived downstairs on C wing and worked in the prison print shop, a rough diamond among the fallen professionals who could not face cleaning toilets or sweating in the kitchen to finance a few comforts.

In a squad of twenty-five players, only Nigel, Paddy, Carl, Rizler, Calvin, Bunny and Jonah could be confident of winning a place in the first team (as could Wayne, had he chosen to play). It was all rather more nervy for the others. Competition was tough. No threats, and no amount of browning of the tongue could influence the manager's selection. They had no choice but to work on their game, and hope for a chance to show what they could do.

It just so happened that on the opening day of the season Luke, the first-choice goalkeeper, was due at an Open University meeting in the visitors' block. So Nigel Zebedee, a forty-four-year-old prison officer, stepped into the breach.

Jonah and Nigel lined up as centre-backs, with Mick, a hefty, thirty-nine-year-old rugby lover, at left-back. Mick was a loner, a miserable bastard, said the reserves who coveted his place. Eddie started at right-back. To anyone acquainted with Scottish football of the 1970s, Eddie inspired memories of small, hard defenders like Danny McGrain and Jimmy Johnstone. Eddie might have been flattered by the comparison, but for the fact McGrain and Johnstone were both legends of Celtic Park.

In midfield, Calvin and Bunny held the centre, with Rizler on the left and Steve, who nobody knew much about, on the other flank. Steve was the only new face, having arrived at Kingston a few weeks previously. His fitness so impressed Nigel that he made his way straight into the starting eleven. This irked a few of his new team mates: Steve was too lightweight for the rough and tumble of league games, they said.

Paddy and Carl were the strikers.

Those who missed out bore their indignation as best they could. Teddy, who was knocking on the door of his fiftieth birthday, may have been the oldest player in the squad but, as Jonah remarked, he had 'a stare on him that could stop traffic'. Teddy was tall, pony-tailed and thick around the waist. He looked like a wrestler. Teddy did not attend the eleven a.m. team meeting. Neither did Duffy, his smaller, younger friend, who was known more for his prowess in the weights room.

All things considered, Morgan and Shaggy were content to be among the substitutes. The bench was no consolation for Scouse, though, who had trained as hard as anyone in pre-season, losing so much weight that he became gaunt. Scouse felt he deserved a place. He wanted to be out there where he enjoyed himself most, the place where he felt he belonged: centre stage.

There was a story about Scouse being driven away from the Crown Court, about an hour into his life sentence. What should come on Radio Merseyside but a news report about the end of his murder trial. A guard went to turn the volume down – a kindness, given the scene which must have unfolded before Scouse climbed into the prison van. In a cell under the court house his family would have said goodbye. They knew that nothing could atone for the outrage their son had committed. But at that moment there was only fear, and the ravaged dreams of parenthood. They moved apart, the mother and father to one fate, their son to another.

So the guard shouted, 'I expect you want me to turn this off.'

'It's all right, mate, let me listen.'

So Scouse heard his fifteen seconds of fame. When it was over he sat back and listened to the roar of the diesel engine, waiting for the system to swallow him whole.

3
CARL

It's been remarked on a couple of times that I do look after my boots. If you look after your tools, your tools look after you. Everything nice and clean. I have a pair of Adidas Quest, size 9. They cost me twenty-five quid from a mail order catalogue.

Because this is my fourth season, some of them that come in to play us, they know me by my first name and I know them. You have two-minute chats. The football allows you to build up some sort of relationship with the outside space. But jail makes it difficult. When we train on Thursday, everything goes well. When we play on Saturday, everything goes out the window. If you tell someone to do something, right, their attitude is, 'Who are you to be telling me what to do?' People are very defensive. Which is sad, right? The amount of time we've got to get fit, we should never lose a game.

I found it hard when I first come here. There was jealousies, back-stabbing and stuff. I had to live with that. My walls was up. I was stand-offish, right, because I'd had a hard time in other jails. It used to be a case of, here's the line, and if you step over you're going to get this, *bam*. Kingston is more a mental jail than a physical jail. Which is a good thing for me – and for most people. They clear the shit out of your system. It's about learning to lose face gracefully.

What I believe, right, is that they send you to Kingston because they're looking to release you but they are not too sure. So they put you in a more relaxed environment so you can be your true self. There's no big lecture, you just pick up the atmosphere. There's sport and stuff. We call the screws by their first names. They ain't chasing you around. They're watching you, like goldfish in a bowl. There's lots of guys who can't handle it, the non-violent confrontation, and they always get shipped out.

In a normal jail there might be 500 cons. People bully you, take things off you. You have to have this attitude: you mix it with me, you're gonna get this, *bam*. If you're in for a dodgy crime, it depends on your conduct as to whether you're accepted. I shouldn't be saying this, but you could be accepted if you got *money*. He might be in for killing a kid, right, but the armed robbers, who are cool, say, 'Yeah he's all right.' But if he never had a pot to piss in he'd get a hard time. Morals goes out the window. It's about size as well. If you're five foot nothing, and you're in for a dodgy crime, and you've got fuck all, you get pushed around, for sure.

Here, right, you get your politicians. 'Don't talk to this guy because he's in for blah blah blah.' Spreading poison. That's the last thing you need, but there ain't so much fighting. In other jails you've got short-term, young guys. They want to make a name for themselves. I took a lifer out! In a jail like that you try to deal with it mentally, but you can't, so you end up dealing with it physically. In my case it all boils down to my offence. I can handle the verbals, but if someone starts pushing you around, you have to defend yourself.

Like when I was in Wakefield, I had a problem with another inmate. I was queuing up for dinner and he pushed into me. I laughed and said, 'What's your problem?'

He said, 'You really think you're nice and tasty.'

His mate then intervened: 'Don't do nothing now because he'll go public.'

So I said to his mate, 'After I've wrecked him, I'm coming for you.'

And he said, 'All right, after work.'

So it's on my mind. I'm thinking, 'I've got to sort this out. Yeah, I'm gonna take him out.'

So I come back from work. I got a friend to watch the door. My mate said to this guy, 'Do you really want to go through with this?' and he said, 'Not really.' It transpired, right, that his mates was winding him up. I said, 'Ah, fuck this man, let's clear the air.' So I've closed the door and we started to get it on, fighting, right.

The situation was this. I've thrown him a couple of blows, yeah, and he's rushed into me. And he's grabbed hold of me. So I thought, 'Well, this guy don't like getting hit.' I mean, no one likes getting hit, but this man *really* don't like getting hit. He's grabbed hold of me and is trying to fling me around the cell. So I start beating on him. He squealed and everything, right. Now, all that time the furniture is going around. The door got tapped; screw coming up. So we broke off the proceedings. I've looked in the mirror to see if there was any damage. I was pretty clear. He was shaken up and everything, but he went back to his cell.

We both got pulled. They tried to charge us with assault. The other guy said nothing – I respected him for that – but I was sent down the block for a week.

Then I got into the next situation with this next person. Now this is petty. But this is how the story goes. I was working in the kitchen and this particular arsehole was trying to give me a hard time. He give me a load of verbals over the landings, and he likes me for some magazines, right. I said, 'I ain't got none.' He never believed me sort of thing. So I added, 'Furthermore, you're getting fuck all off me.'

So he goes, 'Who do you think you're talking to?'

And I said, 'Don't try my patience, else I'll take you out here and now.'

He called me a 'fucking niggah'. Now, back then, anyone said any racist remarks to me, no hesitation, I'd take them out. There was nobody around, so I gave him a little shake.

And then we got banged up for lunch. I'm pacing up and down inside my cell, thinking, 'Should I do something with this guy?' I thought, 'Nah, better cool down.'

I go to work in the afternoon. When I walked past his cell, he said, 'Are you ready for me now, niggah?'

I thought, 'Ah, this man *wants* it.'

And he goes again, 'Are you ready for me now?'

And I say, 'Well, you've come to the right person if you wanna get taken out.'

He had a sock in his hand, with a PP9 [battery] inside. He swung the PP9. I put my head down and it bounced off my locks. As I moved back to dodge another blow, he cut my face with a blade. So I just switched off on him. I disarmed him. I took the PP9 and went smack, smack, smack into his face. Then I got the blade and cut him up.

He said he'd had enough. I said, 'You've had enough when I've had enough.' He was hurt pretty bad. I know it sounds bad, but you have to defend yourself.

I've always been in trouble – being unruly, you know what I'm saying? Getting in trouble with the authorities, shop-lifting, thieving, and all that. I went to some sort of approved school. Going home at weekends and that.

I was born in Aston. I moved to West London when I was a kid. I went to school in North London. My dad is still alive. If I can remember, rightly, he was a foreman on a building site. I ain't got much time for him. My mum died of cancer six years ago. I was banged up at the time. My brother is a year and two months younger than me, then I got my sister, who's the eldest.

My parents split up because my old man was violent towards my mum. Simple as that, you know what I'm saying? My dad never took his hands to me. I remember one incident when he pushed my mum down the stairs. I don't know what sort of emotions he was going through, you know what I'm saying? He used to hit her in the car. He used to slap her and everything. And all three of us was there, me, my brother and sister. I don't think there's any relationship between my dad and what happened to me. It's just down to me. It's a cop-out to say that all my troubles can be blamed on my old man. He didn't bring me up, did he? He was like a flash in my lifetime. By the time I was five or six they were divorced and we moved down to London.

My mum was very generous and kind. She was strong in her own little way. She really did love us. But she never had much money. If I wanted something I'd go and get it. When I was twelve I used to support myself in my own little way. With my mates at the time, right, we used to go shop-lifting and stuff. I ended up getting in trouble for petty crimes and she couldn't cope with me. That's why I went to an approved school. I never got to know her until my late teens, when I lived with her. I started to feel bad – the strain and the pressure I had put on her. As a kid, you don't realise. She gave me a couple of slaps because I was embarrassing her. More out of frustration than anything else. 'Why are you doing all this? You got to sort yourself out!' But she always stood in my corner. Maybe I took advantage of that. I wasn't conscious of it at the time but I always thought she would visit me in prison.

I did see my dad sometimes. One time I almost had a fight with him. We was having a discussion with friends, and I said,

'Fuck off, you're talking crap.' So he stood up, pulled me out in the passageway.

'You got to show me respect.'

I said, 'What do you know, fuck off! If you put a finger on me, you see what I'll do.'

'You think you're a big man now you're seventeen. You want to take me on?'

'I ain't no big man. You hardly know me. You can't demand respect from me. The way you used to treat my mum, you're lucky I don't take you out directly.'

He knew I wouldn't back down, so he let it go.

He visited me once on remand. He told my sister he wanted to visit again. Maybe, right, because I've changed, I should let him back into my life. I don't know.

My brother lives in the West Midlands. My sister now lives in Kent. She's got a young family. I says to her, 'Don't waste the money coming to see me when you could spend it on the kids.' I phone her a couple of times a week, so I got that contact there.

When I went to that approved school, right, the authorities tried to steer me in the right direction but I formed a group of mates, criminal-minded, you know what I'm saying? Basically I never wanted to grow up. I was selfish. And, in a way, spoilt. Looking in the shops and thinking, 'Yeah I want that, but I haven't got the money.' I thought the answer was to take it. I wasn't very successful because we used to get caught.

When I was a teenager I moved on to bigger things. We targeted registered mail bags. A group of us would go to a train station. You know Redhill? Big sorting office. We went for the registered letters, right, for the money. There was lots of money. We'd pick up £300, £600, even £1,000 a time. We used to distract the guard, grab a mail bag, then find an isolated place and stuff as many letters as we could into the sports bag.

Pure cash. Nice feeling.

We'd go back to school with a load of money on us. The teachers found out and wanted to know where it come from.

I got sent to a detention centre. Now that really hit me. Six weeks. When I got sentenced I cried. This was big time, real prison. The stories you used to hear, geezers getting beaten up and stuff. It was bad, bad, bad. I always maintain that if I'd only done a week in DC I wouldn't be sitting here talking to you now. It shit me up bad, bad, bad. Put the frighteners on me. But after seven days, right, I got on top of it. And when I came out I was strong, fit and dark.

I done a burglary in Tottenham during the riots. I got Borstal. Eight months. I wasn't interested in a job when I came out. I hooked up with a friend to work offices in the West End. My friend would distract a secretary, at lunch time or early on, skeleton staff sort of thing. We'd go for the money, petty cash, wallets, handbags, whatever.

I did try the YTS, right. Six months working in a food warehouse. But I got in a fight in the street one day and broke my wrist. So I was off work. And one day my friend says to me, 'Are you coming out?' I was short of money – I used to be a gambler as well – so I got involved.

I went into a hardware shop. There was no one around, so I went behind the counter and bust the till open. This old man, the owner, come out and said, 'What you doing?' We struggled a bit. I picked up a hammer and hit him across the head. He's gone over. I fucked off directly, right. I was thinking, 'Fucking hell, only seventy quid.' Even more of a wind-up.

The thing is, after the street fight in which I broke my wrist, a copper had come to my door to see if I wanted to press charges. I had a plaster cast on. This copper heard the description of the hardware shop incident and put two and two together.

I was eighteen. I got three and a half years.

I started counting the days. I was still going to be a criminal, but *no* more violent crime. Pure fraud was going to be my thing.

I done my bird, right, and come out. I hooked up with my old friends. We started intercepting credit cards. It was the good life. Too good. I got complacent. One time I had three credit cards on me. This tape player cost about eighty quid. I handed over the wrong card. You got six days to use a dodgy card, right, but this one was too old. The bloke in the shop phoned up for authorisation, right. He's looked at me and, in so many words, said, 'You better fuck off.' He knows, right. Normally, when they asked you to wait, I fucked off, end of conversation. This time I waited about forty-five seconds too long. If I'd got to the streets, no one was catching me. I was gone.

I'm arrested. I stalled them with a load of bullshit. Who gave you the card? I told them every basic – he was six feet tall, black hair, blue eyes. I gave them the run-around, looking for an opportunity to escape. But I was eventually charged with fraud and deception. But when it went to court I got a suspended sentence.

So I started hooking up with various women, right, senior to me in age. This one woman was about ten years older than me. She wanted sex and that, right. I had about three or four girls on the go. They was doing well for themselves. They *gave* me credit cards.

Anyway, this one woman, right, started to get serious. Something more meaningful, right, you know what I'm saying? Now me being immature, directly, right, I'm not having any of that. I'm going clubbing and that, and she's trying to bring me down. I told her about the life I'd been living. Blah, blah, blah sort of thing. She said she didn't mind, and the relationship started to develop. What was keeping us together was the sex. There was no love or anything. I wasn't an emotional guy, you know what I'm saying? She was white. She'd been to college and all that. She had ambitions. She was pretty well organised and that. Sorted out holidays and everything. I was a spoilt little kid. Take, take, take. Then we started getting deeper into each other. When I told her about myself, then came the emotions. But she suspected I was seeing other women. At various times she tried phoning, like when she couldn't find me for three days at a time. We started arguing, having fights and all that, you know what I'm saying? After a couple of days she'd come chasing me back. I said to myself, 'No, I don't need this,' but I was getting drawn to her. This was the first time it had happened to me.

Then she gets pregnant. The one thing I don't want. We're fighting and arguing. It got to the point where I said, 'That's it. I don't want to know you.' She's saying, 'But I'm carrying your child.' I says, 'I don't care.' So she's chased me. And I ain't got one ounce of fight left in me. This was a period when I was under some serious pressure. My head was going bam, bam, bam.

The first time I hit her was the month before the tragic incident, right, you know what I'm saying? It was Christmas. I was at her flat and everything, right, you know what I'm saying? And I was just sitting there and everything, right. And we was talking. And we got into an argument over something petty. So she went for a cigarette. And I said, 'You ain't fucking smoking' – she's pregnant, right. I snatched it off her, right, and slung a couple of right-handers in her face, and everything. Slap, slap. She started fighting back. So I pushed her down, kicked her in the mouth and steamed out, right, you know what I mean? She had to go to hospital and have stiches.

I didn't have any feelings, apart from pure anger. It was only when I was travelling home. Then I started to think, 'Fucking hell, what am I doing? She's carrying my child. What am I doing hitting her?' that sort of thing. I felt bad, bad, bad. Next day I chased her. I said, 'Forgive me, forgive me, it won't happen again.' She never let me in, but she talked to my brother. I went to the pub, I couldn't handle the waiting. In the end she let me in. I said, 'Give me another chance . . . blah, blah, blah.'

The next time was at my place. We had an argument about going out. She said, 'Let's go to the pictures. What about this film?' I said, 'What do you fucking know? Get out, I've had enough. I'm taking you to the bus stop and you can just fuck off out of my life.'

So we're going up the street and she's bleating in my ear. I don't love her and all that shit. And I says, 'Listen, I just can't take no more of this crap.' Now I'm blaming her for why I'm in this predicament. My life was pretty nice, directly, right, until she stepped into it and caused me this confusion. So we end up fighting again.

She didn't hit me. I hit her, you know what I mean? I hit her a couple of times, you know what I mean, and everything, right. I must have probably went blank, right, cos I don't remember kicking her, right. But they say I kicked her, and she say I kicked her. She was pregnant all right. Seven months. She cried and cried. I just walked off and left her.

At the time I was hitting her I must have had the devil on my shoulder. As I'm walking back I'm thinking, 'Fucking hell, what have I done?' I go home. I'm sitting in the corner. My brother says, 'What's wrong?' I says, 'Nothing.' But I feel horrible. I didn't want to talk to my brother. Too close. So I knocked on this woman's door upstairs.

About one a.m. the police arrived. They said they got reason to believe I assaulted someone. I denied everything. I just closed down. I knew I did it, but I couldn't believe I was capable of what had happened. I'm going through the most emotions and the most confusion. I've gone a complete blank, right. All I said was, 'I don't know what you're talking about.'

I know what you are thinking: a defenceless woman, she's pregnant, I'm a coward, how could I even think about doing what I did? Fair enough, right. I don't want to lessen the blow.

Anyway, they done an operation, right, but they couldn't save the baby. So I gave her a miscarriage, right, you know what I mean? But I don't believe I've done it, right, because I'm thinking to myself, 'I ain't capable of doing this.' I kept blanking it, kept blanking it, kept blanking it. It went to court and everything. I can't get my head around it. I'm thinking, 'Nah, I never done that,' and I'm blaming her for the predicament.

But anyway, that's water under the bridge. It's gone to court and I've thought, 'I can probably fight this.' So I've gone 'not guilty'. I know now, right, if I'd gone 'guilty' I wouldn't be sitting here talking to you. But because I went 'not guilty' and I got found 'guilty' I got a life sentence. I never got done for murder. I got done under the Infant Life Preservation Act 1979. Cut down short, they call it 'Child Destruction', right, the baby capable of being born alive. The sentence goes from probation to life sentence. I got a life sentence, right, because of the way I played my cards. I had fights with myself, with my brief, trying to come to terms with it, pushing it away, pushing it away. I just couldn't get my head around the offence and the case.

35

For the first three years I wouldn't talk to nobody about what happened. I was basically embarrassed. I thought the doctors done it, gave her an abortion. But you can't hide from the truth. I'm still embarrassed about it now. I know it can't go away. I've got to accept what happened. I think to myself, 'Fucking hell, Carl, you've got to live with this for the rest of your life.'

I don't want to see her. But if I did, I'd say, 'Sorry I caused you so much grief.' Three people's lives got affected, even though I was the cause. Her life got affected. The baby could have been born. And my life. I just hope, right, that she has settled and found a decent person, much better than me at that time.

Of course it preys on your mind. He would have been coming up on ten years old now. But it's just fantasy. Can I put it this way: because I never felt the baby or seen it, it's just like imagination. Say if I'd killed you, beaten you up and left you to die. I can grieve over that because I've seen you. With the baby, right, because I haven't seen or felt it, I can't grieve, it ain't there, physically. Obviously I know I lost something, but I never had it in my hands. I've shown remorse towards the girl because I knew the girl, felt the girl, touched the girl. And, yeah, I'm deeply sorry the baby's gone. But I'm probably more sorry for what the girl went through. I can still picture her in my mind. I cannot picture the baby.

I don't feel sad when I see babies. I see them as a joy. There's a woman having a baby who comes to the [prison chapel]. She sits down next to me. I don't feel any sort of uneasiness. It ain't like any woman I see I'm going to attack. I don't fancy having kids myself when I get out there. The way I see it now, I don't plan to have any, but maybe my feelings will change. I'm in charge of the videos here. I showed *Nine Months* [where the lead male character has unexpectedly to come to terms with fatherhood] the other day. I even watched it. I never felt worried about it.

I don't want to hide at this stage of my sentence. Any time I deal with a woman now, right, I don't want no physical relationship at the beginning. I want to become good friends first, right, before I probably want to cross that road. I've worked out that with women, they want to be friends. My mentality was fuck, fuck, fuck.

That guy – me – was wrong. Well immature. This jail has given me the skills to communicate with people, to be more tolerant and not to be so judgemental. I'm always working on myself. I go to the [prison chapel] a lot. People from the outside partake of the service. Afterwards we talk. I've got friendly with quite a few of them. I've got so friendly with them that they are saying I've got a ready-made family when I leave.

I'm not affiliated to any religion. Catholics, Church of England, Pentecostal. It gives me peace of mind, but what I really get out of it, right, is the contact with the outside people. It helps with my social skills. Talking to the other inmates, right, you just go around in circles. What this guy's doing, what that guy's doing. Round and round. It drives you mad. I want to get out of that prison talk.

This one person I met, I said to the chaplain, can you arrange a visit? So he did. She's been coming in every Monday. I've helped her with certain problems she's had. I can look at it from a more detached point of view. I said it's a good thing that you are married because it cuts out all that stuff. I'm not going to chat her up and that, right. She's forty-four, been married for twenty years, got one kid. She's all right, as it goes, small and petite. She became a Christian two years ago. We talk about a whole range of things. Once a month we talk about wonderful moments that have happened in our lives instead of talking about all the sad moments. Nothing but good. She listens to my life as well. It's give and take.

She was going to introduce me to one of her friends. She mentioned that if I didn't want her to visit no more I should just say so. She said, 'This woman's single, so you might want to use all your visits on her.'

I said, 'You're my number one friend. There's nothing going to get in the way of that.'

4

ST BRUNO

'Okay gentlemen, leave your valuables in the lockers provided.'

The prison officer surveyed the group of twenty footballers standing in the holding area. They looked young and style-conscious. The jostle of suntans and sunglasses smacked of foreign holidays, nightclubs and three a.m. sex. Their hairstyles, slicked back and closely cropped, were High Street contemporary. Even the most casually dressed wore T-shirts and jeans whose colours and fabrics, spared the rigours of the prison laundry, were fresh with a sense of the outside world. A few stubbed-out cigarettes, filter-tipped, of course. Pockets of stale tobacco air clung to their clothes, but did nothing to diminish the luscious aura of freedom shimmering about them.

Plover took their name from a suburban pub. They were regarded as one of the more physical sides in the Portsmouth North End League. Plover considered themselves title contenders. It was a tough opening fixture.

'Has anyone got a mobile phone?' asked the officer, beginning his security check.

Notices warned about taking banned items into the jail. For football teams these included women and children. The instruction sounded sinister and, in a way, it was. Her

Majesty's Prison Kingston contains a number of murder-rapists and child-killers. Nigel preferred to stress that the restrictions existed for other reasons: staff were not in a position to supervise non-essential guests during sports fixtures.

The prison stands on Milton Road, a busy northern route out of the city. It may have been built in 1876 but it resembles a small medieval castle. An enormous perimeter wall extends left and right off the tombstone-grey gatehouse. The effect is suitably forbidding even though, over the course of a century-plus, the surrounding district has been colonised by streets lined with terraced houses and friendly corner shops.

After being counted, the players queued to exit the gatehouse through a tiny door. It led to an open-air compound surrounded by a mass of security fencing. With steel mesh as closely knit as a woollen sweater, the fencing was considered impossible to scale without climbing gear. Still, there had been incidents of prisoners at other institutions almost getting over, equipped with nothing more than desperation.

When Nigel unlocked a gate off to the right, the visitors were inside the grounds where the prisoners, under the supervision of guards and security cameras, were allowed to roam at certain times on certain days. Nigel escorted the party to the dressing room. Walking past the visitors' block – a modest, two-storey structure – provided the first clear view of the cell block. It was part of a huddle of prison buildings, massed together on the left. The wings of the cell block looked like factory sheds, with two decks of small windows. To the right, the football pitch occupied the only open space of any size within the walls. The towering perimeter wall, which ran all the way around the Kingston grounds, boxed in the playing surface on three sides. It also shrouded the near goalmouth, at the Milton Road End, in shadow. Straight ahead, the far goalmouth loomed empty and expectant, the nets already hung. This was the Railway End, where trains rumbled past, out of sight.

Having walked the length of the pitch, a path took the party to the left, behind the main buildings to the gymnasium block where the all-weather pitch, used for hockey and bowls, baked in the sun.

The atmosphere in the dressing room was light-hearted. 'I bet they get lots of volunteers when the ball goes over the wall,' sniggered one man. A second voice mentioned Kingston's recent appearance in the national newspapers. Two nuns had been caught smuggling tobacco and food to inmates. Guards searched Sister Annuntiata and Sister Anna and found two dozen eggs, six packs of bacon, two packs of meats and 2.4kg of cheese, the details all printed in the local newspaper. The nuns, who were in their seventies, had been interviewed by police and banned from prison visiting for life. There was talk of referring the case to the Crown Prosecution Service. 'I said in my paper that one of 'em was nicknamed "St Bruno" by the inmates because she got 'em tobacco,' said another man. Much hearty laughter followed, but then a short, butch character with bulging forearms and a silver crew-cut began arguing with Nigel.

Two referees had arrived. Normally it was the responsibility of the home team to organise the match official (each side provided one referee's assistant). But as Kingston Arrows were granted special dispensation by the FA to play all their games at 'home', there had obviously been a misunderstanding over whether this was a true 'home' fixture or whether it was Plover's 'home' game.

'You're wrong, it's our home game,' said the Plover man, adamantly.

'I checked the fixture list carefully,' said Nigel.

The other man said nothing.

'The fixture list was changed a few weeks ago, maybe that's what's led to the confusion,' suggested Nigel.

There had indeed been problems with the original, which had required Terry Allison to issue a revised fixture list. The trouble was, the defunct schedule was still being used by some club secretaries. Not only that, but the new version required some teams to play each other back-to-back, almost as if they were taking part in a cup competition with 'home' and 'away' legs.

None of this interested the man from Plover. He stared at Nigel, chest pumped out. 'You're wrong.'

Nigel's face began to cloud, but before the Kingston manager could speak one of the referees intervened. 'It's no problem, I'll go home.'

Arrangements were made for the ref to be escorted back to the gatehouse.

Walking up the stairs to the gym office, Nigel nodded in the general direction of the visitors' dressing room. 'He's playing up to his mates. What an arsehole.'

Paddy was already on his way, elbows pumping, eyes glancing back over his shoulder, tracking Jonah's long ball. The inmates crowding the touchlines watched a little more closely, anticipating an early goal. The Kingston captain reached the edge of the box, only to scuff his shot.

All over the pitch, the players wiped away the first sweat of the season. The match had started at a high tempo.

A big crowd, perhaps sixty inmates, created a kind of electricity. A few stood alone but mostly it was groups of twos and threes. It was unusual to see so many lifers in one place. They were not your average football crowd, none singing, none drunk, no women, and not a word to the referee. But they did shout the odd bit of advice to the boys in red.

Plover wore black and white striped jerseys, white shorts and white socks – the colours of Juventus, the style loose and Italian. Kingston toiled in something which harked back to the days when shirts were tighter and shorts less baggy. It looked okay on the players who possessed the vital statistics of mannequins, but clung to the big defenders, Mick and Jonah, and made no allowance for the Olympian thigh muscles powering Carl and Paddy.

On thirty minutes a free-kick curled into the Kingston box. A clump of bodies jumped but made no contact, and in the resulting scramble a Plover forward slammed the ball into the roof of the net.

'Come on Arrows, let's not let our heads go down!' rallied Nigel.

Paddy kept missing chances.

'Everything he hit was flying in last season,' observed Scouse, one of the subs.

On forty-three minutes Carl hit a post. A minute later he had a penalty appeal turned down. And on the stroke of half-time Paddy faced the goalkeeper alone. He shot straight at him.

The players trooped off and drank tepid orange squash from plastic cups. 'We're getting through, we've just got to take our chances,' said Nigel, whose forehead was greasy with perspiration. 'They don't know how to handle Carl and Paddy. We've just got to keep going.'

Since kick-off the crowd had grown. The spectators stood out against the wall. A white strip rose from the base of the bricks to well above eye level. At regular intervals, this band was interspersed with giant red numbers, designed to aid capture by giving prison officers a point of reference in the event of an escape attempt (there had only been one in seven years: the prisoner got away, but was recaptured during a bank raid two weeks later). Traditional goalposts would have been lost against this milky background so, long ago, someone had obtained permission from the FA to paint them blue.

Just after the restart Bunny was chopped down crossing the half-way line. Paddy nodded the free-kick towards the penalty spot, from where Carl gingerly headed home.

'Yeesss!'

On seventy-two minutes Rizler broke down the left, came inside, and whipped a fierce shot on target. Not for the first time, the goalkeeper spilled the ball. Carl side-footed home.

Plover bustled forward in search of an equaliser. With three minutes remaining, Kingston made a mess of clearing a corner and someone called Anthony Drackett bundled the ball over the line. It finished 2–2.

'Typical first game of the season. No one wanted to give anything away.'

Nigel sat on a stool in the Rose and June. The short walk from the prison had done nothing to sap his energy, still flowing from the match.

'Maybe we lacked a bit of concentration. They didn't have much up front, but we still conceded two goals. I wanted Bunny to sit, with Calvin pushing on and Steve and Riz going up and down the flanks. It didn't really happen. There wasn't enough movement.'

Taking a gulp of his beer, Nigel kept his eyes on the television mounted high in one corner of the bar. He was waiting for the football results. Jamie Lawrence had scored in Bradford City's 3–0 win at Reading. Lawrence, a one-time Leicester City starlet, was returning to professional football having served twenty-six months for robbery with violence.

'Shame he never made it to Kingston,' I said.

Nigel laughed. 'Better strikers than him have been inside.' Duncan Ferguson, George Best and Micky Quinn were cited.

His mood changed when I asked him about the nuns. 'They've been slated by the press, who've picked up on something they don't understand. You are talking about people who have done twenty-seven years' good work. To me, the nuns were manipulated by certain prisoners. They wouldn't have appreciated how the stuff would be used. They would have thought it was being divided evenly. A bloody great chunk of cheese, twenty blokes in their class, no harm in it. What they wouldn't understand is that it might never have got to the twenty. One or two might have kept a certain amount and used the rest as currency.'

He kept watching for the Portsmouth result, then added, 'I tell you what, the nuns have done a bloody good job for the prison. They've provided an avenue for inmates who are dying. When it is ony a matter of days, with cancer or some other terminal illness, the prisoners are sometimes released on humanitarian grounds. The nuns take them into their homes so that the blokes don't actually die in prison.'

The thought of it, dying unforgiven, seemed a million miles from *Final Score* and the Saturday shoppers heading home in the buses and cars streaming past the open pub door.

Nigel finished his pint.

'It might be that the stuff got shared out. But I doubt it.'

5

SCISSORHANDS

My name is Eddie and I bin here about a year.

The fitba's great. This is the best set-up I've seen, and I bin inside for eleven years. The training sessions, the kits and all that are great. If there was a league of prison teams I reckon we'd win it easily. But there's no away games, are there, so it's never going to happen. Mind you, you're safer on home ground. There's a lot of inmates who are not strong characters. If we went to other jails I reckon they would sort of go. They would be under extreme pressure. See what happens here, the players are comfortable. They know what they're gonna face all the time. People coming in from the outside on Saturdays. They can handle that. But if you suddenly started moving them about the country, they'd be lost. They couldna handle that pressure.

I couldna. I'd run for it. I've already escaped once, from ma uncle's funeral. And I've bin on the roof. I did a protest at Durham in 1993. I was only up there one day but I caused about £100,000 worth of damage. I smashed it to smithereens, man. I've also done a hunger strike. I stopped that after twenty-nine days because I was injuring myself. I also done a dirty protest. Three weeks – but I couldna suffer that. It was disgusting.

I was on the run for eleven weeks. After I got recaptured I

ended up in a secure unit. When I came here one of the screws said to me, 'You'll never last at Kingston,' but I've kept ma head down. I bin clear of trouble since ma escape. Staying away from drugs and all that. There's a lot of clear-headed people here. The gym is always busy and there's the fitba team of course.

I did ma protests because I'm guilty of killing a man, but no guilty of murder. I killed him in self-defence. There was two geezers attacking me. The one that died pulled a knife.

This geezer worked in a local store on the fruit and veg counter. At the time I was renting flats out for a bloke I knew in Scotland. I also had a small painting and decorating business – that was ma trade. Every day I used to go to this store, me, ma wife and ma kid, and say, 'All right Duncan?' We'd have a chat, pass the time of day. He was forty-seven years old. He was right nice to ma daughter.

One night we went for a drink and Duncan come into the pub. He invited us back to his flat and really, just to be sociable, I went along. We'd left a baby-sitter looking after ma daughter, so ma wife had te go home. She dinae like Duncan, anyway. She says to me, 'That man, he's a wee bit strange.' I said I'll have a drink with him, anyway. I had loads of bottle, then, I'd take any challenge.

So I've accepted his invitation, right, and everything seems all right. We're drinking whisky and all of a sudden he puts his hand on ma knee. You want to know why I dinae just say, 'Sorry mate, you've got the wrong idea,' and leave? That's what everyone asks. That's the mistake I made. I could have got up and left. But I says te him, 'Look, I'm not into all that business, man. Dunie touch ma leg.' I still dinae realise exactly what he was getting at. I'd never bin propositioned before, never had anything like that happen to me.

It turned out there was five men in this flat. They were away to their bedrooms when we arrived. They left us alone –

47

and remember, I've no twigged that he's bent or anything, I've just shoved his hand out the way. At the end of the night I went to the toilet. I met one of the other flatmates. I says to this geezer, 'Is he bent?' He says, 'No, no, no.' Anyway, I went back to the sitting room and, as time went by, fell asleep.

I woke up with this Duncan at my side, with a knife in his hand, and one of the other guys was sat over the backs of ma legs, holding me down. There was a struggle. I used a pair of scissors to defend myself. That's why they called me Scissorhands in the papers. I was lashing out in the dark. All of a sudden this knife appears again. I just lunged and the knife . . . I'm not quite sure how I stabbed him, but it was only once, and it was with the knife. I must have used ma left hand.

Within about half an hour I was found in the street with the injuries to ma fingers. There was blood all over the sitting room door, blood all over the front door, where I'd panicked to get out. In the photographs you could see I'd panicked to get out.

I feel hard done by because from day one, when the coppers came to question me in hospital, I said, 'All right, the bent bastard attacked me and I must have killed him.' But it was never murder. He pulled the knife and I grabbed it. Ma fingers were actually hanging off. I had eleven hours of micro-surgery. And the guy who done the operation said it was a defensive wound. The jury wasnae told that the doctor had said any of that. When you come up against top judges and legal people you've got no chance.

Ma dad was a railway painter, mum a housewife. We lived in Edinburgh. I've two brothers and three sisters. They're all straight pegs. Honest, hardworking people, never bin in trouble with the police.

I dunie know if I was adopted. That's under debate right

now, so I couldna answer that honestly. I can't ask ma mum. She's terrified of revealing things. I've always been the black sheep. I was the only one in the whole family who was locked up at a very young age. You know, because I was uncontrollable. Ma mum had ma three sisters and two brothers and I was just everywhere. She had to keep two hands on me and two eyes on the rest of them. I dinae know why I was a problem. They reckon I was slow at school. I seem to be more educated than the whole family put together now. Whether that's true or not I dunie know.

Ma step-dad used to beat me up. Belts and slippers. For not going to school. For any stupid reason. He just went over the top. Stripped me naked and lashed me with a leather belt until I was absolutely black and blue. He'd just keep whacking me until I stopped crying. He was an evil man. He wasn't a pervert, he was just violent. I dunie know what's happened to him. I'm no interested. The thing is, I do wonder what happened to him as a kid. It's a vicious circle, isn't it?

I remember the day I was taken away from home. It was a bad day. I was screaming ma heart out. I was in a convent from when I was aged eight until I was twelve. I think ma mum got rid of me for protection from all the beatings. They were the best four years of ma life. If I'd have stayed there right up to age sixteen I reckon I'd never have bin in trouble. It was like a family, with the nuns and the other members of staff.

I used te go home every fourth weekend. All ma brothers and sisters had their own agendas. I was left on ma own. There was no big effort to include me. I can understand it now. It's the way things were structured. I canie blame them if I feel I'm no part of the family circle. I've never bin there. If you take a kid outa the family, if you stop trying to work with the kid within the family, then what happens is that his brothers and sisters grow up and they're not used to having him in the family anymore. And I grew up not used to being with them. So we dinae develop like a family. The rejection, that's the biggest part of it, innit? If you've got three sisters and two brothers who all grew up living at home, you're always looking at them from the outside in. It makes you feel strange, different, like you've got a mental disorder.

I was a crazy teenager. Always in fights. Always breaking someone's bones. Me and ma pals used to rob everything in sight. We were like street urchins. Whenever we saw a delivery van, TVs, videos, whatever, we'd wait until the guy was outa the way. Then we'd be in it.

The first major thing I stole was a cash box from a double-decker bus. It caused chaos. The bus driver chased us for miles, man. He caught us in this back garden. We had all these bags of silver coins. He went a bit over the top, angry-wise.

I'm thirty-four. I got married aged nineteen. I was divorced last year – that's no bad for someone who's bin in jail a long time. I've got one daughter who's sixteen. She's from a previous relationship. I got another daughter, fourteen. They come down – not as often as I'd like – one from Scotland, one from London.

Ma wife had the same sort of childhood as me. We got together after meeting in the street one night. I seen this geezer punching her. I went over and beat the shit out of him. I still remember this guy. I steamed into him. I took her home, got her washed up and let her sleep on ma settee. She was so quiet. It was like having a broken sparrow. She had a bit of a reputation at the time. She was a loner looking for company. You would find her in the strangest pubs. Smoking, taking drugs.

I remember taking her to see *Fatal Attraction*. I was wrecked. I thought I'd crash out and she could watch the film. I stuck ma feet on the seat in front. I fell asleep, and the next minute I've got this geezer shaking me, right, cos I've taken ma shoes off. He said ma feet smelt. I said, 'I've just woken up, man, I've got a hangover and just who the fuck are you?' So I stuck the nut on him. That is the kind of guy I was.

Ma wife always thought there was hope. I told her from day one, you've got a life, I can't expect you to do ma sentence with me. She hung on to false hope. She was destroying herself with drugs. Now she's met someone else and has settled down.

If I had kids – well, I've got kids, but if I was on the outside, I'd make sure I was there for them. I'd let them know that I love them and they've got someone to defend them. If I seen a kid, the same as me in the street, I wouldna go near that kid. But I would say something to his mum and dad. The kid needs his own family to put him straight. I'd tell the parents to point him in the right direction. Give the kid a wee bit more attention. Then he might not behave in a certain way to get attention from other people. Too much blame, I think, goes on the kids. You're just a kid, for godsake. The likes of Jamie Bulger and those kids. How can anyone justify putting kids away for life? It breaks ma heart. It's just totally inhuman. All right, I know what they've done. Their mums and dads have got to be approached. Someone should say, 'Well, listen, we want to know how you raised these kids up.'

I've spent a lot of time in children's homes. That makes me angry. I think people could have done better when I was younger. They could have studied ma case a bit better, bin a bit more professional. The thing is, I feel the direction I've got now I only got in Grendon, the therapeutic jail where they send you to talk about your problems. If somebody had spotted certain things when I was a kid I'd never be in jail today. That makes me angry because I've wasted half ma fucking life in places like this. These people say they are fucking professional. They take you out of the family circle and they stick you in a fuckin' children's home.

I'm different now. Before, if I had an argument, my instinct was: never back down. I'd fight that feeling of being stood on. Like for my offence. I could have defended myself and then just left the flat. I dinae attack the victim. He attacked me. But to leave him with a couple of cuts just wasn't good enough. Ma anger was so bad that the end result was that he died. It was still self-defence, regardless of how it happened. It was definitely self-defence. His intention was to hurt me. But ma reaction was, there's no fucking way this is going to happen, and I went over the top.

I done eighteen months at Grendon. It's a good set-up but it's not a nice place to be. It's nay fun listening to paedophiles talking about raping kids and stuff. That's probably what calmed my anger. To actually sit there and listen, you realise that other things are minor. It makes you think you are losing your temper over nothing.

There's no much trouble at this jail. The majority of lifers are afraid to misbehave. There's a minority who do have bottle. They're angry at the system. There's other people like me, who won't sit back and take being wrongly convicted.

Don't get me wrong, I like it here. The people are nice. It's much better than in Scotland. Scotland is fucked. With Aids. With drugs. The culture's too harsh. You can imagine what the jails are like. Suicides every week, man.

There's a couple of nuns who come to visit me from the convent where I was as a kid. I only got in touch with them by pure chance. It just so happens I was up in the prison chapel one day and I heard this Christian lad talking about this nun he'd met. It so happened that her name rang a bell. I spoke to the priest and he contacted her. And she's come to see me. That was four weeks ago. I hadna seen her for twenty-six years. So I'm starting to find out things about ma past.

I take responsibility for everything I've done. I canie blame anyone else. But I sometimes sit in ma cell and think, 'Well, I've three sisters who never come to visit, and two brothers who couldna give a fuck anyway.' They think that when I want to see them it's just for money to buy material things. Nothing could be further from the truth. When I sit back and think about it, I've spent half my life in children's homes and places like that, so they are not used to seeing me. There just doesn't seem to be a bond.

I dunie blame ma mum. Well, she is to blame, but I dunie want her to feel she's to blame. I've seen ma mum go through some terrible times. I don't want to blame her. It doesn't make anything any better, does it?

It seems to me the powers-that-be, the judges and that, they've never really bin inside a jail, they dunie look into the backgrounds of the people they are dealing with. You done this, you're going away! They want to clean the streets up. They jam-pack the jails. And the staff haven't got the facilities to spend time with the lads to try to rehabilitate them. I mean, getting people to interact with each other, and with outside people as well. That's where the fitba's good, though. At the end of the game we all shake hands. Always at the end of the game there is respect. It's good.

6
ALARM BELLS

Thursday's basketball session drew to a close. All ten players were psyched into the contest. They wanted more. Geordie Foster stood in the centre of the sports hall, considering the request.

It was a tricky time, the end of a session. Tired players making one last effort before the finish. Tempers frayed, incidents could occur.

'All right lads, let's play on for one more quarter,' said Geordie, making no show of his wariness.

The thirty-six-year-old PEI refereed the match. At the start he had removed his panic alarm. It was supposed to be worn whenever on duty. The trouble was, the belt-mounted device was not designed for sport. Geordie discovered this out on the hockey pitch. Twice he had accidentally knocked the alarm. Twice a group of prison officers tumbled out of nowhere, rushing to the aid of an officer in distress. Sorry, false alarm – again. They saw the funny side of it, but Geordie was not happy to be crying wolf. A few months previously an inmate had plunged a pair of scissors into a Kingston officer's neck. The quick response of his colleagues may well have saved his life.

Wayne, who loathed Paddy's reproaches so much that he dropped out of the football team, protesting about his captaincy, was on the same side as Bunny. They bickered continually. When the session ended, it was Bunny's turn to voice one criticism too many.

'Shut your fackin' mouth,' yelled the ex-soldier.

'Don't you dare cunt me off,' spat back Bunny.

Chests out, eyes blazing, they were face to face, pushing and shoving.

Geordie dived in. 'Come on guys, knock it on the head, it ain't worth it, the game's finished.'

Wayne relaxed his aggressive posture. 'Awright, it's gone, let me go.'

Wayne left the sports hall, heading down the long corridor back towards the cell block. Before he was out of earshot, Bunny was at it again.

'Fuckin' tosser . . .'

Wayne turned immediately and ran back, shouting, 'I'll 'ave you!' Geordie struggled to block the sports hall entrance. Arms flailing, Wayne was now out of control, screaming threats and abuse. 'Cunt, cunt, you facking cunt. . .'

'Look man, leave it. Calm down!' bellowed Geordie.

'Take it *easy*,' urged Scouse, the football team substitute.

Geordie decided enough was enough. Using his control and restraint training, he knocked Wayne to the floor and reached for the panic alarm. That was when he remembered he'd left it on his desk. He could just about reach an alarm on the wall. He punched the red button. Help would come now.

Teddy, the middle-aged reserve defender with a wrestler's physique, held on to Bunny. To most of the cons, Ted was simply a 'big old boy' who'd been there and done that, as far as being a hardcase was concerned. The guards picked this up, of course. 'Ted's mature, he knows the score,' they would say, sounding relieved. But to outsiders he was Ted

the Merciless, who could have put Big Daddy and Giant
Haystacks in a half-Nelson, and whose huge knuckles and
mangled fingernails commanded attention. Teddy's grey
pony tail swung from side to side as Bunny bucked and
cussed in the clinch.

'I ain't afraid of fighting no screws, bring on as many as
you like!' he wailed. 'There're ain't enough screws in this
fuckin' nick to control me.'

Teddy looked agitated. 'No need for alarm bells, Geordie.
We got this under control.'

'Bollocks,' replied the PEI.

Three minutes passed but no one arrived. There was
obviously something wrong with the sports hall alarm.
Geordie felt bemused but the moment was passing. Wayne
and Bunny had already turned their minds to the possible
consequences of the fracas: a loss of privileges, fines, or
something much more serious. Geordie could write a report
accusing them of violent conduct. It would be on their
records the next time either man came up before a review
board. 'If you can't behave in here, why should we believe
you can behave on the outside?' And that one schoolboy
tussle could tip the balance, consigning them to two, maybe
three more years inside the concrete coffin.

'There was no need for that,' Geordie scolded. 'You're
lucky the alarm bell hasn't gone off, otherwise you'd both be
in deep shit.'

Wayne and Bunny said nothing. After a moment's silence
the session broke up. A group of players escorted Wayne back
to C wing. Geordie and Ted the Merciless followed behind
with Bunny, heading for D wing.

Later, Geordie stuck his head around the door of one of
the wing staff offices. 'Any of you fellas hear an alarm bell?'

The looked blank.

Another prison officer entered the room. 'Have some trouble down the gym?'

'Yeah, you could say that,' laughed Geordie.

The man was puzzled. 'Well, I looked down the corridor and thought I could see something going on, but I wasn't sure.'

'So you thought, "Oh, I won't bother having a look," ' suggested Geordie, sarcastically. 'I could have had my arse shagged with a wire brush for all you care.'

'Were you wearing your personal alarm?'

Geordie held up his hands, fed-up with the whole episode, and left them to their tea and biscuits.

Back in the gym office Geordie got changed, strapping on the black belt, which anchored his chrome key-chain and personal alarm. His dark blue tracksuit, polo shirt and training shoes attracted much less hostility than the uniforms worn by the prison officers on the wings. They bristled with authority in black trousers, ties and shoes, white shirts, and outdoor jackets the colour of dry coal. The black and white symbolised right and wrong. There were no grey areas, no mitigating circumstances.

It was different in the gym. Over a cup of tea Geordie said a report was unnecessary, but he would draw upon the incident when making his assessments of Bunny and Wayne. He appeared hardened to confrontation. A few weeks previously Carl and Morgan had squared up during football training, the latter signing off with, 'Don't call me a wanker. Don't call me *anything*.' Paddy and Micky the Surfer (so-called because he once rode ocean waves, as opposed to the Internet, a cultural phenomenon which meant nothing in prison) had also threatened to come to blows. Mickey, tall and statuesque, looked more like a lifeguard than a lifer, and could be seen about the prison grounds reading books about

J. S. Bach. He was doing an Open University music degree, and only occasionally trained with the squad.

'On the out, if someone is a complete tosser you can just walk away,' reflected Geordie. 'In here you're stuck with him. The cons have to learn how to deal with that. So, yeah, there are bust-ups, personality clashes, whatever, but, to be honest, when it comes to football the cons are better behaved than some of the lads they play against. You'd never see an inmate kicking lumps out of the opposition because he knows it would be a serious problem, one that's going to affect his future.'

Geordie's blond hair was prematurely grey and looked ill at ease with itself, somewhere between too curly and not straight enough. He sought to control it with gel. His face was not especially expressive, and his eyes were a cold blue. It was all at odds with his warm, generous nature.

The son of a fireman, Geordie's given name was in fact Wayne. He had stopped using it at fourteen, when his family moved away from Newbiggen, a jobless former mining village a few miles north of Newcastle. Geordie tried several vocations, including lorry driving, before becoming a physical education instructor. There were stints working for the Territorial Army and at adventure holiday centres in Cornwall and the Brecon Beacons, teaching canoeing, sailing and wind surfing. He took a short-term engagement as a Lance-Corporal in the regular army, warming up soldiers prior to the Gulf War. Once that was done, he settled on the prison service. In some ways Geordie was still an outsider. His accent was at odds with the soft Hampshire burr of his colleagues, people who would say 'I knows' instead of 'I know'.

Geordie was married and had two sons and a daughter. He made for lighter company than Nigel, but his poker face was harder to read. There were times when Geordie's expression suggested he was wrestling with private dilemmas, only for it to become apparent that he was thinking about Newcastle United's next match. Reading out loud from the sports pages was another proclivity: 'Alan Shearer has signed for Umbro – until he's forty-two!'

The two PEIs got on well enough, but might not have chosen each other as friends had work not brought them together. Nigel was the first to admit to having interests that extended no further than his job, his family and his love of sport. Geordie was more introspective, and had a taste for adventure. A large framed photograph of Captain Scott's ship the *Terra Nova* surrounded by Antarctic ice fields looked down on the reproduction furniture in his dining room. 'I like it because someone had to get out of the ship and walk all the way around here to take the picture,' Geordie explained. Paradoxically, while Nigel had spent years thinking about rehabilitating offenders, Geordie was much more circumspect. A lot of them were too self-obsessed for his own down-to-earth sensibilities. 'What's an inmate's favourite topic of conversation?' he would scoff. 'Himself.'

The players gave Geordie a hard time when he arrived, five months previously, from Guy's Marsh, a young offenders institution. Paddy questioned his every decision. Calvin, shaven-headed and gold-chained, acted bored and arrogant. So Geordie found himself 'dishing out a few home truths'. Calvin was told that it was all very well putting across his own point of view, but he had to listen to what others had to say. Paddy was advised to calm down. 'If someone makes a mistake, Paddy's on their case in a flash, even if they're one of the old boys who's only come out to make up the numbers for hockey.'

Geordie never played for Kingston Arrows. The idea of following Nigel's example and coming into the prison on his own time was out of the question.

It was all going wrong for Eddie.

The second game of the season, against Grant Thornton, was slipping away. The visitors, who represented the local branch of a national chain of accountants, went 2–1 up at the start of the second half, but the score did not reflect their dominance of the play. Paddy missed the few chances Kingston managed to create, and as the match wore on, the service dried up. That was when Nigel decided to change things around.

Calvin and Bunny were outnumbered in midfield. Steve, having scored an early goal, had 'gone missing' on the right wing, while Rizler was marked out of the game. Nigel switched to an impromptu 3–5–2 formation, pushing himself into midfield. The back line was reshaped, with Eddie, because of his pace, positioned between the two big defenders, Mick and Jonah.

The change backfired almost immediately. Grant Thornton sent a long ball down the middle. Eddie, the last man, mistimed his jump. One of their strikers darted forward and smacked the ball past Zebedee. 3–1.

The mistake rattled Eddie. One minute after the restart, he again went to block a pass, but miskicked wildly. Once again the ball was loose in the space behind the Kingston defence. It was a straight race between Eddie and one of their forwards. Considering he had to turn, Eddie performed heroics to get there first. But then, flustered, he hit a feeble back-pass. The forward pounced again to make it 4–1.

Unbelievably, Eddie underhit yet another back-pass two minutes later, and Kingston were 5–1 down. Stunned silence. No one said anything to Eddie; it was just too embarrassing for that. And when a cross was headed home to make it 6–1, Kingston looked like collapsing completely, but the goal was disallowed. Eddie was substituted. His face a mask of self-disgust and misery, he trudged towards the touchline, pulling off the black leather gloves that he wore to protect his scarred hands.

Carl got one back late on, but a 5–2 hammering was no one's idea of an entertaining Saturday afternoon.

When Nigel and Zebedee emerged from the showers, the inquest began.

Zebedee was not sympathetic. 'Eddie's all right as an attacking full-back, sitting on his man, but that's about it. He can't read the game.'

Nigel towelled himself down in silence.

'It's always the same with Grant Thornton,' continued Zebedee. 'They've been coming in here for years and going home with all the points. They're our bogey team.'

Terry Allison, the league official, dictated his match report over the telephone to the local sports paper, the *Football Mail*. When the call was completed, he was keen to offer his own theory.

'You need someone in midfield who can play the easy ball,' said Terry, brightly. 'I've seen David Batty destroy teams with passes from here to that radiator.'

7
PADDY (1)

It rained last night. I could also hear the road. It's weird – you get used to the background noise. When I first went to the Scrubs, it's right on the flight line for Heathrow, so I heard planes all the time. When I first came here it was trains. It felt like I hadn't slept a wink. To be honest, I don't sleep much now. I woke up at three a.m. on Friday. There was a thunderstorm. I got up and watched the lights for about twenty minutes.

On remand you've got people playing stereos all night, people screaming and shouting across the wings to each other. You've got loads of people who aren't going to be there that long. The pace of life is different. There's not that consideration for other people that there has to be on a long-termer's wing.

It's quieter here, but it's still hard to sleep. In the summer, when it's really hot, you are snatching an hour here and there. In the winter they pump hot, dry air into the cell. You can't sleep then, either. But my biggest gripe about my cell is that I haven't got anywhere comfortable to sit. You are on your bed or sat in your little chair, trying to read the paper or a book, but you just can't get comfortable. You're always leaning on your arm, or getting a crick in your neck. What you want is your favourite armchair. You haven't got that, and you're never going to get it.

I was at the Scrubs for three and a half years. The only football they had was a kick-about on an exercise yard the size of a postage stamp. It makes our tiny pitch look like Wembley.

I enjoy being captain, but there can be a bit of a hassle. Some of the lads have only ever played football in prison. They haven't learned the little things that make all the difference. I suppose everybody expects people to be able to do the same things that they can do. It's very difficult. I want to enjoy my football. I do enjoy it. But sometimes it's frustrating. I upset people; I'm aware of it. I'm having a go at someone for something they can't do. You don't think about it until afterwards. I'm not saying I'm right, but if I make a run to the far post, and they drive it to the near post all the time, that's frustrating. I can't just say nothing, I'm the team captain. But I don't like the niggles and friction. Why should I fall out with people over the football? I've got to live with them.

I know my football, I've played with some good footballers. I'm not being big-headed, but I feel I'm the best goal-scorer we've got. The first year I was here I scored thirty in sixteen games. Last year I scored nineteen. Had things been different, I could probably have gone to a higher level than I did. I went for trials at Southampton when I was a nipper. I didn't get selected. I played at right-back. I was no great shakes, not big for my age, although I've always had long legs. I played for the area rep side. Francis Benali was in the team. I mean, he was a man at fourteen.

We all need something we are good at. It's a self-esteem thing, especially in prison, after all you've gone through. It's like an identity crisis. There are all these things that I am now that I never was before. Or that I could never imagine myself being. Sport has enabled me to retain some good feelings about myself, instead of going to the other extreme and ripping myself to pieces.

One of the beauties of football is that whatever level you play at, it's your FA Cup, your European Cup, your World Cup. It's not less than playing at the top. It may only be one game but it's with you all week. On Monday you've got the last match, thinking about what happened. By the time you get to Wednesday and Thursday you're looking ahead to the next one. There are eleven players on the pitch but it has a knock-on effect. A lot of the guys watch the football.

We are not all best mates in the team. The C wing guys – Teddy, Duffy, Scouse and Wayne – spend all their time together. Riz is on the fringes of that group. Jonah goes his own way. I get on with all of them – apart from Wayne, who's a little bit strange, to say the least. Calvin, Bunny, Carl and myself talk but it's a bit of an anticlimax after games. We tend to go our separate ways.

I used to be particularly friendly with Griff, the gym orderly. At the moment I'm just doing my own thing. I'm not one for getting involved with big heavy friendships. I'm not a loner, I'm just happy with my own company. It's almost like there's a prison attitude, a mentality, that I don't feel I have. Certain people have been in and out of prison, and it's kind of like arrested development. They are all eighteen years old. And they'll never get any older. I find that quite scary. Some of them are genuinely nice people, but I don't want to spend time with them.

It's amazing how quickly you adapt to your environment – because you have to. When I first went to the Scrubs, from Winchester, it was like, oh God. I'd never been in prison, but I'd heard of the Scrubs. One of those 'orrible places in London where they beat you to within an inch of your life every week. I remember thinking I was going to be on a wing full of murderers. Then it dawns on you: 'No, you can't think like that, you're one of those now.' Although it sounds a bit strange, I missed Winchester. I knew most of the staff and was kind of settled. That was important because everything else in my life was going down the tubes.

Within about four to six weeks of arriving at the Scrubs, that's when it hit home that this was going to be my life. That was the roughest patch. There were a couple of guys who helped me in the right way. They said, 'This is the way it is and you've just got to get through it.' They were honest. When you survive the bad spells it gives you some reference points. You think, 'Well, I've been here before and this time it's not so intense.' There are people who become so depressed it becomes mental illness. There was a time when I thought I'd never cope. There's the whole wrench of being taken away from your family and friends, your environment. The woman who lives at the end of the road; you don't know her name, but you say hello to her every morning. All those little things are part of who you are. When you're taken away from that, it's like, 'Who am I? What do I amount to?'

I can only talk from personal experience, but I suppose if you are that bit older, you're a little bit more established as far as who you are, then it's not so tough. I was twenty when I came in. A great deal of my sense of self was based around my father and the group of people I associated with. When you lose that . . . it's like a mid-life crisis – you don't know who you are. But maybe that's not the case, maybe it's harder if you're older. There's a guy here who was a building society manager. I'm sure he was a good building society manager. I'm sure people came in and he treated them well. He's always got time to talk and listen. A great bloke. But if you've done that for twenty years and then end up in a place like this, that's got to be difficult.

When I first came inside I was bursting with tears. For

nights on end you can't sleep. Your mind won't switch off. You can go weeks without having a really bad time, and then one night something sets you off. There's always a part of you saying 'I've got to deal with this, I've got to survive', because you want to survive. There's another part that says, 'Look at what you've done. How could you have done that? It's terrible.' And then there's a part of you that thinks, 'Look at what your mum and dad and your grandmother and your sisters and your friends are going through, and it's your fault.' You'll pull yourself apart.

At the stage I'm at now it's less raw and emotional. You don't try to justify what you've done. You can't keep knocking yourself all the time. You have to be able to live with yourself. It sounds so glib to say you have to go on, but if you can't forgive yourself for what you've done, you can't hope for other people's forgiveness. All you can do is say, 'Look, what I did is terrible, I didn't think it would happen, I wish it never happened, I still feel bad about it, even if not in the same way, but the only thing I can do is make sure that it will not happen again.'

I'm reasonably confident, but sometimes I find that something happens and it knocks my confidence and starts off this whole spiral of 'How do you know who you are? This is who you thought you were before, but it turns out you've killed someone.' I never thought I'd get into a situation where I could kill someone. You don't think of yourself as a potential murderer.

People in here don't want to know your problems. On the outside people make more time for you. If you split up with your girlfriend, your mates will say, 'Let's take him out. Have a few beers.' You never get that release in prison. You drag your problems around with you. I've been inside for eight years. Sometimes I think I can't keep dragging myself along. The days are so similar. Over and over again. You have to

become accustomed to prison life to survive, but you don't
want to. There's always a fear of becoming institutionalised.

8

MANSLAUGHTER UNITED

Of course none of the players meant to commit murder. That is to say, it was a momentary loss of control, a struggle that got out of hand, one mistake that changed the course of dozens of lives. Even those men who apparently demonstrated obvious 'intent' – putting a gun to the head of a shop owner who refused to open a till, and pulling the trigger – were able to cite mitigating circumstances. 'The gun just went off in my hand . . .'

Most of the players accepted responsibility for the physical act of killing. It was just that they felt manslaughter to be a more accurate reflection of the nature and circumstances of their crimes. That was natural enough: a murder conviction carries a mandatory life term; manslaughter, on the other hand, gives the judge discretion. The sentencing options range from life all the way down to an absolute discharge.

There are 7,000 crimes, ranging from minor regulatory offences – concerning, for instance, traffic and the operation of pubs – through property offences, public order offences, moral offences such as prostitution, offences created for the protection of the state, and offences involving violence. In the UK, the mandatory life sentence reflects the assumption that murder is a crime of such unique heinousness that the offender forfeits his right ever to be set free.

The players did not find the verdict easy to live with. Most told themselves that the 'murder' they had committed was somehow an accident of fate, that everything would have been different had the victim not appeared at that precise moment. These sentiments were dismissed by corrections officers as predictable attempts to minimise responsibility, but it was almost as if the players never recovered from the shock of discovering that the law is a blunt instrument when it comes to dealing with homicide. They were appalled to learn that demonstrating they had not *wanted* to kill was almost irrelevant. In court, the central question is simply whether the defendant had *intended* to cause death or serious injury. And as Lord Bingham stated in a landmark ruling (R v. Moloney, 1985), it is quite possible to intend a result which you do not actually want. He gave the example of a man who, in an attempt to escape pursuit, boards a plane to Manchester. Even though he may have no desire to go to Manchester, that is clearly where he intends to go.

With the exception of Jonah, the players had all pleaded not guilty to murder. A few maintained genuine innocence, but in most cases the plea was part of a strategy. The players were united in the vain hope of getting the charge reduced to manslaughter.

At Crown Court, a defendant listens as the prosecution sets about proving its case beyond reasonable doubt. To win, the prosecution is obliged to score twice. The first goal is establishing 'factual cause' – demonstrating that 'but for' the conduct of the accused, the victim would not have died as and when he or she did. The second is 'legal cause', the sometimes more murky question of whether, in law, the defendant is liable for murder.

There are three ways for the prosecution to establish legal cause. It can show that, at the time of the victim's death, the original wounds or injuries inflicted by the defendant were still an 'operative' cause of that death (as opposed to any misfortune which might have struck the victim following those original wounds). In doing so, the barristers are able to refer to precedent, such as R v. Smith (1959) where a soldier was stabbed in a brawl. He was dropped twice as he was being taken to hospital, only to suffer a long delay before being seen by a doctor, as staff mistakenly thought that the case was not urgent. When the soldier eventually did receive treatment it was 'thoroughly bad' and might have affected his chances of recovery. He died two hours after being stabbed. Nonetheless, the court took the view that the original wound was still an operative cause of death and the accused was liable for murder.

Alternatively, the prosecution can establish legal cause by demonstrating that the death was 'reasonably foreseeable'. So, if a defendant had knocked his victim unconscious and left him or her lying on a beach, it was reasonably foreseeable that when the tide came in the victim would drown, and he would have caused the death. However, the defendant would not be liable for murder if the victim was left unconscious on the seashore then killed by a car running out of control off a nearby road. Clearly, the intervening act could not have been said to be reasonably foreseeable. Finally, the prosecution can invoke the 'thin skull test'. This meant the players had to take their victims as they found them. So, if, for instance, one of them struck his victim over the head with the kind of blow which would not usually kill, but the victim had an unusually thin skull which made the blow fatal, he would be liable.

Before their cases came to trial the players became aware, if they did not know already, that there are three types of unlawful homicide: murder, voluntary manslaughter and involuntary manslaughter. Again, murder requires malice aforethought – the defendant *intended* to kill or cause serious injury. But the definition is misleading: his motives need not have been malicious. Deliberate euthanasia prompted by a motive of compassion satisfies the malice aforethought requirement quite adequately. Voluntary manslaughter means that the intent to kill or cause serious injury existed, but the court accepts there were mitigating circumstances which reduced the defendant's liability. These relate to his mental condition. No one is ever charged with voluntary manslaughter; the defendant faces a murder rap and puts his defence, hoping to get the charge knocked down to voluntary manslaughter by entering a plea of provocation or diminished responsibility. (*In*voluntary manslaughter relates to cases where there was no intent to kill or cause serious injury – for example, where death resulted from negligence of some kind.)

Once sentenced to life the Home Office can keep prisoners incarcerated for as long as it deems necessary. The minimum term to be served, the tariff, is decided by the trial judge in consultation with the Home Office. This figure is sometimes revised (upwards) by the Home Secretary. The effects can be dramatic. John, one of the Kingston reserves, was given a fifteen-year tariff for standing by while his accomplice suffocated three elderly people during two burglaries. David Waddington, Home Secretary at the time, doubled his tariff to thirty years.

The route into the prison system is always the same. From Crown Court detainees are taken to a local jail where they are assessed as to the likelihood of escape, and the danger they would present if they did get out. There are four security categories into which prisoners are placed: A, B, C and D.

Category A prisoners spend the majority of their time in isolation, and consider themselves fortunate to see natural daylight, much less exercise.

Category B prisoners are deemed not dangerous enough

to demand the very highest conditions of security, but escape must be made extremely difficult.

Catgory C prisoners cannot be trusted in open conditions, but do not have the ability or resources to make a determined escape attempt.

Category D prisoners represent the lowest security risk, and can reasonably be trusted to serve their sentences in open conditions.

Kingston is a Cat B prison. Most of the players started their sentence in one of three English jails: Wormwood Scrubs, London; Gartree in Market Harborough, Leicestershire; or Wakefield in West Yorkshire. Being lifers they were regarded as a special needs group, and these institutions had specialist lifer-induction units. 'Staff must recognise that prisoners serving indeterminate sentences have a need for support and guidance beyond that required by fixed-term prisoners, even long-termers,' cautions the Home Office in guidance notes to staff. The fact lifers are given single cells is more a practicality than anything else – they have more belongings.

Having been appraised by psychologists, each prisoner is given a sentence plan. Put bluntly, it tells the recipient what is wrong with him. The diagnosis comes in the form of a list of 'risk factors'. These could be anything about the prisoner that contributed to his offence. Each is required to take part in psychotherapy and group counselling to address his behaviour. If the case has a sexual connotation, the inmate is referred to the Sex Offenders Treatment Programme (SOTP). The other courses include Relationships, Cognitive Skills, Drug Awareness and Alcohol Awareness.

The course work was completed by the players over the years as they left the three induction jails and moved into the prison system. Some of them were transferred to HMP Grendon, in Buckinghamshire, a unique British jail run along the lines of a therapeutic community. Inmates take part in intensive group therapy aimed at unravelling, understanding and changing anti-social behaviour. The rationale is that unexpressed anger contributed to their offences. So the inmates go through a variety of role-playing exercises to relive painful experiences from their past, with the specific intention of emptying them of anger.

In 1997 there were some 4,500 lifers in UK jails. By conviction, the population broke down as 85 per cent murder, 6 per cent manslaughter or other homicide/attempted homicide offences, 7 per cent sexual offences, and 2 per cent arson. The one thread linking the majority of homicides together was loss of control, so Anger Management courses were all but mandatory. At Kingston, these groups were attended by about eight inmates at a time. The tutor took them on a grand tour of anger, beginning with a few basics: anger could be the result of hurt pride, of unreasonable expectations, or of winding themselves up with hostile fantasies. Apart from employing anger to get something they wanted, the tutor suggested that the players might have used anger to blame others for their own shortcomings, to justify oppressing others, to boost flagging egos, and to hide other emotions (such as fear). Any situation that frustrated them was a potential trigger for anger and aggression, which was defined as an action intended to harm someone. The tutor distinguished aggression from assertiveness – a person tactfully and rationally standing up for his own rights. (Assertiveness was the subject of a whole other course.) The fireworks began when each man was required to discuss his experiences of losing control, prompted by questions along the lines of, 'Was it like an electric charge going through you? Or did you go blank?' They hated talking in front of each other, but failure to participate was a stumbling block to progress through the system.

There were periodic review boards. The panel searched for signs that the players accepted absolute responsibility for their offences. Anyone who attempted to avoid blame by placing emphasis, for example, on the goodness of his cause ('I was protecting a friend'), or by degrading his victim in any way (he or she somehow 'deserved it') was not, in theory, going to advance.

The Kingston Arrows had all come up against acerbic characters like Theodore Dalrymple, the *Spectator* columnist and prison psychiatrist who gave short shrift to sob stories. The players *were* allowed to have come from troubled backgrounds – perhaps they grew up accustomed to violence, in a family where a raised voice became a verbal attack which escalated to a raised hand which led to a shove, then a slap, and finally severe beatings. But lifers were gambling with their future if they used these issues to avoid taking responsibility for their own failings. It was the job of the review board to make sure an inmate did not think of himself as a victim of circumstance, because such a scenario would mean that he was not a bad person or a failure; indeed, he deserved sympathy. Mistreated by a cruel world, the prisoner might even reach the conclusion that he did not need to change.

The discussion group approach represented remarkable progress from the days when a lifer only had to stay clear of trouble, keep his cell tidy, and convince the prison chaplain of his penitence, before moving on towards release. But it was severely criticised by some psychologists. Courses were designed to train offenders in empathy, putting them in touch with their feelings and helping them to develop a conscience. This approach was based on the assumption that the offenders had simply gone off track and needed re-socialisation. It might work in some cases, the critics argued, but would be useless when dealing with an offender who had psychopathic tendencies.

The criteria for diagnosing a psychopath vary around the globe, but there is a consensus that psychopaths willingly cause pain and suffering. They know how much it hurts only in an abstract intellectual sense; they are unable to construct an 'emotional facsimile' of others. About 15 to 20 per cent of prisoners are thought to have psychopathic tendencies. The disorder is common among drug dealers, spouse and child abusers, swindlers and con men, gang members, mercenaries, terrorists and cult leaders.

'In a frantic search for understanding, we blame upbringing, poverty, flawed environment, or an ineffective criminal justice system,' suggested Robert Hare, Professor of Psychology at the University of British Columbia, in *The Harvard Mental Health Letter*. 'All these may be important, but we tend to ignore the suffering inflicted by a few people whose antisocial attitudes and behaviour result less from social forces than from an inherent sense of entitlement and an incapacity for emotional connection to the rest of humanity. For these individuals – psychopaths – social rules have no constraining force. Lacking in conscience and feelings for others, they take what they want and do as they please, violating social norms and expectations without guilt or regret. They often pass through a variety of treatment programs without success. They learn enough psychiatric and psychological jargon to convince therapists, counsellors and parole boards that they are making progress, but they use that knowledge only to develop better ways to manipulate and deceive.'

9

BAD DOGS

Scouse rolled his eyes in disbelief. The hours in the gym, pounding the punch bag, doing the circuits, shedding sixteen pounds – it was all for nothing. Nigel completely rearranged the team for the third match of the season, changing tactics and personnel, but there was still no place for the defender, who was again named as a substitute.

Scouse approached winning a position in the starting eleven with the same logic that might be applied to a bus queue. That two reserve-team players leapfrogged over him was beyond belief. 'I've got the skills and the commitment,' he would tell anyone who was prepared to listen. A raw, hard edge carried his voice. Scouse sounded like a factory machine which had been grating away for years, its owners having neglected to provide the proper amounts of oil and grease. Maybe it was just that he assumed he had to raise his voice to be heard. After all, the other players said he had 'a heart of gold'.

Scouse was thirty-three and ten years into a life term for a murder he committed during a burglary. He never said so directly, but he gave the impression that the break-in was related to the need to finance a heroin addiction.

The frustration of missing out on selection shrank the pupils of his blue eyes to pinpricks, so that his face, with its pale, rough skin, seemed especially harsh. His blond hair was shaved to stubble. The severity of the cut made his skull resemble an old white tennis ball which had been left outside too long, the surface fabric worn away to reveal the blemishes and marks underneath.

Scouse was lucky to have any hair. Like the other inmates who had been Young Offenders before committing the offence which landed them a life sentence, he was covered in scars. As a teenager he stole an RS Cosworth from outside a recreation centre in Chester. During the ensuing police chase Scouse lost control of the sports car and crashed into a concrete plinth. Something came through the windscreen and scalped him. When he woke up in hospital, Scouse yanked a drip out of his arm and tried to run for it. That was when he discovered that one of his knees was smashed, and that the top of his head was a pulpy mess that throbbed like it had been tenderised with a butcher's hammer. A white, lifeless scar marked the line where a surgeon reattached the scalp.

Carl was sitting in the gym office when Scouse appeared, a towel around his neck and a film of perspiration glinting on his clean-shaven jaw. The punch bag had been jabbed, hooked and cuffed for about twenty minutes.

'Morgan – plays like a mule, and he's put him in instead of me, fuckin' stupid twat,' said Scouse, quickfire.

'Yeah?' said Carl. 'You rubbed your name off the team sheet, didn't you?'

'Don't matter.'

'You putting it back on?'

'No.'

For a moment Scouse brimmed silently with the injustice of it, then he continued. 'How could he pick Morgan over me?'

'Well, you know what I mean, it's up to you Scouse, innit?' replied Carl, a smile trickling across his face.

'No, it's not up to me. I don't pick the team. I've proved my fitness. I'm quicker and more committed than Morgan. All day, Carl. You saw how he done on that run last week. He's a fuckin' ming.'

'What, the run on Thursday?'

'Yeah.'

'You done better than him?'

'Fuckin' right. I beat him every time. Every time, Carl. And I'm not even going to argue with you, Carl, because I know I'm better than Morgan. I know. I mightn't be as good in the air as him but I'm a more complete player. I'm more committed. I'm not fuckin' frightened of getting injured. I'm not *scared* of the opposition.'

The need for two team changes had given the cynics a field day. What a surprise: Jonah, the hypochondriac, had picked up an Achilles tendon injury. As for Steve, the only thing more predictable than the squad's newest member becoming its first drop-out of the season was his lame excuse. Steve said he no longer wanted to play because of a 'long-term groin injury'. The grapevine told a different story. Steve was stuck in the dinner queue when he overheard Carl, a few places behind, rubbishing his contribution. 'Headless chicken, bottling out of tackles . . .' Steve took it all to heart.

When Nigel heard the news he sought Steve out, but his mind was made up. For him, coming to terms with a life sentence was hard enough without having to worry about the petty politics of the football team. His head couldn't take any more. He didn't want to be considered again.

Nigel was disappointed, but in the wake of the Grant Thornton defeat had already decided to revamp the midfield for the second visit of Plover (whose prompt return was a legacy of the rearranged fixture list). To this end, he was switching to a 3–4–1–2 formation. It meant there were fewer opportunities for squad members, like Scouse, who were not considered up to the task of playing anywhere other than at the back.

There was Jonah's place, but this went to Ted the Merciless. Morgan, a thirty-five-year-old D wing resident, replaced Steve. A ringer for Action Man's wayward cousin, having the same square-jawed, outdoorsy appearance but none of the trademark muscular cladding, Morgan's lack of fitness usually kept him on the bench. He was plastered in tattoos – including a spider's web on his neck.

Morgan was given a holding role in the centre alongside Calvin. Bunny was switched to the left side of midfield. Eddie moved out of defence to patrol the right flank. Much to his annoyance, Paddy, leading scorer for the past two seasons, was pulled back to float between midfield and attack, supporting Rizler and Carl up front. Ted, Nigel and Mick formed a three-man defence in front of prison officer Zebedee. Luke, the first-choice goalkeeper in pre-season, had yet to start a match.

'Why couldn't he have slotted me in?' demanded Scouse. 'That's pushing me nose out of joint. Obviously me face don't fit.'

Carl giggled, glad that for once it was not him bumping along the bottom, the whole world on his shoulders.

'It just don't matter what I do, I'm not going to get in the fuckin' first team,' lamented Scouse.

'You *are* in the first team—'

'But I'm not gonna get a *start*. I'm more committed than half the team—'

'Yeah, but you check it out—'

Scouse cut him off again. 'I carry on all game. All game. I never fuckin' give up. I never give up. That's all I'm saying. I keep going for the ball, even when I'm not going to get it.

I never give up. I think the team should be picked on that, not on who can jump higher than me.'

'You started the last friendly—'

'Yeah, and he made me captain – but he's put them reserve lads in over me.'

Carl spun himself round on Nigel's ancient swivel chair. 'Look, I don't know where Nigel's coming from, but he's not gong to pick you if you rub your name off the Availability List.'

'Yeah, but I put it up every time. Every time. And that's the third time he's ignored me.'

'But didn't someone put your name down and *you* scrubbed it off?'

'So what! Someone put me name on, and I scrubbed it off. Then I put it back on meself.'

Scouse looked sheepish. No one had the right to put his name down on the Availability List. That was a liberty.

'I've sat on the subs bench every game this season. Morgan's not even put his name on the list *once*. As soon as he does, he gets picked.'

'But—'

'*No*, Carl. Nigel said to me at the beginning of the season—'

'Yeah, but Morgan's playing in midfield and you're a defender.'

'Big deal. He could have taken someone out of the back and put them in midfield. Nigel told me. He said, "It's only Eddie keeping you out of the team. As soon as there's a place, you're in." Ted got in ahead of me – and I'm not talking behind his back.'

'Yeah, but Ted's improved, hasn't he, really?'

'Yeah, but even Ted said I should be playing before him. Why did Morgan get picked the *first* time he puts his name on the fuckin' list? You haven't got an answer have you? I have: it's because I'm on fuckin' C wing.'

Carl scoffed. C wing was second class all right, but that was where Ted lived, wasn't it?

Scouse showed no sign of flagging. 'Geordie phoned Nige last night and said, "Who are you putting in, Morgan or Scouse?" And Nige said, "Fuckin' leave Scouse on the bench."'

Carl laughed. 'You heard that?'

'Fuckin' Geordie told me.'

At that point Geordie appeared. With perfect comic timing, he shot back, 'I told you nothing.'

Later, when the match kicked off, everything was wrong with the world.

'Riz is not well,' sighed Scouse, standing on the touchline. 'I don't know what's wrong with him.' A few moments later he added, a touch ominously, 'There's a lot of unrest in the prison at the moment. Too much change.'

The rumour of the week suggested Kingston was moving away from its exclusive life-only status. The prospect of living alongside a bunch of fixed-termers, who could entertain themselves by baiting men with everything to lose, was not Scouse's idea of an encouraging development. Worse still, the football pitch might be scarified, with a new wing built on the sacred rectangle.

Such hearsay was not taken lightly. Luke, the goalkeeper who, like Scouse, was perplexed by his continued non-selection, wrote to Richard Tilt, the Director of the Prison Service, expressing his consternation at the proposal. Luke even received a reply: his query was being forwarded to the South Coast Area Manager.

There was an alternative prediction. An inquiry into an IRA breakout from another English prison had demanded enhanced security measures at all prisons holding Cat A or Cat B inmates. For Kingston, this could mean a second perimeter wall being built inside the existing one. This new obstacle would infringe on the pitch. As every available square yard of land for the playing surface was already exhausted, the long-term future of Kingston Arrows appeared to be in some jeopardy.

'You see we're all naked, aren't we?' declared Scouse, when asked whether it mattered. 'People don't want to know us. People don't want to know our problems. All they want is the prison service to lock us up and throw away the key. That's all that matters.' He shook his head. 'You can't lock a bad dog up and expect it to be good on its own. If you just leave it, nothing will happen. It will stay a bad dog. What happens when they let it out?'

Scouse told a story about making friends with a man convicted of rape, the point of which seemed to be that not all lifers were such bad blokes. 'Cracking lad, from Liverpool, good footballer, getting on a bit now. Him and this other lad burgled this house. There was a woman in the place, early hours of the morning. They put a blade on her neck, and started looking for a safe. And she was in her knickers and bra. This lad was out of his fuckin' head on coke. He's come to the end of this fuckin' burglary and this bird's said, "I suppose you're going to rape me now." He'd never even thought of it. But, cos she's given him the idea, he's fuckin' shagged her anyway. She even made a plea to the judge, asking him not to life the fella off.'

The referee, a thin, pale figure, jogged past. Having done little to stamp his authority on the match, reckless tackles were exchanged as acquaintances from the first game were renewed. A Plover defender tumbled as Carl barged past. They squared up, but stood down following the mandatory exchange of industrial language.

After twenty minutes, Kingston settled down, playing some incisive, counter-attacking football. It set the pattern for the match. Inaction Man was doing a sound, if unspectacular job, but Scouse was not prepared to concede that Morgan's presence gave the side a more solid look.

Carl and his marker continued niggling each other. The Plover captain cautioned his team mate to 'calm down'. The marker muttered something about Carl throwing his weight around. 'I know, it's what they're in here for, innit?' replied the captain.

On thirty-five minutes Calvin dispatched a grass-cutter behind the defence. For once, Carl read the pass early. Easily beating his marker for pace, he latched on to the ball, drew the goalkeeper and scored.

At the start of the second half, Rizler poached two quick goals to make it 3–0. Eager to make up for the Grant Thornton débâcle, Kingston kept pushing forward. Carl and Eddie both scored before Paddy made it 6–0, hitting the target with a low, patient drive into the corner. The captain may have finished the previous season as top scorer with nienteen goals, but he had been missing everything since the opening game. Paddy allowed himself a smile on the walk back to the half-way line.

'Well done Pad,' shouted Scouse. 'Keep them shootin' boots on.'

Guessing that, with the points safe, Nigel would give the substitutes a run, Scouse began warming up. With twenty minutes remaining he duly got his chance, replacing Teddy. There was no public address system to mark this momentous event, and no thunder from the crowd. But Scouse was on, and that was all that mattered. With his forearms out in front, like Pinocchio, he ebbed back and forth, never straying into the opposition half, his gaze switching between the action ahead, and sideways, checking Nigel's position.

Scouse was just beginning to look comfortable when a striker weaved the ball towards him at speed. Scouse might have jockeyed him to the touchline. Or into the centre of the pitch where Calvin and Morgan were on patrol. Scouse could even have attempted a tackle. In fact, when the moment came he seemed unsure what to do. So he jumped into the player. It was a car crash of a challenge, shoulder into body. The striker collapsed, winded, astonished.

'Sorry lad,' said Scouse.

Teddy watched all this with mild amusement. He was not yet so old that anyone would chance flying into a reckless tackle with him. And he loved it. Some of the inmates, like Paddy, moved briskly around the cell block, reluctant to linger on the open landings. Teddy strolled down the centre of whatever space he occupied, head upright, shoulders rolling, surveying all before him.

Teddy turned down all requests for interviews, though he did once ask if I had met The Spice Girls. He was two-thirds of the way through a thirty-year minimum term for shooting dead two security guards during a robbery. Scouse and his other C wing neighbours tended to defer to him, partly because he was older, but also on account of the severity of his sentence. 'Ted's done a lot of bird,' they would say. Ted could not actually count on being released in ten years. Before the child killer Myra Hindley reached her thirty-year tariff the Home Office revised the figure upwards so that she would remain in prison until her death. The Court of Appeal upheld the decision.

Teddy also lived with the knowledge that the people who would decide his fate were not interested in taking risks. The Home Office knew all about the mistakes, the lifers who were granted their liberty only to reoffend. A commissioned study had revealed that 1,329 lifers were released on licence between 1972 and 1991. Of these, 23 per cent were reconvicted of some sort of crime. Of the reoffenders, 3.8 per cent were reconvicted of a 'grave' offence, i.e. homicide, rape, robbery or aggravated burglary. The remaining 77 per cent did not reoffend during the study period.

Kingston housed at least two men who had served one life sentence for murder, been freed on licence, and then killed again. One man had murdered his wife during an argument. He went through the whole shebang, doing fifteen years before the parole board judged him eligible for release on licence. Then he married again but, during a fierce disagreement with his new partner, killed her, too. Perhaps unwilling to extend the ritual of criminal discovery and investigation any longer than was absolutely necessary, the man simply walked into a local police station and said, 'I've done something to my wife.'

Teddy, mopping sweat from his forehead, approached another inmate, a bald, hunched figure whose face was deeply lined. He was Scrotal Bill, the unofficial club official. On match days Bill took it upon himself to make a flask of tea for Terry Allison. A D wing resident, he was in the habit of making gloomy predictions. Even when Kingston were leading 6–0, Bill would mumble, 'Well, they might get a result today, but what about next week?'

Teddy asked Bill the time.

'Whatcha wanna know for?'

'Because I'm catchin' the 4.40 p.m. to Waterloo. Why d'you think I wanna know?'

'Five minutes to go,' said Bill, remembering the importance of avoiding showing too much attitude while addressing cons twice his size.

Teddy wandered off, laughing softly, as if to say, 'The people you have to put up with in here . . .'

Shaggy and Duffy had followed Scouse into the fray. The substitutions produced a riotous climax to the match as

Kingston suddenly lost grip in midfield, and Plover surged forward, pulling two goals back in the last few minutes.

Still, with a 6–2 victory no one complained too loudly, least of all Scouse, who walked back to the cell block nursing his ribs and chatting with Nigel.

10
SCOUSE

I always wear a sports label cos that shows who I am. I read 4–4–2 and Britain's biggest non-league football magazine. You've got to keep the contact with the outside world. It's like a big umbilical cord. If you lose that, you've lost everything. Since I bin away I've started writing to people who I'd never have come across in my outside life. I've got a pen friend who's a consultant surgeon. He knows me mum and heard about my case through the media. The letters help, and it makes a change to get along with people who I wouldn't have even spoke to outside because, really, I only speak to my own. I don't trust the papers. They tell lies. Or the near truth. Look at Ravanelli. He was going to join Everton. I'll say no more. That was going on for months and he's ended up in France. He's at Marseilles. France was never mentioned. That's how good they are.

I miss my family, Goodison Park – obviously, and my pals. I miss shaggin'. The first couple of years away me 'ead was on women, but after a while . . . you're still the same person, but you've gotta get by without them. I miss male company more. Goin' out with the boys and having a good scream. Like today, Everton, we're at home. Fuckin' hell, I'd make me way to the Blue House for about noon. Have a pie or whatever, then go to Goodison. I used go to every game, home and away. That would be my life. I'd be a single fella, going to football at the weekend, working in the building trade.

I work with the gardener here. I like being outdoors. My dream job would be to work as the groundsman at Goodison. But I might as well dream on. The Home Office let you out when they want, mate. To be honest, I don't think about it, I just crack on. I've got to go with the flow. Done ten years already.

My risk factors are violent behaviour, alcohol and drugs. Take alcohol and drugs away from me and I'm all right. That's bin the problem all my life. I can make you a bottle of prison grog that'll be ready in five days. A couple of cups will put you on your arse. So you can't say that temptation doesn't exist. Here, in prison, is the hardest place to say no. It's a way out, an escape. If I took heroin then I'm no longer in jail.

You've got to work hard to get to a place like Kingston. You've got to address your behaviour. No Class A drugs. No violent behaviour. People think we have an easy time. We fuckin' don't. No one's behind that door when we're banged up. I don't want to be on my own all my fuckin' life. I like being around people, I want to be with people. I *can* do it. But I've had to go through unbelievable emotions.

It took me four years to get into my sentence. You've got to come to terms with becoming a murderer. I'm a murderer. I'm not a murderer. I am. At first you just go round and round. The second stage is dealing with it, and I suppose the third stage will be going back outside. People are going to know.

I've committed the worst crime. I'm never going forget it. I live with it every day. I've not slept right since I bin in prison. That's right, so what? It's not going to bring no one back. So what if you break down *completely*. Fuck you. Fuck you! You killed someone.

What is the point of remorse? Well, the system expects you to show remorse. But how can you show remorse in a man's world? I showed my remorse, done all my suffering behind that door. I don't want to share that with nobody. Before I came here I never shared stuff with nobody. Now I let bits out. Only the things that are important to the system. The other bits are private to me. Every year I have to see the probation officer, a psychologist, case worker, education, the PEIs and tell them the same fuckin' story. But it's done. You can't keep repeating yourself. Why can't they just get last year's reports and read them? They're exactly the same.

I don't want to talk about my offence.

I *can* talk about it, but there's no *need* for me to talk about it.

I never meant to do it, but I did it. I lost it. You know, bad. With one of my family members – well, a family connection. The way I look at it everyone's allowed one major fuck-up in life. I've made mine. It's sad. All murders are sad, but some good's got to come out of it else it's a waste of time sending people away.

I'm starting to reap the fruits. I feel a better person.

I used to have a short fuse. It used to be about a quarter of an inch but now it's huge. You've got to change. You can't be that fuckin' fella on the street any more. I've learned to control myself.

My family are all good people. My dad had a plastering firm. Oh aye, I was a right fuckin' handful. Seeking attention, a lot of it. Didn't want to go to school. Didn't mean nothing to me. I was good with me hands – car mechanics, woodwork. But I've always been a bit of a rogue. Since I was about ten.

I've bin married. It done me 'ead in, mate. I was twenty-three. I was bored. I didn't need her. I only married because she looked good. We have a son.

I grew up with drug money. Money, money, money. Loadsamoney. I used to work for these fellas. They'd give me a tenna a week. I never had fuck all, so it were easy. They were on my estate. 'Want a job?' What is it? 'Putting envelopes through doors . . .'

I didn't want to be like everyone else. I've gone the other way. I was aggressive and boisterous. I liked being able to spend, spend, spend and not worry about it. The trouble is, it don't matter how much money you make, how high on the ladder you go. When you come to jail you're on your own, back down at the bottom. All my family are in jail because every day they've got to think of me being in jail.

Drugs mess you up and put your family under tons of fucking stress. The lifestyle ruins people. It was a fuckin' nightmare, really. I was getting plenty of cash but you can't spend it happy. You just get involved in drinking sessions and card schools. It was all fucking bollocks. I'm flamboyant. I like to be noticed. I couldn't mix with non-criminals. It's a terrible life, because you know that's all you've got. You were dealing with people who would rob the eyes out of a blind man. Who would fuckin' rob you now, in this room?

I've known guys in jail who mugged the telephone repair man. It was at [HMP] Full Sutton, which is a hardcore jail, people pissed up and drugged up on the landings. The fuckin' phone man come on the wing because the card phone was dodgy. So these two lads have come along, put a blade to him, took him in a pad, took his rings and chains and watches, then fucked off. I was laughing. I watched the whole scam go down. The screws didn't know who done it. Two black fellas; it coulda bin anyone.

Prison is an aggressive, violent place. I come from a hard estate but there's nothing as aggressive as the lifers' wing at

Full Sutton. You might see someone get hit in the face in a pub now and then, but it happens every day in jail. You've got to deal with that. It don't matter who you are. If a smack head wants to rob you, he'll rob you, then you've got to deal with that.

At the end of the day I can do as many courses as they want but there's no telling if I'm going to reoffend until I get out. There's courses that you can't do. You might be sitting next to a fella who never broke the law before he committed the offence that got him lifed off. I've gone the other way. I've come in jail having been a villain all my life and will go out the other way.

I don't want to be a villain any more. Because it's fuckin' jail, innit? I can't stand it any more. I've been in and out since I was fifteen. I can't stand it. I fuckin' *hate* it. I can go outside now and I know I'm fucked. No one wants to know a murderer. I know I can't do anything, but I'm happy about that. I feel with the confidence I've gained since I bin here that I don't need drugs for people to like me. That's all I used to do it for a lot of the time, to socialise. But it don't matter any more. I've realised since I've bin sober that people are into the real me. So when I was trying to buy people off, trying to get involved, that was all bollocks. People like me anyway.

I'm fucked on my own. I've done three years in segregation. I had this big fuckin' attitude. I hated everyone. I was pissed off with the world. Pissed off with myself. I done three years on my own. I learned a lot about myself. It was like a marathon. Can you hack it? I still get that now. Can I go on? Some mornings I get up and I just can't fucking deal with it any more.

11

HEROIN AND GRASS

A clear October morning broke over Portsdown Hill. Abruptly, the screen of motorway embankment came to an end, revealing miles of open, sloping countryside. A panorama of Channel coastline filled the prison Transit. Portsmouth, five miles ahead, occupied the centre of a flat plain which stretched out of sight to the left and right, and was bordered only by the sea. At this distance the city displayed a kind of industrial grace, the outlines of roads, factories, office buildings and, to the west, the naval docks, evidence enough of the people's work ethic. A passenger ferry crept towards the horizon.

Raphael Rowe, handcuffed in the back of the van, stared at the scenery. Apart from a few hours transferring between jails, the last ten years had been spent within the confines of Dartford, Wandsworth, Swaleside, Wormwood Scrubs, Leicester, Durham, Gartree and Maidstone.

Raph knew the drill well enough, but each move was still a milestone. In the previous few days some of the Maidstone inmates – not exactly close friends, but his associates of three and a half years – had gathered, vaguely aware of the need to spend time with him. Saying farewells, they embraced, and told Raph that if they ever saw him again, they hoped it would be on the *Six O'Clock News*, standing outside the

Court of Appeal in London, surrounded by his family, friends and the supporters of the M25 Three campaign. A free man, vindicated at last.

Kingston offered the prospect of a friendly welcome. Raph, who was thirty, knew Calvin and Teddy from the Scrubs. Duffy had left him behind in Maidstone. There was also the football team. 'A couple of guys in Maidstone had been at Kingston. They told me Nigel was a nice fella, that he run a good football team. I heard that he done football training, and teams come in from the outside, and that Nigel was once a semi-pro himself. All that appealed to me. I thought, "Yeah, I gotta get there and play football with these guys." '

Raph claims to be the victim of British injustice. His conviction for taking part in a series of violent robberies in 1988, which left one man dead, had always been controversial. The villains were dubbed the M25 gang because they used London's orbital motorway to speed between attacks. The victims provided descriptions of two white men and one black man. The three men convicted are all black. MPs from all sides of the House of Commons expressed an interest in the case. Nelson Mandela wrote Raph's family a letter of support and, amazingly, the National Association of Probation Officers expressed misgivings about the conviction. With his dreadlocks and pretty-boy face, it was no surprise that television producers were watching developments with a view to making a drama-documentary, should Raph be released by the Court of Appeal.

He moved in upstairs on C wing. Duffy met him with a big embrace, Teddy a firm handshake. They were glad to see him healthy. Raph's hunger strike, in April 1997, had made the newspapers. He stopped eating in protest at his treatment by the Home Office. Raph was given assurances that a decision on referring his case back to the Court of Appeal would be made before 1 April 1997, the date when all claims relating to potential miscarriages of justice transferred to a new body. The Criminal Cases Review Commission (CCRC) was set up to prevent innocent people spending years behind bars in the manner of the Guildford Four, the Birmingham Six and others. Raph did not want his case referred because for three years it had been in the hands of C3, the Home Office unit which was being phased out. Getting the CCRC involved would mean going back to square one. And that was what happened: a Home Office recommendation never materialised and the case of the M25 Three was referred to the CCRC. Raph claimed the reason for the delay was that the Conservative government did not want the release of another group of people failed by the justice system on the eve of the May 1997 General Election. So Raph stopped eating for two weeks. His hunger strike ended when he was given a personal assurance by a CCRC commissioner that the M25 case would be dealt with promptly.

The day after his arrival, some of his C wing neighbours took Raph on a tour. The visitors' block was clean and hospitable. His guides said there was none of the oppressive security that humiliated family and friends. Raph noticed the little things: menus on the table; the chance to buy refreshments for people who might have travelled a long way; and you could even pay at the end, rather than have a prison officer standing over your guests, demanding payment as if you and your kind were scum bags who would cheat the Home Office out of the price of a cup of tea.

Raph shook his head, remembering Swaleside. That was a cons' nick. Inmates walking around the exercise yard with clothes on a hanger, trying to sell them so they could get money for drugs. Guys getting beaten up in the yard. A physical place. Kingston looked different.

The highlight of the tour was the directors' box. Its official title was the quiet room, a place to read or think outside a cell. It just so happened that its big picture windows offered unsurpassed second-floor views of the football pitch. Over the years Raph had heard other cons describe it. He assumed they were exaggerating.

When he finally pressed his face against the glass he said: 'All I've seen is barbed wire, concrete and bars . . . and now you're showing me this.' The lush rectangle stretched out before him. Calming, inspiring, quiet with dreams; it was like staring at the ocean. The perimeter wall loomed over the playing surface on three sides, but it focused attention on the grass, the empty stage.

Thursday training began with light jogging. Nigel then divided the squad into four groups for a passing exercise. A player stood on each side of a square, marked out with cones. The idea was to control and pass the ball with only two touches. A fifth player in the centre harassed the man in possession. If he gave the ball away, or took more than the requisite touches, he swapped places with the piggy in the middle.

Raph was not able to take part. A back injury – a consequence, he said, of being handcuffed and dragged backwards down the stairs during his arrest – had flared up. It would be some time before he was ready to challenge for a place in the team.

The squad moved to the other end of the pitch. In relays, they raced each other, dribbling balls around cones. Then chaos reigned, footballs flying everywhere, when Nigel staged a passing shuttle involving hitting a moving ball.

Training finished with a full-scale practice match. The dissident Wayne still refused to make himself available to the Kingston Arrows in protest at Paddy's captaincy, but he showed Nigel what they were missing, his feet jabbing for the ball like angry wasps. Eddie was also on his game, dribbling at such speed that one would have thought the entire Hampshire constabulary was in pursuit.

Afterwards, Calvin, showered and changed, sauntered over to the hockey pitch. His gold rope chain glinted in the sun, and his bald head appeared even more glossy than usual. He was only of medium build, but his body was so well proportioned, his arms, legs and torso just exactly the right size, that he seemed quick and mobile on the pitch when he was not especially so. As usual, he was smartly dressed, wearing a grey sweatshirt and matching baggy shorts. Big, uneven teeth complicated his smile. The healthy afterglow of training added to the illusion that he'd just stepped off a Caribbean beach.

Being locked away for a minimum of eleven hours a day was torture for some lifers, but not Calvin. 'I quite like the bang-up,' he said. 'I can write my letters, read, listen to music.' He took so long forming and delivering sentences that he appeared to lack confidence speaking. But when the words came, they were direct, consise and frank. For the uninitiated, his intent, watchful caginess was disconcerting.

Calvin was half-way through a sixteen-year minimum term for a murder he committed during a supermarket robbery. 'The deceased was stabbed seven times.' He said it as if he were reading it out of a newspaper, an event unconnected with himself.

Did the victim try to stop the robbery?

'Yeah.'

A vision of Calvin thrashing a knife into his victim and then making his escape, hurdling shop counters, blanked out everything; all I could think of to say was that he must have been a frightening guy on the outside.

'You would have been right to be scared [if you had met me], but I would say the vicious side of me was more of a

96

front. When you got to know me you would realise that there is another side to me.'

Why was he vicious?

'Protection.'

Calvin spread out his hands, inspecting his fingernails. They were clean and neatly trimmed.

'Where I was growing up, on an estate in Battersea, I used to go to parties and get into fights. It just carried on as I was growing up. I started carrying a knife when I was fifteen. I was still carrying a knife when I was twenty-six. What I'm saying is, when I used to go to parties, I saw people getting stabbed just for stepping on someone's foot.'

Did he feel bad about what happened?

He said nothing.

Did the victim ask for it?

'No. I wouldn't say he asked for it. I didn't mean to do it . . .' Calvin paused. 'Yeah, there have been times when I've thought about him, but I got to be honest, I've got other things to think about. I've told everybody how sorry I am. Which I am. But I can't still feel the same sorry I felt when it happened. Time has gone past. The prison keeps pushing what happened at you. When you talk to them you've got to tell them how sorry you are. But you can't put anything into it because years have gone past.' His tone became decisive. 'I thought about it when it happened but it can't have had that much effect because I carried on doing what I was doing – robberies and stuff. It was six weeks before I was nicked.

'I wasn't really into drugs. For years it was just a bit of smoking, and now and then a bit of Class A. But I'm doing a drugs course now. I've done other courses. I don't see them doing anything. At the end of the day it's my choice to stop doing drugs or whatever. I haven't taken any drugs for seven years. I made that decision because I had to change my life. The thing about being in prison is that you've got time to think. I decided I can't go back on the streets the same way I came in. So I knocked that on the head for a start.'

What other changes had he made?

'I think about my reactions. On the out, if somebody said something that I might not approve of, I'd lose my temper and that would be it. A lot of it comes down to maturity. You have to work to get what you want. I didn't used to think that. I was just lazy. Where I grew up everybody was into something, and there wasn't a lot of people into work. I hung around with the guys on my estate. We was all into stealing, violence – everything.'

His school days were a disaster for all concerned.

'After being expelled no one would take me because I was disruptive. I got into a lot of fights. They just couldn't take it any more.' Calvin laughed. 'I spent most of my school days out of school. I didn't have no time for it. I realise now that my teachers never really understood me. They needed to understand that some kids get bored easily. You have to make lessons fun. They expect kids to come to school every day. The way I see school is that they're just teaching you so you can get a nine-to-five job. If you're not interested in that, well, there's no way you're going to be interested in school.'

Calvin was doing a finance course at Kingston. 'At my last jail I did book-keeping. They teach you to keep the accounts of a small business. I enjoyed it. I was surprised. When it comes to the homework I don't find it hard. So I said to myself, "Here's something you enjoy, take it as far as you can." I wouldn't say my maths are that good. But with finance, you've got a calculator and the figures are in front of you. The main thing is just knowing where to put the figures.'

Education, though, was hard for Calvin. This admission came without warning. He was not a man known for his humility. He was vice-captain of the football team but rarely contributed to the debate at club meetings, and generally made it obvious that he had no interest in what the other players thought. Calvin got away with it because there was not a trace of affectation in his manner – he really was nonchalant. And also because he was important. A composed figure in central midfield, he went about winning the ball and passing without any fuss and bother. He was good, and he just got on with it. The upshot was that no one had a bad word to say about him. Calvin was cool.

'Even now, I find it hard to learn certain things, but the difference is, now, if I don't understand, I let people know.'

When asked about his family, he smiled again. 'My dad used to work for British Aerospace. He knew how to enjoy himself. My mum is very strong, very quiet. She lives in Florida now. Everything flows through my sister. She's in control.' His biggest regret was missing his ten-year-old daughter growing up. 'I get regular visits, once a month. My sister brings her down.' He added, 'I never knew what love was until my daughter come along. I'm still on a high two days later after I've seen her. It's hard, every day she's not here.'

Calvin found it impossible to talk about the future. His best hope was that he would be released in his early forties. First, there were people to convince that he was not a danger to the public. 'The only way you can show them is by doing these courses. I'll go there, sit down and put my point of view. [But] they ain't teaching me things I don't already know. I figured out what I need to do. And what I need to do is not the same as what Jack over there needs to do. The things he needs are totally different. What I needed to do, as well as cutting out the drink and drugs, was to grow up. I know in myself that it needed a prison sentence to get me out of the rut that I was in. The only problem is that it was a life sentence.'

The Portsmouth North End League held a meeting on the second floor of the Co-op Social Club. Gaining entry required passing through a dark, smoky room dominated by two snooker tables. Aficionados lined the walls, holding pints of beer, ignoring trespassers. Bright lights cut through the gloom above each green felt, creating the impression that the tables were shrines, and we were disturbing the members of another sporting cult going about their business.

Having arrived late, straight from work, Nigel stood at the back of the function suite. A row of middle-aged men, including Terry Allison, sat at the top table. They faced an audience of forty-five club managers, secretaries and referees. Someone was in trouble for fielding an unregistered player. A transfer dispute and routine disciplinary matters were also on the agenda. The chairman read out charges and heard the excuses. Justice was swift, and fines put to the vote: 'Five pounds against H&S Aviation for turning up late last Saturday – all in favour raise hands.'

When it was over we headed for the bar downstairs. The manager of St Helena, Bobby Williams, a big Asian bloke, perhaps fifty years old, wandered over to say hello to Nigel. Bobby's black leather blazer had a certain Sunday market trader chic. His fuzzy grey hair brought Don King to mind. Having been promoted as runners-up of Division Two the previous season, St Helena were now being taken apart every week. Bobby hoped to get a result against Court House. The previous Saturday Kingston had beaten them 2–0 in a limp, one-sided contest notable only for goals from Carl (his sixth in four games) and Morgan, plus ninety minutes of bickering between Paddy and Rizler. Court House had held the highly rated George and Dragon to a goalless draw on the opening day of the season, but it had been downhill ever since, with players failing to turn up and some defecting to other clubs.

Still, they, like Kingston, had points, which was more than could be said for St Helena:

	P	W	D	L	F	A	PTS
George and Dragon	4	3	1	0	17	3	10
Plover	5	3	1	1	14	12	10
H&S Aviation	4	3	0	1	17	12	9
Kingston Arrows	4	2	1	1	12	9	7
Rimor	4	2	0	2	14	15	6
So. Co-op Dairies	4	1	1	2	12	8	4
Grant Thornton	3	1	1	1	10	11	4
Court House	4	1	1	2	6	11	4
Magpie	4	1	0	3	15	12	3
St Helena	4	0	0	4	2	26	0

Past midnight, Nigel and I crept back into his three-bedroom terraced house, carrying brown paper bags laden with take-away curry. His wife and two daughters, aged five and twelve, were asleep upstairs. On a kitchen wall there was a strip of pictures of them making faces in a photo-booth. The back door was painted with a DIY marbling effect. Save for the hum of the refrigerator, the house was quiet. After a day in jail, it all felt reassuring and comfortable.

In the company of inmates Nigel avoided mentioning his home life. If he ever took a personal telephone call in the gym office, he was careful to close the door. But that did not mean his job gave him nightmares about his family's safety. 'I think fear of crime is rammed down our throats, it's all overplayed,' he said, handing me a plate and a beer. 'The media make out that every time you step outside the front door you'll get mugged.'

Journalism was not a profession Nigel held in high regard.

The story about the St Bruno nuns just served to confirm his reservations. A few years previously the *News of the World* published an account of a stag party held at the Kingston staff club. The building is outside the prison walls, so the presence of a stripper could not be said to represent a scandal, much less a matter of national interest. It was just another stag party. Nevertheless, the newspaper did not allow that to get in the way. For the purposes of its 'undercover exclusive' the club was relocated to within the prison grounds:

> The screws at HM Prison Kingston certainly try to live up to their name – and give a whole new meaning to the expression being banged up. During the day they guard lifers, many of them rapists and sex perverts. Last Wednesday night, two saucy strippers provided them with a little public exhibition of their own. It included oral sex, hand relief, lesbianism – and acts too disgusting to detail in a family newspaper. The evening – £7.50 all in – was organised by the warders' social club, situated behind the walls of the Portsmouth jail.

The idea of someone from a national newspaper creeping around a staff party with a camera concealed in his tie was deemed so bizarre that most of the officers laughed off the incident. But others, notably the governor, were weary of such cheap shots. Like the one that seemed to occur every December, when a newspaper would get hold of a prison menu for Christmas Day. The story was always the same: convicted murderers living it up on turkey and roast potatoes, played off against pensioners unable to afford heating, much less Christmas lunch. Nigel referred to the tabloids as 'the hang 'em and flog 'em brigade'.

The son of a brick-layer and a holiday camp chalet maid,

he grew up on the Isle of Wight, which he called 'the island'. The eldest of three brothers, Nigel sat entrance exams for the Royal Engineers, but backed out at the last minute, having had second thoughts about leaving his friends and his football. He played semi-professionally for Newport in the Wessex League, occasionally crossing paths with ex-pros like Ted McDougall, formerly of West Ham and Norwich. Football dominated his universe until, aged twenty-one, Nigel broke his leg and was unable to work for four months. The injury came at a time when he wanted to sort out a career and spend more time with his future wife, who he met at a disco on the night of his twenty-first birthday. The prison service was a chance to work in a sports environment.

Once Nigel had completed his training there were grants available to finance a place on an FA Full Licence course – English football's principal coaching qualification. Nigel's fellow pupils included Mick McCarthy, later to become the Republic of Ireland's manager, and Peter Taylor, the England Under-21 coach. The first part of the course alone featured eighty subjects, including defending corners, switching from defence to attack, and set-pieces. Nigel was in football heaven, and it didn't matter that these skills were not going to be used on the best and the brightest footballers, but on some of the most disruptive members of our society.

The known facts about prisoners' offences were available on file. Both Nigel and Geordie were ambivalent about the value of this information, preferring to take inmates as they found them. 'It's not my job to punish them,' said Nigel emphatically. 'People are sent to prison *as* punishment, not *for* punishment. My job is to provide a PE programme, and the football team falls under that umbrella. I treat the inmates the same as I treat everyone. I'd be unprofessional if I acted any other way.'

The received wisdom among social workers and other

people working with offenders is that sport (and similar 'positive' experiences, such as trips to adventure training centres) might reach those inadequate personality types who find it difficult to cope with life. Plagued by a lack of self-esteem, these people are prone to dependence on drugs and/or alcohol. This dependency not only draws them to crime, but makes them repeat offenders. Sport, the theory goes, is one means of attacking the cycle. The modicum of success that comes with taking part can provide a foundation from which offenders go forward to tackle other weaknesses.

Nigel thought this all made sense. He wanted to believe that sporting values – fair play, adherence to the rules, and respect for opponents – put something positive into the drip feed of experience that affects the way people behave. But eleven years in the job had not furnished him with any grand visions about changing lives, and he never lost sight of the fact that some of the inmates he worked with had very serious behavioural problems. 'Some blokes rehabilitate themselves. Some are probably beyond reach – your hardcore criminals. I'd love to think that we make a difference, but you just don't know.'

We talked on into the early hours, cluttering the table with empty beer cans. Nigel seemed content to turn over his thoughts about his job, the part sport played in the process of rehabilitation, and to tussle with the contradictions inherent within the criminal justice system.

'We've got a lot of blokes who, for whatever reason, have not taken part in team games before they've come to prison. I find that quite sad. I've been involved in sport all my life and know that it can keep you out of trouble. What made survival easy for me as a kid was that I always had the status of being the football team captain. With sport, if you give a good account of yourself and if you are committed, some of the bullies at school, for example, would rather be for you than against you.

'Sport is like life – you've got to meet your ups and your downs. Some of those disappointments might come in the form of being dropped from the team. The next time you get your chance, you might play well. Silence your critics. It gives you an opportunity to develop your character. Or, if not develop your character, at least to demonstrate it.'

We called time and stumbled upstairs, where Nigel pointed me in the direction of a small pink bedroom, vacated for the night by his eldest daughter. Pre-teen idol Peter Andre stared back from the bedroom door. I looked at Peter, thought about Nigel, and wondered whether role models could teach bad dogs new tricks.

Earlier in the day I had caught a glimpse of Scouse's cell. The feeling that he would have been comfortable not just in Nigel's house, but in his life, had been with me all evening. His cell seemed to be a microcosm of a working man's home, a reincarnation, as best Scouse could manage, of a three-bed semi where he could put his feet up after doing a shift alongside the prison gardener. School photographs on the sideboard. A table lamp. A worn-out sofa with matching chairs. A kitchen where everything had its place. A bed where he could sleep next to a woman who wanted to share her life with his, for one night or more. None of these things was present in Scouse's cell, but in the simple arrangement of his belongings there was a sense of them all the same.

His cramped little bunker was also a place to face torments alone. And what torments: the walls and ceilings of one life collapsed in ruins, the construction of a new one bound so tightly by rules that Scouse could not so much as step outside unless they said so. To say nothing of the bitter irony of confronting the junkie rationalisation that ordinary life amounts to nothing more than spirit-crushing game shows and a routine so stifling that heroin is the only logical solution.

Scouse gave me a book of his poems, entitled *Behind the Keyhole*. The inscription read: 'Something I done after seg. I had plenty of time on my hands, and went very deep into my soul.' There were nineteen poems. The most accomplished was entitled 'No One Like Me':

> I walk in the open spaces of my domain
> I am meant to be working
> (If you can call picking up litter, work).
> Every day's the same
> Or so I think
> Till I take a breather
> And sit on a patch of grass.
> There's a bald patch where I sit.
> I pick at it with a splinter of wood.
> Ten stones I find today
> In this patch of soil
> When my work is done.
> I go back to my cell
> And place the ten stones
> On my bed. I pick one out
> and call it me
> As I'm the same as no one else.

This was the Scouse who thought of himself as a character removed from a Lowry painting. A melancholy, unfortunate figure who belonged in a cityscape of terraced houses, smoke-blackened churches and looming factories, but who was instead trapped by the slamming of prison doors. This Scouse still wanted to stand on a box and shout at the world, 'I'm here, I'm workin' class and you can't ignore me!' He could channel his energy, he had control, he was his own man.

But Kingston Scouse was banged up, same as always.

12
RIZLER

I heard them opening my door this morning. I thought, 'Nah, I'm not getting up, there's no football.' The match is postponed, waterlogged pitch. I was knackered anyway. I played a video game, Sega, until about two a.m. On weekends some of the guys are still in bed at noon. You have to be quiet. It causes friction otherwise. People have been up all night, writing appeals, letters to girlfriends and family.

There's no electric on C wing, and we can't afford batteries, see, so what I do is unscrew the light and pull out the little wires. You got to go right inside the ceiling rose, find the live and the earth. You make your own plug out of the flexible tubes you get in biros. It's not dangerous if you know what you're doing. The first time I tried it I blew the lights right across the landing. Everybody was laughing and going mad at me. I've been done three times for messing with the mains – a two-pound fine each time. Sometimes they have your radio. Or maybe take a visit off you. For people who ain't been working, or who are financially embarrassed, two pounds is a lot of money. I get seven pounds a week. I'm a wing cleaner.

I spend a lot of time playing with Tiger, my budgie. My mother bought him for me. He's mad. Whenever I get chips I've always got to break a bit off for him, otherwise he'll crap on my food. He's a great bird. He feeds on normal bird seed. I also get him a tonic for his feathers. He'll go on my finger, my shoulder, walk along the floor. He's a pied. That's the make of the bird. You get some greens and blues. There's all kinds of birds. They are copy cats. If you are a boring person, they'll pick that up; if you are bubbly, the bird will be too. If I put my music on, Tiger's up and away, chirping and flying around the cell.

I was a kid when I came in – nineteen. That was ten years ago. I dunno how I handled it. I said to myself I had to keep busy. But I was in Cardiff, and you can't keep busy because you are banged up all the time. Terrible place, filthy, full of cockroaches. You get one book a month. Never see a paper. When I'm not busy I get in trouble. I'm awful for it. I dunno – I just go on a wander and see what I can . . . not pinch stuff but, you know, find myself mischief. I always have. I think I always will.

I lived in South Wales. Years ago my mum worked in a chicken factory, but that closed down. We used to have a big grate in our house. She fell and hurt her head on it one time, and that messed her up. She's not been the same since. My father never worked. He's always been on the hobble – the dole – and doing a little bit on the side. My family have always been poachers. They've gone out and knocked a couple of deer down, or rabbits, or got a couple of salmon out of the river. It was mining country, like, so there was loads of fields. That's how we used to earn our money.

My father was a drunk. He wasn't physically damaging towards the family, but it was the atmosphere, the smell of the drink on his breath early in the morning. He'd be out all night, causing trouble for us. There was times when I'd be in bed, and I'd shout downstairs, 'Shut up, you bald-headed bastard!' He slapped my old girl around. She came out of hospital once, having had an operation on her gall stones.

109

She was doing the washing and he come in all pissed up. He couldn't have known what he was doing, but he just lashed out and kicked her. She went unconscious on the floor. There was blood coming out of the stitches. I ran across to my neighbours and said, 'Quick, my mum's dying.' It was pretty sad.

We lived in a council house on a small estate, with a little shop at the top of the road. We had to walk about half a mile to the town. Lovely place, lovely people. I worked in a slaughterhouse, cleaning mostly. They was doing sheep and cows. I couldn't even chew gum in there, it was that disgusting. One bloke would stand on this big girder with this bolt-gun. When the animal came through, he'd shoot it in the back of the head. The animal would fall on its side. Sometimes they were still kicking. So I had to get this metal rod and push it in down in the hole to kill off all the nerves.

That's how my life went. My trouble started after my fiancée went off with another bloke. It was the first relationship I was really strong about. She was a pretty girl. Half-caste. She was in her last year of school. I was pretty messed up in my head. I burnt all her clothes. And then one night I come back from a night-club with these two older guys. I was intoxicated with drugs. Sitting on my wall, one of them said, 'Let's do a burglary.' We goes to my house. In my kitchen I've got this pick-axe handle. There's me, big Riz, saying 'We'll take this,' not knowing the consequences of taking it and saying those words.

The house was two doors down. I'd known the bloke all my life. There was a window not properly closed. So we goes in. Pitch black inside. Went upstairs, bedroom door locked. What's going on yer? We didn't think the guy was in the house – sometimes he stayed around the corner with his relatives.

We went back downstairs and was looking around when he

appeared. I hit him twice on the head with the pick-axe handle. I chucked it down and then just bolted. He was sixty-five years old.

Don't get me wrong, I knows what I done. I was on the window sill. I had my head in my hands, saying 'I killed him, I killed him.' The others were saying, 'Nah, you just knocked him out.' But I'd seen blood splatter all over the wallpaper and he was out on the floor.

So we gets in this car and drives to London. There was no plan, nothing at all. Just go, first instinct. None of us thought to get an ambulance. We was three-quarters the way to London when one of my co-accused says, 'I've got to go back. I'm up in court tomorrow for burglary.' All through the night we're driving back. I gets home. Gets out of my clothes. Later on that day I go out and meets this guy, Alvin, who used to work with me at the slaughterhouse. I tells him, 'Alvin, I think I killed somebody last night on a burglary.' That's the only thing that got me caught.

The victim used to be a cleaner in the army. His wife died many years ago. He had a grandson, but nobody living with him. I think we picked up twenty quid in cash. That went on the petrol. Behind my house was a neighbour who I hated all my life. We fought day and night. He used to chuck rubbish over our garden and we'd send it back with interest. I had cause to kill him; I wouldn't have, but I would have felt better about it. I liked the man I killed.

That night they found the body. Nobody had seen him all day, his dog was howling, so somebody knocked on his door.

I was at this fish shop, when someone comes up and says, 'Riz, there's coppers all outside your house.' It didn't even register. I goes home with a couple of my mates. One of them says 'They're waiting behind the door for you.' I says, 'Don't joke, don't take the piss.' The coppers are on to me straight away. 'Where were you last night?' I says I went to

London. 'What for?' 'To find a job.' I wasn't thinking straight. They went away.

I slept all that night. I slept right through. The next morning my mum's called up, 'Riz, the police are here, they want to talk to you again.' I walked downstairs and they said, 'We are arresting you on suspicion of murder.' I shouted, 'I've not killed no one.' They said they were taking me in anyway. I could have bolted. They would never have caught me. I'd have been over the back of the gardens and into the fields. But there were four of them, and they handcuffed me. Anyway, they take me down the cop station. They called me 'a right bastard', and said, 'We're gonna kick the shit out of you.' They pushed me into a cell. About two or three hours later they came back. I found out later that they had already picked up one of my co-accused and he spilled the beans, like.

I wasn't thinking straight. They even offered me a manslaughter charge at court. I'd have served the ten years and I'd have been out by now. But I ended up convicted of murder.

I'd been in jail twice before: twenty-four days for kicking a guy in the jaw during a pub fight, and six months for wrecking cars. This guy gave me money to spray all these cars and slice up their canvas roofs. MGs, they were. He wanted to fuck someone bad. He gave us twenty quid, and we caused about £30,000 worth of damage.

It took me about seven years to come to terms with what I done. They sent me to Grendon. Before that I was just messed up on drugs. I had no professional help in Bristol or Cardiff. Grendon was the best jail I have been in, but I got kicked out for smoking too much cannabis. I was nicked loads of times, and also got in trouble because they found these instructions in my cell: how to beat a drug test.

I like it yer. The football team is great. Paddy does give me a fair bit of stick. First of all I was going to play left midfield, but I thought that's mostly defending. There's guys who are better than me at defending, so I says to Nige, 'Why not push me on?' I know Paddy don't like it. I think he went and spoke with Nigel as well.

The lifer people say I got an adverse reaction to confrontation. I don't like people taking me for a fool. I've had it all my days off my father. But since Grendon I haven't lifted my hands to anyone. I've been to anger control groups. Now they want me to do a Relationships course. Maybe I am immature. Maybe I still got that in me, but what do they expect in an artificial environment? It's hard to grow up in prison.

13
GIVE AND GO

Kingston were due to play their fifth match of the season but the team that had beaten Court House 2–0 and Plover 6–2 was suddenly depleted: Mick, one of the hefty defenders, had had his request to be transferred to a lower-security jail granted.

Nigel apart, no one else in the squad had turned out more times for the Arrows. Yet within a couple of days Mick was all but forgotten. There was nothing unusual about the indifference towards his departure: a lifer marked his own time and no one else's. Mick, in any case, would not have wanted to be remembered. Most mornings he could be seen leaning against the D wing railings, staring at the scene below. In his five years at Kingston the view scarcely changed: the pool table, out of bounds until lunch time; the telephone booths which did not receive incoming calls; the metal cell doors, painted purple and spaced out like the compartments of honeycomb, leading up to the hub where all the wings converged; the snooker table in the centre of the hub; prison officers talking among themselves; Carl checking the VCR kept in a cupboard next to the noticeboard where the team sheet hung; the inmate kitchen, quiet for now. The same view as yesterday. The same view as always. Mick had the stillness of a broken clock. It was as if the hopelessness of his situation, of all the years irrevocably lost, rooted him to the spot.

Chunky black spectacles dominated his boyish face. Every now and then Mick's fingers brushed his flat, mousy fringe back into a side-parting. His voice was deep but, like his face, lacked colour and animation. The story he told was of a boy, born in Oxford, who had never quite fitted in. Mick's family 'moved around the country a lot' during his childhood. He described himself as 'one of those bright kids who dropped out during his A-levels'. A couple of friends still visited, but part of him wished they would stay away: 'It's a cop-out, I know, but it makes it harder; you miss people more.'

His only child was now seventeen. After separating from the boy's mother, Mick lived in a bedsit, unemployed, alone. One night he decided to rob his neighbour. The man returned and, during the ensuing struggle, Mick beat him to death. Dealing with the reality of 'losing control to that extent' was one of the hardest truths to face. Violence, he felt, was 'out of character'.

At Kingston, Mick looked and sounded on the point of being lost to the world, and gave the impression that football was one of the last threads keeping him attached to the rest of us. When challenged, he could just about bother to defend himself, and on these occasions he became surly and contrary. It was impossible to know whether the life sentence had broken him – the sense of his resignation was over-whelming – or whether he was just like that.

At the time of the offence nothing had stood in the way of him fleeing the country. Mick did attempt to see his son to say goodbye, but when this half-hearted venture came to nothing he simply walked around in a daze for two days until someone called the police. After the arrest Mick was desperate to be alone, someplace quiet where he could figure out what had happened. So he got off to a bad start when the police doctor asked him if he was suicidal. 'Well,' Mick said, 'I don't know, I've never felt suicidal before.'

During a rain storm the roof leaked. The resulting flood damage put the satellite TV rooms out of action. It represented a potential crisis for Carl, until he found out it was possible for the decisive World Cup qualifier between Italy and England to be screened in the canteen. The inmates crowded in to watch the first half before the nine p.m. bang-up, and followed the rest of the match via radio.

Carl had been TV and video monitor for over a year. 'I get the Sky listings magazine and go through once a month deciding what to tape,' he explained. 'We've got two machines. Tonight I'm showing *Braveheart* and *Richard III* – that's a Shakespeare one. I've taped *Executive Decision*, but I'm saving that for Christmas Day.' The job paid £1.50 a week, which was on top of the money he got for working in the laundry. 'The best thing is that anything I want to watch, I can tape and watch at my leisure in one of the education rooms. I like sports programmes, and sci-fi ones, the *Star Treks*, and the documentaries on Discovery.'

Carl also decided what would be shown in the Sky TV rooms. And if something came on Sky Sports which clashed with his advertised plans, there could be trouble. When Middlesbrough played Stockport in an unscheduled fixture, Carl refused to abandon his timetable. Some of the cons threatened to report him to the Governor. 'I was thinking to myself, *Cops* and *Speed* start at eight p.m. Middlesbrough was on at 7.30 p.m. What should I do? About twenty people wanted to watch the football. They come to me and said, "Don't put a film on tonight." I said, "Nah, film come first." So they've gone to my boss, Brendan Martin, a screw. He says, "What are you going to do?" I reply, "I made my decision and if I start changing it's a slippery road." He agreed. Now, it transpired that only five people wanted to watch *Cops*. But I didn't change the schedule. A couple of people said, "You did right there." A couple gave me some crap. I told them, "You got football Monday and Wednesday – let other people have access to the Sky television. You've got to learn how to compromise." '

There were people on the outside who thought it was outrageous that prisoners had access to satellite television, but they were not involved in the pragmatic business of managing offenders. The Home Office was even considering putting TVs in cells, the rationale being that it would make it easier to leave inmates banged up for longer periods, so fewer staff would be needed on duty, which would reduce costs.

Geordie was not working the evening of Italy v. England but he was on duty, attending his father-in-law's sixtieth birthday party. 'One of my boys was a bit poorly so we put him in the spare room and I said I'd keep an eye on him,' he explained, clenching a mug of milky tea. 'There just happened to be a portable TV in there.'

A pack of sandwiches wrapped in silver foil and the *Daily Mail* lay open before him. We were lunching in the gym office, waiting for Nigel, who was cycling to work on his day off to play against Southern Co-op Dairies. Geordie, for the moment, was more interested in Florida than football. Without knowing of each other's plans, both he and Nigel had booked family holidays to Disney World – they would take turns to be away in March.

Jonah's Achilles problem had eased, allowing the big defender to return alongside Nigel and the middle-aged Teddy (who kept his place in the absence of Mick). But Jonah was feeling peculiar when he appeared after the lunch time bang-up. 'Blimey, I put me head down for a quick kip last night and next thing I knew, the door opened and it was breakfast,' he said in a rush of words. Jonah had already seen the nurse. 'I said, "Is there any chance of doing one of those diabetic tests?" The symptoms of acute diabetes are being thirsty and tired. Well, for the last couple of weeks I've been bloody knackered. And I'm always dry in the mouth.'

Geordie was sceptical: 'If he was a horse they'd shoot him.'

Scouse had not put his name down on the Availability List. For some unspecified reason Eddie was also unavailable. His league performances had been muted since the Grant Thornton fiasco, but Shaggy, who stepped up from the reserves to start at right wing-back, appeared apprehensive at the prospect of deputising for the Scotsman.

Small and wiry, Shaggy was probably in his thirties, but it was hard to tell. His flaxen hair might have belonged to an eight-year-old, but he had the crumpled face of a grieving old man. Shaggy rarely made eye contact, much less spoke.

When Nigel addressed the players on the pitch just before kick-off – the eleven a.m. meeting was cancelled on his days off – Shaggy became the focus of attention. 'Listen, you've got a lot of work to do on that right side,' cautioned the coach. 'I'm not worried about your fitness, but your head. People aren't getting at you if they tell you you've got to do something, it's just that the role you've got is important to the team.' Shaggy nodded grimly, apparently accepting that he had some work to do when it came to taking constructive criticism.

Southern Co-op Dairies wore a green and white kit even more dated than Kingston's, but such considerations quickly became irrelevant. They poured forward, knocking the ball about with bravado. Kingston players tracked runs and competed as best they could, but in the opening exchanges it was all they could do to hang on.

Scouse wandered along the touchline, unshaven and spaced-out. His beloved Everton were playing Liverpool. He was wearing pocket radio earphones, awaiting pre-match news, apparently oblivious to what was already shaping up to be Kingston's match of the season.

Once the home side got the measure of the Co-op's adventurous style of play, Calvin's tackling and Paddy's passing and movement inspired a series of counter-attacks. The captain might have been disillusioned at being taken out of the firing line, but he was making things happen.

The chances came thick and fast. The visitor's goalkeeper, under pressure, made a hash of clearing his lines and Rizler intercepted, only to shoot into the side netting. At the other end someone steamed past Teddy but smacked the ball against a post. A couple of deep crosses might have been converted but for Zebedee, who turned one snap-shot wide and – just – managed to smother another.

Bunny then crossed into the path of Paddy. The captain latched on to the ball, darted around the goalkeeper, and side-footed home with all the instinctiveness that had been missing in earlier games. It was his third goal in five matches, but it still came against the run of play, as the Co-op-supplied linesman reminded everyone. 'Best we've played all season. Keep it going,' he hollered at the Dairies side.

The most exciting exchanges took place down Kingston's left. Bunny and Jonah faced the Co-op's best player. He wore white boots and had dark, shoulder-length hair. With step-overs, drag-backs and feigned changes of direction, he had plenty of tricks to lure them into challenges, only to pull away with a burst of acceleration. His name was Colin Pack. He looked like David Ginola. Bunny seemed roused by his outrageous performance. Soon he, too, was demanding the ball and hurdling tackles on swashbuckling forward runs. Jonah, fearful of having to match the visitor for pace, sat back. The upshot was that the Co-op man ran riot in the space. 'We'll have to do something about him, he's taking us apart,' noted Geordie.

On twenty-one minutes, another counter attack: Bunny released Carl, who held off a clutch of defenders and dummied the goalkeeper before scoring. Miraculously, Kingston then went 3–0 ahead, Carl finishing a glorious high-speed exchange of passes between Rizler and Calvin.

Co-op pulled one back with a penalty and the contest was still wide open at half-time. Feelings ran high. 'Don't push on so much,' Nigel told Bunny. 'We're 3–1 up. There's no need to chase the game.' Bunny slumped to the floor, disgusted.

After the restart Paddy took a couple of hefty knocks and faded. 'He doesn't like it when it gets physical,' cautioned Geordie. Co-op were dominating possession, but just as Geordie was moved to observe that 'they're like Liverpool, they're doing nothing with it', they scored. At 3–2 Nigel issued more urgent instructions to tighten up the midfield. Kingston were under siege.

With three minutes remaining, the pressure finally told. The Co-op's David Ginola lookalike headed home a corner. There was no doubt he had been the star of the 3–3 draw. At the final whistle, one of his team mates ran over to contragulate him as he walked towards the dressing room.

'We played well going forward,' the man said brightly.

'You're telling me,' said Colin Pack. 'We're just shit at the back.'

14
BUNNY

For the last two years I've been saying, 'Look, Nigel, we've got to start playing more football.' I'd sooner lose 20–0 knowing we are playing good, attractive football where everyone is enjoying themselves, than hit a few long balls and win 1–0. Having said that, a lot of our guys are not football-minded. Paddy, Calvin, Nigel, Jonah and myself. We think football. We can read the game. But some of the others haven't got a clue. Carl is very fast and Nigel uses that, but he can't head the ball, he can't trap it. All you've got to do is put the ball over the defender and he'll get it. To me, he's not a football player.

I come from Harlesden, so QPR was my local side. But Spurs have always been my team since I come to England. They just had something about them – flair, charisma, wonderful football. Jimmy Greaves, Dave Mackay, Joe Kinnear, young Stevie Perryman, Martin Chivers and all that lot.

When I was fourteen years old I was at Queens Park Rangers. I played in one of their youth sides for eighteen months. They were always working on ball skills. I met quite a few first-team players. Gerry Francis had just come into the side. There was Ian Gillard, Terry Venables. I can remember having a conversation with Stan Bowles about his dribbling skills. He was a very laid-back character. A gifted man. But it was hard for a black guy coming through the ranks. In those days there was Clyde Best at West Ham. Another one named Coker. That's part of the reason I got enticed out of it. I didn't see a lot of my own kind in the game. I started getting into trouble instead. I had a chance and I blew it.

I come over from Jamaica at the age of eight. Once Jamaica got independence it was very easy to come to England. Try to make a better living for yourself. It was hard to settle. It was so cold. 1963 was one of the coldest winters England's had. I used to wear three pairs of socks to keep my feet warm. We had a few friends – there were people who came over with my mother and father and cousin. We lived in Kensal Rise. My old man used to work for Schweppes. He died of cancer twelve years ago. He was very laid back, then he'd explode. My mother was a nurse. There was no beating about the bush with her. She is still alive.

It started to go wrong for me because I wanted to be one of the boys. I wanted nice gear but I was skint. I allowed myself to get involved. The first serious thing was in 1970. With a few friends I robbed a post office. We got about £7,000. We didn't have no tools. In those days you could just walk in and put a bit of pressure on them physically. There was a man and a woman in the post office. We jumped over the counters – they had low counters in those days – and just intimidated them. I got a kick out of it – easy money, you know? The adrenalin was pumping, and I wasn't scared of getting caught. I just thought about the rewards.

But we got caught. One of the guys was walking around spending money which he shouldn't have done. His mother took him to the police station and eventually he came out with it. I was sent to Borstal. I thought, 'Fuck me, I'm in jail! The system has done me wrong.' It was like I had to get back at the system. As I said to you, I wasn't very intelligent in those days. I was very naive.

You learn things in Borstal. If you've got good people behind you, you can get out of a rut. But if you've got negative influences, it's not so easy. When I came out I couldn't get a job, so I did illegal things. Burglaries and robberies. I got done for drugs offences – intent to supply. I did four years for robbery; we went into a house and tied someone up, took all their money and jewellery. After that stretch I stopped. I was just selling cannabis and stuff to survive. I didn't want to put myself on the line to come back into one of these places.

I worked in the music business for a long time. I started off as a roadie, humping all the gear. I thought I had more intelligence than that, so I took a sound engineering course. I worked with Aswad for about four years – I've known them since boyhood. I also worked with groups called Sernace, Maxi Priest, Burning Spur and Sham 69. I done an Amnesty International tour with Peter Gabriel. All around Europe, as well as America and Japan. Travelling with the music suited me. The banter between the guys. You got the roadies and the band, we're all one unit. It's down to us to get everything working properly, and to enjoy the fun after. I made good money. I'd come back with several grand in my pocket. That was the most enjoyable part of my life.

I once worked alongside Bob Marley at Crystal Palace Bowl. I used to play football with Bob and a few of the lads in West London. He was a brilliant footballer. Bunny Wailers is a good player as well. He could keep a ball up all day. You know the Scrubs prison, in London? We used to play football in a park at the back there. Bob stayed in Ladbroke Grove whenever he was in London. And when I was in Jamaica, I used to visit members of his band. Marley was true to the person that he portrayed. The last time I saw him was before the cancer; he was playing football. People looked up to him, but they weren't in awe of him. In Jamaica he had an open house. 'If you ain't got food – *come*!' He'd feed ya. He was a true man of the world.

I was out of trouble for a long time before I committed my offence. Then my sister was assaulted and robbed. The police didn't want to know. They thought it was a drugs thing. My sister had just come back from Jamaica. These people seen her in Jamaica. They thought she was bringing back cannabis. When they came back to England they went to her house. Three geezers and this woman. And because there was no drugs, they bashed up my sister and smashed up her house.

I'd just come back from Holland – touring. I was at home with my two children. It was a May bank holiday. My nephew come round and told me, 'Ooh, you better come, Isa has been bashed up.' As soon as I arrived I could see the chaos. There was a trail of blood, windows smashed, the door smashed, loads of things turned over. And my sister's a very neat person, you know. And I just felt bad. I've only got the one sister and I thought it was my job to protect her. I said, 'Fuck this, I've got to sort this out.'

I knew these people had guns, so I went and got a gun. These people don't mess around. They'd kill you as soon as blink. I went with three pals. What happened is that we went to their house about eight a.m. It was basically in darkness. From what I've gathered since, they didn't have no electricity. We knocked on the door and put on a child's voice. The woman looked through the spy-hole but we were crouched down. She fell on the floor when we barged in. I had a gun on her, and I'm talking to her, right, saying, 'Don't you fucking do what you did to my sister,' and all this, you know. I heard someone running down the stairs. So I spun around. Because it was an air trigger, the slightest touch, the shotgun just went off. Somebody fell down – I didn't know who at the time. I didn't know who. She kept screaming at me, 'Don't shoot my husband, shoot me, don't shoot my husband, shoot me.' She's on the floor. And she's grabbed the gun. So I fired the second barrel, and it hit her in the leg. Her husband had run into the bathroom. He was hiding under the panels – from what I heard after.

I didn't know then that the person I'd shot was the boy – he was a sixteen-year-old boy – or that he had died. I knew I'd shot the mother and that, with my record, I was in serious shit. So we ran off. I tried to keep calm because the others were all panicking. To be honest with you, I was shit scared. I knew I'd done something bad. I hoped it was the husband, you know. I knew the kid. I knew him like he was my nephew. At one time we lived next door to each other. I used to take him out with my nieces, take them swimming, and play football with him. The thing is, I had somebody check this place out. He told me that the children were living with the grandmother.

When they arrested me, at home, about 6.30 a.m., it was very heavy. The first I knew of it, my missus was screaming. I pulled on my pants and got out of a ground-floor window. There was a lot of police. I thought I was going to die. I tried to climb a wall but they was all pointing guns. They called my name and said, 'If you move, you're dead.'

The mother committed suicide because of what I done. I don't know how she done it. All I know is that one day when I was in [HMP] Long Lartin I got a phone call to say she'd killed herself. People say I try to make it simplistic, but I think it was partially her guilt. The grandmother of the boy sent me a message to say that she forgave me because she knew that I cared for this kid, and that it wasn't intentional. But I've still got to live with it. I've looked into myself. I've got children. I know what I would feel like if someone had taken a child of mine.

From the day they told me in the police station that it was the boy that died, I broke down. I wasn't putting it on for the sake of the police. I knew I'd made the biggest mistake of my life. I knew I was going to pay for it big time.

These people don't let you forget about it. You'd never forget about it anyway, but they force you to talk about it continuously. It's always there. I tell myself I've done some good things in my life. I've been in a situation where I saw an inmate going to stab a member of staff, and I've come in between and said, 'Nah, don't do that.' I see both sides. There's also loads of guys that I've met who have been worse off than myself, emotionally and physically. I know I done bad. But the people closest to me, the people that I've worked for, know the good in me. They stick with me. Some of the people I worked for still send me money because they've known the good in me.

This prison has done things for me. I've improved my education. I've got certificates for things I never had before. I'm more knowledgeable about myself. Before I was a bit selfish. I wasn't taking into consideration people's feelings. I used to break into people's houses and take their stuff. There was no consideration.

But I don't like it here. People try to put you down. At other nicks I've known guys who've done forty-odd years, but they were still compassionate. They'd help you build yourself up again when you got down. Here, there's guys who come to you week in, week out, asking you, 'Lend me half an ounce, lend us a tea bag?' They never once give you anything back. I don't give to receive. But it's got to be a two-way street. People here are very two-faced. Someone will say, 'I think he's a cunt,' and the next minute you see him talking to the fella. I feel like going to the Governor and saying, 'Get me out of your fucking prison because I don't like hypocritical people.' The trouble is, it's no longer my life. It belongs to the system.

15

DO YOUR JOB

There was no comfort in the low, grey sky. The lack of blue spaces, where clouds drifted and aeroplane contrails dissolved, oppressed the spirit. Even the wind kept away. Blowing in from the Channel, it gusted across the three miles of townscape from Portsmouth's sea-front Victorian hotels, buffeting street signs and stirring litter, passing down roads lined with convenience stores, newsagents and pubs before encountering the unyielding walls of the prison.

The pitch was deserted, but the empty space was fringed here and there by inmates wearing black donkey jackets. In ones and twos they wandered the extent of the touchlines with all the solitude of the last men on earth. Their gaze combed the grass, rather than up towards the dull, heavy sky which was yet another reminder of their confinement and culpability.

Being late October, regular downpours threatened fixtures, but this was British football weather. There was something about a muddy pitch, about brisk temperatures and darkening afternoons which formed an integral part of the season. In the days running up to league games the players' thoughts never strayed too far from the forecast, hoping the turf would drain and the match survived; remembering the voices of loving girlfriends, wives and mothers, the people who would have asked, 'You're not going out in this?'

Raph was still injured, and deeply frustrated about the lack of news from the Criminal Cases Review Commission. The newspapers were full of reports that the family of Derek Bentley, the last man to be executed in Britain, might be in line for compensation after the Appeal Court belatedly quashed his conviction. Home Secretary Jack Straw had granted the family a private meeting. Derek was nineteen when he was hanged for the rooftop shooting of a policeman in 1952. His co-defendant, sixteen-year-old Christopher Craig, who fired the gun, was too young to swing. He was sentenced to be detained 'during Her Majesty's pleasure', and later released. The Bentley case became a *cause célèbre* among opponents of the death penalty. Derek, who had a mental age of eleven, was convicted on the basis of the words 'Let him have it, Chris,' which he uttered some fifteen minutes before the policeman was fatally wounded. But all that was ancient history, as Raph pointed out in a letter published in the *Guardian*:

I clap my hands to applaud Decca Aitkenhead [who had previously written for the *Guardian* about the Bentley case] – 'Leave the dead alone. There are enough living victims who need help . . .' I'm one of them. And it makes me so angry to read that the Criminal Cases Review Commission has used its limited resources on hanged people's cases rather than those languishing in jail today. Ten long years I have campaigned to have my case reopened and wrongful conviction quashed. When the CCRC took over the M25 Three case from the Home Office it was asked to deal with it urgently. At the time I was on hunger strike and prepared to die in protest at the continuous delays. The commission responded that my case would be dealt with as a priority. That was 16 months ago. Now the CCRC resources have been concentrated on the dead, rather than the living hundreds of people who can be saved.

Raph did not have much interest in the squad players who were frustrated at their lack of first-team opportunities. A run-out in the Sunday reserves was all very well, they said, but these matches were infrequent and the worsening weather made them susceptible to cancellation. Scouse was as vocal as ever, but Luke, Duffy, Ian, John and Matty also made it known that they were now running out of patience.

Scouse wrote a report covering the sixth game of the season, the return visit of Grant Thornton, composed following another fidgety Saturday afternoon on the bench:

GT scored on 18 minutes. A minute later Nigel headed down the left, Riz picked up the ball, turned two players, then slotted the keeper. 1–1. After 30 minutes GT shot from the left to the right side, beating Zeb. 1–2. Just before half-time a penalty was awarded, handball against Jonah, booked for dissent. Zeb saved it. GT came out firing for the second half. Our defence was all over the place, hence another silly goal. 1–3. Then Riz came from left to right, and scored from the edge of box, making it 2–3. We put loads of pressure on. Their number seven had been booked in the first half. He went in for a tackle with Paddy and fell on the floor. Paddy took the ball around him, and the GT player lashed out with his feet. The ref had no other option, he had to walk. There were about six of us clapping the lad and giving him a bit of banter. He was shitting himself, as once he's off the pitch he's on our turf. But he was okay. It's just football to me and most of the other squad members.

Next to the words 'Subs Not Used', Scouse drew an unhappy face.

The manager's official position was that he would not change a winning side. When Kingston Arrows lost, it became apparent that Nigel reserved the right to qualify this principle: 'The players had done nothing wrong and deserved another chance.' Consequently, the use of substitutes became a big issue. For the most part, Nigel only made changes when injuries forced him to do so, or when the result appeared beyond all doubt. This caution, Nigel gladly admitted, stemmed from the three substitutions he had made against Plover the previous month; Kingston, leading 6–0, had promptly conceded two goals. Nigel did not want a repeat of the shaky conclusion to that match. It was a reminder, he said, of how the introduction of a fresh player was not necessarily a shot in the arm for a flagging side. Whereas the other players were tuned in to the pace of the game, the newcomer was not. And during his period of acclimatisation, the pattern of team play was often interrupted.

Each of the squad players could come up with reasons why he deserved at least forty-five minutes. Luke, who was thirty-three, prematurely grey, and slight for a goalkeeper, haboured the strongest grievance. On seeing the team sheet for the previous match, against Southern Co-op Dairies, a quizzical expression on his face had dissolved into contempt. This transformation was disconcerting. For starters, Luke was known for his civility. And then there was his response to rejection in the past to consider.

Luke thought of himself as a model prisoner. He helped inmates with legal problems – like Rizler, who wanted to appeal against his tariff, but did not understand the forms. As a solicitor and scout leader, Luke had once been a summation of everything conventional and upwardly mobile. He styled himself with a kind of Marks and Spencer respectability – jeans, woollen jumpers – and was the sort of man some women would be pleased to introduce to their mothers.

That made the circumstances of his offence even more shocking. His wife, a twenty-four-year-old nurse, came home from a nightshift one morning to say that she was leaving him to set up home with another man – one of his friends. She broke the news in the garage where Luke, clutching a lump hammer and a masonry chisel, stood renovating a pile of bricks. He smashed her skull with sixteen or seventeen hammer blows. Some landed as she staggered backwards. Others as she collapsed to her knees. A final salvo as she lay on the floor.

Luke's efforts to prevent himself being identified as the killer – staging a break-in and appearing on television, stricken with fake grief, to appeal for witnesses that did not exist – demonstrated his capacity for self-control. They also ensured his case a degree of notoriety above and beyond that normally attracted by a domestic murder. And having maintained his innocence throughout the trial, and for months afterwards, a number of unanswered questions remained. That is the way of it with murder; sometimes, no matter how much evidence can be gathered, the only people who know precisely what happened are the victim and the perpetrator, and only one of them is still around to talk. As far as the evidence was concerned, there was the matter of how Luke managed to avoid getting blood on his clothing. One theory held that he must have carried out the murder naked. The prosecution also pointed out that if the attack was frenzied, it was not so wild that the blows fell anywhere other than on his wife's head. The wounds suggested she had been subjected to a methodical assault, rather than a burst of unrestrained flailing, which would have left injuries elsewhere. One of the impacts almost severed an ear.

Luke became a born-again Christian about two years after conviction. He appeared to have resolved to tell the absolute truth, no matter how damning. So when asked about his risk factors he simply replied, 'Over-controlled personality. Jealousy. Possessiveness. Obsessiveness. Manipulation. And use of a weapon.' His voice remained uniformly quiet and calm as he related the indictments against his character. Luke concluded with a little grin: 'I can see where [the psychologists] are coming from.'

There was no sense of potential violence about Luke, but his show of emotion at being left out of the team sharpened the senses. And that voice of peaceful prayer vanished when he talked about Zebedee, his prison officer rival for the goalkeeping jersey. He felt Zeb had broken a mutual understanding: 'At the end of last season Zebedee told Nigel he didn't want the full-time commitment any more. So Zebedee asked me, "Do you want to take it on?" I said, "Of course I do – but there are going to be times when I might have visits, so I'll need cover." Zebedee was happy to be the cover person. Now he's gone back on his word. The difficult comment for me came when Nigel Wheeler said that if I'd played the first game of the season I'd be in the side now. But I couldn't play because of a long-standing Open University commitment. Obviously Zebedee went in goal, and I haven't had a look in since. I asked Nigel after a couple of weeks, "What are my chances of getting back in?" He said, "At the moment I don't want to change a winning side." It's all just a total reversal of what I'd been told. I'd even written to family and friends asking them to change visits to Sunday. I don't know how Zebedee can look me in the eye. I'd like to believe he's not thinking he can walk all over me because I'm a con, but I don't know. The bottom line is that I can't make waves.'

Neither Zebedee nor Nigel had much to say about the situation, beyond pointing out that the door was not closed on Luke, and that the player in possession of the goalkeeping jersey, as with all positions in the team, was entitled to a degree of loyalty. Paddy had an interesting perspective on the matter, though. 'The first consideration is that, as goalkeepers, they are much of a muchness. I thought Luke should have started the season. He explained to Nigel that he had an appointment, and I was expecting him to come back in for the next game. But Zeb's played okay, so he's stuck with him. The thing is, Luke has made himself unavailable. For one of the games Nigel told me he was going to drop Zeb and play Luke. When I saw Nigel on the Thursday, it turned out Luke had arranged a visit. So he put Zeb back in, and since then Nigel doesn't feel Zeb has done anything to justify being dropped. I agree with him. I mean, if Peter Schmeichel arrived here, I'd say, "For fuck's sake, let's get Zeb out of there." But that's not the case. Luke is a good goalkeeper, and with a good run, and a boost to his confidence, he'd do well. But one Saturday Nigel wanted him to sit on the bench. Luke said, "I'm not doing it, I'm having a visit." I don't blame Luke; I'd have done the same. But it's not canny. Nigel likes people who are committed. It was almost like Nigel was feeling him out to see what his reaction would be. So Luke's shot himself in the foot.'

All predictions for the seventh match of the season centred on damage limitation, and what effect a second successive defeat would have on the manager's selection policy. The George and Dragon were league leaders, and Terry Allison had heard they looked 'something special'. It was not an opportune moment for Jonah to get another heel injury. Carl was also missing, having hurt his neck in training. Scouse and Duffy were named as replacements.

Since learning that he was playing Scouse had been carrying himself like a sprinter on the eve of an Olympic final. His body became a temple, not to be abused with anything which might sap his strength. He decamped to the weights room, stretching and taxing muscles, but carefully so. He was tuned in for the big game.

The revised striking partnership of Paddy and Rizler, with Duffy playing in the 'hole', exposed wing loyalties. Many D wing cons thought Ian, who was in his late forties, was the obvious candidate to replace Carl. The manager did not. 'Ian's ball control and awareness are superb – in the reserves,' said Nigel. 'But his legs wouldn't hold up. You get chased all over the pitch in league matches. A full game like this one would fuck him for a week.' So Nigel drafted in Duffy, who belonged to the same C wing clique as Scouse, Teddy and the squad rebel Wayne. They pointed out that Duffy lacked nothing in terms of fitness and commitment. The D wing cons, on the other hand, said that Duffy was the Artless Dodger: he could run all day, but had no idea how to use the ball.

There were lots of bruised egos, and it hardly helped matters when Nigel confessed at the team meeting, 'Duffy's not a natural footballer – I've just asked him to get in there and break up their rhythm.' Bunny took greatest exception: 'It's a fucking joke. Duffy runs around closing people down. He's not going to create anything and he's not gonna win many tackles. Have you seen the way Ian knocks the ball about?' Bunny's tone was indicative of a wider disaffection with the manager. He thought Kingston sat too deep whenever they went ahead, inviting the opposition forward, asking for trouble.

The George and Dragon arrived in the style of champions

– late, and accompanied by a noisy entourage equipped with all manner of fancy sports gear and accessories. Two men carried a milk crate containing an impressive array of luminous water bottles. 'Oh man, they got all the gear,' laughed Jonah, who stood on the sidelines, hands dug in pockets.

It turned out that Jonah was not missing the game because of his Achilles, and tests had not revealed any sign of diabetes. 'I've had a bad knee for years,' he said, rolling up a trouser leg. 'The cruciate ligament is X-shaped. One bit of mine has ruptured or snapped. I've seen a doctor but because it was deemed a non-essential operation they won't operate. It's playing up at the moment.'

Terry Allison was jolly with gallows humour. 'I think Kingston will do well if they get something out of this one,' he said, as Scrotal Bill, the unofficial club official, poured hot tea from a flask and nodded sagaciously. So they were stunned when Kingston raced into a 2–0 lead. Paddy turned in a corner on three minutes; then Calvin threaded a pass to the captain, who took one touch before crashing home his second from outside the box.

Calvin, allowed time and space in the middle, was running the game. On twenty-three minutes he sent another pin-point pass down the left. Paddy, who had spun out from the centre, stretched the defence before cutting it back to Rizler. With his first touch the Welshman took the ball around the goalkeeper. With his second, he scored.

It was smash-and-grab football, and Kingston were 3–0 up.

At half-time Nigel was beaming. 'We've just got to keep it going,' he panted, his face flushed. 'Anyone who's tired, let me know. I've got blokes on the side raring to go.' Even Geordie was impressed. 'It's good to watch. You're all up for it.'

After the restart the George and Dragon battled their way back into the contest. On fifty-one minutes a long throw dropped into the box. One of their forwards arrived late, outjumped Nigel, and made it 3–1. The fast, flowing football that had taken the visitors to the top of the league spread unease along the touchlines. 'This is the time to take off Duffy,' mused Jonah. 'These lads have got over the shock of coming in here. Time to play.'

George and Dragon won another corner. Again, the same forward made a late run, outjumped Nigel, and scored. 3–2.

Consternation. For a moment, everyone seemed to be blaming everyone else. The shouting quickly boiled down to Nigel versus Bunny.

'Do your fucking job,' sneered Bunny, going for the last word.

After the briefest of silences, Nigel beckoned the referee. 'Hold on, ref, substitution.'

Nigel looked at Bunny and pointed towards the touchline. Bunny sloped off, angrily shaking his head. Paddy and Calvin exchanged glances. It was obvious just by looking at them they were contemplating whether Nigel had overstepped the mark, using his status as a prison officer to settle what had been a football argument. 'Betcha they walk off in support of their mate,' said Jonah. Bunny, his long arms swinging like pendulums, turned and gestured at Nigel – wanker. His team mates were looking at each other as if no one was sure where all this was going, but the match restarted and the immediate needs of surviving the visitors' onslaught galvanised the home side. Whatever inquest there was going to be would have to wait.

Big and strong, the George and Dragon players chased down everything in search of an equaliser. And with two minutes remaining, Scouse lunged for a ball that was never his, and the forward surged away into space and shot powerfully at the Kingston goal.

A jab of apprehension and disappointment . . . as the ball soared beyond Zebedee's reach . . . and the best performance of the season was dissolving into a draw . . . until the post went SMACK!

'Stop being a pussy, get in there for the rebound!' someone screamed.

Danger cleared.

Morgan, out on his legs. 'How long, ref?'

Two minutes of injury time passed before the man in black finally blew. Scouse and Rizler, excited little boys, hugged each other.

'Fuckin' well done.'

'Magic.'

The 3–2 victory meant Kingston had three wins, two draws and two defeats from their opening seven games, and they leapt to second in the table. But as the pitch cleared in the gathering twilight, Bunny confronted Nigel.

In eleven years working with the team no inmate had ever laid a finger on Nigel, and shuffling Bunny did not seem the obvious contender to land the first blow. But there he was, leaning over the manager, wagging a finger in his face, unable to lose his fury. There were prison officers in the vicinity, but none directly at hand, and none apparently aware of what was happening. Of the inmates, Paddy, Jonah and Luke might intervene as peacemakers if a fight broke out. Of the others, carrying with them all their years of grudges, harboured frustrations and knock-backs, who could be sure?

Nigel was talking, 'I hear you, I hear what you are saying, but this isn't the time or the place to talk about it, Bun. We've got the points. We've won the match, and we can talk about everything else later.'

Bunny turned around and marched towards the cell block.

Nigel, plastered in mud, finished taking down the nets and made his way around the back to the gymnasium. His face was red with anger. 'There is a line and he's just crossed it,' he said, his studs crunching on the concrete path.

16

LUKE

Nigel asked me if I wanted to go on the subs bench. I said no. This is not a childish stomp because I haven't been picked. I just feel that I have been messed about. If Nigel was testing my commitment, I don't think that was necessary. If I'd played I would have been fully committed. More committed than some of the challenges I've seen from Zebedee.

I don't mind playing in the reserves. The only trouble is you can get a bit of a Mickey Mouse defence. You get some of the first-team players – like Scouse, Teddy and Morgan – but people make more errors. Stupid passing, or trying to play one-touch football on your eighteen-yard line, when your first touch takes the ball six feet away from you.

I've always been a goalkeeper. I played Lancashire schools football until I was sixteen. Then I got a cartilage injury. A big crunch tackle, studs from the other fella straight across my knee. My bottle went. I didn't play again for about two years and by then I'd been left behind; other players progressed ahead of me. I was in the Territorial Army for three years when I was at university. I played for them when we went on a fortnight regimental camp. When I qualified as a solicitor it was just the odd five-a-side game in the evening.

I don't mind telling you my story, but please change my

name. Not so much for my sake, purely for my wife's family –
and my own. My mum still gets a lot of flak from the local
press. Any chance they get to report about my case they take.
This is the last letter they sent to me:

Dear Luke,
We'd like you to consider a request for an interview,
angling on your views of what has happened in the last
few years, your life before that and your reasons for the
terrible events. A member of staff would come and visit
you at your convenience.

There really is no point in replying. To whose benefit is it?
It's not for mine. People have either judged me or forgotten
me, or aren't bothered.

The notoriety of my case made things difficult at Walton,
the local prison where I was sent after my conviction. The
fact that I was a former solicitor, some accepted, some didn't.
And then you had the stupid kudos of being a lifer. In spite
of what you've done, people respect you because of the
length of your sentence. It was very useful. I can remember
on one occasion someone started a fight with me, but was
pulled off by others and given a good slapping. Not at my
request, I hasten to add.

I should have gone on to Wakefield, but a lifer wrote to
me, the first person to do so after my conviction, suggesting I
try to get into Gartree. He read about my case in the
newspapers. He was a former professional, worked for the
Post Office for twenty-odd years. He felt sorry for me and
wanted to help guide me through some of the pitfalls. He's
been very kind. He suggested that I write to the Home
Secretary to request Gartree. Felt it would be better for me.
They obviously listened. I had three decent years at Gartree.
There was an opportunity to do things. I got a BA degree in

economics from the Open University. I'm just about to start a degree in theology.

I didn't attend the chapel events early on in my sentence. But I always felt there must be something that was superior to me. I wasn't sure what. I went along with the usual sceptical mind, trying to shoot everyone down in flames. Asking all the usual questions – why do people suffer when God is supposed to love us, and things like that. Then, one morning, I went to one of the services. I'll never forget it. There was a black evangelical pastor preaching. More than anything, I remember his black patent shoes, which seemed totally incongruous. I just walked away from that service realising what God was offering me.

I met my fiancée three years ago. She was one of the prison visitors at Gartree chapel. She has two daughters. As I've got a potential ten years more to do, it's going to be a long engagement. We are both Christians and want to walk into church together without having the hassle of officers around.

Our relationship raised a few eyebrows originally. I certainly wasn't looking to have another person in my life. I think we both made efforts to avoid it, but if people are drawn to each other, it's hard to avoid. We've got a lot in common. We've got a lot of differences as well, but we've certainly got a strong relationship. The biggest concern for me is that I'm not there to offer support. If anything would have kept us apart, that would have been it. It's not as though the sexual side of the relationship is important. We've been able to form a relationship as friends, though it is frustrating now that we can't take it further forward.

I'm on a waiting list to do a Relationships course. At Gartree I did one called Handling Conflict. It was an amalgam of the Anger Management and the Assertiveness course. I've also done Violence Against Women. That was very intensive. Very heavy duty. It was excellent. There were certainly aspects of the relationship I had with my late wife that were a lot clearer to me after that course. They put me in with a former prison officer who had killed his wife, on the basis that we were both in for cases with similar backgrounds, and we might not have as much reticence opening up as we would with one or two others. The two probation officers were both women, and we could have an open session without fear of other inmates being indiscreet.

Looking back at my career, I hadn't quite reached the point where I wondered why I'd done it, why I was there. But it was a boring job. At the time of my offence I was earning quite good money, not bad for someone who had only been qualified for one year. I was motivated by material things. I'm not now. I think my offence and my Christianity have brought out a different perspective on things.

At the time of my offence I was married to a girl I had been dating since I was sixteen. So the relationship was about eight or nine years old. Without looking for excuses, and I'm not, really, we took too much on in terms of financial commitments. By the time of the offence we had about a £100,000 mortgage. Although we weren't in the red at the end of each month, we didn't have anything left over. It sounds a feeble excuse, but it's a part of it. There was a lot of pressure on us and we were too young and inexperienced to handle it.

For whatever reason, we had been growing apart over that last year. We just stopped talking. The nice little things stopped. Our sex life went down the tubes – too tired. We were just coming home and working on the house. Everyday life became mundane. I had always seen my wife as a great friend. When the problems came along, I hadn't got anyone I could turn to.

On the morning of the offence my wife said she was leaving me for a good friend. Makes it sound very blasé, but I just totally lost it. I hit her with a hammer a number of times. And she died. I had to decide there and then whether I held my hands up and got on with things. Or not. I tried to cover it up. I concocted a story to get out of it which was quite plainly false and was eventually seen through.

When she told me I felt angry, shocked and rejected. In some ways it wasn't a surprise; I'd suspected something a few weeks before. I'd confronted her, and she'd told me not to be so stupid. I can't remember exactly what I was thinking in the few seconds before the offence happened. With hindsight I can say I imagine I would have felt this and this because I feel them now. But I can't say what my thoughts were at that particular time. I just got so angry I lost control. It was just seconds. I'd got the hammer in one hand, the chisel in the other hand, lashed out, and just carried on lashing out. Ten seconds, it was probably all over.

I was aiming at her head, I can't say I wasn't. I don't remember it being frenzied, I don't remember it being controlled. Obviously they are saying all the blows hit the head. I must have put the chisel down somewhere. I swung the first [hammer] blow with my right arm, sideways, I think, up towards her head. From then on it was just repeated and repeated. In spite of the amount of blood that was around my wife after she died, there wasn't a lot of blood lost as the offence was happening. Although there were some splashes, there wasn't a great dramatic fountain of the stuff all over the place. The blood on my clothing was minimal. Looking back, I'm surprised myself.

I put all [my] clothes in the washing machine. The police had a very young, inexperienced female forensic scientist. [She] made the mistake in court of saying the blood could not have been washed out of the clothes. Obviously, I knew it could have been and must have been because I knew what

144

was on the clothes when they went in the machine, and I knew that there was [no blood] when they came out.

The first half-hour afterwards, I don't remember thinking anything. I spent about a quarter of an hour or so sitting in the kitchen, then putting the clothes in the washing machine and starting it, then going upstairs and sitting with the cat on the bed. I was physically numb. I just lay back against the headboard, wondering what to do, toying with giving myself up and trying to explain what happened. That would put it at about 8.30 a.m. in the morning. It wasn't until after ten that I rang the police.

There must have been a point where I knew I'd have to own up or construct something. I do remember thinking that, because of my legal background, I wouldn't be offered any grace or favours by the police. I wouldn't be offered manslaughter, so I might as well run it as not guilty. In domestic situations like mine, people are sometimes found guilty of manslaughter. But not in enough cases. With hindsight, I was right. If I had admitted it from the start I wouldn't have been offered manslaughter. I felt I had nothing to lose so I thought I might as well try to get away with it. A warped process, I guess, but that's how it was. I remember crying for ten or fifteen minutes and then thinking 'Stop, pull yourself together.' In that sense I accept being controlled. I'm not the sort of person who readily shows emotion. The fact that I cried was indicative of how bad things were. But from then it was a question of thinking, 'Well, I've always been a coper, so let's cope.'

After that first fifteen minutes I started to concoct a story that was feasible. One of the options was to have the door between the garage, where the offence happened, and the kitchen locked [and for the key to be missing]. And also the key for the door [that went from] the garage into the back alleyway to be missing. The idea was that my wife would have come in from the back alley, been killed by the intruder in the garage, who then fled, locking the outside door as he left. The only way to do that was to lose the keys somewhere in the house. It was too risky to go outside. I might have been seen. I couldn't have been awake at the time of the offence. I set the alarm clock to go off at ten a.m., and then was able to say I only woke when the alarm went off. I go downstairs, find the kitchen door locked, wonder why, discover the body, and ring the police.

I was pretty certain I'd be a suspect. In domestic murder cases the spouse is usually the principal suspect. I went into the station in the afternoon voluntarily to give a statement. Over the coming months the house was ripped apart by the police – door frames, the lot – looking for the keys. The advantage I had was that I'd been involved in so much of the renovation that I had a fair idea of where things could be hidden. I buried the keys under the floor. There was a pipe, and I stuffed them inside. Even when they found them, the officer admitted it was luck. He saw something glint, which turned out to be a piece of broken glass. It led him to the keys.

From the moment I was charged, there was no other explanation as far as my wife's mother was concerned. I was remanded in custody for the first month, then got bail. I think I got bail because the prosecution case was purely circumstantial. I also think the prosecutor offended the judge, so he spited him by granting bail. I was on bail for fifteen months. I lived with a friend in Birmingham.

I sold my wedding ring – I needed the money. I bought six pairs of socks with it. I just had to get rid of it. It was too much of an emotional burden when I was pleading my innocence. Trying to concentrate on a future when you're wearing this sign of the past. The stress of maintaining the pretence of innocence was incredible. Not being able to talk to anyone about it. I didn't want to put anyone in a position where they were compromised. I really don't know how I got through it.

I pleaded not guilty but was convicted after a full trial, which lasted just over three weeks. I've got a fifteen-year tariff, so really I should be serving fifteen years before I'm released, although I may go over that. As a life-sentence prisoner there's no guarantee. There are people who have had ten-year tariffs who have done twenty years. There is no automatic release.

Her mum and aunt were at the trial most of the time. I know some lifers have had to [meet] their victims' families. My outside probation officer had to [talk to them] about my sentence. During that conversation my wife's mum said she didn't want any contact with me. In a way it was a relief. But, at the same time, I felt sad that she was going to cling on to the bitterness she's got against me, justified or otherwise. I feel sad for her that she can't let that bitterness go. It must be horrible to hold on to something so horrible. I'm not bothered for my own sake. If she wants to go on hating me, I suppose that's her choice. But I know that if ever I've felt angry at someone and it's lingered, it's not felt nice for me. I don't want her to feel lousy. She's quite a nice lady really.

It wasn't for months after my conviction that I told my friends and family. I'd gone into the shocked, coping mode at Walton. I just thought, 'Well, I've got what I deserve, I just better get on with it.' Once I got to Gartree I began to get my head together. I realised I had to start telling people. I don't think it was a shock to them, but they were glad to hear it from me. Certainly, telling my mum and brother was the most difficult part of it. That was one to one. My brother is five years younger than me. I don't know what would have happened had I got away with it. I'd have been a mess, trying to live with it. But I was close to getting away with it.

I actually like myself more now. The person you are talking to hasn't got any airs and graces. He's doing everything that he does for himself. I'm doing things because I want to do them. Going into the legal profession was expected. Going to university was expected: there was a pressure to conform at sixth-form level. My choice would have been to do technical drawing and go into design.

Most of the officers here are okay. A few of them struggle with me – they don't know how to take my level of education and intelligence. They are very cautious. If you look at the mix of inmates we've got, it's not much different to the comprehensive school I went to. A mixed bag. We are allowed personal clothes. My room is cleaner and more homely than the room I had at university. I never get bored. It's a question of having the right mentality. You have to want to achieve, to do something with your time. I work during the week in the prison workshop, basically doing anything that a desktop publishing and commercial printers would do. We produce all the forms and documents that the prison service uses, like canteen forms and the mandatory drug test register. I work Monday to Thursday 8.30 to 5 p.m. Fridays we finish at lunch time because there's an afternoon lock-up. From the football team, Jonah and Steve are also in there.

I can't honestly describe the nightmares. I just know that sometimes I've had a bad night, woken up in a cold sweat, not knowing exactly what the dream was about, but having a fair idea. I don't have flashbacks. I mean, I can be sitting at my desk and picture the offence, but it's not what people would think of as a flashback.

I will never forget my wife, or the impact on my family and her family. I did love her, but that love was tarnished by what happened. I have forgiven her for the adultery, though I'm not sure sometimes. Sometimes, in my really-feeling-sorry-for-myself moments, I'm angry at her still. I don't want to be. Generally, it's more anger at myself for committing the offence. As everyone in here should be able to tell you, you are responsible for your own actions. At times like that I'm castigating myself rather than having a dig at her.

I don't think a day goes by without me having a thought about her. Generally, the thoughts are good ones. We had a lot of happy times. If things could have been different, we could have had a happy future together. At the same time, you've got to be a bit selfish in a place like this, otherwise you get squashed. That selfishness in me, and I recognise it, says you can't forever punish yourself. I think my Christian faith helps. I'm not using it as a crutch, but I really feel as though God has forgiven me for what I've done. I've got to try to forgive myself for what I've done, and I've also got to forgive my wife for what she did in our life. Most of the time I have. But it's a continuous process. It's not like you forgive and that's the end of the story.

As a Christian, I believe that Christians will go to heaven, and people who haven't given their life to Jesus won't. I wouldn't like to speculate as to what heaven will look like, feel like, or what the experience of it will be. I do believe that the experience for me is going to be the pinnacle – what I'm working for, effectively. I don't think it's going to be lots of people walking around in white gowns on fluffy clouds. It's more spiritual than that. At the same time, I think it's going to be a meeting up with the spirits of former Christians, and Jesus himself. That prospect is an exciting one for me. To meet the great prophets from the Bible like Moses and Isaiah.

I'd be thrilled to bits if my wife were there. I like to think that she went in the same direction as I'll eventually go. And I'm not trying to underplay what happened. I honestly think that meeting her would not be the problem that we'd have were it a reincarnation event on earth, in human terms. I'm not trying to use that as an excuse to [avoid] thinking about it. I really believe that it would be okay with her. I know that sounds horrible in some ways – 'Hello darling, how are you?' – but it wouldn't be like that. It would be far more spiritual. I would simply say I'm sorry. I don't think I can say any more. To start going into some great diatribe about what happened, there's no need. She knows it anyway. She didn't deserve what happened.

She was a warm, bubbly character. A church-goer from a church-going family. But I don't know what her real core belief was. I suppose I would say that I am an evangelical Christian because I don't keep quiet about it. I don't go around thumping people over the head with the Bible, but I'm not afraid to talk about my faith.

I think every Christian has to be born again. I know that people can be baptised as children, brought up in Christian households, go to Sunday school and church, but at some point in their older life, when they are socially and morally aware, that is the only time you can become a Christian. You have to make a choice to follow Jesus. If that sounds exclusive, well, it is. You have to make your mind up. Not many people get saved.

I don't know how you can show remorse. That's one of the things I'm concerned about. Should you wear the biblical sack cloth, walking around totally dishevelled because you are feeling remorseful? Or are you allowed to dress smartly and cleanly and just say so? I do feel remorse. I wish my wife was still alive. From a more selfish point of view, I wish I had not committed my offence. I'd do anything to bring her back, or to stop the hurt that has been caused to both families. But I can only say that. I can't say I'd give my life to bring her back. I want to live. I think I've got a lot to live for. I don't think I could do that.

I have been called cold, yeah. But I can't say I'm

devastated because I'm not. I feel dreadfully sorry for what I've done and the hurt I've caused. But I've always been a person that tends to cope. I'd like to think that doesn't mean I'm a bad person. You can be overemotional. That can be a risk factor.

I've not spoken to my father properly for years. He was a solicitor. His split with my mum started in my early teens. Our relationship is strained, mainly because he doesn't know how to deal with what's happened. My mum worked in the printing industry, then had a part-time job as a doctor's receptionist. She's mainly the one, in terms of visits from my family.

The rift with my dad opened up during a telephone call when I was at Gartree. He said that I was the cause of his and my brother's problems. It just so happened my brother had already told me he had gone for counselling because of problems in his own life. He said, 'It's not just you, but you are part of it.' And I've accepted it. I've caused a lot of hurt. I think my dad's ashamed because he wasn't there for us more. He's feeling sorry for himself, a failure as a dad. I wouldn't say that it was totally cold, but his idea of good parenting was to make sure we had everything materially. All I wanted to do was play football with him in the garden. I can't tell him that, though. It would just send him off the deep end.

I have felt there was a link between my upbringing and my outburst of anger, and I spoke to a psychologist at Gartree about it. I felt that because my parents' marriage failed, I didn't want my marriage to fail. It wasn't the adultery so much as the failure and rejection.

I've been totally open with my fiancée. I've made sure that any reports about me, she's had a copy, so has my mum. I have been totally and utterly open. Every avenue she wants to walk down, she can. She's said to me in the past, 'What you said on the phone was a bit harsh.' And I said, 'Okay, but it was honest.' In the past I've suppressed things.

I know the world is full of people looking for affection outside their marriages, but I don't think my fiancée would be unfaithful. Without sounding blasé, I think I could handle being told about an affair now. I feel more mature. 'Let's sit down and talk, not be confrontational. How did it start? What do you want? What have we got for the future? Have we got a future?' The very nature of my offence is sufficient motivation to get it right next time. Or, if it's going to fail, to see that it fails in a decent way, and not in some horrible, violent mess.

17

THE WASH

Nigel stared at a portable television in the kitchen; his youngest daughter sat on his knee, eating toast. *Breakfast News* carried reports of a prison officer taken hostage at Durham jail.

'Bet he's sweating,' said Nigel, to no one in particular.

The Nigel versus Bunny inquest was saved for the drive into work. A couple of days after the match, the two men had met to 'have a word'. The matter was now resolved, the wanker gesture forgotten. 'I was very offended,' Nigel explained. 'I could have probably put up with some verbals over my performance as a player, but I thought "Do your job" meant he was having a go at me as a manager. So it was like two planets colliding. I wasn't going to back down.'

Paddy, as team captain, had been put in an awkward situation by the row. 'I've had three seasons here and that's the first time I've seen Nigel take someone off like that,' he said. 'It did smack a bit of, "I'm the boss, if you challenge my authority you're off." Afterwards I saw Bunny having a go at him. It wasn't like he was offering Nigel out, but it was going that way. It's difficult because Bunny is someone who I speak to a quite a lot and Nigel is a good bloke, too – but he's staff. There's always going to be that friction.' He paused. 'Nigel is a great organiser. The thing is, if you are going to organise everything you've got to put your hand up if you make a mistake. Whether he did or not, I don't know, but it's a thankless task being a manager. You have to have someone calling the shots, and whether Nigel's made the right decision or not, someone can always say, "Yeah, well, a screw, what do you expect?" Most of the guys don't think that way about him. Nigel has most people's respect because of his attitude to the game. But Bunny felt he was looking for a scapegoat.'

Clearing the air did not extend as far as Bunny apologising. 'All I was saying to Nigel was that we were defending too deep, and he's not listening to me. He's just giving people verbals. So I said, "Do your job." He took the wrong end of the stick. He thought I was cunting him off about his team selection. The thing is, quite a few of us [in D wing] had got the hump that Duffy was in. He ain't a footballer. Before the game I went to see Geordie and said, "What the fuck is Duffy doing in the team?" That got back to Nigel. He also had Scouse bending his ear. Anyway, I was cunting him off because he let the man come in front of him – twice. It's a team game. I'm entitled to say to Nigel whatever I feel is good for the team. And he's entitled to say to me, "Fucking hell, Bun, shut up and get your arse up and down the touchline." '

Bunny's protests about Duffy's inclusion had not gone down well on C wing. One inmate, insisting on anonymity, suggested Bunny was talking himself into trouble. 'You don't mess about with this guy,' he laughed ominously. 'Duffy's a fucking major league drug dealer with connections all over the place. He blew his best mate's head off with a shotgun because the fella stitched him up. Duffy has already been to Bunny's pad once and said, "Have you been slagging me off?" And Bunny denied everything.'

I had no idea about the truth of what I was being told.

Duffy, a Londoner in his early thirties, was a central figure on C wing but a fringe member of the squad, and we had yet to meet. He was unexpectedly boisterous, which could put an outsider on guard – it's not what you expect, a laughing and joking lifer. Duffy also seemed to inspire devotion. It was said that Wayne would do anything for him. Some of the other inmates, though, were rather too keen to emphasise that they got on well with him. 'Duffy's very lively,' remarked Luke, gingerly. Asking either Duffy or Bunny whether they had had some sort of confrontation ran the risk of identifying the source. So I asked Bunny if he was concerned that his criticisms might be taken personally. 'A lot of the guys worry about things like that,' he said, defiantly. 'I can only be me. People say I'm too outspoken, but I'd rather be outspoken than two-faced.'

At the team meeting Nigel brought the 'do your job' incident out into the open. 'I know me and Bunny had a bust-up last week. That happens in games. We've had a chat about it and sorted out our differences. It's all in the past. To be fair, I probably reacted a little bit more than I should have done. But Bunny knows I can't have too much dissent during a game. It's got to be us focusing on beating the opposition, not beating each other.'

'It's called passion,' murmured Eddie.

'If it comes out in the wash I got no trouble with it,' said Nigel brightly. 'It was a good all-round team performance, let's not forget that. That lot were top of the table.'

'Fuckin' brilliant,' said Scouse.

They talked on, knocking backwards and forwards compliments, rebuilding the team spirit, making the peace.

'Eddie, your discipline was excellent,' enthused Nigel. 'Paddy, you added a dimension to your game. You were winning tackles, making balls in the air, closing people down, setting an example. Bunny, you were forcing them to play it.

I know you were getting frustrated because they were knocking the ball around you, but even when you didn't win it, two, three passes down the line, by forcing them to play it quicker we were gaining possession.'

The players had studied the league table and, for the first time, shared a real conviction that this season might turn out to be special. The improbable George and Dragon victory – secured with a weakened team which withstood a second-half pounding – seemed like a turning point. Kingston had also had the better of the new league leaders. Plover had reached the top with five straight wins since their 2–2 draw and 6–2 defeat in the prison. If Kingston could stop letting teams back into matches, there was no reason why they could not sustain a title challenge.

	P	W	D	L	F	A	PTS
Plover	7	5	1	1	28	15	16
Kingston Arrows	7	3	2	2	20	17	11
George and Dragon	5	3	1	1	19	6	10
So. Co-op Dairies	7	2	3	2	21	14	9
H&S Aviation	4	3	0	1	17	12	9
Grant Thornton	4	2	1	1	13	13	7
Rimor	4	2	0	2	14	15	6
Magpie	6	1	1	4	19	19	4
Court House	4	1	1	2	6	11	4
St Helena	6	0	0	6	4	39	0

For the return visit of lowly Court House, Paddy was pushed forward to join Carl and Rizler in an ambitious 3–4–3 formation.

'Let's attack them in the first twenty minutes like they haven't been attacked all season,' said Nigel.

There was need of another reshuffle at the back. Teddy had broken a foot in training and Jonah's Achilles was playing up again. It could have been a mini crisis, but Wayne had decided to rejoin the fold. There was no grand speech. His boycott of the team had not been supported by anyone else, and judging by the stick Paddy gave Rizler for drifting out of matches, nothing much had changed. The captain was not going to bite his lip. Wayne may have felt he'd made his point, or had simply got bored on the sidelines. But whatever the reason, he went straight back into the team, on the left side of midfield. Bunny was moved back behind him in defence. Scouse hung on to his place on the right of Nigel.

After the meeting, Scouse stood at the bottom of the stairs which lead up to the gym office. He was already wearing his kit, a full two hours and forty-five minutes before kick-off. The previous week someone had written 'Two left feet' by his name on the Availability List. Seven days on, Scouse could laugh about it. Sort of. 'I was right fed-up about that,' he said. 'The bastards haven't seen the work I put in to get in the team.' One of his front teeth was missing, left in a jar somewhere, but there was no mistaking the grin, the glow of satisfaction. 'To tell you the truth, it got me fired up for the George and Dragon. And I feel fired up now. It doesn't matter, does it, if someone's got a bit of jealousy? And I don't care about the injuries to Jonah and Ted. I want to keep my place. I want fuck all else. I'm having a good streak. I'm thirty-four this year. It was twelve years ago that I was told I wouldn't play football again after my car smash, cos of the scars on me 'ead. I say, fuck it, slap a bit of Vaseline on there. As long as it's not opening up, it don't matter.' Scouse was starting to become philosophical. It wasn't so bad being a washed-up drug dealer with no future, as long as you were in the team.

Later, in the gym office, Nigel and I were talking about his

157

plans for the weekend. As a surprise retirement present for his father-in-law, a snooker fan, the family had hired Willie Thorne, ranked fifty-first in the world, to play a couple of frames against him at the local club. Nigel was half-way through explaining this when Paddy appeared. Nigel faltered for a beat, wondering whether to continue talking about a family matter, but ploughed on. Paddy stood there, smiling keenly, looking at our faces as the plans for the big night were outlined, excluded by everything, but wanting to join in.

'Willie Thorne, eh?'

Some weeks before I'd asked Nigel why he had reappointed Paddy as captain when it seemed to cause so many rows. Surely it would have been better for all concerned if someone else did the job? 'It's not a popularity contest, it's about strength of character,' bridled the manager. 'You need someone who can be his own man, who doesn't run with the crowd.' What about the business of bawling out players who made mistakes? 'I think Paddy needs to understand that he's not doing himself any favours with the other lads. As for the rest of it, he maybe stands there with his hands on hips three times in a game. And that's out of frustration – he makes a lot of runs and never gets the ball. Those times get highlighted because Paddy is the type of guy who'll tell people if he's frustrated, and they feel they have to have a go back. He rolls up his sleeves and works as hard as anyone.'

Once Nigel left us to our meeting, Paddy said that he was glad Wayne had rejoined the squad. 'He's very good at getting a foot in. He's not like Calvin, he doesn't make big tackles. Wayne just wears people down, harassing them the whole game. He doesn't normally waste the ball either.'

Fresh-faced and trim, Paddy was in even better shape than at the start of the season. Save for his tracksuit and T-shirt, which were loose and well worn, he would not have looked out of place at the training ground of a professional club. With four goals in seven games, he had not quite lived up to his hotshot billing, but he was at least going back up front. 'I wouldn't have minded so much being in the withdrawn role if we had a bit more link-up play. But Carl and Riz are both the sort of players who want the ball over the top so they can run on to it and have the shot. I didn't do so well in the opening couple of games but, to be honest, I also feel our pre-season was poor. That's where you get your sharpness from, especially up front. We just didn't play together. We sometimes had only three first-team players and everyone else was just making up the numbers.'

Raph's back problems had eased enough to allow him to appear at training. Everyone who saw the session reached the same conclusion: here was the missing link, the playmaker Kingston sorely needed. 'He'll give us a lot more in the middle,' said Paddy. 'Part of the reason we've played so much long-ball football is that the midfield tends to be weak. If Nigel gives the ball to Morgan, we'll not only lose possession, but it'll start knocking Morgan's confidence. And confidence is important. Nigel is not going to make someone with no ability a brilliant player overnight. But if you can play a little bit, confidence is probably 50 per cent of the battle.

'It's the same with Scouse. He was thrown in at the deep end. He's stopped trying to do fantastic things. He's realised that just holding your position and knocking the ball away is adequate. I think Scouse feels he's started to hold his own. He's been on for a few games now and not embarrassed himself. People are starting to treat him as a regular. When the Availability List went up the other week, I said to him, "Are you going to put your name down for the Sunday friendly?" He said, "Nah, I'm a first-team player now." He loves it. Without sounding condescending, I think that's great. He loves his football. He's sincere about it. After that

George and Dragon game he had a grin on his face for the rest of that day. And the next.'

I mentioned the touchline observation that Paddy 'didn't like it when it got rough'. He paused, taken aback. 'I certainly don't go out onto the pitch worrying about getting hurt. I feel that over the course of the season I take my fair share of stick.' Paddy screwed up his face. 'There is this kind of attitude that says, "Well, if you haven't got bottle, you're not a man, you're nothing." It's almost like you've got to put your head down for someone to kick it off. If I play up front my job is to score goals and make goals for the other forwards. To be honest, if I don't think I'm going to get the ball, I'm not going to get in there. If the ball *is* there to be won, I try to win. I don't pull out of tackles. You've really thrown me. It's not something I've thought about.'

His eyes drifted away, contemplating a massing of his sneering critics. Who would question his commitment when he worked hard to stay sharp, as opposed to just turning up on a Saturday and hoping for the best? When he played on and off the ball for the full ninety minutes, giving the team everything he had? Wayne? Teddy? Rizler? The guys that hung around with them? Surely not Raph, already?

Abruptly, Paddy made his excuses and left.

Later that afternoon he scored eight goals. It was a blitzkrieg performance, laying waste to Court House, who were beaten 11–1.

In the last minute Paddy was booked for making a late tackle, and on the final whistle he made straight for the cell block, avoiding the circus of players wanting to celebrate how good they felt about their biggest win of the season.

18

WAYNE

I don't want to say nothing controversial about Paddy. It come down to politics. I was sick about the way it was run. At the start of the season I had a word with Nigel and said I didn't want to play any more. I told him exactly how I felt. If one person has the captaincy for one season then he should give someone else a chance – it would give that person better experience in leadership and confidence. You probably think we should be able to sit down and talk about our differences, but life ain't like that, unfortunately. Paddy's very arrogant in the way he talks to people. The only person he wants to listen to is Nigel. But it don't matter how high you are, I feel that if you're playing a game, screaming up the pitch at people who make mistakes, it don't help.

I come from Shepherd's Bush in London. Me and my dad are Arsenal supporters, and all my brothers are Chelsea. I used to go to Highbury, get kitted out – pathetic, eh? I remember when Chelsea won the cup in 1970. Our school was near Chelsea football ground. We took the morning off to watch them all coming back on the bus. It was the Leeds final. The replay was at Old Trafford. I liked Leeds at the time – you had Madley, Lorimar, Clarke; there's a lot of names I've forgotten. We were trying to figure out the first black man in football the other week. The only one I could think of was Clyde Best, but Leeds had Paul Reaney, didn't they?

I'm not one to dwell on the past. What's happened has happened. I can't change it, I can't bring him back. My wife said after the incident in which I was involved, 'Either you were going to die or he was going to die,' and she was happy it was him. It's something I can't change. My mum died twenty-five years ago, and if I could've brought anyone back, believe me, she'd be here now. So we know we can't change things, and I'm not going to dwell on it.

It was a fight. I went back with one of my mates afterwards. It was stupid really. I knew I was drunk but I didn't know he was drunk. My mate said, 'Here you are, have this shotgun,' and because we were drunk, I said, 'Yeah, that's a good idea.' The guy who I had been fighting with had a car. I was going to blow it to pieces. His brother came round the corner. I was saying, 'Yeah, you bastard, you can't come near me now,' but he come forward, didn't he, and *bang* he went down. He was dying. The Old Bill were there in seconds, and so was an ambulance, but they couldn't save him.

I've lost my wife, I've lost everything. At first, she said, 'I'll always be here for you.' But it got to her in the end. She's married again. I'm quite happy, I'm quite pleased about it. The selfish reason is that having a wife and feeling someone's out there and having her crying on the phone is a real bad strain on top of a life sentence. I haven't got those worries no more. I ring people every week. I ring my brother, my sister, or me nephew's wife. Some people one week, other people the next week. It's good to find out what's going on.

I'm doing a BA in art. I'd like to do my Masters degree and teach one day, but when reality comes in to it, maybe not. They ain't gonna let me, are they? Just for something else to do, I work on the computers here as a draughtsman.

I've got technical drawing and design qualifications since I come to prison. We put building specifications into computers, everything down to the last hinge and screw. It's all put on to disk and sent to the Home Office. The pay is crap, eight quid a week.

I was in the Royal Engineers for six years. When I went down to Aldershot, I was no more than nineteen. They give you basic army training for six months, and then you do your engineering training, which is building bridges, basic demolition, bomb disposal, that kind of stuff. After basic training I was super fit. It made you much more mentally and physically alert. It made you feel like you could do anything. I'm thirty-eight now but I won't give up my fitness – that's the army in me. They teach you that you can go beyond the boundaries of human expectations; when you're dropping, when you think you can't go no further – that's the time to kick hard. You never give up. I got married and we didn't want to move to Germany. I decided to leave the army, but it was a big mistake.

Most prisons are hell holes, out of control, drug-infested and everything. You come here and it's so calm, it's gone right to the bottom of the scale. Nobody wants to move to a C Cat because if one of those lunatics on a fixed term with nothing to lose wants to get at you, and you protect yourself, you'll end up worse off. It could put back your chances of getting released by five years or more. He knows that. The system will tell you, 'Well, you should have done this, you should have done that,' but they've never had anyone jump on them, have they?

19

NOW OR NEVER

The late November return of Southern Co-op Dairies was Kingston's ninth match of the season, and marked the half-way point in the fixture list. The visitors picked up where they'd left off during the first game, a 3–3 draw, but this time it was Wayne enduring a fearful chasing from the David Ginola lookalike. Three, four, five last-ditch tackles from Nigel halted the onslaught in the opening ten minutes, but the team around him groaned as it dilated. A goal was coming.

Paddy relieved the pressure. On the touchline, just inside the opposition half, his chest cushioned a driven cross-field pass from Bunny. Two men in green and white advanced, closing down the space and trapping the captain. Using his body as a shield, Paddy bounced the ball on his knee, then let it drop on to the white line. He took perhaps half a second to set himself before back-heeling the ball, spinning around and sprinting away, leaving his markers flat-footed. Within a few paces Paddy hit an early cross, catching the defence stretched. Rizler, first-time, flicked the ball left and shouted, 'Bury it!' but Carl blazed wide. Goal of the season, had it gone in.

A hand here, a punch there, at the other end Zebedee resembled the star of the beer commercial in which a German goalkeeper leapt about the Moehne dam, diverting bouncing bombs. And it went on like that, the two teams swapping punches like final-round boxers slugging it out for the knock-out. Finally Co-op got through scoring the first goal, Paddy equalised, then the visitors scored again to lead 2–1 at the break.

It had been fast and furious – and that was not Morgan's type of game. Nigel, to general touchline exasperation, did not substitute him. 'We've got to work together to win the ball back,' he said, winding up the players as they returned to the pitch. 'Come on, I know it's like the Alamo out there, but we need quality in the middle. Let's get Wayne and Eddie into the game.'

Calvin roused Kingston with a couple of stirring, defiant tackles. And suddenly they were back in it, Carl chasing down a long ball and threading it past the goalkeeper for 2–2. Zebedee, Bunny and Scouse made decisive interventions as the visitors attacked from all angles, sending in another barrage of crosses. And on seventy minutes, the sucker punch: Morgan, of all people, nudging home Paddy's low centre to put Kingston ahead for the first time – 3–2.

The visitors continued to press forward. With five minutes remaining their sheer determination brought its reward. Scouse finally made a mistake, a weak clearance finding the feet of a big, busy forward called Michael Marsh, who gleefully completed his hat-trick.

Relief, as much as anything, greeted the final whistle. The players shook hands – exhausted, taken to the limit, and perhaps glad that they had seen the last of each other for that season.

The following week Kingston moved to the top of the Portsmouth North End League. Surprisingly, nobody made much of this development, achieved with a point from another 3–3 draw, this time against Magpie (Paddy scored twice, Morgan once). Kingston led 3–2 until the final minute. The frustration at the concession of yet another disastrous late goal simmered for days afterwards. Without being aware of it, they were behaving like champions. A draw simply wasn't good enough.

Magpie, promoted the previous season as champions of Division Two, returned seven days later, so prompt atonement was at least feasible. Bunny was one of many players who thought Nigel should hold an open meeting to try to thrash out their problems. They all knew they had the makings of a good team but, for some reason, they kept letting the opposition back into games that were all but won. There was also the question of whether Nigel would stick with the same 3–4–3 formation. Playing with three out-and-out strikers placed extra demands on the midfielders and defenders when the other team had the ball. The formation would be an expensive luxury if the front men could not get their act together. As far as changing individuals was concerned, the manager's options remained limited. There was no easy way to bolster midfield, where Morgan was increasingly seen as a liability. Raph, the great hope, was following an exercise programme in an attempt to remedy his back problem, but would not be available until the New Year, a month away. Nigel wanted to try Jonah as midfield anchor. His mobility was no better than Morgan's, but he was much more effective on the ball. The trouble was, Jonah's Achilles injury had still not properly healed.

Standing by the D wing pool table, Morgan bore the uncertain smile of a man who knew his place was under threat. He had been to see the captain for reassurance. None was forthcoming. 'I told him to get down the gym and work on his fitness,' Paddy explained later. 'Morgan just stiffened up and said, "Whadda ya mean – I'm fit."'

Some of the players punctuated descriptions of their daily routines with references to 'having a quick wash'. Their clothes never appeared grubby. They often shaved at the weekends. And they made Morgan, who tended to loaf around the cell block, seem like poor white trash. Except that Morgan was kind of swarthy, and Bunny teased him about that, saying he must have 'a bit of traveller' in him. The other prisoners found nothing to dislike about 'friendly' and 'placid' Morgan. He had lots of friends and could talk for hours about his tattoos. But the fact remained he'd spent over half his life in jail. And when asked about the consequences of that, Morgan would put his hands behind his head, stretch back on his duvet marked with stains of an unknown origin, and say, 'Nah, I ain't worried about becoming institutionalised.' Talk Radio jabbered in the background; even banged up for eleven hours a day he couldn't be bothered to read books. On a shelf his toothbrush lay among ancient piles of budgie excrement, deposited by Lucky, his inappropriately named cell mate.

'There's been a couple of games when I've not been up to scratch,' sniffed Morgan, his grip-hands cupping a pool cue. 'All it is, right, is that sometimes you go out there and you have a good game. And sometimes you don't. Last week the pitch was heavy. It was hard work. Everyone played terrible. Magpie ain't a team we ain't capable of beating. If anything, I've been trying too hard. I think I've been chasing the ball rather than keeping my position.'

The second half of the season presented a potentially easier fixture list, but there was a sense that the title was already on the line. Kingston had completed more matches than the other main contenders: Plover, the George and Dragon, and Southern Co-op Dairies. While they were unbeaten against the best teams, they had suffered the two Grant Thornton defeats and dropped eight points in four drawn games. The concern was that come the title run-in, Kingston would be overtaken when their rivals played out games in hand.

'We are in a good position, much better than I expected,' said Nigel, ahead of Thursday's training session. 'But we've got to stop giving away silly points. Any more slip-ups and we can forget about the league. There just isn't that much margin for error.' He was contemplating having it out with the players, but wanted to think about what to say, and decided to keep his powder dry until the Saturday morning team meeting.

Carl and two of the reserves, Ian and John, missed Thursday training, their presence required at an Anger Management course. Ian leaned over the balcony as we trooped out of C wing. 'I wish I was coming with you rather than doing all this bollocks.'

Waiting for the outside gate to be unlocked, Duffy bounded up. A regular in the weights room, his shoulders and upper chest were pumped up out of all proportion to his slight frame and puny legs. Duffy was not the youngest member of the squad, but he gave that impression. His face was small, pale, with brown eyes and short, mousy hair. He could look like an orphan, with an expression which tended to switch between wide-eyed curiosity and abject vacancy. When Duffy was up, everything was a joke, and he was a puppy in your face, which made him popular with his C wing neighbours.

'Whaddaya talkin' about?' he asked Bunny.

'Darren Peacock.'

'Who?'

'Geezer plays for Newcastle, stupid hairstyle.'

Duffy looked blank for a moment, snorted out a laugh, lost interest and turned to find somebody else to talk to.

Eddie captained one of the teams for the eight-a-side game, picking Paddy, Nigel, Geordie, Scouse, Duffy and

Shaggy, plus an inmate from outside the squad. Bunny chose Calvin, Jonah, Wayne, Rizler, Morgan, Taffy the prison cook – and me.

The goals came thick and fast.

'What's the score?' Duffy asked Rizler.

'4–3.'

'Huh. Bad cantin' that is. Try 5–3.'

A little too determined to play as I would on the outside, a heavy challenge sent Duffy crashing to the sodden turf. When he turned around there was a moment when I wondered if the wildest speculations about him were true, that Duffy had indeed been a shotgun-toting drug dealer on the outside, a delinquent who let his fists do the talking, being the product of a dysfunctional family heralding from some toxic corner of South London where pavement vomit, fighting dogs, domestic violence, alcoholism, burglary, terrorised bus conductors and smack heads were part of the fabric of life.

Duffy laughed, dusted himself down, and carried on with the game.

It was quiet that afternoon on C and D wings. Most of the inmates were working or in the education rooms. Eddie was on a break from laundry duty. It turned out that one of his old acquaintances had made the headlines. Charles Bronson, often described as Britain's most violent prisoner, had attempted a world record for physical endurance with the help of staff at Belmarsh prison in south-east London. Bronson – known as Michael Peterson before adopting the name of Hollywood's *Death Wish* actor – completed 1,790 sit-ups in an hour while catching and throwing an eleven-pound medicine ball. He was awaiting validation from the *Guiness Book of Records*. Bill Duff, governor of Belmarsh, told the *Daily Mail*, 'We believe that if a man looks after himself physically and treats himself well he may be more inclined to treat others well.'

Some years before, Bronson had given Eddie one of his paintings – a self-portrait – and a copy of *Concrete Coffin*, an anti-crime booklet he'd written. Bronson, forty-five, from Luton, was sentenced to seven years for armed robbery in the early 1970s. All but sixty-nine days since had been spent in jail, his incarceration extended again and again for assaults on staff and inmates. An eighteen-stone body-builder, with a shaven head and ZZ Top beard, Bronson looked like a Victorian circus act (see a man bend iron bars with his bare hands). Bronson was kept away from other prisoners because of his unpredictable behaviour. He had spent twenty-one out of twenty-five years in segregation (solitary confinement in all but name) and been 'ghosted' – moved between jails without warning – over fifty times. Bronson once felt so isolated he asked for a blow-up doll; not for sexual gratification, but to talk to. During his first hostage-taking incident he throttled a deputy governor. In the course of the second, he barricaded three Belmarsh inmates inside his cell (two Iraqis accused of hijacking a Sudanese passenger jet, and another con described as his Scrabble partner). Bronson threatened to kill them all and eat one of them unless he was given a helicopter, two Uzi sub-machine guns, 5,000 rounds of ammunition, a cheese sandwich and some ice-cream. He wanted to be flown to Cuba or Libya, where he would seek political asylum. Officers were warned that if his demands were not met within the hour, 'I have a blade and will cut them up . . . even if it means me taking [a bullet] in the head.'

'He's one terrifying guy,' said Eddie, thoughtfully. We were sat in the D wing office – a converted cell, furnished with two chairs, a desk and a panic alarm. 'The first time I met Charlie was in the exercise block at [HMP] Franklin. I'd

170

bin banged up fur hours and I was dying te get outside, even though there was snow about a foot deep on the ground. The block was supposed to be empty for him, but the lock on the gate letting me out had frozen and the screw couldn't open it in time. Charlie comes running into the pen. He just stopped and stared at me, with steam coming out his nostrils. He shouts, "What are you doing in ma cage!" I was fuckin' shitting myself, man, thinking even the screws were terrified. But Charlie burst out laughing. And he comes over and gives me a cuddle. And from that day on we were mates. The thing is, I was the only one who got on with him. When he wanted something he'd use me so that he didn't have to talk to the staff. One time we were stood by this screw and he said, "Ask the screw if I can have a visiting order." I did, and this screw said, "Fine." So I turned to Charlie, and he goes, "What did the screw say?" '

Eddie also talked about the inmates he'd rather not have met. Like Bungle, a grave-robbing necrophiliac, and Forty-Two, who looked like Donny Osmond on steroids, and was said to masturbate the aforementioned number of times a day. Forty-Two had raped and murdered a woman and then ejaculated on her corpse. He was marrying his penfriend. Most Saturdays they could be seen in the visitors' block, kissing like they were trying to resuscitate each other.

Given the chance, Eddie would tell the juvenile delinquents who were given tours of Kingston about Bungle, Forty-Two and the others like them. They went too easy on the kids, he thought. 'The last time they brought one of these groups in here, I happened to be on the punch bag. I could spot straight away who was the top kid. He had his shoulders back, walking round like it was no big deal being in jail. My first instinct was to punch the fuck outa the bag and stare at him. Because they never show these kids what it's like. They took that group to the cell of this con who works in the kitchen – a well-paid job. You open the door and this guy's got so much gear you'd think he was the Sultan of Brunei. They should take them te the worst fucking cell in the whole nick, and then let me have a chat with them.'

Telling the story about Charlie Bronson had raised a weak smile, but otherwise Eddie was subdued, and slumped in his chair. His only friend at Kingston, Cardy, had recently shipped out. 'You make a good mate and the next minute he's gone. That upsets everything. You go to the gym with your mate. You play football with your mate. When you get food, you cook together.' There were two other Scottish inmates, neither of whom he bothered with. 'One of them's a sex case. The other, an old guy, is all right. But I don't want too many of these people in ma head when I get outa here.'

He ran a scarred hand through his red bristle. His green eyes were desolate. 'It's not easy to talk about your problems. Going in offices with members of staff. People think, "What's he talking about?" And the other cons have got their own problems. I mean, Nigel asked me to see you a few weeks ago but ma head was shot. I've just been divorced. My kid who has bin down here for eight years is going back te Scotland. My mum's ill, you know. She had a hysterectomy and it's bin down hill ever since. I've got a sister on drugs and stuff like that. When I call home it's expensive, and I got the sound of my mum coughing herself into the grave, and ma kids causing trouble in the background. And there's nothing I can do. I'm stuck in here, fucked up on a life sentence.'

Money problems backed Eddie still further into a corner. He borrowed from other cons. Eddie recognised that this was a slippery slope, that debts could become insurmountable. 'I borrow four quid and never go over that,' he said, quickly. 'I've got it under control.' Eddie was hoping to get a better-paid job than the one he presently held, earning seven pounds a week as laundry storeman. Tuesday, when he went around the cells delivering clean sheets, was the only bearable shift. 'I sit there with nothing to do for an hour sometimes,' he said, amazed that such idleness was possible in the workplace. 'I've just filled out an application for the kitchen. I've worked in there before. It pays sixteen quid a week. I'm no frightened of work. I'm a good grafter. The thing is, when I was in the kitchen before, as a cleaner, there was a guy who I was clashing with. I've only been in there three days, and he's shouting, "Where's this fuckin' cleaner?" And I'm just learning the job. Little things were building up and I thought if I don't get outa here I'm going to end up fighting with this guy. That's the last thing I fuckin' need. He's since been kicked out because of his attitude with the staff.

'All these things build up, you know. You get to the stage where you go, fuck it, bang the cell door, and you don't want to come out again. There's times when I want to abuse myself with drugs. There's some days when I think, *fuck* it. Other days you get up and think, okay, man, let's go. There's no pattern. Sometimes I drag everything outa ma cell and scrub it clean. I strip ma whole cell and rebuild it. I don't know why, it makes me feel better.'

We left Nigel's wife watching early-evening television in the lounge, draped across the sofa. Geordie, whose birthday we were celebrating, met us in a local pub. Four pints later we worked our way through the network of residential streets that stood between the pub and the Taj Mahal. The freezing December night made the trek laborious. Nigel, wearing a shirt but no jacket or overcoat, walked with hands in pockets and chest to the fore. A bloke on a bloke's Friday night out. Around 11.30 p.m. the dimly lit curry house had the feel of a suburban party where half the expected guests had not turned up, but those strangers who had were at ease in each other's company. Everyone appeared a little drunk. One table was occupied by some players from St Mary's Arms, a Division Two club. They bantered with Nigel. Geordie, arms resting on the white linen, studied the menu.

After a few more drinks I wondered what a satellite view of Britain taken at that very moment would have revealed about how people exercise their precious freedom. The blackness of midnight dotted with the glow of street lamps, taxi ranks, service stations, twenty-four-hour supermarkets and bed-room windows. And if the lens zoomed closer still it would find pockets of people like us, sat in cheap restaurants, using the place to mark the successes and failures of another week, a kind of diving bell where the purpose was not to remove excess nitrogen from the blood, but to dissipate the bends formed by unopened bills, ambitions, difficult people and awful weather. Everything dissolving in alcohol, companion-ship, spices and food colourants. And, for us, a little football talk. It was depressing and heartening all at the same time.

The crunch meeting took place the following morning, ahead of Kingston's eleventh game of the season, the Magpie return. Word had gone around that Nigel was going to be blunt and unforgiving addressing problems before Kingston embarked on a championship challenge in which they could ill afford to throw away points. The advance billing also suggested that the usual paranoia about players being openly critical would be swept aside.

By eleven a.m. it was standing room only. The full squad crowded into a small room. Nigel stood in front of a white board facing an audience arranged in the shape of a horseshoe. Duffy, Teddy and Raph were among the crowd sat to his left. Carl leant against the wall behind them, having glided across the floor like a sulky gigolo, wearing a grey sweatshirt and skimpy lilac shorts. Scouse, Rizler, Paddy and Eddie were in the group opposite the manager, at the back of the room. Bunny, Calvin and Jonah were to his right.

Nigel plunged straight into the subject of Morgan, who had struggled in recent games, the nadir arriving with the 3–3 against Magpie. Inaction Man scored, but otherwise covered the ground so slowly he might as well have been twelve inches tall.

'We've got a lot of competition for places and Morgan, you know you had a 'mare last week. The way I see it, I'm sticking by you, mate. I didn't look upon you as a first eleven player this season. Same as Scouse. But you've not let me down, or the team down, or yourself down. You've done well. I feel anyone is entitled to one bad game. Last week's just bypassed you. You've got to—'

'He scored a goal,' interrupted Carl.

'It don't matter to me who scores the goals,' shot back Nigel. 'I'm more interested in the guy who lays on four or five goals. I'm more interested in the guy who comes off the bench and runs around stopping them scoring rather than the guy who just stands there and touches it in. It's a team thing. It's about hard work.'

Carl said nothing.

'Now look, it's easy for me to say, "You're crap, you had a shit game," ' continued the coach, referring to the team as a whole. 'But I'm not just going to slate you. I'm going to tell you how to improve.'

They waited to see where the finger would be pointed.

'The one major area where we can really improve – and if we get it right, we are going to rip teams to pieces – is up front. There is not enough movement from the front three. There are no exceptions. You've got to work as a unit. We've got Carl on the right because he's right-footed; Riz on the left because he likes cutting inside on his right foot; Paddy in the middle. You've got to rotate. You've got to draw people out. Scouse will tell you, Teddy, Jonah, Bunny, myself – anyone who plays at the back – if my attacker stands still for the whole game, what a lovely game that is. I don't have to run about. I don't have any problems.'

Paddy, Carl and Rizler said nothing. Nigel was obviously going to stick with the attack-is-the-best-form-of-defence formation and would give them another chance together.

'It's not just the strikers,' continued Nigel. 'If they are pulling the defenders around, the rest of you have got to exploit the gaps. I want this interchange of movement. If Paddy makes a run, that's left space for someone else. It might be that you carry the ball into that space. It might be that the ball is played in there. It might be that you make an unselfish run, opening up a space for someone else. One movement sets off a chain reaction.'

Nigel walked Carl through a demonstration of how to position himself when being marked, so that he was easier to pass to. Given the sullen expression on Carl's face, there was no telling how he would react to being spoon-fed a few basics in front of everyone else, with the manager holding his arms and moving him around like a mannequin. But he said nothing, just nodded occasionally.

'Instead of thinking, "Right, I'm going to turn and take the bloke on," when you get the ball, look for Calvin, Morgan or anyone else who has moved up behind you. If you are in the first two-thirds of the pitch, lay the ball back to them, and move forward. It's simple. Last week when Duffy came on he played the simple ball. He made about ten passes. We retained possession. It was very effective.'

'I do lay it off,' blurted out Carl.

'A lot of times when you lay it off it's because you haven't been able to run with it, and by then it's too late. The person was free, but now he's been closed down. The moment has gone.'

Rizler, an unlit roll-up hanging from his mouth, mumbled, 'No disrespect Carl, but it's no good just standing there.'

Now it was Eddie's turn: 'Carl, last week at the start of the game, I'm looking for you te lay the ball, so you can make some room, and I'm gonna fuckin' feed the ball back to you. But you're trying te take on two or three—'

'Nah, nah, nah,' said Carl, shaking his head.

Paddy too was keen for Carl to concede the point. 'It's not a question of anyone slating you. We've all got areas of our game we can improve. You've got to be honest and say, "Okay, I do this well but I don't do that well." Every single one of us can improve our game.'

'All I'm saying,' insisted Eddie, 'is give me the ball, roll off and make some space.'

Carl, back against the wall, remained silent, chewing his lip and avoiding eye contact. Of course his show of obstinacy only made matters worse, making him the focus of the team's problem. It all seemed a bit unfortunate. Carl usually worked harder off the ball than Rizler, who could not kick the habit of accepting criticism during meetings, but rarely doing much about it on the pitch.

'A lot of the time we pass the ball and then just stand and watch,' Nigel continued. 'But it's just not good enough to look at your striking partner and think, "Look at him go, he's working hard today." '

Laughter ripped across the room.

'Bunny – now, he got caught, what, three or four times last week, playing the ball across the middle. Sometimes we play too much football; it's too tight. But sometimes we've *got* to try to play our way out, even *though* it's tight. What we need is movement from everyone. That's why I criticised you, Morgan. If that ball goes out to Eddie or Wayne, you can't just be standing there thinking, "Blimey, he's making a good job of holding off them defenders." '

Morgan raised a hand admitting guilt – more laughter.

Nigel then went on to the importance of warming up properly. It just so happened that Carl was the worst culprit. 'You've got to remember, lads, fail to prepare, and prepare to fail. So Carl, when it's two minutes to kick-off, we're all ready and you come out late, haven't even got your shirt on, fag in your mouth—'

'Nah, I never have no fag in my mouth,' said Carl, decisively.

'Another thing,' said Nigel, ploughing on. 'Let's warm up *sensibly*. Eddie, I don't need to see you booting the ball over the wall.'

Ironic cheers of 'Eddie!' filled the room. They went on for some time. It became the open, constructive dialogue everyone wanted, with players airing their views about problems and making suggestions as to how they could improve. They talked about defending as a team when the opposition had the ball, and how to attack when Kingston were in possession. By the end, it was almost evangelical.

'Everyone's got to have the winning spirit,' declared Duffy. 'Gotta wanna win.'

'Well said,' barked Scouse. 'We're all in this together. It don't matter – just get out there. Eleven fuckin' lads on the pitch.'

It was becoming a full-blown bonding session, and a strange one at that. In the normal course of events there would have been nothing to draw these individuals together. Life on the wings was harsh, governed by a survival instinct which said to each long-term prisoner, 'Look after number one, because no one else cares.' Who knows what they would have done with their time had the football team not existed. Some might have found something meaningful to do on a

Saturday afternoon. Others might have gone to the other extreme of taking drugs, or remaining in their cells, sitting there for month after month, deteriorating to the point where the personality began to disintegrate. But most would have probably just returned to the same old routine. Nothing would change.

Spirits were so high come the end of the meeting that Nigel even chanced a joke. 'It's like I say to them at the gate. "Don't worry about a valuables bag, lads – they're not thieves. Just murderers.' On any other day it would have bombed. But only Carl did a double-take. Teddy turned to his friend and laughed. 'Poor bastards. A lot of 'um come in here and must shit themselves.'

Calvin, the only player to remain unmoved by the feel-good session, led the march to the canteen to watch Manchester United play Liverpool, scheduled for a Saturday morning at the behest of Sky television. It was a big room, with white walls and a blue polished floor. Some months previously a disgruntled arsonist had started a blaze which caused so much damage the canteen had to be completely redecorated. So the decor was clean and newish. The easy chairs were all occupied. Latecomers sat on the same small upright wooden chairs that were found in the classroom.

At 11.30 a.m. a large hatch opened revealing the kitchen, and a queue formed for lunch. Paddy, a Liverpool fan, appeared with a plate of mashed potato, tinned tomatoes and a rectangular beefburger. We sat and watched as Andy Cole wasted chance after chance, while Liverpool conceded soft goals from set-pieces. Paddy looked unperturbed, picking half-heartedly at his food, making excuses for Liverpool's disaster-prone goalkeeper, David James. With tape recorders and questions put to one side, we sat chatting, enjoying the first half, two blokes watching a game of football. Just before noon the warders appeared and ushered Paddy and everyone else towards the cells, and me back to reality.

Terry Allison arrived at 1.30 p.m. So did the referee who, even before changing into his kit, caused a disturbance.

'I don't like it when they turn up looking like a bag of shit,' muttered Terry. 'It looks bad from the off. I like referees clean and tidy. Maybe I'm old-fashioned.' Geordie laughed, which only encouraged Terry. 'When you see him walking in, he's got that silly motorcycle jump-suit on and hair all over the place. It don't give you a lot of confidence.' With his red spectacles, grey hair slicked back with Brylcreem, and long nylon sports coat over tracksuit bottoms, Terry was a stranger to Savile Row himself. Still, he was not in charge of the match.

When everyone went outside it became apparent that Geordie had left the referee locked in the changing rooms. 'An innocent mistake,' he said, grinning.

Les Hyson, the Magpie manager, walked out to the pitch with Terry and me. He said he enjoyed bringing his players into the prison. 'Some teams do object, but they only complain when they are losing. Belle View protested last year. Said they didn't like it because they felt intimidated with the inmates all around – you know, the ones watching as well as them playing. I always think there's a lot less hassle when we come in here.' A couple of weeks previously Magpie had beaten Plover 2–0. 'Because they didn't have their own way on the pitch, they kicked the shit out of us,' said Les. 'That would never happen in here.'

Carl was the last to arrive on the pitch. If he was making any kind of statement, refusing to bow to the will of the coach, it backfired. Having forgotten his shirt – he always put it on at the last moment – Carl had to run back inside with undignified haste.

It was an action-packed first half, Kingston twice going behind to penalties, but a curling free-kick from Paddy and a spectacular overhead kick from Rizler brought them level. Nigel got booked for what the referee described as 'giving him an aggressive look'.

Just after the break Paddy smacked home yet another penalty. But at 3–2 ahead, and with some thirty minutes remaining, the verve went out of Kingston's play. After all their talk about working together they were anxious about throwing away another victory. The trouble was, the 3–4–3 formation and the personnel were better suited to attacking than to soaking up pressure. Magpie seized control, and by the time Paddy dropped back into central midfield with about ten minutes to go, Kingston were under siege.

Geordie rubbed his hands anxiously. 'Not looking good, eh?'

Until the eighty-ninth minute it still seemed as though Kingston would hold on for a win. And then the visitors won a corner. Nobody jumping made contact, and the ball spilled to the feet of a Magpie player. Nigel charged towards him to block the shot, but the player miscued and the ball spun towards the penalty spot. One of their players reacted first. He hammered it into the net. Zebedee, hands on hips, was incredulous. 'What happened? The angle changed and it just went past me . . .' Nigel, Bunny and Scouse could scarcely look at each other. All that resolve about working together, keeping it tight. They'd blown it.

Stony-faced, Paddy organised the restart. With no stoppages to speak of, a matter of seconds remained. He worked the ball out to the right, midway into the Magpie half. Eddie won a throw. He sent it long, the ball dropping towards the centre of the pitch. Suddenly, there was Rizler, impishly advancing into space. He let it bounce once and then, about a foot off the ground, slammed his foot into it.

How beautiful the ball looked arching across the sky, following an even trajectory, the strike perfectly weighted. It thudded against the left-hand post but, amazingly, cannoned sideways into the net.

Eyes bulging with manic joy, Rizler ran towards the touchline, fists clenched, as Carl and everyone else gave pursuit.

Geordie was grinning. 'Can you believe that?'

And then the final whistle.

Scouse was ecstatic: 4–3; they'd saved themselves. He ruffled the hair of a young Magpie player slumped on the turf. 'Eh, mate, we're not as bad as they say. Don't believe everything you read in the papers.' The player looked utterly baffled. He went to speak, but Scouse was already on his way.

20

MEN OF EXPERIENCE

'You only got two cups there, Geordie. There's three of us. Where's yours?' Carl was sat in the gym office, enjoying pushing his luck.

'Come on,' he moaned. Geordie squeezed the life out of the tea bags, and remained silent as he deposited them in the waste bin.

Carl smiled, big and lazy, tilting his head so that his dreadlocks swung to one side. He was wearing his skimpy lilac shorts again, exposing almost the full length of his sinewy legs. 'Ah no, it's my favourite brand, Tetley.'

Finally, Geordie laughed. 'I'm not making you tea, Carl.'

'I'll make it then.'

Geordie put the milk back in the fridge. Mug in hand, he made his way downstairs to where the contents of the PE store room were spread across the sports hall floor. A health and safety inspector had visited Kingston during the week and insisted that the locker be tidied. Geordie was given the honour.

The death of an inmate at another jail had created other management concerns. The man had dropped a weight on himself while bench-pressing. The PEI in charge of the session was answering the telephone at the time. As a precaution, Nigel and Geordie were issued new guidelines.

No one could use the sports facilities unless directly supervised. It meant a huge change in working practices; PEIs could no longer open the weights room and then, for example, referee a hockey match. 'The area manager has brought it to our attention that we could leave ourselves wide open to litigation,' said Geordie. He and Nigel had spent hours fending off the staff and inmates who wanted to grumble about how this restricted access affected them.

Later, in the D wing office, Carl wanted to put his side of the story about the Magpie team meeting. 'What Nigel was saying was a load of bollocks,' he declared, with unexpected gusto. 'I took exception when Nigel said I come out on the pitch smoking. And he never had a valid point, directly, right, about my work rate, either. The problem was between Rizler and Paddy. They was having little digs at each other and I thought, "I'm not getting involved in that," and stayed out on the flanks.'

Sat beneath a red plastic sign, the words NO SMOKING engraved on it in white letters, Carl lit a roll-up, his long fingers cradling the white sliver as he pulled hard. 'At the end of the day I'm the longest-serving member of the side, a 4–4–2 sort of guy. Get the ball up there, no mucking about, and *bam*. I don't like passing to Riz because he holds on to the ball too long. He's not interested in one-twos. The thing is, we're all different players. As much as I want us to be successful, I can only take so much personally. What you got to realise is that I'm a man of experience. Whenever I knock it back to Eddie, who's behind me on the right, he runs off with the ball. He don't know what to do with it. Now, if I get the ball and turn, there's more chance of something happening. Last season I had Wayne behind me. Beautiful. Lay the ball off to him, you get it straight back. He loves passing.'

I asked him if he accepted Nigel's criticism about his lack

of movement. Carl thought for a while, his big brown eyes rolling up to the ceiling. 'Nigel had a point, right, but he never wanted to have a go at Eddie. Keep the peace. I don't think Eddie can handle the criticism. There's a lot of people who can't handle criticism. Nigel don't criticise Scouse, just to keep the peace. He had a go at Morgan. I said, "Hang on, he scored the goal that brought us back in the game." Nigel gave us all this bollocks about it don't matter who scored. He should have praised him for scoring. Morgan's the top-scoring midfielder.'

There was also the matter of Carl's willingness to accept reproach. He laughed. 'It's funny you should say that. Just before the last match, Nigel came up to my cell and said, "Well done for taking criticism." '

This management doublespeak bore the hallmarks of necessity. Prison officers approached their jobs in one of two ways: they could be a guard, whose function was to lock and unlock doors, count inmates and follow procedures to make sure security was maintained – which was how Zebedee saw himself; or they could be like Nigel, who was willing to have a more interactive relationship with the cons. During the bang-up he would have made his way along the D wing landing, knocked on Carl's door and gone inside to talk things over. It was a case of trying to reach Carl with a few words of support while nudging him towards change and reality. And that required keeping the lines of communication open.

Nigel was reluctant to discuss his approach. He bluffed, saying it was just sound football management. He could not afford to have one of his best players feeling alienated – and since the Magpie meeting Carl had been pouting like a supermodel whose limousine was late. What also seemed true was that Nigel was self-conscious about how his actions might be viewed. He'd been in enough situations on the outside where somebody had asked him what he did for a living, and when it eventually came out that the prison had a football team, people got that look: Prison, murderers, playing *football*? Is that what we pay taxes for? And there were plenty of prison officers who thought that doing anything beyond what was stated in the job description was just asking for trouble. After all, in some countries Carl would have been ten years' dead, the subject of a state execution, maybe Chinese style, a bullet through the back of the head, his last mark on the world an iridescent stain on a concrete floor somewhere. There would have been no talk of football, no hope of redemption.

So Nigel kept his mouth shut and got on with his job in the way he saw fit. And his approach took into account the reality that some inmates, like Carl, were responsible for crimes which attracted so much revulsion that they exhibited a kind of involuntary shut-down whenever confronted by personal criticism. If you wanted to work with the good in Carl, to encourage the reason, the honesty and the self-discipline, if you wanted to help Carl mature, that sometimes meant going further than you wanted to go. And that was the way the Kingston manager went about his job.

Carl was by no means the only lifer who found criticism unbearable. But so much antipathy seemed to have flowed his way that he developed a coping mechanism based on childish denial. He was right and everyone else was wrong. Sometimes Carl's stories and mannerisms carried hints of the inner world into which he retreated, where he was smarter than the average con, a senior member of the football team, whose sexuality once made him a trophy-fuck for white professional women. Carl often talked about the times he indulged himself with the trail of credit cards they laid to their doors. Shopping and fucking.

The gates to his kingdom, the Don't Mess With Me

Republic, swung a little further open when he was asked how he would react if punched during a match. 'I'm not in the business of turning the other cheek, and I'm not in the business of seeking out trouble – someone has got to draw first blood,' he proclaimed. So he would defend himself physically? 'Of course.' Carl accompanied the words with the suave wave of a playboy sanctioning the purchase of the most expensive champagne in the house. Carl was given to such gestures, highlighting his taste for doing things with style.

He was fascinated by himself, and would often stand in front of his shaving mirror talking about self-improvement. 'I'm starting to grow as a person,' he enthused. 'I want to discipline myself. I say to myself, "Right, that means doing things I don't like." Like, for instance, I don't like getting up in the mornings. So I said to myself, "Right, any time seven a.m. comes you've got to get up regardless. Get up, have a quick wash, brush your teeth." Give me the most time to clean up my cell, clean myself, write anything, so when the door opens, I'm organised.

'I'm also denying myself certain things. I says, "Right, what do I like?" Pornographic magazines. I used to have a good selection. So what did I do? I just gave them away one by one. I gave my last one away the other night. This is ironic, right. I'm going back to my cell to get banged up. John goes, "Here, Carl." He give me a magazine in a paper bag. I thought, "Fucking hell, man, I want this." It was a good magazine. Tempted. "Shall I take this back to my cell tonight?" ' Carl shook his head. ' "Nah." I passed it to my friend, Dave. I said, "Take this for tonight, Dave. I'll take it off you tomorrow and give it back to John." So when I got banged up I had nothing at all. I was doing the right thing: disciplining myself.'

He was making other changes. 'I've had a big clear-out and got rid of all my shopping catalogues. When I first came inside I had the most material things. You get hardened. You don't need it. You deal with what's important to you now. But it ain't easy getting rid of stuff. It ain't like when people get a God trip, and throw everything away. They are punishing themselves. I'm doing it gradually.

'I want my heart and mind functioning as one. I want my aura just right. I want to start respecting myself, because charity begins at home. I look in the mirror and say' – he put on a schoolmasterly voice – ' "Are you still ready to continue to lie to yourself? Because if you can lie to yourself you're *worthless*." So I says to myself, "No, I'm not going to lie to myself at all." And when I'm not lying to myself, I'm finding respect is coming from other people. Everything run nice.'

Confirmation that Carl was getting somewhere came at a recent review board. Carl felt he held his own in the intimidating circumstances. 'For the first time in my life I had control of it,' he said proudly. 'I have been consistent in my dealings with people. They was pretty pleased with that. I know for a fact all the work I've done will push me through when the big one comes along for me to be considered for release. I'm still embarrassed by what I done, but I've learnt I can walk tall.'

21

IT'S A WONDERFUL LIFE

The door opened just before eight a.m., sending a shard of electric light into the gloom. Lying awake in bed, Paddy turned on his radio. Christmas Day is a time for being with the people you love, he told himself. There was nothing to celebrate.

A home-made curtain covered the Perspex observation strip in his cell door. During bang-up the warders were supposed to look to check inmates had not escaped or killed themselves. Paddy had been fined two pounds for drawing the curtain, but found the idea of not having any privacy such an affront to his dignity that he was prepared to risk further sanctions. The curtain stopped him feeling like an animal in a cage, and meant he could complete his ablutions in private.

The eight feet by twelve feet space was crammed with books – mostly contemporary fiction, courtesy of the local library – and family photographs. The wall above his bed featured his sister, big and hearty, laughing in a kitchen somewhere; his younger brother, with arms around their parents; Mark, an old friend, holding a carp caught on a fishing trip taken with Paddy years before. Two young boys, his nephews, beamed out of a couple of frames. As did the son of an old girlfriend. There were also two brightly coloured landscapes – postcards his brother sent from holidays in the Bahamas and the Florida Keys, images truly from another world. On the opposite wall, above his desk, there was a series of fantasy illustrations. The sword and sorcery artwork was not to Paddy's taste, but the pictures were a present from a Scottish inmate whom he befriended in Winchester. Paddy said they reminded him of the start of his sentence. Next to his desk there was a wash basin and shaving mirror. Opposite stood a small cabinet, overloaded with old sports magazines. At the foot of the cell, a partition obscured most of the toilet.

Paddy called on one of his neighbours to say Happy Christmas. Griff, the gym orderly, was a 6ft 2in wall of muscle who once belonged to the French Foreign Legion. They'd been close friends until Paddy said something out of turn during a hockey match. Griff finished the row by dismissing Paddy with the words, 'The trouble with you is that you are everybody's mate and nobody's friend.' They had patched up their differences, sort of.

Making his way downstairs for breakfast, Paddy considered his options. Over the Christmas and New Year period some special activities were scheduled. For Christmas Day and Boxing Day these amounted to snooker, pool and chess tournaments, and Carl was screening the latest videos rented from an outside store: *Batman and Robin*, *The Nutty Professor*, and *Con Air*. The gym was closed, but there was to be a Superstars contest on New Years' Eve, based on the 1970s TV series in which sports celebrities competed across a series of disciplines, including squat-thrusts and sit-ups. Paddy had decided to enter. Griff would take some beating. Duffy was no push-over, either.

The queue for the phones that morning, and the disembodied sounds of the free world when the connection home was finally made, sank the spirits of those lifers who bothered. At lunch time Luke got through, planning a reconciliation with his father, only for all the old arguments to come pouring out. 'I've not spoken to him properly for years, but I think I got him at a bad time – he'd been drinking,' said Luke. 'It was quite plain he didn't know what to say to me. Then he swung everything around and said that I was the cause of all his problems, and the problems my brother is having. I told him that that's not the case and that since I wasn't prepared to take that, I was hanging up.'

Luke was never going to be one of the eighty or so prisoners a year who topped themselves in British jails, but the implication of his father's words – that it would have been better for all concerned had Luke never been born – certainly stung. So he turned to the Bible. 'My favourite passage is from the Book of Romans, chapter eight, verse twenty-eight. Basically, in all things God works for the good of those who love him. That's very uplifting when things are against you. They will turn out okay in the end because God has a plan for our lives. It's not that I believe in predestination – within his basic plan we have choices – I just think God knows what choices we are going to make.'

Luke had 'a calling' to be a minister. Assuming he was released, there would of course be problems answering this. People-based occupations were usually restricted under the terms of licence. And no amount of grovelling prayer to the Lord would make the average parishioner welcome the counsel of a man convicted of breaking the sixth commandment. Luke knew this. 'I feel my calling is not precise. It may be as an ordained or as a lay minister. I want to investigate ordination, but it's not everything.' He took inspiration from the letters of the apostle Paul. 'He wrote most of them while he was in prison, but he retained a massive faith and basically developed the Church from his prison cell. And then you have Jesus's direct teaching about forgiveness: if someone hits you on the cheek, offer the other cheek.'

Luke was not the only footballer at the Christmas Day chapel service. Carl was there, practising his social skills. 'It was done by the Catholics and was about having respect for your neighbour,' he said. Afterwards, Carl decamped to a friend's cell. They ate sweets and compared presents. The previous weekend Carl's sister had visited, bearing gifts. These were unwrapped by the guards for security checks, but then Carl stashed away the cassette-radio, chocolates and photo album, saving them for the day. Carl had also swapped presents with his visitor-friend. 'She got me a denim shirt. In reply, I gave her a jail-made box of chocolates, with a picture of her and her son stamped on the box.'

All around the wings the cons were playing cat and mouse with the screws, who were attempting to enforce a drug-free Christmas. The previous year Eddie had spent the day out of his head. Now he wanted to focus on preparing for the Superstars contest, and forgetting that he had not bought his children presents. 'I made a major mistake,' he said. Eddie's expression appeared even more gaunt than usual; he could not forgive himself for being so hopeless with money. 'About three months ago I bought a keyboard and a computer. They were going cheap in here, so I grabbed 'em. I sold ma stereo to pay for 'em. And I handed them out te ma kids. The thing is, if I'd used ma nut, I coulda used 'em as Christmas presents.' Eddie had not found the time to make anything in the workshop.

In prison, given the lack of space in cells, wooden stools were a prized item of furniture. Calvin must have had this in mind when he made one for his daughter, although what she made of it was anyone's guess. 'It's for her bedroom,' he said unselfconsciously.

By the nine p.m. bang-up Scouse was careful to be in his cell. Christmas or not, he made a point of closing his door, thinking that some of the officers got a kick out of locking him away, twirling the keys, making a meal of it. Paddy, too, pulled his own door shut. Having grown tired of reading, he listened to the radio until the early hours, trying not to dwell on the question of how many more Christmas Days would end like this, with only his books and photographs for company.

The Over-35s versus Under-35s football match was part of the festivities. It kicked off on the morning of 27 December. The old boys started well enough, Bunny orchestrating play from the back and Carl looking sharp in central midfield as they put three past Luke.

That was when Carl got sent off. Little Chris, a recreational player rather than a squad member, skipped past him in the centre circle. Carl stuck out a leg to win the ball, but missed. As Carl withdrew his foot, he caught Little Chris, who crashed to the turf.

Rizler took this as his cue to push Carl in the chest. 'You're bang out of order, swiping the back of his ankles,' snapped the Welshman.

So Carl slapped Riz across the face.

Geordie blew hard on the whistle. 'Right, Carl, that's it – you're off.'

'You didn't see what he did!'

'I don't care. I don't want to know. If anyone smacks anyone in a PE session, he's going off.'

Little Chris examined Riz's face for marks. It was as cadaverous as usual.

'Don't worry mate, it didn't hurt,' said Riz, hands on hips. 'I could have reacted. I could have hit him back. But I want to play football.'

'You fucking little arsehole,' yelled Carl, as he trudged off.

Bunny and the other Over-35s argued with Geordie. They wanted Rizler red-carded too. As a concession – it was, after all, supposed to be a light-hearted friendly – Geordie said they could bring on Morgan as a replacement for Carl. The appearance of Inaction Man, however, made no difference. The Under-35s ran away with the second half, and won 5–3.

'I've noticed in league games that Carl's raised his hands a couple of times,' reflected Geordie afterwards. 'It's something he's prone to do. It was only a slap, but I will bring it up in a report. You don't come out and say, "Carl's got a short temper" – there are ways and means of putting things across. Sport's different to the situation on the wings. It brings out the aggression in people, the competitive spirit. If it's not going your way, the slightest thing can set you off. You see professional footballers lose it all the time.'

Carl was not the only one who had been gambling with his future. Aubrey, a Pakistani inmate, who was often a friendly, humorous presence on the touchline, attacked another con with a snooker cue. A petty argument had got out of hand. Aubrey inflicted cuts and bruises before being overpowered by guards. He was shipped out of Kingston the next day.

Later that afternoon, Rizler walked over to D wing to apologise.

'Fuck off,' scowled Carl. 'You're just trying to justify yourself. It's over and done with, but keep out of my way.'

Peace and goodwill to all men.

22
FIGHTING TALK

On New Year's Eve Eddie put everything into winning the Superstars contest. He was to finish second behind Griff, but he pushed himself so hard he threw up in the sports hall. A couple of days afterwards Eddie saw the medical staff. What happened next was the subject of conjecture. The only established fact was that Eddie had been shipped out of Kingston.

'It's all just hearsay,' said Paddy, in the gym office. 'The story is that Eddie went to the infirmary complaining of stomach pains. The [medical staff] wouldn't do anything for him. They tried to fob him off, saying, basically, he was a malingerer. They treat you like that. They very rarely think there's anything wrong. And even if there is, their attitude is, here's a couple of paracetamol, piss off. Anyway, Eddie got into an argument. There was some sort of confrontation. Eddie was taken downstairs. They kept him in a holding cell overnight and got rid of him first thing in the morning.'

The departure sparked a rumour frenzy. The most fantastic of them suggested the Governor had got wind of an escape attempt. Eddie was supposed to have finalised this with an outside contact during his last visit. It was to be a snatch-and-grab operation, somewhere en route to the local hospital. A variation on the theme had it that Eddie managed to smuggle a gun into Kingston. And there was another explanation: Eddie had run up debts he could not pay, and engineered the confrontation to ensure he was moved before facing a severe beating for defaulting.

Whatever the truth, Paddy took the incident to heart. 'You get used to people disappearing, but it really does hammer home that it could be you. From what I can make out, Eddie was in pain. He's blown up at the doctor, so they've got rid of him. That could have been me. If I'm ill one night and I go to [the medical staff] and say a little bit too much, get a little bit cocky, I'll be on my way.'

The prison medical service is separate from the NHS. Most of the inmates were suspicious of being treated by people who, they said, were not 'proper doctors'. There were lots of stories like the one Wayne told about a man he'd known at another jail. The inmate complained of searing headaches only to be ordered back to his cell, where he suffered a brain haemorrhage. The Home Office dismissed any suggestion that the service was inadequate, and governors regarded such criticisms as blatant attempts to exploit the system in some way. But the Chief Inspector of Prisons, Sir David Ramsbotham, still wanted some changes. He was on record describing the fact that NHS medical records were not transferred to prisons as 'absolute madness'.

'Eddie was a bit fiery but he'd calmed down a lot,' reflected Paddy. 'He was a pussy cat here, really, going about his sentence the right way. I say the right way. I mean the way they wanted him to go about it. As far as I know this was his first fuck-up here. He certainly hasn't been, like, throwing punches at screws and climbing on the roof. It's sad. It seems to me that after all he's been through, he finally got himself to a jail that's good for getting your head together. And now they've sent him backwards.

'When Cardy, his best mate, left you noticed Eddie was

down. I think Eddie had that sort of temperament; he was always going to have a few spells when he felt down. But Cardy kept him on an even keel. Normally, when one of them was ranting and raving, the other would listen, and he could get it off his chest. With Cardy gone, Eddie was a little bit alone.'

It had been five weeks since the last league game. The break allowed the injured defenders, Jonah and Ted the Merciless, to recover from injuries. Raph, whose supporters held a vigil outside Kingston in December, protesting the innocence of the M25 Three, was finally ready to make his debut. In fact, he took Eddie's place at right wing-back. Nigel (so as not to disturb a winning team) put Jonah and Ted on the bench, alongside Duffy. The back three of Scouse, Nigel and Bunny remained unchanged.

'I'd have put Raph in the middle with Calvin,' said Paddy. 'We are crying out for someone skilful in there, and people accept that Raph is a very good footballer, so there's no problem him coming straight into the side. I know there's talk about being loyal, but if good players turn up, they get in the team, don't they? Morgan just has to accept that.'

The shock of Eddie's departure, and the long break since the last league game, appeared to have strained Paddy's regard for Nigel. It all came out when he talked about how relations between the strikers had plummeted to a new low with Carl and Rizler's bust-up in the Over-35s v. Under-35s game. 'The real problem,' said Paddy, 'is that I don't think they're going to become better players. The way the gym programme is going, Nigel's not here to do the coaching. This is the worst season for training I've known. Rightly or wrongly, I don't think Nigel's as interested as he has been. He's got other things on his mind. I won't say it has affected his game – he's still 100 per cent – but the extra stuff has just gone by the wayside. Maybe Nigel is fed up. Some people are not willing to listen. I mean, Carl has always had a bad attitude like that. You can't tell him anything. But there are all these things that need working on. We go 3–0 up and then camp out on our own eighteen-yard line, inviting teams to come at us. We've been doing it all season and no one even mentions it. It annoys me the amount of times we've lost and drawn when we should have won. In the grand scheme of things I know it doesn't matter. But football is the focal point of my week, so I get frustrated when problems go unresolved. Someone in the team has got to mould the individuals into a cohesive unit. But that's not my job.' Paddy, I thought, might have been more forgiving had he known just how protective Nigel was when others bitched about him.

Outside, it was a damp January morning. At the Milton Road End Geordie was busy in advance of Kingston's twelfth match of the season, the visit of H&S Aviation. In the centre of the goal, teetering on a wooden chair, he hooked the net to the crossbar. Whenever Nigel performed the ritual, Morgan was eager to help. Now Morgan stood, arms folded, watching Geordie edge his way across the muddy goal-mouth.

Inaction Man was going to be free soon. 'I've got a letter to prove it,' he grinned. 'I've been offered a deal. I ain't made up my mind yet if I'm gonna accept. If I says yes, that means I'm admitting to sumthin' I ain't done.' Morgan believed he was going to be released on appeal, his conviction reduced to manslaughter and the sentence downgraded to the ten years already served. Morgan did not want anyone else to see the letter – it was 'confidential'. The fact that he had shaved, though, did lend some credence to the story.

'You can't go, Morgan, you're our top-scoring midfield dynamo,' said Geordie.

Morgan wanted to change the subject. 'We ain't played for weeks, and the lot that's comin' in today are supposed to be sumthin'.'

'Morgan's looking over his shoulder; he knows he's in the autumn of his career,' murmured Geordie. 'Raph's coming into the side now.'

'Geordie can't even get on the bench,' jeered Morgan. 'He's not passionate about his football. Watchin', yeah, that's okay, but playin' is what it's all about.'

'I still get paid,' said Geordie.

Back in the gym office Nigel was fishing around in a bag that had returned from the prison laundry. Carl had been sacked from his position in the wash house for failing to turn up to work on a couple of occasions. Teddy applied for, and got, his job. Judging by the damp football kit, Ted had not quite got the hang of it.

'I've minimised changes because we've only played one friendly since our last league game,' said Nigel, ironing his top dry. 'Raph can do what Eddie did for us on the right. He's got the vision to see the gaps for the forwards. But I don't want to put Eddie down – he did a lot of hard work for us.'

The big news was that Nigel wanted to move back to the Isle of Wight, returning to the place where he and his wife grew up. His house was under offer, and he had found somewhere to buy. Nigel planned to commute on the ferry but, long-term, was looking for a new job at one of the island's three prisons. The player-manager was also hanging up his boots: 'I don't think it's right that I should be coming into the prison on my weekends off. You can't pick and choose when you play. That wouldn't be fair on the other people in the squad. So this will be my last season.'

Nigel accepted the grumbles about the amount of coaching he had done. He gave a helpless shrug. 'After Geordie started working here he had to have some leave because his wife had a baby. And I had already been eight months, working on my own, doing the job of two men.' He broke off with a tight smile that said: 'I've done the best I can.'

H&S Aviation wore yellow shirts, blue shorts and blue socks. A works side, their players overhauled aircraft engines. 'This is a big test for us,' said Graham Underwood, club secretary. 'We've been promoted every year since we formed and all we want this year is to consolidate in this division. We know we're not going to win the league. We know they are a good side. They've always been in the First Division, and if we lose we won't be too surprised.'

Having been involved in the worst case of indiscipline of the season – three of their players were among the five sent off when H&S met the George and Dragon – Underwood's team were missing a number of regulars. 'We've all been banned, fined and Christ knows what,' he laughed. 'I've got a thirty-five-day ban and twenty-pound fine for having a go at the referee. Our striker, Paul Roberts, got a forty-two-day ban and a twenty-pound fine. One of our centre-backs hurt his foot during the game. He was lying on the floor, and his leg was blowing up. So he said, "For fuck's sake, ref, can I have some water?" And he got red-carded for that. When we walked off at the end everyone was saying, "What on earth was that about?" The ref had a bad day. He was only a young nipper. I think he's trying to make a name for himself in the refereeing ranks.'

Scrotal Bill's pessimism was finally getting to Terry Allison. 'I think Kingston could struggle today,' cautioned Terry, offering a bag of boiled sweets to Bill and Old Stan – one of the regular spectators, a huge E wing inmate from Yorkshire, sporting thick glasses and a fine handlebar moustache – who were sat alongside him on the bench. 'H&S hammered Plover, and Kingston haven't played for ages. What with Eddie gone and Nigel going, and Bill says there's unrest in the camp, I don't know how they'll go.'

The concerns about players being unsettled were dispelled before a ball was kicked. When Paddy appeared out of the cell block, he found himself walking on alongside Wayne, whose head was bandaged, Van Gogh style, after a clash of heads in training left him with a split ear. The two men made eye contact, said a few words, and briefly embraced. The last few days had served as a reminder to the inmates that they were all on the same side of the wall. The two men were not friends, but had resolved to settle for a truce.

The match started at a high tempo. Rizler cut in from the right on fourteen minutes, and drove the ball under the goalkeeper to put Kingston 1–0 ahead. Then Paddy chipped the H&S goalkeeper. The ball hit the crossbar. Carl brought the rebound down with his first touch and flicked it home, slipping as he ran away to celebrate, leaving a giant smudge of mud up his back.

Raph, all deft touches and short passes, did not have Eddie's inclination to dribble. Rather, he ushered the ball in from the flanks, and linked up with the strikers. On twenty-one minutes he marked his debut with a goal, turning sharply and shooting inside the box. Carl poked home a loose ball to make it 4–0 and, just before the break, Paddy, with defenders giving chase, chipped the goalkeeper. Again, he hit the bar, but this time he won the race for the rebound. 5–0. Easy.

'Who's the fucking ref? He's taking the piss,' said Calvin, breathing hard at half-time. 'The fouls they're committing, I can't believe they're getting away with it.'

'Forget the score,' said Nigel, beginning his talk. 'Everything you've done to achieve it is brilliant. The movement off the ball has been superb. The forwards, I've not seen you make so many diagonal runs – you're making it a lot easier for midfield. Carl, I've never seen you lay the ball off so well. Well done, mate. Midfield, you're supporting brilliantly. Just keep it going. On the defending side, just be a little bit cautious. They see the game as lost. They'll start throwing people forward. So let's keep our shape so that we don't get caught. If we keep going we'll create chances. All the hard work you've done, you've got to build on that.' As the gathering broke up, Paddy put an arm around Morgan. 'Excellent. Keep it going.'

The second half was a cruise. Paddy and Rizler made it 7–0. The substitutes came on and a clean sheet looked feasible until the last couple of minutes. Zebedee shouted at Jonah to leave a cross, but then changed his mind, and remained rooted to the goal line. A striker nipped in between them to score. And almost on time, Colin Archer, H&S's leading scorer, cracked a shot against the underside of the crossbar. It hit Zebedee's back and rebounded into the net.

'That's the difference between playing with Jonah and playing with you,' Zebedee told Nigel in the office afterwards. 'I know with you that if I call for the ball, but you're already set, you'll still play it. I didn't see Jonah moving out of the way so I thought, "He's going to head this bastard."'

Geordie scoffed. 'We've heard this story twice already.'

'Yeah,' agreed Terry. 'Pain in the arse.'

A new computerised switchboard at the local newspaper was perplexing Terry. 'Ah no, they got one of these answering things,' he cursed, fumbling with his note pad. 'Press one if you want this, two if you want that . . .'

In Terry's estimation Plover were now title favourites. 'Kingston beat and drew with them, but Plover never stopped winning after that. The one thing that helps Kingston is that Plover and Southern Co-op Dairies, who have also got a decent chance, have to play each other twice, which'll mean someone dropping points.' Terry thought that if Kingston won their six remaining games they would be champions. It wasn't as improbable as it sounded. Five of the fixtures were against modest opponents: the return of H&S Aviation; two matches against St Helena, who were bottom of the table; and two against Rimor, a mid-table side of no great repute. The one to worry about, which would take place half-way through the remaining programme, was the return of the George and Dragon. That contest, scheduled for St Valentine's Day, bore all the hallmarks of a champion-ship decider.

As it was a Saturday night, Luke was cooking an Indian meal with three of his friends. They had all murdered their wives. David, a plump former Woolwich building society manager, was probably in his late forties, as was Steve, a gruff and bearded former print industry executive. Tony was clean-cut and in his thirties, once a horse racing photographer. Luke completed the social circle. Wedged into David's cell, they dunked naan bread into steaming, fragrant dishes.

David, a Spurs supporter, looked for a photograph of a Rotary Club trip he once organised, taking a group of underprivileged children to see the FA Cup on show at White Hart Lane. Birthdays, cheque presentations and an enlarged print of him with Steve Perryman and Ricardo Villa flicked past before David found the one of the kids with the trophy. 'The FA Cup was kept in the most tatty box you've ever seen,' he said, brightly.

Afterwards, Luke crossed the D wing landing to his cell. On his desk, next to a Christian newspaper, was a framed photograph of two women. One was tall, young, fresh-faced and attractive. She stood next to a well-to-do-looking older woman.

'Is that your mother?'

'No, she's my fiancée, and that's her daughter,' he said.

Luke seemed untroubled by my gaff. But then lifers who formed relationships with women prison visitors were accustomed to scepticism. Periodically, newspapers featured stories about women who fell into the thrall of men behind bars. There was the thirty-two-year-old academic, about to get her Masters degree, who risked everything for the love of an armed robber. She was caught smuggling cannabis while visiting him on remand. The QC defending told the court, 'This young lady is intelligent and hard-working, but emotionally vulnerable.' Maybe that was it. Carl, who had his own friendship with a visitor, never sounded more cynical than when he offered his own theory about women who got themselves involved with prisoners. Carl said they all fell into one of four categories: 'Low self-esteem; do-gooder; likes talking dirty about sex; member of the press.' Having already suggested to Luke that he was only interested in the Church because no one else would have him, it felt abusive to enquire which category, if any, was appropriate for the new love of his life.

And anyway, Luke had been writing letters again. The goalkeepers at England's top football clubs had received requests for gloves which would be auctioned for charities supported by the prison. There was no doubt that Luke could have produced a copy of his request. His cell was meticulously organised. There were just the right amount of personal effects so that the available space was not jumbled. A sensible number of personal items decorated the walls. The light from his table lamp was soft and scholarly. Luke kept copies of outgoing correspondence filed alongside case papers and incoming mail. 'I said that I was a life-sentence prisoner and that I liked to play football as much as I can. I explained that we have close contact with a school for mentally handicapped kids, and made a joke about the prison's goalkeeping gloves, which are so old the latex was dripping off. I asked them to send one pair of their gloves for the appeal, and one for myself.'

Shaka Hislop was the first to write back. A handwritten note was included with three pairs of expensive-looking gloves, strengthened so that a firmly struck ball could not bend fingers back to the point of a break or dislocation.

Luke,
I loved your letter and I'm glad to do what I can to help. I've enclosed three pairs of gloves. One's signed as requested. Both the other pairs are used. At the moment I'm short of new gloves. One is in better condition but has a tear along the left thumb. A needle and thread would probably work wonders. Good luck for the rest of your season, whatever's left of it. I would love to hear from you from time to time to hear how things are going and how you are getting on.
   Anyway, bye for now, sincerely
   Shaka Hislop
   Newcastle United FC

Mart Poom at Derby County, Nigel Martyn at Leeds United, and Tim Flowers at Blackburn Rovers also sent two pairs each. 'The only problem with the ones Tim Flowers sent is that they are not so clever in the wet,' remarked Luke. 'They're okay when it's damp, but when they get mud on them they become slimy.' Nothing at all from Ian Walker at Tottenham. 'All the lads, Bunny especially, are joking that even if he sent, they might tend to make things fly through my hands.'

That evening I also met Jonah playing pool in C wing. We

talked about the Christmas snooker-cue attack, which happened outside his cell. 'It's quiet here, but it can go any time,' he said, narrowing his blue eyes. 'If it's one of your mates, you might want to help, but you got to be careful. It all gets written down. Now, if someone has a go at me, I try to talk. If he don't want to talk and he's aggressive, I say, "I know that trick and trade, and it don't work." I say, "That's how I used to deal with things, screaming and shoutin', and it ain't the answer – but we can always go somewhere quiet if you want to." '

Jonah was thirty-seven. He had spent eighteen years, almost half his life, inside for a murder-rape. The result was that he was a cockney Crocodile Dundee, assured in his own world – prison – but baffled by much of what went on beyond the perimeter walls. He was straightforward, with endless innocent cheek. ('Cor, what does your wife think, spending the weekend with a load of bloody murderers?') His big rubbery face, with a forehead that was a great slab of flesh and bone, was strangely handsome, and not much of an emotional mask. Whatever Jonah felt – boredom, amusement, frustration, anxiety – it was there for all to see. He also didn't know his own strength, as I'd already discovered when, with the grip of an iron clamp – 'Com'an 'ave a word with this geezer' – he took my upper arm.

Jonah kept out of the C wing football clique. 'As you get older and wiser you tend not to take mates on board,' he explained. 'With a mate you want to sit down and share everything that is private and personal. A trusted companion. You might take someone on board in here, but he has got his best mate. So what you're sharing with him, is he sharing it with his mate?' Family was strictly taboo. 'I can only speak for myself, but I've heard from a high percentage of inmates, "Don't trust other cons with that information." You might say, "I can't play football today because I got a visit" – but nothing more. They can see afterwards that you got a spring in your step. It's because you've seen a bit of what's classified as normality.'

23
JONAH

I've had a lot of injuries this season so I'm watching me weight. I'm cutting down on the tea. You see a lot of guys in jail, they smoke or have a brew just for the sake of it. I'm quite pleased with my form when I 'ave played, though. I've been trying to be calm on the ball. It helps having someone like Nigel around, who makes himself available – you've always got an outlet. I also think this new fella, Raph, will be something special.

When I was growing up in East London the family all supported West Ham. I got dragged along. When me mother and father's divorce was going through, I moved to West London – it was the only place where me father could get a job. I used to work for him on Saturdays, shunting lorries around a depot. One Saturday he said, 'Why don't you go to a football match?' I went to Chelsea and liked what I saw. Chopper Harris, Osgood. All the faces. I followed them home and away for a season. It was too much on the pocket, though, and I was losing girlfriends left, right and centre, so I gave up going.

I was charged with murder. I'd been in a pub drinking with a girlfriend. I had an argument with her, took her home. I went back to the pub and met another girl. We went to a secluded place, a churchyard; an argument took place and I just beat the living shit out of her, to put it mildly. It was sort of like deemed a build-up of things, because I didn't have the assertiveness to talk to people as a young kid. I used to absorb things and bottle them up, and try to unwrangle them in me own head. Rather than try to talk to people, it just come out in an aggressive, frustrated manner. I was my own worst enemy. I was eighteen.

I pleaded guilty. I accepted what I'd done, I just wouldn't talk about it. The Old Bailey was so intimidating; being the focus of everyone's attention. And when you go downstairs, you're asking your solicitor, 'What does this mean?' All you heard were the words 'life sentence'. And you think life is life, no hope of ever getting out. And then you go into a cell. About twenty minutes later my mother and father was there. When I saw them it just slaughtered me.

When the judge done my tariff he said that this was an extremely brutal crime, but because of my youth and my plea of guilty, he could see no reason why I couldn't serve a normal sentence. The Home Secretary asked the judge what he classified as a normal sentence. The judge said twelve to thirteen years. The Home Secretary said it should be thirteen to fourteen years, and they split it at thirteen. I've now done eighteen and a half years.

I come in immature. I could hardly read or write. You get involved in all sorts of disturbances. Fights. Aggressive comments. It was just fun and games, jail. It wasn't until you realised that you weren't getting home leaves, or released for compassionate visits. You see other cons go and come back, and you think: when's this going to happen to me?

I also got a summary in my reports. There's some remarks that was put in there years ago. Like a summary of all my upbringing and everything, and my court case. I disagree with it. Some of it is completely false. So I've had to get a solicitor. Now what the solicitor does is contact the people here, who'll then contact the Home Office and, hopefully, they'll change it. What they are saying is that when I was taken to the police station I was alleged to have said that I dragged her in [the churchyard]. My depositions have gone walkabout so, at the moment, I can't prove what I said. No one can find them anywhere. Now we got to contact the Old Bailey and ask the secretary to go into his vault, and would he please go into my depositions. I have it written down – in press cuttings, and various reports – that I'd taken my girlfriend home, and then come back to the pub. I knew a party of girls, nurses, in the pub. I sat down with one of them and we was kissing and cuddling. We left the pub laughing and joking. She was even pulled by the barmaid, who said, 'Do you realise what you are doing? You're two-timing your boyfriend.'

The parole board want a full view of the story. Well, I've given it them. I sat down for six months and done a full account of my history and my offence. But this particular bad remark [made by the police] is still in there. So I've got to get this solicitor to give my view over. I've said they can do what they want: hypnosis, truth drugs, whatever.

My father's been a rock to me. Solid, you know what I mean? Whatever I want, albeit within the space of his wallet, he's got me. I have tried not to make excessive demands on his pocket or on his head. I found out during the trial that he was not my natural father. They read out that I was illegitimate. I was saying to my brief, 'What does that mean?'

As regards my step-mother, I didn't see eye-to-eye with her when I was out there. That was a major contribution to me building up a lot of problems. With me bringing home girlfriends, and her being heavily pregnant, it was sort of like she was doing my washing, ironing, cleaning my room, and I used to take advantage. I didn't have no respect for how hard it is, you know what I mean? When her first baby was born and she fell pregnant again virtually straight away, it was a case of total ignorance for how she felt. It was always me, me, me. Selfish.

I'm not in touch with my mother. I'd dearly love to make contact. But she's one of those people; once she gets what she wants, she forgets where her family is, where her roots are. That's what caused the breakdown of her marriage. She done that with my father – she went with another guy when he was inside. He did a bit of time for impersonating a police officer.

Once, my mother and father turned up on the same day for a visit. She said, 'I don't want him here. It's *my* visit.' I said, 'You're supposed to cheer me up, keep me informed about what's happening out there, not give me a hard time about me dad.' It was very stony after that. Three weeks passed and I heard nothing. I was very concerned because my mother is not the Elizabeth Taylor of jewellery, but she does like a bit of Tom, as we say in London. I was a bit scared she might get mugged and beaten up for the jewellery. I always told her, 'Come up with your husband or leave the jewellery at home.' Anyway, three weeks passed and I had no letters, no visits. So I got the welfare to phone her and a piece of paper come back, no bigger than the size of a cigarette packet. It said, 'Your mother doesn't want to see you until you cease your relationship with your father.' I thought: I'm not going to get tied up in any of that, I'm just going to leave it. I told the probation, 'I don't want you to be a go-between but if you want to pass on a message, this is what I have to say: "I'm not going to be belittled. I'm not a little boy any more."' I can see now that she was always looking at me as her little child.

There was a gap of about six years before we started talking again. Nothing had changed. She was making excessive demands, putting all her troubles on me, because I'm the only son. I said, 'Mum, I'm doing a very stressful course here, I can't emphasise that enough. I'm bringing back all the old vibes, from as far back as I can remember. I can go back to the time when the old man used to chase me up the stairs as a young kid, and when you and the old man were going through the divorce and the judge sat me on his lap and said, "Who do you want to go with, your old man or your mother?" ' It was obvious I wanted to go with my old man, but he was in jail. Anyway, she hit the roof. 'I ain't mental, I don't want to talk to the Samaritans.' She kept slamming down phones on me. I said, 'Mum, if you keep using this approach as your method, nothing's ever going to get solved.' That was about three years ago. No letters, nothing at all since.

It wasn't until about eleven years after my conviction that I started talking about my crime. One day I spoke to this probation officer, his name was Officer Wicks. It was one of those situations where you felt confident. He was very relaxed in his job and his approach. I just broke down and told him the actual story. It was the first time it had come out from A to Z. I was still using a lot of distortions about why I committed the murder. Blaming people, you know what I mean? But the floodgates opened, believe me. That was my first sign of remorse, in terms of talking about the crime and breaking down. He just let me get on with the story. Afterwards he took me back to my cell. Obviously he notified people; there was a lot of people coming back to me saying, 'Are you all right?' and everything. They knew it was the first time I actually spoke about it. It was then continuously on my mind, you know: life means life and all this business. And I've taken someone else's life. You can't replace it. You recognise that you can't replace it.

I've done Anger Management, Alcohol Awareness, Assertiveness, and SOTP [Sexual Offenders Treatment Programme]. I'm a Cat C inmate and I'm only here because it's the best place available for me to do some more course work. They unravel your brain. It's really serious psychology. They are going through all your ways of thinking. If you have any fantasies, whether they are deviant. The course I just done was thirteen months talking about asserting yourself. Taking responsibility for things. Getting rid of distortions. Like at the time of my murder. Because of my childhood upbringing, which was very severe, I was passed around, sent around like an unwanted parcel. But I shouldn't be saying that in connection with the murder. Putting the responsibility on me mother and father. I should be taking full responsibility.

If I didn't get my own way as a kid, I wasn't happy, I'd say, 'Well, fuck you.' I couldn't keep still. If someone said, 'Don't do that,' I'd probably do it. I was just too immature to recognise that I was the cause of a lot of my own problems. I could have sat down and talked to people. I wanted a stable background more than anything. When I used to visit my mates I got this impression, even in chaos, that in other people's households and families there was a solidness and jovialness, a togetherness. There was a different sort of 'good morning'. Mine was sort of like 'Welcome to Anthrax Island'. Growling from my dad, from everybody. When you opened your mouth, it was a case of 'Shut up!' As a kid you absorb that. Fighting in my house, outside my house. My old man storming out, the old dear's taking it out on me. Okay for the next couple of weeks, then my old dear comes out of the kitchen with a carving knife, after my old man again. Every time my old dear had the grumpy, PMT as it's called now, I became a bit of a burden. Every time she wanted to go out I was a burden. I was an inconvenience. She was twenty-six and wanted to go out. So she off-loaded me to my old man's parents. Then in foster homes. So I was running away. And when they asked me what the problem was, I couldn't tell them. From the age of six to eighteen that's how I conducted myself.

Living with my nan and grandad was one of them times when you felt stable. They were always around. For them to take me on, and me to still be around for eighteen months, two years, was a miracle. After three months, six months, land mines should have been going off, trouble. But they were very good for me. I started to look after me own bedroom. Maybe it was their maturity. A calming influence. There was always someone in the house when I wanted to talk. My mum was one of those Hilda Ogdens who'd scream out the window, 'Come back in this facking 'ouse.'

At the time of the murder I was lashing out, because of all the nonsense I had taken in my life. I bottled it up. And just that one derogatory remark I received on that particular night gave me permission to explode.

I only learnt about six months ago how her family feels. The probation service don't go around to the victim's parents every time you go up for a review board because it reminds them about the crime, and you got to let them get on with their life as much as possible. But they are never, ever going to forget the horrific nature of that murder. They got all the constant reminders around them, her loss. But it came as a dreadful shock to me that they are still having dreadful thoughts, finding it hard to come to terms with what happened.

I tried writing a letter. The first one – it was just a letter as far as I was concerned. In terms of remorse, it was heartless. The second time we was given guidance. It took me twenty-two days. Cor, it slaughtered me, believe me. You just don't know what to say. Who am I to say, right, this is why I done it. They know you taken their daughter's life. They don't want to hear the horrific nature of the crime. It comes across heartless. You don't know how to say sorry. I met a lot of guys, every time they talk about their crime they burst out crying. I feel I've done my crying. All I can do is try to be honest. What can I say? I wasted someone's life. I've destroyed someone's family. I've destroyed everyone's belief. It goes on and on.

When I talked about it the first time I could feel it rise, a ball in my stomach and chest, and then it happens, and it all comes out, a load of blabber. You can't talk. You can't speak. Whatever you try to say makes no sense. The best you can do is try to calm down. Then you are into the heavy sobbing. The probation officer says, 'Let it go . . .' And Christ, you go again. You can only go on for so long; your eyes hurt, your throat hurts. He gets you a drop of water and asks you how you feel. You're sobbing when you talk. You feel withdrawn, like you don't want to talk about it any more. That's the time when you should talk, because if you want to know the truth, that's when the truth will come out.

I went into this little pub. I was rowing with my girlfriend. Stupid, stupid rowing. I went to the bar to give myself a breathing space, and I'm thinking, 'Do I really want to be with this girl, or do I want to get rid of her?' When I got back to the table she started straight away. I slapped the drink on the table and said, 'Drink that up, I'm taking you home, I can't handle this.' What I should have done is took her home and accepted that the night had turned rough, it was bad. But what I've done is gone back to the pub. What they teach you is that a Seemingly Irrelevant Decision – it's called a SID – has been important. So even though I'm telling myself to go home, the pub's a draw. I know I'll have a good time in there. I walk back through the door and I see these two girls. Walked up to the bar. Someone says, 'Can you turn around?' Bang, flash in the face, someone's took a picture. So immediately I've said, 'Do you want a name on that photograph?' That's it, the introduction out of the way. She said, 'Yes, come over, sign the photograph.' And I just plonked myself down next to her.

On the course they say, 'Did she invite you or did you sit down yourself?' Well, obviously I just sat down myself. I was a really confident teenager. They ask, 'Do you feel that you forced yourself on her?' It was a bit of both. When I sat down she moved along next to me – and when I say that, they are saying I'm still blaming the victim, but it's a fact. They are also asking if there was any body language or mannerisms which said she wanted me to leave. No. I blanked her friend because I was focused on the girl. She was pretty, you know what I mean? She could have told me to go. In that sentence alone they say I'm still blaming my victim. My case tutor came up to me during the course and said, 'You didn't really mean it that way, did you?' But in the eyes of the course, it's all about accepting responsibility. They like you to use phrases like, 'At the point of being photographed I targeted the girl . . .' I say it was social. They say, 'You murdered the girl, so it ain't social.' There was no deviant way of thinking. I was just a young lad, my hormones going overdrive.

About an hour later, we were having such a good time, we left. There was nowhere in particular to go. I wanted to get in this girl's knickers. I pick up the body language I know in my youth: arm around back of bench seat, and there's no shrug of the shoulders on her behalf; holding hands. I'm thinking, 'I've cracked it.' There's three places I could go: car park by river, car park by woods, or this graveyard.

We've gone in the graveyard. Straight around to the back, straight against the wall, I've lifted her up and we're doing the business. My arms are getting tired, so I put her down. Obviously she's uncomfortable. Because I'm going to town with the anger inside me, with the girlfriend and what's previous, I'm probably most definitely portraying it in the act of intercourse. So when I put her down she gets a bit of gravity and pushes me away. I'm sort of like not satisfied. All I can think about is me, me, me. So I comes forward again. She says, 'If you want any more, go and see that slag of a girlfriend of yours.' My girlfriend was fast approaching sixteen and I'm eighteen myself. With all the nonsense going through my head, I hate my step-mother, I hate my father . . . everyone who fucked my life up. So to hear this was the last resort, you know what I mean?

So I just lashed out, believe me. When she's in the air I let off four to six punches before she fell to the ground. She was unconscious as soon as she hit the ground. I knocked her scatty, believe me. I'm kicking, I'm stamping on her forehead, all around her chest, probably her arms and legs. There had been light rain, and as she's hit the floor, I'm slipping everywhere. I've dragged her to an area of gravel. I've tried to have my wicked way because I'm so focused on what I wanted to do. I thank my lucky stars that she was unconscious, so hopefully she didn't feel any more than she did. That's the only thing I'm thankful for on that night. I tried to have my way with her, but all I could see was this person beaten to a pulp. She was still breathing. You get a thing called a death croak, like a gargle. Whether it was blood or fluid, there was this gargling happening. I got up. I'm sort of infuriated, wild, because I couldn't get what I wanted and I'm thinking about what she said. And then getting all these – not pictures, it would be stupid to say pictures, but these thoughts, all these people around me that's created my life as hell. It's given me permission to go ahead and hit her and punch her again. So the worst thing I did was start up again. I wanted to hurt her internally, so I went over to a tree, broke off a branch and I just stabbed her between her legs. The autopsy proved that it went into her anus. I just wanted to hurt her. That's when the reality started to come into my brain. I'm in more trouble than I've ever been in my life. It's all self, self, self. I'm in serious trouble. I've killed this person. I better clean up.

There was a canal nearby. I've gone down, cleaned myself up. No traffic about, no people; 12.20 a.m. at the latest. From what light there is – yellow, hazy street lamp – I'm saying to myself, 'Right, I've done a good job.' It's not until I've got on the bus I can see that I've got little splashes of blood on me. So I've got on the bus. The conductor has moved right away from me, as far as possible on the bottom floor of a double-decker. Scared. Picked up the vibes. And maybe seen the blood on me jacket. The driver's looked around. Now I'm wishing this bus would speed up and get me home. Now it was seven to ten stops maximum, but every stop they are stopping just for the sake of it. It seems like I'm on the bus for hours.

I run home. I'm flustered, where's my keys? I'm dropping everything in my hands and I'm shaking. Once that door's closed it's relief. I turn the light on. I can see I've got spots of blood smeared on my beige Harrington jacket. Brownish red. I couldn't wait to get these clothes off and have a wash and a bath. I got in bed after and went to sleep immediately.

When I woke up in the morning I haven't thought about the clothes, I've just left them where I threw them. I made myself a cup of tea. I know what I've done. The first thing I want to do is avoid people. I'm nervous, I don't want to admit what I've done. People might pick up the change in me. I've gone into work and got on with it immediately, which was irregular. I worked for a cargo handling company. I started making boxes for machinery. The theory in my mind was I wanted to keep away from the others. We had a little hut. We used to gossip about West Ham, anything. I wanted to keep away from newspapers, too. I knew it would be a focus of attention.

The police came the next morning. I was arrested because I was the last person she was seen alive with. 'Do you know what it's about?' Automatic denial. I don't want to be associated with it. The police straight away were very heavy with the body language. Carried out, tightly gripped by my biceps, guns trained on me.

I'm in denial for two days. Very arrogant. 'You'll get nothing out of me.' But they've done a search of my bedroom and come up with these clothes, blood on my jackets and trousers. In my own mind I thought I'd be okay if I kept quiet. Doctor takes forensic swabs, hair clippings. It's all new to me. I've been questioned and had the verbals. The coppers said, 'This is the most brutal crime I've ever seen in my life.' Looking back, yes, they were right. Maybe six of them around me at any one time. When I was put in a cell, I thought, 'Blimey, thank God for that, get a break.' Soon as the door closed, and I'm getting down, the door opened again. I was getting the treatment. On day three they got me at my worst and I gave them part of the story: yes, consensual sex, no, I didn't hurt her. But I was stupid. They had all these clothes. Looking back it was odds on they would come for me. They didn't have to be Sherlock Holmes.

Years ago I would say that a life sentence was too long. You always say, 'Well, you've committed a murder, you realise what you've done and there's no way you're going to do that again.' But at the end of the day, having done this course, you ain't got just the one victim. You've got your actual victim and then you've got the mother, the father, her sisters, everyday people that mixed with her. They're all victims. So then you have to put yourself in their position. If that was to happen to my father, my mother, how would I feel? Well, you'd want to actually physically harm them.

People talk about letting Myra Hindley out. Can you see Myra Hindley walking down the road without getting a clump around her head by someone? It's not possible.

It would have been nice to have a fixed sentence, so there would be some light at the end of the tunnel. But you have to ask, would that necessarily make people learn from the bad they've done? You'd get some guys who'd just sit back in their cells for fifteen years and do nothing. Is that rehabilitation? Of course not. It happens. There's guys still protesting, saying, 'I didn't do this and I'm going to die in prison,' when the information against them is completely and utterly overwhelming. When they tell their side of the story they are stuttering and sweating profusely, and they are just backing themselves into a corner. They are still blaming people. You don't recognise this until you've done certain courses. And when people talk to me, I listen and think they are blaming people, they are not taking responsibility. But you have to bite your tongue.

Would I give my life for hers? It's just never going to happen, is it?

24

THE EXPLODED BOMB

Raph had jarred his back making his debut against H&S Aviation, so was not available for the first visit of Rimor. Nigel decided to try Jonah in a midfield holding role.

Jonah felt rough on the morning of the game, having been up for much of the night preparing a letter to his solicitor, but was looking forward to it all the same. 'I spread my case papers all across me bed and the floor. But being hunched up has done me back in.'

His cell was spartan, with only a map of North America, given to him by another inmate years before, and a couple of Page Three girls on the walls. Status Quo tapes sat on one shelf. The careworn faces of his father, who was not his father, and his step-mother smiled out of a solitary photograph. They looked like Sid James and Barbara Windsor.

Jonah was five years over his tariff. There were two issues as far as he was concerned: clearing up the mistake in his police records which stated that his victim had not willingly accompanied him to the graveyard, and finding a place on a course he was required to complete. Did the parole board think that he was a danger to women? 'Nah, it's nothing like that,' he said, taken aback. After spending many hours explaining the antecedence of his offence, the idea that a stranger, hearing it all for the first time, still might not understand made him nervous. Jonah considered himself to be a decent man on the basis that he had accepted responsibility for his crime, and developed the emotional maturity to have some idea of the horrors he inflicted on the victim's family – even if that was a long time coming. He wanted to distance himself from the psychopaths he'd met during sex offenders counselling. 'On the Assertiveness course I've just done, they pointed out some areas that I need to do a bit more work on. They want me to do an extended [Sexual Offenders Treatment Programme], because of my quietness and keeping everything internal. It's sort of like internal trouble. It's a matter of building up confidence. I'd never done course work with more than one person. So to go into a group – seven other inmates, and three tutors – the situation was very daunting.'

At a previous jail Jonah had been allowed out on a day-release scheme. He did chores in a carpenter's workshop, 'because, when it does end, I have to be able to do something'. One lunch time he was taken into a pub in Roehampton, Surrey. To his astonishment, Colin Stagg, the man acquitted of the murder of Rachel Nickell, who was stabbed to death in front of her three-year-old son on Wimbledon Common in 1992, was sat a few tables away. 'The pub was called the Maltese Cat. A friend of my dad's said, "Do you know who that is over in the corner?" – out loud, so everyone could hear. "That's *Colin Stagg*." So everyone looked around really slowly. So Stagg's got up very slowly. And my dad's friend shouts, "I hate people who hit girls." And when Stagg's going out the door she says, "And don't come back you fackin' 'orrible bastard." Apparently Stagg's windows had been smashed in, and he'd been moved around a lot for his own protection.' Jonah made no connection between himself and the outrage committed against Nickell. It never occurred to him that when he was released there was a danger he'd receive similar treatment if people found out why he had spent over half his life in jail.

Being a Cat C prisoner – Jonah was only at Kingston for logistical reasons – he was the closest of all the players to release on licence. If his reports were satisfactory, the next step would see him downgraded to a Cat D and a move to an open prison. Within about two years of that Jonah would begin the process of starting a life on the outside. It was not going to be easy. He would be an alien figure, with no personal history he would want to speak of, no memories he could casually bring up in conversation, no jobs, no friends, no nights out to recall. Lifers are required to tell potential employers why they have been in jail. About 90 per cent of people leaving prison do not get jobs, and sex offenders are considered almost unemployable. Whatever personal qualities they may seem to have, the stigma of their crime is overpowering.

Criminal psychologists are apt to point out that understanding is not the same as forgiving; in fact, understanding can increase our awareness of the shortcomings of offenders because we see them as human beings, not monsters without morals and responsibilities. (And from that awareness the knowledge gained might prevent others from following the same path to destruction.) Ervin Staub, whose work *The Roots of Evil* explored atrocities committed in Nazi Germany, believed we needed 'double vision' when considering these offenders: a search for understanding while acknowledging human responsibility. The curious thing is that a single atrocity is sometimes harder to understand than a million or more. Over the broad sweep of the twentieth century, with its wars, concentration camps and endless human rights abuses, the answer to the questions 'How?' and 'Why?' can be deduced from a framework of historical events and

223

characters. On the level of one murder this information does not always add up to much.

I thought Jonah would spend the rest of his life trying to explain, without ever being understood. He clung to the answers of counselling sessions, that his inability to express his frustration at his treatment by his parents turned him into a bomb containing eighteen years of anger. It was an explanation, but it required concentration. Blink, and once again it was impossible to fathom how a night in a pub involving a group of apparently unremarkable young people ended in rape, murder and mutilation.

Later that morning the Governor, Stuart McLean, remained tight-lipped about Eddie's departure. The matter was confidential. The only rumour control he could provide was that once A wing was restored it would house more lifers rather than the fixed-term prisoners who so concerned Scouse. The pitch was also safe; coiled barbed wire was being added to the top of the wall. With other enhanced security measures, he thought it unlikely that a second perimeter would be required.

An overcast morning added to the impression that his office, all dark oak panels and burgundy carpeting, was small and government gloomy. Mr McLean – for that is what Nigel called him – was a tall, slim fifty-three-year-old. A gentlemanly manner went with a cinematic face and rough skin. His steady, intent gaze put people on their mettle, as did his accent, which was slightly pinched and hard to place.

It was Saturday, and the administration offices were deserted. 'I like coming in at the weekends because I have a chance to get about the place,' he said, making coffee. 'There are a lot of rumours [among staff] in a place like this because a lot of them are simply waiting around in case anything goes wrong. It's my chance to talk to them.'

Having grown up in what became Zambia, he joined the UK prison service in 1978. Kingston was his first governorship. It seemed to be his kind of jail – quiet and civilised. 'All prisons have their own character – it grows out of historical reasons, where they are in the country, and the effect of individual governors,' he said. 'When Kingston opened in the function it currently has [it housed young offenders until 1971], it was a domestic lifers prison, where the inmates had, by and large, killed their wives. With that sort of population you find that the majority of them don't have a criminal background. So the relationships that developed between the staff and the prisoners are quite different because on the whole these people really were remorseful. Now we take a more mixed population, but somehow, because the feed of new prisoners into the place has always been relatively slow, instead of Kingston changing to the way the new prisoners are, they have adapted to the Kingston way. I'm sure they come here and think, "This place is too quiet, we'll set it alight." But after they have been here a while they are glad not to have the aggravation, all the head-to-heads. Some jails are very hectic. You get a lot of young men who act before they think. We've got young men who fall into that category, but there's a sort of unofficial structure in [the cell block] that if they start rocking the boat, other prisoners, will say, "Calm down. If you approach the matter in this way or that way you'll probably get the result you want." '

Being a governor was a complicated management job encompassing the roles of chief executive, civil servant, social worker and security guard. Along with Nigel and Geordie, fifty prison officers, four healthcare workers, three catering staff and assorted administrative clerks reported to Mr McLean. 'We're dealing with people's lives, and that's a very complicated business,' he pointed out. 'You can have all the rules in the world, but you're always going to come across someone to whom, because of their particular circumstances, the rules don't really apply. You've got to balance the human need with the security considerations and the needs of the prison service.'

Mr McLean believed in rehabilitation. 'It's all very well people saying, "Lock them up and give them bread and water." But if you do that, all you are going to do is turn out bitter people. Everyone who comes into prison, by and large, goes out again. If they want to perpetuate this cycle of people coming into prison, doing nothing with them, sending them out, unskilled, going back into crime, if we're prepared to pay for that, that's fine. But I suspect we're not. I want to see prisoners treated humanly and decently, but that's all. There should be no wonderful privileges. But we've got to keep them in touch with what's going on outside, try to educate them, and give them something that helps them lead an honest life.'

It was not his job to worry about whether sentences were adequate. 'For the victim's family, I guess nothing you could do would ever satisfy them, although some have actually forgiven the person who committed the crime. What I do know is that the life sentence is not an easy option. Some people spend a long time in jail, some a relatively short time. But it doesn't end when you leave prison. They're out on life licence and the controls are there. They've got to conform, or the supervisors can have them back inside quicker than a flash. And the reality is, if they are recalled it's not a matter of a couple of weeks to test them out, you're talking years again. They are on a very tight rein.'

He wandered along the touchline later that afternoon, prompting a few grins from the inmates, sheepish in the presence of authority. Mr McLean had gone back to his paperwork by the time a Rizler volley put Kingston ahead against Rimor. It was 3–2 at the break, Carl and Rizler twice restoring the lead. Kingston took the contest to another level in the second half. Paddy struck twice before Rizler completed his first hat-trick of the season. It finished 6–2. Paddy's nineteen goals made him the league's leading scorer, and with Carl averaging one a game, Kingston were still on track for the title.

	P	W	D	L	F	A	PTS
Kingston Arrows	13	7	4	2	54	31	25
Plover	10	7	1	2	40	20	22
So. Co-op Dairies	10	4	4	2	39	19	16
George and Dragon	7	5	1	1	26	9	16
H&S Aviation	8	4	0	4	27	26	12
Rimor	7	4	0	3	24	26	12
Magpie	11	3	2	6	32	32	11
Grant Thornton	6	2	1	3	16	20	7
Court House	8	2	1	5	15	39	7
St Helena	10	0	0	10	9	60	0

25

REASONABLE DOUBT

On the night of 15/16 December 1988 three violent robberies were carried out in the Surrey suburbs. One man was murdered and six other people brutally attacked, most of them woken in their beds by masked intruders armed with a machete and a gun. The police deduced that one gang had committed all three attacks. A chain of stolen cars linked the incidents.

The rampage began when the gang, who started the night driving a stolen Triumph Spitfire, pulled up beside an Austin Princess parked off a country lane. It contained two men: fifty-seven-year-old Peter Hurburgh and forty-two-year-old Alun Ely. Both were dragged into a field, beaten and doused in petrol. One of the gang members jumped on Hurburgh's chest, staving in his sternum. He died of heart failure.

The green Triumph Spitfire, with a small Union Jack sticker on one side, was then abandoned by the gang. They took Hurburgh's Austin Princess and headed for the village of Oxted, seven miles away, where they broke into the home of a retired couple, a Mr and Mrs Napier, and their visiting son, forty-year-old Timothy. The Napiers were beaten and robbed. Timothy Napier fought back and was stabbed repeatedly for his trouble, losing four pints of blood. When the gang left, pausing only to rip his mother's rings off her fingers, Timothy managed to dial 999, but was so weak all the operator could hear was heavy breathing. Police traced the call to the house.

The gang dumped the Austin Princess and stole Timothy Napier's Toyota Corolla. They drove twenty-four miles to Fetcham, where they broke into the residence of Rosemary Spicer, thirty-five, and her boyfriend Peter Almond, thirty-six. The couple were tied up and gagged while the gang spent the next hour looting their home. The attackers left the Toyota and fled in the couple's Vauxhall Cavalier and Renault 5, with jewellery, credit cards and cheque books among the stolen property.

The villains were dubbed the M25 gang because they used London's orbital motorway to speed between attacks. With targets apparently chosen at random, and the robberies pointlessly violent, as if the perpetrators enjoyed terrorising their victims, it was a big story. No one, it seemed, could sleep safely until they were in custody. There was a £25,000 reward for information leading to the conviction of the gang, including £10,000 from the *Daily Mail*.

In January 1990, just over a year later, Raphael Rowe sat in the dock at the Old Bailey and heard himself described as the mastermind behind the offences committed on the night of 15/16 December. From the moment of his arrest Raph vehemently maintained his innocence. There was no forensic evidence linking him to the murder and robberies, and for a time he seemed to have a cast-iron alibi. But along with his friend Michael Davis, and another man, Randolph Johnson, he was sentenced to life imprisonment. It was an 'orgy of offences', said Mr Justice Auld. No one could fail to be affected by the 'total horror' of what had happened.

We met in the gym office. Raph sloped in, wearing a loose white T-shirt, grey tracksuit trousers, and carrying a mug of tea. He stood 5ft 8in, with a compact, muscular physique, and a watchful face. His shoulder-length dreadlocks were gathered in a pony tail. It was obvious from the outset that Raph was different. Raph was not a guilt-ridden lifer who worried about rocking the boat. He was cocky, bitter, but more than anything else determined to clear his name.

His reputation preceded him. Not only had the case of the M25 Three been in and out of the newspapers for ten years, but prior to his arrival at Kingston the grapevine had buzzed with reports of his football skills, hitherto demonstrated during inter-wing games at Maidstone prison. It was also known that his cousin, Carl Hutchings, was a professional, on the books at Brentford.

Raph and Michael Davis, supported by their families and friends, campaigned vigorously to prove they had been wrongfully convicted. (They were not in contact with Randolph Johnson, who made his own representations.) They were waiting on tenterhooks to see if their case would be sent back to the Court of Appeal, a decision that was in the hands of the Criminal Cases Review Commission (CCRC).

There was a time when the existence of a quasi-government organisation such as the CCRC, going around questioning whether the police and the courts had handled cases fairly, would have been unthinkable. But by the time of Raph's conviction, in March 1990, the reputation of British justice was at an all-time low. A succession of high-profile cases – the Guildford Four, the Birmingham Six, the Cardiff Three, the Bridgewater Four, among others – severely damaged confidence in the police, the judiciary and the Home Office. In some cases, evidence pointing to the innocence of the defendants was found to have been withheld. New ways of testing documents demolished the authenticity of a number of 'confessions' by suggesting the police records had not been made contemporaneously, as was always maintained in court. It was revealed that Carole Richardson, of the Guildford Four, had been injected with the opiate drug pethidine before making her admission of 'guilt', just one of many astonishing disclosures that forced a huge sea change of opinion within the legal system. Judges had to recognise that police evidence might not always be reliable. And then there was the complacency of the Home Office, which was found to have ignored compelling new evidence to re-examine cases. Stefan Kiszko spent sixteen years in prison for the sexual murder of a child that DNA testing revealed he could not have committed. Kiszko's mother devoted herself to save her son, but both were to die just two years after Stefan's name was finally cleared.

It hardly helped, too, that juries appeared to have abandoned the requirement to prove guilt beyond reasonable doubt. During his time in Maidstone prison Raph formed a friendship with Winston Silcott, whose conviction for the murder of PC Keith Blakelock during the 1985 Tottenham riots came to represent the sheer flimsiness of the 'evidence' on which a defendant could be found guilty. In the event, Silcott's conviction was overturned by the Court of Appeal, but the fact he had ever been found guilty raised concerns. Silcott was not connected to the policeman's death by any forensic evidence or any eyewitnesses, and he did not feature in the video footage or the thousands of photos at the scene. The conviction was based solely on the strength of an unsigned statement which read: 'You can't pin this on me, no one will talk.' As David Rose points out in his book *In the Name of the Law*, the trial was flawed. 'Jurors were allowed to hear a mass of highly prejudicial allegations against Silcott, including the claim he planned to parade PC Blakelock's head on a pole, a claim which had been made by thirteen-year-old Jason Hill, who had been questioned about the murder. The judge ordered the jurors to acquit Hill. But they were not in court to hear him dismiss Hill's account as "fantasy", the result of oppressive and illegal treatment (the boy had been held incommunicado for three days wearing only his underpants and a blanket, stained with his own vomit).' The fact Silcott was convicted of another murder in an unrelated case should not make the circumstances of the Blakelock wrongful conviction any more palatable. People need confidence in the police and the courts. A country without justice has about as much going for it as a football match without a ball.

Of course, there were many reasons why a prisoner, especially one convicted of murder, might falsely claim to be the victim of a miscarriage of justice. If he could find a loophole in the evidence, the conduct of the trial, or something wrong with the original police enquiries, there was always the possibility of tipping the balance of law in his favour. A murder charge beaten down to manslaughter – or perhaps even quashed. In his book *Inside Time*, Ken Smith suggests that a number of prisoners persist in claiming innocence out of stubbornness, maintaining the front constructed during their trials. Others do so because they are capable of great self-deception. And a few because they are innocent.

It is beyond the scope of this book to investigate the M25 case, but a team of researchers from the BBC's *Rough Justice* programme did and uncovered what it called an 'avalanche of inconsistencies' in the evidence that got Raph and Michael Davis convicted. They concluded that the trial of the M25 Three was 'profoundly unfair'.

It is a complicated case, so campaigners tend to stress the most obvious concerns about the conviction. They include the fact that the police were looking for two white men, one of whom had blond hair and blue eyes, and a black man. These descriptions were even broadcast on the BBC's

Crimewatch. But by the time the trial came around a dramatic transformation had taken place. Three black men stood in the dock. The jury *was* told that two white men and one black man had been sought, but they never heard the victims' detailed accounts recorded in police notebooks, simply because the defence was not told that this material existed.

Then there was the timing of the crime. There were seven witnesses, whose testimony was not disputed, who could establish the whereabouts of Raph and Michael Davis between about 8 p.m. and 1.30 a.m. According to Alun Ely's first account of the crime, Peter Hurburgh was killed at about midnight, so Raph and Michael Davis seemed to be in the clear. But fifteen days after the attack, Alun Ely changed his story. He altered the times, saying the murder must have happened two hours later, putting it after two a.m. This removed both men's alibis, even though there was still nothing to place them at the scene of the murder or the subsequent robberies.

In their efforts to get the case returned to the Court of Appeal, the BBC researchers found another witness who confirmed the timing of the attack as given in Alun Ely's first statement. A woman had been driving back from a horse show at Olympia. At around 12.30 a.m. she went down the country lane. At a T-junction she saw the abandoned green Triumph Spitfire. Her husband even remarked on the small Union Jack sticker on the side. As the Spitfire had been dumped by whoever killed Hurburgh, this piece of information alone could have unravelled the whole case against Raph and Michael. They could not be in two places at once. In court, Ely said he hadn't told the truth about the timing of the attack in his first statement because he had not wanted to reveal that he and Hurburgh had been having sex in the car.

It was partly on the basis of Alun Ely's revised timings that the three men were convicted, but the mystery was why the jury gave them credence. Under cross-examination, Alun Ely admitted that he sometimes had problems with the truth.

'Do you agree that when it suits you can handle the truth carelessly?'

Alun Ely: 'Yes.'

'And invent all sorts of colourful incidents that never happened and describe it all in a logical progression so that anyone listening would be completely taken in?'

'Yes – unless they knew me. Family or friends would turn around and call me a liar.'

Raph and Michael Davis lived at a ten-bedroom hostel in Sydenham. The change in Alun Ely's story opened up the possibility that both men, and Randolph Johnson, could have taken part in the murder and subsequent robberies. But that's all. Campaigners are quick to point out that the bulk of the prosecution evidence came from three other men who lived at the same hostel, and who were originally arrested as part of the M25 inquiry: Norman Duncan, Shane Griffin and Andy Jobbins, all of whom are white. On the face of it, they appeared to be prime suspects. They admitted to being accomplices to the M25 crimes, but that much was almost academic: a number of knives and home-made weapons were found in their rooms when the hostel was searched. And when police raided the home of a girlfriend of Andy Jobbins, they found goods stolen during the Fetcham robbery, as well as an air gun, later identified by Timothy Napier as the weapon used by the gang. Duncan, Jobbins and Griffin admitted that they had stolen the Triumph Spitfire, and Duncan's and Jobbins' fingerprints were found on the car at the scene of the Peter Hurburgh murder. They also confessed to dumping the Cavalier and Renault cars stolen during the final robbery, and had no alibis, yet all charges against them were dropped.

They offered the only evidence which directly linked Raph, Michael Davis and Randolph Johnson to the M25 crimes. They alleged that Raph had paid them to steal the Triumph Spitfire, and that explained why their fingerprints were on it. They also alleged that Raph had asked for help in disposing of the stolen goods. But as the BBC's *Rough Justice* explained, there were glaring contradictions. Duncan and Jobbins could not agree on when they had stolen the Triumph Spitfire. They also disagreed about what Raph was wearing when he went out. When first interviewed, Andy Jobbins even put the wrong man up for the job, naming Michael Davis's brother. This man, it turned out, had an alibi. The next day, when interviewed again, Jobbins substituted his name for Randolph Johnson – a change that went completely unchallenged by the police. *Rough Justice* suggested the Duncan group of witnesses had difficulty with their story because they were describing events that never happened.

There were lots of other problems with the case, including custody records suggesting that lengthy unrecorded conversations had taken place, breaching police procedure. And during a failed appeal in 1993 it emerged that there was information relating to the M25 case which had been kept from the defence. At that appeal the judges had gone into private session with the prosecution, barring the defence and the public. The conclusion they came to was that some of the evidence in the case was so sensitive it could only be revealed to the defence if they promised not to show it to their clients – an offer which was declined. The court justified its secrecy by invoking a Public Interest Immunity (PII) certificate, a highly controversial means of circumventing the need to have the facts of a case established in open court. M25 campaigners believe the PII related to the question of who had received the reward money, and that its use was unfair, denying them the opportunity to question whether the cash had a bearing on the reliability of key prosecution witnesses. In the event, covert operations by *Rough Justice* researchers later established that Norman Duncan had received the £10,000 reward from the *Daily Mail*. They were not able to find out what had happened to the other £15,000. The use of the PII prompted a submission to the European Commission of Human Rights. It has decided that the British government has a case to answer in respect of whether the M25 Three received a fair trial.

At the 1993 failed appeal, Michael Mansfield QC sought to demonstrate there was a lurking doubt about the soundness of the conviction of Raph and Michael Davis, based on the general unreliability of the Norman Duncan group of witnesses, as well as inconsistencies in timing. He also produced the police notebook that had not been disclosed at the trial; it contained notes from interviews with Mrs Napier describing in detail the gang being composed of two white men and one black man. The three Appeal Court judges were not convinced by these points, ruling that the non-disclosure of the police notebook was an 'irregularity' but not a 'material irregularity'.

The strangeness of the entire case was summed up by the prosecution making much of the fact that Raph's skin colour – he's from a mixed-race background and his features could be said to be more Caucasian than African – might conceivably have allowed him to pass as a 'white' man. What the prosecution could not explain was, if Raph *was* one of the 'white' men who fitted the descriptions provided by the victims, who was the other white man? Michael Davis and Randolph Johnson are unmistakably black. Deputy Lord Chief Justice Watkins, in his summing up at the Court of Appeal, described this as a 'mystery'.

If Raph was innocent of involvement in the murder and

robberies, the last ten years must have been hell. 'Nobody fights my case more than me,' he said firmly. 'I've got solicitors, campaigners, but nobody can understand my case like me because I live and breathe it every fucking day.' He sounded as bitter as if the conviction had happened yesterday. 'When I first come inside my attitude to inmates and staff was horrible. I didn't have the skills to fight my case any other way. Now, over the years, I've learnt to use the computer, my mind and other people to better advantage, whereas before I would just steam into a screw. Along the way I met people like the Birmingham Six. They'd been in the system a few years longer than me and were older and wiser. They showed me the way, to be honest. They said, "You need to set up a campaign." I used to think, "It didn't help you lot, why the fuck is it going to help me?" I got on best with Paddy Joe Hill. Although he was older, he had such a vicious attitude. His attitude was the same as mine: fuck 'em, fuck 'em, fuck 'em. Very angry. Some of the others, Billy Powell and Richard MacKilkenny, they were more diplomatic. They allowed the campaign to do the work. Eventually that was the way I went.'

Raph claimed to have been assaulted by officers at Wormwood Scrubs (his was one of fifteen complaints about the segregation unit, which prompted an official investigation, the results of which are not yet public). 'Horrendous things have happened to me. I've been beaten by the screws, put in a straitjacket, brutalised. But never from the day I was locked up have I ever cried, because if I started I'd never stop. They've damaged me. I've never been in love. I've missed out on all these experiences and I think it's drained me of my natural feelings. I know I'll never be the same person again, but ten years of my life have been ruined so far, and I don't want to go out there and destroy myself.' Raph believed he was on the verge of freedom, but admitted to moments of terror as the decision loomed. 'I'm confident my conviction will be quashed, but I'm so scared of hearing that decision.'

26

ZERO TOLERANCE

St Helena should have been a trouble-free game. Without so much as a point all season, they were plunging towards relegation, having conceded sixty goals in ten games. That made it a case of the worst defence in the league coming up against the most potent attack, Kingston having hit the target fifty-four times in thirteen games. And, as it turned out, the St Helena players did not cause any problems. Kingston's did.

The match turned ugly five minutes before half-time. Teddy and Duffy had been named as substitutes. Jonah was back in defence, replacing Nigel who'd taken the day off to finish moving into his new home on the Isle of Wight. Teddy was running the line when Paddy questioned one of his offside decisions. The captain shouted something. It seemed to be, 'You've got to be kidding.'

Teddy's reply: 'Fucking cunt.'

Teddy barely raised his voice, but managed to infuse each syllable with enough hatred to turn heads. Along the near touchline faces were suddenly alert, sensing that something was about to go off.

Teddy stood erect in a green lightweight rain jacket and blue tracksuit bottoms, gripping the line-flag in his hand. He got louder. 'Fucking wanker. Shut the fuck up. Fucking little wanker.'

From the penalty spot, Paddy glanced in the direction of the abuse. Teddy's face was naturally hard and angular, the broad sweep of his forehead underscored by high cheek-bones, leathery skin and a pointed chin. One look at his teeth-clenched fury made it obvious an explanation was in order.

'Hey, I was talking to the ref.'

'Fucking cunt,' shouted Teddy. He was chewing vigorously on some gum, his pony tail bobbing with the pounding of his jaw.

Duffy had been sulking about being on the bench. He happened to be approaching when Teddy's outburst began. 'What's up?'

'That little cunt has been giving me lip.'

'Well,' snorted Duffy, looking up at his taller friend, 'if he's giving you backchat you gotta deck him, aintcha?'

Duffy and Teddy went into a huddle with another con. This man was a fiftysomething Londoner who had a reputation for getting his kicks from winding up situations, then standing back to watch the show. The three of them might as well have chanted the mantra: 'Paddy, fuckin' little cunt, Paddy, gonna fuckin' 'ave ya, Paddy, fuckin' little cunt, Paddy gonna fuckin' 'ave ya.'

Not that Duffy needed any encouragement. He had already approached a group standing on the touchline to voice his contempt at Nigel's team selection: 'Don't change a winning team, says Nigel. I been in three winning teams, so how's that make sense?' Duffy had replaced the injured Carl during the George and Dragon victory back in November, and had twice been summoned from the bench when matches were all but won. No one wanted to point out the absurdity of taking the manager's remarks quite so literally.

The blankness of Duffy's expression discouraged further discussion. So Duffy walked on, fuming.

Kingston were 2–1 ahead at the break, but Wayne and Paddy's goals hardly mattered. All eyes were on Teddy, and what would happen next.

As the players gathered on the side of the pitch, Paddy marched towards him. His stride was forthright, but gave no clue of his intentions. At the last moment, Paddy held out his hand. 'Let's forget—'

Teddy stepped back. 'No way! Fuck off you cunt. You fucking wanker.'

Paddy shook his head, said, 'All right then,' and moved on a few paces. He sat down on the frozen ground.

Geordie appeared with the drinks and said a few words about the performance, but everyone was tuned to the brooding silence between the two men.

The bad feeling spread in the second half, with petty arguments punctuating three more goals from Paddy, and one apiece from Carl and Rizler. There was a reply, taking the score to 7–2. And now Zebedee and Scouse were arguing about who was to blame for that. The game restarted and Jonah asked Scouse to mark someone. That was too much for the man from Merseyside, and he immediately asked to be substituted. 'I'm sick and tired of people talking like this.' Scouse was up for some trouble, too. As soon as he was off the pitch he set about demonstrating his solidarity with Duffy, who, by now, was on the point of losing it completely.

When the score was at 3–1, Duffy approached Geordie. He wanted to know when he would be brought on.

'It's still a bit tight,' said Geordie.

'You're just a fucking cocksucker.'

Geordie, in the midst of a light-hearted conversation, was caught off guard. His cheeks flushed. 'Oh, that's very nice. You think that's going to get you in the team, do you?'

'Geordie is a cocksucker! Geordie is a cocksucker!' Duffy walked away backwards, hands in jacket pockets, shouting at the top of his voice.

Scouse was soon by his side. They marched around the touchlines, matching each other's stride and hunched pose, sullen victims, staring at the turf.

When the match finished, Duffy strode up to Geordie. 'If this was on the out I'd take you out.'

'Are you threatening me?' replied Geordie.

'Are you taking that as a threat?' said Duffy.

They stared at each other, as if assessing the possibilities of violence. Then Duffy thought better of it, turned around and headed back to the cell block.

With only twenty minutes before bang-up it seemed unlikely that the main protagonists, Paddy and Teddy, would attempt to resolve their dispute. I wanted to find out if there was anything going on behind the scenes which would explain why the day had turned sour, but had to wait until evening association, the hours between five and nine p.m. when the cons were allowed out of their cells.

When it came around, Paddy was sat on his bed, trying not to sound like a fugitive. 'It's happened a couple of times – Teddy takes it personally if anyone disputes a decision.' He screwed up his face. 'It's difficult because I couldn't see what he was getting worked up about. I felt like saying, "You're telling me you're going to smash me up because I questioned one of your decisions?" He kind of made it worse by completely dismissing me when I approached him. There was no need for that. I don't want to come across as the big hard man, but I'm not going to be running around, skulking in the shadows. And at the end of the day, if Ted wants to get funny about it, there's not a lot I can do.' He smiled knowingly. 'I don't want to fall out with him. He's a big old bloke, you know.'

With hot water from a flask, Paddy made coffee.

'Prison can be a violent place, but no more so than the outside. It's just a microcosm. There's no real trouble here. There are tobacco barons, drug barons, whatever. People get themselves in debt, same as outside. It's just that the collection methods are a bit more unpleasant. A lot of it is symbolic. I've seen people almost apologetic because they've had to give someone a hiding over a fifty-pound debt.'

No reserve match was scheduled for the following Sunday afternoon. The freezing temperatures meant that only twelve people bothered to turn out for the football session Geordie had scheduled instead.

Walking out of C wing, there was none of the usual banter. Geordie greeted Scouse, who was coming down the stairs. He was ignored.

Once outside, Geordie decided not to play the full length of the pitch. The lack of consultation upset Teddy. 'You're not at Guy's Marsh [Young Offenders Institution] now, you're dealing with men,' roared Teddy, belting the ball into the stratosphere.

Geordie made up the numbers, starting on the opposite side to Duffy. When they first challenged for the same ball, an innocuous enough tussle, Duffy said, 'Oh, so you're kicking me now, are you?' The fireworks, however, were exhausted. The session passed without further incident. By the end, the falling temperature and the hardness of the pitch took its toll. Everyone trooped back inside quietly.

The night before Kingston's fifteenth match of the season, the St Helena return, Bunny was shuffling about outside his cell, polishing a teak and mahogany coffee table. It was a wedding present for someone in his family. 'When I was at school I liked carpentry,' he said. 'I'm starting to pick it up again. We have a woodwork class, Tuesday and Thursday.' There were no special security measures. 'Everything's locked up, but once you are in there you can use whatever tools you want. There's no screws, just Eric, who takes the class.' Bunny made eye contact. 'People are a bit more mature in here. We've all done fucking horrendous crimes, but some-where along the line we got to be trusted.' At the Monday night upholstery class he had made a green velour bed-head studded with matching buttons. 'A couple of guys have offered to pay me to make them one,' said Bunny, trying hard not to sound pleased with himself. 'I can't be bothered; they're a lot of work.'

There was a dusky ambience in his cell, created by the green, yellow and black Jamaican flag which was suspended beneath the ceiling light. Nelson Mandela's *The Long Road to Freedom* lay half-read on a book shelf. Bikini-clad women, posing on tropical beaches, lined the walls. Bunny motioned towards one of the posters. 'She was my girlfriend.' Really? He searched around for the evidence. And there they were, cuddling in a photo, back in the days when Bunny had dreadlocks. He turned to the last page of the album. 'This is a very special photo I'm going to show you.' A shot of his girlfriend's full-length profile filled the page, her face turned towards the lens. She was clutching a chiffon scarf in a way that did nothing to cover her breasts and pubic hair. Bunny reversed through the album. Bob Marley was nowhere to be seen, but backstage at the London Palladium there was a photograph of the comedian Lenny Henry – Bunny at his shoulder, squeezing into the frame.

The rift with Nigel, he said, was long forgotten. 'I've had a go at him. Other people have had a go at him. He's had stick about who's in the team – and, at the end of the day, it's his job to take that flak. But Nige has done excellent. We have gelled as a team. I think he's feeling comfortable and giving us more space to play football. He's enjoying it more, too. If you watched us last year, Nigel was very aggressive. You wouldn't see him smiling during games. This season, I've seen him laughing and joking.'

With the George and Dragon showdown only eight days away, competition for places was reaching a peak. Bunny's position was beyond question; his form had been good enough to prompt jokes that 'he must be on something'.

Duffy's row with Geordie had reminded me of the rumours which suggested that earlier in the season Duffy had visited Bunny's cell to threaten him about his criticisms. (Bunny was in the habit of saying, 'Duffy ain't a footballer.')

'Nah,' Bunny scoffed. 'I wouldn't take that off him.'

Later, we went downstairs to the cell-block kitchen. Duffy was making himself something to eat. Bunny told him what I'd asked. The skin on my neck pricked.

'If you want to know something about me,' said Duffy, swaggering forward, a finger tapping the centre of his chest, 'ask.'

A meeting was arranged.

Come the hour, Duffy was upstairs, leaning against the railings which overlooked the snooker table. He was not alone, but Teddy and the older Londoner who had a reputation for stirring up trouble did not raise their gaze.

Peeling away, Duffy said, 'I've got nothing to say to you.'

What was the problem?

'I don't want you portraying me as a bully.'

I said that asking whether he had threatened Bunny was not the same as calling him a bully. It was just a question.

'Well, you would say that, wouldn't you?'

There was a pause. Then Duffy added, 'I don't suppose you're gonna tell me who said it?'

No, that was not possible, got to protect sources.

245

The meeting was over. I went back downstairs, feeling their contempt with every step.

Jonah, playing pool on the C wing table, stopped to say hello. We had a cup of tea in his cell. I told him how I'd talked myself into trouble, that the issue of Duffy and Bunny was taking on a life of its own. Jonah laughed. 'That's bloody jail for you. Now you see what I have to put up with.'

I saw him again the next morning. Jonah said that everyone was buzzing with the news that Duffy had given me a hard time (I doubted those were the actual words used). The implication was that Duffy had scared me. Which, of course, was true.

When I reached the gym office it was a relief to see Nigel cleaning his boots. I told him about Bunnygate. He listened without comment. Zebedee, to my surprise, was sympathetic. 'You've got to be so careful what you say.'

It turned out that Duffy had come close to being shipped out over the St Helena substitution row. On reading Geordie's report, the governor's verdict was that Duffy would go if the PEI thought it was necessary. A big decision. In the event, Geordie concluded that the best course of action was to try to keep Duffy in the fold. This was rehabilitation in action. 'We've got to deal with it,' said Geordie briskly. 'Make him see that you can't blow up like that when things aren't going your way. I think Duffy's aware of the situation now. If it happens again, he's gone.' Duffy even kept his place in the side, which upset the D wing reserves. 'It looks like you're rewarding Duffy for bad behaviour,' one of them moaned. So Geordie took time out to explain the situation.

Still, the matter had not ended, and at the pre-match meeting Nigel made a point of the fact Duffy was in the team on merit. But even that wasn't enough. On the touchlines the D wing rumour mill had gone into overdrive. It was put about that Duffy had been dealt with leniently because he was under some degree of stress. There were some family problems and he, like some of the other C wing cons, was making a big effort to get off cannabis. The introduction of mandatory drug tests gave them little choice. Failing or refusing a test meant being shipped out of Kingston, a fate they were desperate to avoid.

Jonah was missing the St Helena return, having arranged a visit. Given that there were no more games before the biggest match of the season, the decider against George and Dragon, this seemed reckless indeed. Jonah appeared unaware just how much pressure was building on the 'don't change a winning team' policy. Everyone else, though, was aware, and they were already trying to pre-empt Nigel, making their way one by one to the gym office to argue their case for inclusion. No one wanted to miss out. Scouse and Morgan looked more anxious than anyone – they were out of the St Helena game because of ankle injuries.

Terry Allison arrived with news that Court House were considering dropping out of the league. This was bad news. Kingston had beaten them twice, but the George and Dragon had only drawn with Court House on the opening day of the season. So the Arrows would come off worse if the results were expunged from the records. The George and Dragon game really was win or bust.

St Helena arrived with only ten men, and then had a player sent off. The match became a turkey shoot as Kingston romped to a 12–0 victory, the goals coming from Paddy (8), Raph (2), Calvin (1) and, to all-round cheers, Duffy.

In the directors' box, Scouse pressed his face against the window. In silence we watched the players shaking hands at the final whistle.

The league table published later that day confirmed that Kingston needed to prevent George and Dragon getting anything out of their St Valentine's Day rematch. If the Arrows went on to take maximum points from their remaining two games, the fall of the fixtures meant that they would be guaranteed the runners-up spot, and they stood an excellent chance of becoming champions.

	P	W	D	L	F	A	PTS
Kingston Arrows	15	9	4	2	73	33	31
George and Dragon	10	8	1	1	33	11	25
Plover	12	7	1	4	44	27	22
So. Co-op Dairies	11	5	4	2	43	21	19
H&S Aviation	11	5	1	5	37	37	16
Rimor	8	5	0	3	28	29	15
Magpie	12	3	2	7	33	34	11
Grant Thornton	8	2	2	4	18	24	8
Court House	9	2	1	6	20	45	7
St Helena	12	0	0	12	11	79	0

27
PADDY (2)

I've had my last review board here. I've been recommended for a C Cat but I've asked to stay until June – I'm doing A-level Psychology and want to finish that here. There are three types of review boards: an induction board, which you normally have six months after arriving in the establishment; an interim board, a year later; and then an F75, eighteen months after that. At the Scrubs you faced a panel including one of your wing governors, probation, psychology, chaplain, outside probation, Uncle Tom Cobbley and all. Without sounding too cynical, there are only certain people who actually get to know much about you. For example, Nigel knows me much better than the chaplain. I don't go to church. The only time I see the chaplain is if he walks past me on the wing and I'll say good morning. Unless I use the facility he offers, there's not much he can say about me.

You're supposed to do certain work [regarding] your offence. You go on courses. Two of my risk factors are loss of control and alcohol awareness. Loss of control – well, I'm better than some, worse than others. The fact of the matter is I got involved in a fight and killed a guy. Alcohol Awareness – I'd been in the pub before I committed my offence. There's a genuine need for courses, but they are a token gesture. You get maybe two members of staff who run an

Anger Management course for a week. It's the first one they've done, they've been away for a week's training. To me, if you are sincere about it, you need to treat people on an individual basis. You can't sit twelve guys around a table from different walks of life. You get people who went out and had one drink sat next to a guy who's been an alcoholic for twenty years. That's where there's resentment. I'm willing to do anything that I think is relevant. Not because I'm a poor, sad wretch and need to do all these things, but because I feel I need to make the effort. In the cold light of day we can all improve ourselves. It's difficult sometimes because you think, 'Well, I'm no worse than so and so and he doesn't have to do it.' I'm sorry, but that's human nature. There's a guy losing his rag and throwing snooker balls around and *he* doesn't have to do an Anger Management course. And I do.

They have to offer you something. The bottom line is that, if you are going to release guys after fifteen years or so, people are going to want to know what has been done with them. They can't just say, 'Well, we've kept him locked in a room and now we are going to let him out.' The majority of violent crime is committed by young men between the ages of eighteen and twenty-five, so you don't have to be Einstein to figure out they are going to be about forty when they get out. What are you going to do with these people? To me, fifteen years is a long time. But out there, fifteen years, it comes around. People are outraged that lifers are released, but the images and perceptions of people who commit murder are kind of ludicrous. They are all supposed to be mad axe men. They are not human. You don't want them to be human. The truth is every case is different, everyone is an individual. I know that sounds obvious, but it's the first rule.

If you killed my brother, I can't sit here, knowing all I know, and say I wouldn't want you to die for it. I can't say that because it's not true. Much as people like to be enlightened, your first thought would be, I hope you die. That's human nature, the way we are. But it doesn't change the fact that people have always killed each other and always will. So what do you do about it? There are no winners. If I serve fifteen or twenty years and they let me out, I'm not a winner.

I'm not the brightest person in the world. I have my faults. I'm no different in that sense to the people I went to school with, my friends. Why did I end up here? Why do people end up in prison? Violence is part of the male psyche. I don't know if it's genetic or whatever, but men certainly have a propensity for violence. Some people are more violent than others. Some blokes you've only got to look at them cross-eyed and they're trying to stick a pint glass in your face. When I committed my offence, I'd been drinking, and what I did was not nice: I kicked a guy in the head four or five times. It was way over the top for the situation I found myself in. On the opposite side, right, getting kicked in the head when you go down in a fight is not that exceptional.

I wasn't really heading anywhere at the time of my offence. I suppose it all stemmed from the fact I never really applied myself at school. When I first went to comprehensive school I was in the top set for all my subjects. Gradually, as I went on, it was almost like there were other things that I was doing. School didn't hold my attention and I didn't do the necessary work. I couldn't see what the big deal was. I left school with two O-levels and seven CSEs – really, if I'm honest, pissing around and not bothering. Part of the problem was that people were on my case. It was almost pig-headedness. The more you keep on at me, the more determined I am not to do a stroke. My father's a very strict, authoritarian guy, so there was something liberating about going to school. The teachers didn't have the power over you that parents had. Long term, the only person it affected was me, but at the time it's great to be able to say, 'Well, no, fuck it, I'm not going to do it.' Had I realised how important school was, I'd have been more willing to apply myself. But as so often happens, you lose sight of the actual issues and it becomes a battle of wills. What you are arguing about becomes lost.

I've got an older sister and a younger brother. I'm only thirty-six months older than my brother, but I did everything first. When your brother does the same things it's not quite so dreadful. He's the youngest, so he didn't cause my parents so many problems. When you're young you have these weird ideas about family dynamics. Sometimes I felt my brother could do no wrong, while my sister got what she wanted, and I got all the flak. Looking back, it was very rarely like that. But when you are fourteen the whole world is against you.

There was a stage where I did take stick. I'd get into fights. I was a bit of a soft target in the respect of being in one of the few coloured families in the area. I just learnt to stick up for myself. I didn't take shit off anybody. And maybe that almost becomes an attitude. It's almost like you say, 'I'm not out for trouble, but I refuse to take shit.'

It wasn't until I was a bit older that I realised my dad tried to bring us up the way his parents brought him up, you know, very strict. I don't know how many Afro-Caribbean families you know, but there is a very strict, Bible-based discipline. It's very simplistic in some ways. I'll give you an example. I don't want to make my dad sound like a monster, but he would lose it if I left a door open. Or walked around without my slippers. When I visited my friends' houses I used to think, 'I can't believe what you are getting away with – you want to come round my place.' He used to rant and rave a lot. He wasn't a particularly violent father but he used to carry on a lot. When you are young that's quite intimidating in itself.

My dad is very good at certain things. He's not particularly academic. My mum is more academically gifted. She's not a rocket scientist, but she did pretty well for herself. Had she not married my dad so young she might have gone on to university.

I don't want to paint too bleak a picture. I get on well with my dad. There wasn't a great deal of tension at home. I had quite a good family life, although I had problems, like a lot of people. I did have some awful rows, mainly as a result of frustration. I didn't know what I was going to do. If I'm honest, I don't know what I'll do when I get out because things have changed quite drastically. I can remember my dad slapping the kitchen table and saying, 'You better decide what you are going to do when you leave school.' This was like when I was about fourteen, when I had to decide which subjects I was going to do in my exams.

I don't know what I could have done. When I got a bit older, maybe I would have grown up a bit and gained a bit of insight. There was nothing to stop me going back to college at twenty-five. Some of the jobs I did when I left school – landscape gardening, labouring – I really didn't want to be doing at forty. I worked at a furnishings factory, making mattresses. I installed and sold double glazing. I did telephone sales for a kitchen company. All sorts of jobs that I could just walk into. I wasn't heading anywhere, but it didn't feel like that at the time. I was quite happy. I had money in my pocket. I lived at home. I had everything I needed. I was involved with certain girls at certain times but I wasn't looking to get married off. Like any eighteen-year-old bloke, I just wanted to get my leg over at every opportunity.

Even now I find some of my dad's attitudes strange. It's very difficult to sit and say things about your parents. You feel guilty. I suppose it's a culture shock, something that's hard to come to terms with. You've been told things about the way you should behave. Very old-fashioned: all adults should be addressed as 'Sir', and you think, 'That's nonsense, what are you talking about?' But I suppose most blokes have got unresolved issues with their fathers, haven't they? I feel at the moment I have quite a good relationship with my dad. I only see him about once a week, for about two hours. I get on very well with him. I'm almost loath to say at such and such a time in my life I hated you, and I wish you hadn't done this and that. If I could go back and have my childhood again, I would say to him, 'I wish you could see that the way you are treating me is unsettling me,' or whatever.

Very few people have an idyllic childhood. It's quite a traumatic experience, trying to establish a sense of identity. There's a tendency to blame all your problems on your parents, but you have to take responsibility for yourself. I wasn't abused as a child. I wasn't systematically beaten. I don't believe that me ending up in prison is their fault. It's not valid to say, 'Well, because you hit me when I was eight years old, I went out twelve years later and hit somebody and ended up in prison.' They are good parents. They have got their faults, like so many other people. But having kids – it doesn't come with a manual, does it? They have always been there to offer me support. I can remember being at the police station: 'Do you want us to contact anyone?' And I'm thinking, 'I've got to let my mum and dad know, but how can I tell them?' How do you face it? They never sat down and said, 'How could you do this?' The fact is, I'd done it. It's very difficult for them. They have helped me in every way they can.

The future is very tough to think about. Some guys don't think about anything more than what they are doing at that moment, or what they are doing in the next hour. They are doing their sentence now, but it's probably not crossed their minds that even if they do get out, somewhere around their tariff, they've got a whole world of new problems. They don't appreciate how difficult what they've done is for their families.

I'd like to work with special needs kids. It's something that I've enjoyed doing in here but, realistically, any people-based occupation is going to be a problem for me. I've toyed with the idea of working at a young offenders' place. But automatically that puts up a lot of barriers. I would have the qualifications sporting-wise to work at an Outward Bound centre, but if you were the boss, would you take a chance on me? Regardless of whether people like you or not, it's not a sound risk financially. Leave yourself open to litigation. So I'm probably excluded.

The truth is, if they let me out and said, 'Got a job for you stacking shelves at Tesco's – you've got to do it,' I'd do it. Now, I wouldn't *want* to do that because prison is so repetitive and so boring, I'd hope not to have to do something so tedious on the outside. But I'd do it. There are terms and conditions when you are released, but the other thing is people's attitudes towards you. People will already have judged who I am and what I'm about because you're supposed to tell people that you've been a prisoner, that you're a lifer. If I just said to you, a stranger conducting a job interview, 'Oh, and by the way, I killed someone,' it would be a case of 'Next!'

You want to know what I dream about? Just being outside at night. Just thinking, 'Right, it's two a.m., I'm taking the dog for a walk.' 'It's five a.m., pissing down with rain, but I'm going out for a run.' Because I want to. Because I can.

28

ENTER THE GEORGE AND DRAGON

When the sun burned the fog away the football pitch, cut and rolled, looked immaculate. The gardeners had been busy. Everything was set for the biggest match of the season.

Nigel broke the news in private. Jonah, Morgan and Scouse were not in the team to face the George and Dragon. Teddy and Duffy were selected. The rest of the squad heard the news at the eleven a.m. team meeting.

'Where's Jonah?' asked Paddy.

'He ain't coming,' said Rizler.

'You're kidding?'

Rizler shook his head.

Jonah could not believe that Teddy and Duffy had been chosen ahead of him. He was so upset he told Nigel he was dropping out of the squad. Kingston would have to finish the season without him.

'There's been a huge debate about the team selection,' began Nigel. 'Everyone has got their own opinions. There are seventeen names down on the sheet, including myself. Everyone wants to play. I've had to make a decision. I've wrestled with it. I've decided to keep the policy I've had all season, which wasn't easy, looking at the importance of the game. Duffy and Teddy came in last week for Jonah and Scouse – and I'm sticking with them. It's hard on those left out, but I know that everyone who is going out there will give me 100 per cent. You owe that to what you've achieved so far.'

They set about plotting the downfall of the championship favourites. 'It's a big game, we need to win, so let's remember that it might not all go our way,' cautioned Nigel. 'There's no two ways about it, George and Dragon are a good footballing side, and things happen in games. We don't want to get freaked out and start shouting at each other. We've got to unsettle them. When they've got the ball, we've got to close them down and stop them playing.'

Nigel did his best to mix in some confidence boosting with the game plan. 'Front three, you're our first line of defence. You've got to work together. Midfield, same thing. One of the great things since Raph has come into the side is that we've been able to keep the ball and build the play. Wayne, listen, unsung hero. You are tight down that left-hand side with Bunny. You two have got that sewn up. Look to get the two lads in the middle showing for you, so you can release the ball, play your one-twos, and knock it into the forward line. Same for you Duffy, on the right.'

The goals Kingston had conceded during the first encounter with the George and Dragon had provoked Bunny and Nigel's 'do your job' row. They wanted to avoid a repeat.

'Can I say something?' asked Bunny. 'We've got to be aware of their number eleven coming in on set-pieces. I know Wayne is going to mark him, but that bloke done us last time. He stays out until the last possible minute. That's why he's jumping in higher. Wayne needs to give himself a couple of yards so he can attack the ball.'

And on they talked, working through the things that needed to be said, listening to each other, having a laugh. A good meeting.

Only Scouse looked strained. Before picking up the ankle

injury which kept him out of the St Helena 12–0 win, he'd made eight consecutive appearances, never finishing on the losing side. 'This season is near enough over, right,' he said, his voice creaking with the effort of remaining gracious. 'I think, personally, next season, if we have got a team, you must have a rethink about this dropping people policy. I don't think I deserve to be dropped. I've took it, else I wouldn't be here. But I don't deserve to be dropped cos I've missed one game. Cos I picked my injury up giving 100 per cent. If lads know they are going to be dropped if they pick up injuries, they are not going to give you 100 per cent – you'll get 90 per cent. Now, I've had my say in front of all the lads. I've said nothing behind anyone's back. And that's all I've got to say.'

'That's fair enough,' said Nigel. 'And I respect you for being forthright. I wouldn't ask anything of you that I wouldn't do myself, and I can only say that I would not have started the second game against St Helena, having missed the first, but for the fact you, Morgan and Jonah were unavailable. I'd have been on that bench, having travelled over on my weekend off.'

The players were losing interest in Scouse's heartbreak, so Nigel wrapped it up. 'Listen fellas, you've got yourselves in a brilliant position. I have no doubt that we will win. And then the pressure is all on them – and they have some difficult games coming up.'

Bunny, punching his own hand, said, 'Let's kick ass!'

They drifted away from the meeting in twos and threes, with hands gesturing, acting out who liked the ball played where.

During the lunch time bang-up Griff was allowed out of his cell to help with the final preparations. Under a clear blue sky the gym orderly pushed a small cart around the carpet of green. At the pull of a lever, the mixture of one part chalk powder, twelve parts water, left pristine white touchlines in his wake. Nigel posted the corner-flags and checked the nets. There was no banter, none of his normal match day cheerfulness; he was deep in thought, reflecting on what must have been an awkward meeting with Jonah. Everyone else's tension was getting to him.

After a time, Nigel said, 'To be honest with you, I'll be glad when this game's out of the way. The level of expectancy is so high.'

How had the players who were missing out taken the news?

'Morgan was sat on his bed. He said, "Well, it's policy, Nige, fair enough." Scouse was the same. Jonah was upset. I gave him the option of being a sub because I'd like him to play, but he wants to keep out of it.' Nigel paused. 'I'll give him a bit of space.'

After the Anger Management and the Assertiveness courses that Jonah had attended he was primed to express his frustrations and resentments. I was sure he'd given Nigel a mouthful, told him exactly what he thought of his management style in general, but I was only guessing. Nigel, out of loyalty, would say no more about what transpired. It was a private matter between the manager and the player, not a shout-and-tell confrontation of the Hoddle–Gascoigne variety.

Did he think Alex Ferguson would have picked Jonah?

'Yes.' Nigel answered like it was an unfair question. 'The pros are paid to get results and that comes before everything else. If a player doesn't want to be at that club he can go somewhere else. These guys can't. The last two or three days, I have wrestled with it. At one stage I thought, "It doesn't mean as much to me as these blokes." I considered pulling myself out, and playing Jonah in my place. And then I thought, "I've got to be fair to myself. I want to play."

While it might not be on the level of some of the games I've been involved with in the past, it's every bit as important to me. I've had a policy all season and I'm going to stick to it.'

At least, I suggested, everyone knew where they stood.

'I don't make decisions to be character building, but you've got to be consistent,' said Nigel. 'Being fair and honest and doing things with integrity, that's not bullshit. That's the truth. And if you bullshit in here you get found out.'

We walked to the other end of the pitch.

'I just wish Jonah hadn't taken his visit,' he reflected. 'Jonah would have played instead of Teddy last week – I told Ted that. But I can't fault Teddy and Duffy. It's not their fault St Helena only had nine men; 12–0 was a good performance. Although the result was a foregone conclusion, those goals could make all the difference.' The manager wanted to be positive. 'Duffy will be okay on the right. To be honest, that is probably one of two positions where he won't get found out too much – because of his tenacity, his fitness and his attitude. He *has* got a brilliant attitude to sport. Duffy was chasing back when we were 11–0 up last week. Things like that get noticed. Bunny stopped running as if to say, "Let 'em have a goal, what does it matter?" Duffy was giving his all. He's taking nothing for granted.'

Paddy shook hands with the George and Dragon captain. Waiting for the kick-off, the visiting players did stretches, shook hands and pumped themselves up. They looked big, strong and together. All of a sudden Kingston's 3–4–3 formation seemed much too cavalier for comfort. Scrotal Bill agreed. We were apprehensive.

The visitors put Kingston under pressure from the start, competing for everything. Paddy, Carl and Rizler were clamped by a well-organised marking operation, and Raph and Calvin given no time in the middle.

On fifteen minutes Raph attempted to pass to Calvin, standing in the centre circle. The ball was intercepted and played forward quickly. A deep cross swung towards a striker arriving on the penalty spot. Zebedee braced himself for the volley, but could not have expected what happened next. The forward sliced his shot. The ball looped upwards, over Zebedee's outstretched arms, and into the net.

Almost from the restart, Paddy went close, crashing a shot against the goalkeeper. Wayne might also have pulled it level, scuffing a shot at the far post. Paddy and Carl then exchanged passes, but the finish was again wayward.

By half-time, Kingston appeared to be pinned down and out of ideas. Nigel stressed the need to make better use of goal-kicks, but he seemed pensive, talking while trying to figure out a way back into the contest. There was a lot of chatter. Zebedee wanted to explain the goal. Duffy was asking whether he could leave the man he was marking.

'Come on,' said Teddy. 'Let's listen up to what Nige is saying.' He clapped his hands. 'Listen up!'

'Okay,' said Nigel. 'Charlie [the visitors' player-manager] is winning a lot of ball which, really, he's got no right to win. So Calvin, you gamble, push on, and Raph can sit in. Calvin, you've got to get up and win that ball.'

Calvin looked sceptical. 'What happens if I don't get it?'

'It's okay. Wayne's free a lot of the time, so he can cover you. Right, Duffy, if the ball's free, you can move off your guy. No one's going to slate you. Use your initiative. Riz, you made a flying start, but it's all petered out. I know it's hard to keep it going, but that's what I want from you.'

'I think we're a bit tentative,' said Paddy.

'Yeah,' added Raph. 'We're allowing them to have a lot of the play.'

Nigel nodded. 'Look, we've had our chances. The main thing is we're creating things. Come on, heads up, we can win this.'

Two minutes after the restart, disaster. Another deep, swinging cross was smacked home by one of the George and Dragon strikers. At 2–0 down, Kingston needed something quickly.

Scouse grew hoarse, shouting as his team mates struggled.

'Come on boys!'

'Win the ball, Raph!'

'Well in!'

'*Come on*!'

Scouse got a message to Nigel, asking about a substitution. Word came back that another central defender was just about the last thing Kingston needed.

'You've done fuckin' nothing for me!' yelled Scouse.

There was too much going on for anyone to take an interest in his outburst.

In the sixty-seventh minute Calvin won a huge tackle just past the half-way line and played the ball into the path of Carl. Holding off a defender, and facing the onrushing goalkeeper, Carl slipped the ball into the left-hand corner. Beautiful.

But they were still 2–1 down.

The George and Dragon were content to defend in numbers. They kept working hard, closing down the play, and it appeared hopeless until, with five minutes to go, Kingston won a corner.

Rizler played it to the edge of the box.

Duffy was unmarked.

'Leave it,' screamed Raph.

Duffy stepped aside.

Raph stopped the ball, looked up, then drove it through the crowded box.

At 2–2, there was no time for celebrations, they just wanted to restart. Around the touchline some fifty cons willed Kingston forward for one last effort, pinning their hopes on a burst of speed from Carl or Paddy, some Riz trickery, or maybe a touch of Raph's skill. But the George and Dragon stood firm and the referee blew the whistle. It was over. At the Railway End, Paddy and Calvin slumped to the turf, utterly deflated, reluctant to go back inside just yet.

'They're a good defensive unit,' sighed Paddy, who had endured a long, frustrating afternoon. 'You've got to pull them about a bit, play the quick one-twos. We never did that. It wasn't that bad a performance. The fuck-ups where we've dropped points will cost us now.'

In the crowded gym office, the air was thick with disappointment. Nigel had started the season with no real expectation of success, but by December he knew he had a team on his hands, and the run of nine unbeaten games, laden with goals, had offered real hope of a title. His frustration came out with a rant about the refereee and a heated exchange with Terry Allison, which began when the league official said Kingston had been played off the park.

'I tell you what,' Nigel spat back, 'we had the best chances to win the game. Paddy had a couple of one-on-ones. Wayne missed when he got into the area. Rizler was in there. You can have all the possession you want. It's about creating chances and scoring goals. At the end of the day we had the better chances.'

They knocked it backwards and forwards over ten forlorn minutes. Terry, a gentle man, came off worse. As we walked towards the prison gates, he said, 'Nigel's like my son – you can't tell him anything.'

Zebedee, walking a little further on, knew all about the Scouse incident. 'He come behind my goal with about twenty minutes to go and said Nigel was a cunt and that. I said, "What's getting under your skin now?" He said, "Ah, fuck Nigel. He's just a wanker." Earlier in the season, when Scouse didn't think he would ever get a game, and Nigel put him in, Nigel was the best thing since sliced bread. But now because Nigel wouldn't put him in today, he's the biggest cunt under the sun.'

Nigel stood by the gate. It had been a long day. 'What does Scouse expect – a written guarantee? He was playing to the crowd. Jonah, I'll give him his due, he had his nose put out of joint today, and he didn't go to no one. He told me straight how he felt. He handled it like a man. Different kettle of fish.' His face was clouded with disbelief. 'Scouse even chucked his boots down there on the astro turf.'

Nigel blew out hard. A championship contender no more.

29

SORTING OUT TIME

The playing season was drawing to a close, but at least England were going to the World Cup. Their opening group games against Tunisia, Romania and Columbia appeared negotiable. From that point on, France '98 looked uphill all the way. Bunny, who was supporting Jamaica, drew satisfaction from calculating the nightmare draw for England: the team required to overcome Argentina and Holland in order to face Brazil in the semi-final, an achievement which would equal the best performance of any England side on foreign soil. The alternative route – Croatia in the second round, Germany in the quarter-final and the hosts in the last four – appeared a little less daunting.

'They got no chance,' said Bunny, grinning.

Morgan remembered watching England and Argentina's last meeting in the World Cup – the quarter-finals of the 1986 Mexico tournament. Both countries qualified for the 1982 finals in Spain but were kept apart by the draw, which was just as well given that 242 British soldiers, most of them shipped out of Portsmouth, and more than 700 Argentines had been killed a matter of weeks before, fighting over the Falkland Islands. Morgan's brother, a sailor, was involved, his colleagues on the submarine HMS *Conqueror* sinking the cruiser *General Belgrano*. Presumably that made it 7–0 to

'Our Boys', the *News of the World* having printed a scorecard the previous day reading: 'Britain 6 (three warplanes, two airstrips, and South Georgia), Argentina 0'.

Four years later, at Italia '90, England faced another old enemy, West Germany, this time in the semi-final. It was one of those epic games; everyone remembered where they watched it.

Wednesday, 4 July 1990

England grinds to a halt as the country is allowed home early to cheer on Bobby Robson's battling team in the World Cup semi-final. The journey to the last four of Italia '90 has seen England cope with the premature loss of their captain, Bryan Robson, fail once again to get the best out of John Barnes, make tactical U-turns, and twice survive being taken to extra-time. So much for the rollercoaster, now it is sorting out time. They face West Germany, the powerful and ominously rhythmic tournament favourites, described by Bobby Robson as 'good enough to take the game to any opponent'.

Paddy leaves work at four p.m. On his way home he wonders how England will cope. Des Walker, a battered leg, and Mark Wright, a gashed eye, are carrying injuries. They face the quicksilver Jurgen Klinsmann and the master poacher, Rudi Völler. Then there is the relentless drive of the captain, Lothar Matthaus, the player of the tournament. England's best hope? Probably Gary Lineker and Paul Gascoigne.

One hour before kick-off the World Cup chief, Luca di Montezemolo, arrives in the half-empty England dressing room at the Stadio delle Alpi, Turin. He is accompanied by the president of Juventus, Giovanni Agnelli. Gascoigne appears. He makes Bobby Robson laugh by saying to Agnelli, one of the world's richest men, 'Hello mate, how are you?'

Gascoigne puts his thumbs up as he says it. Agnelli, accustomed to people bowing and scraping, is delighted.

Later, Gascoigne is taken to one side by his manager. 'If you play like you did in the first hour against Cameroon we will be in trouble,' cautions Robson. 'If you disappear, Matthaus will come through the gap like a cobra and put us out of the World Cup.'

Gascoigne is unfazed. 'Boss, leave him to me.'

Paddy leaves home, heading for the best place he knows to watch the game, a pub managed by a friend. Not only is the venue lucky – he watched the Belgium second-phase match and the Cameroon quarter-final there – but the facilities are well-planned. The rectangular room is separate from the main pub. A wooden floor means nobody has to worry too much about spilling beer, and the screen is high up on the wall at one end so everyone can see.

And it is a stunning opening thirty-five minutes. England surge forward, playing the Germans at their own game, the axis of Beardsley, Gascoigne and Waddle opening up the favourites, who fear Lineker and the hard-running Platt. Wright, with seven stitches in a head wound, commands Klinsmann, while Stuart Pearce shows Brehme there is more than one decent left-back in Europe. The Germans force their way back into the contest before the interval. Both teams leave the field to a thunderous ovation.

Early in the second half Brehme strikes a free-kick from outside the box. Paul Parker charges down the shot, there is a huge deflection, and Paddy watches in disbelief as Peter Shilton, caught off his line, cannot back-pedal fast enough before the ball squeezes under the crossbar. The Germans lead 1–0.

So tight is the contest, no one can look away. The Germans are shading it when, with ten minutes remaining, Köhler, Augenthaler and Berthold make a mess of clearing a

Parker cross. In full flow, Lineker takes it on his thigh, wriggles past them and fires the ball beyond Illgner.

Extra-time, and the Germans are everywhere. Klinsmann is denied by a magnificent Walker tackle. In the next attack only Shilton can stop him. And when he gets through again, Klinsmann shoots wide.

Gascoigne slides for the ball, misses, and catches Berthold, who makes a meal of it. The German bench are up in protest. England's finest is in trouble. A yellow card.

'That'll mean he'll miss the final if we get through,' says someone in the pub.

In the clear, the goal mouth beckoning, Waddle slams a shot against the inside of the German post. Platt scores from a free-kick, but it is disallowed, offside. Shilton keeps out Thon. Buchwald shudders the woodwork. Whoever loses will know that they were taken to the limit, that the teams gave everything they had.

The final whistle. Gazza is in tears. In the pub everyone hears the injured England captain Bryan Robson, watching the game in a TV studio, plead, 'Take the camera off him.'

England pick Lineker and Pearce for what Bobby Robson estimates will be the toughest penalties in the shoot-out, the first and the fourth turns where there is often most pressure.

The contest begins.

Lineker scores. Then Brehme, then Beardsley, Matthaus, Platt and Riedle. Shilton and Illgner have no chance. The scorers drift back towards the half-way line, glad that they have done their duty, that whatever happens, they will not be the villains of the piece.

The fourth penalty. Everyone expects Pearce to score. Illgner saves with his feet. Thon makes it 4–3. Waddle must score. The waiting is unbearable. He runs up and sky rockets the ball over the bar. History is written. England are out.

Matthaus, the victorious captain, delays his own celebrations to console the vanquished. And the party breaks up in the pub, the realisation sinking in that England's best efforts were not enough, but also that it was a performance of strength and verve, something to be proud of.

Paddy is too drunk to drive – six pints of beer between 5.30 p.m. and 10.30 p.m. With his friends, he heads for a take-away restaurant. They meet another group, including his sister and some of her friends, also returning from watching the game. Nine of them begin the twenty-minute walk towards the estate where they all live, singing and taking turns to push each other along in a shopping trolley.

Paddy gets carried away. He pushes the shopping trolley into a gate, then grabs hold of a wooden fence. He shakes it backwards and forwards. On a street corner two local men are upset by the disturbance. One of them shouts out something about breaking the fence.

An argument begins. Everyone is talking at once. Shouting, pointing, threatening.

One of the men is saying, 'What do you think you're doing?' The other says almost nothing, watching and listening.

The air is charged with potential violence. Everyone knows there is going to be a fight. The more voluble of the two men takes his jacket off. The quiet man slaps Paddy's sister across her face.

Later, Paddy thinks the victim, outnumbered eight to two, panicked. But at the time, Paddy is in a punching rage.

The quiet man goes down.

Paddy goes for his head. Maybe five times.

Muscles whipping and bunching.

Kick, kick, kick.

Stamp, stamp.

A police car pulls up. Paddy is taken away. The charge is suspicion of causing grievous bodily harm.

Sometime after midnight the quiet man dies. The police say he suffered a brain haemorrhage, caused by a sharp, twisting movement, the rotation of his head on the neck causing a small tear, which bled into the brain.

At four a.m. Paddy is charged with murder.

Much later, Paddy is advised by his barrister to plead not guilty in the hope that the charge can be reduced to manslaughter. The prosecution portrays Paddy as a football hooligan, a rabid dog, part of an angry mob out looking for trouble. Paddy says that's just not the truth. Yes, he did hit the man, but not because of football. It was a fight. An ordinary fight. But he sits in the dock, doomed, knowing he is going to be found guilty. He thinks the proceedings are not so much a matter of finding out what actually happened but a case of there being two stories, the defence and prosecution, of which one is going to be believed. The truth, Paddy tells himself, is probably a combination of the two. But the harsher truth, that the victim was no real threat to him or his sister, sank in long before he faced the jury. And that feels worse than anything.

A week or so after the George and Dragon return, Nigel and Terry patched up their differences. Nothing of substance was said. They merely made the effort to be sociable, to ignore their disagreement. What friendship they had recovered.

Jonah stayed away from the squad. Scouse kept a low profile.

In the final two matches Kingston swept aside H&S Aviation 5–1, and Rimor 3–0.

A good football team, competitive in all areas of the pitch, the Kingston Arrows had made great progress since the start of the season. But not enough: Southern Co-op Dairies were

to win the championship, on goal difference, having finished
level on points with the George and Dragon and Plover. The
champions received a trophy and the runners-up consolation
medals.

There were to be no team photographs of the Kingston
Arrows, 1997–98, to hang on the wall in the gym office, a
reminder of the players who, by and large, gave a good
account of themselves.

With twenty-nine goals, Paddy finished as the Portsmouth
North End League's leading scorer, ahead of Jim Pegg of
Magpie (20) and Colin Pack of Southern Co-op Dairies (18).

Nigel was pleased for the winners, 'the best footballing
side that come in here this season'.

Kingston would have been champions on goal difference
had they turned just one of their five drawn games into a win.
As it was, the final table stood like this:

	P	W	D	L	F	A	PTS
So. Co-op Dairies	16	10	4	2	60	30	34
Plover	16	11	1	4	59	36	34
George and Dragon	16	11	1	4	46	26	34
Kingston Arrows	16	9	5	2	70	35	32
Grant Thornton	16	6	3	7	48	43	21
Magpie	16	5	2	9	52	64	17
H&S Aviation	16	5	1	10	42	51	16
Rimor	16	5	1	10	40	57	16
St Helena	16	1	0	15	17	92	3

Court House record expunged

POSTSCRIPT

In April 1999 the Criminal Cases Review Commission sent the case of the M25 Three back to the Court of Appeal in London. The case was expected to be heard in Autumn of 1999.

James Nichol, solicitor for Rowe, provided the CCRC with documents which he said showed that the main prosecution witness, Norman Duncan, who was originally a suspect, had been paid £10,000 by a national newspaper, and £300 by the Surrey Police. 'This information was withheld from the defence in 1990, and again by the Court of Appeal in 1993,' explained Nichol.

By the time jubilant campaigners heard this news, the European Commission of Human Rights had already ruled that the M25 Three did not get a fair trial and referred the case to the European Court of Human Rights. On hearing that the case was finally going back to the Court of Appeal, Raph's mother, Rosemary, told David Taylor, of the *Daily Express*, 'He rang me this morning and just said, "Mum, we've got it!" I started shaking and went all cold.'

Solicitor Jim Nichol said. 'I confidently expect Raphael Rowe and the others to be exonerated and their convictions quashed.'

In the summer after the 1997–8 season ended, Carl was

shipped out of Kingston in disgrace, following an incident involving a Roman Catholic priest. The *Daily Telegraph* reported that Father Derek Reeve, sixty-seven, had been banned indefinitely from Kingston prison for taking in prohibited articles. Governor Stuart McLean described the incident as a breach of trust: 'Once someone has been involved in the very serious matter of trafficking, they are vulnerable to blackmail.' No further details were available.

Paddy and Bunny also left the team, progressing to Category C prisons. Calvin took over as captain.

Jonah returned to the side at the start of the following season. He took Nigel's place, as the manager stuck to his decision to hang up his boots. Zebedee also retired; Luke was restored as first-choice goalkeeper. Having often complained that Zebedee was 'uncommitted' when challenging for the ball, Luke was injured in his first game back, damaging his ribs sliding into a striker. So he missed the start of the new campaign. Grant Thornton, as usual, secured the points, a late winner making it 4–3.

Duffy, Eddie, Mick, Morgan, Ian, Rizler, Scouse, Shaggy, Teddy and Wayne got on with serving their time.

When we last spoke, Nigel mentioned that Geordie had been coming into the prison on his weekends off. Just to watch the football. 'It stops being a job after a while, and gets under your skin,' said the manager.

Making Peace
HEALING A VIOLENT WORLD

Edited by Carolyn McConnell
and Sarah Ruth van Gelder

from *YES! A Journal of Positive Futures*

Positive Futures Network

is an independent, nonprofit organization
that supports people's active engagement in creating a more just, sustainable,
and compassionate world.

Darkness cannot drive out darkness;
        only light can do that. Hate cannot
drive out hate; only love can do that.

Reverend Martin Luther King, Jr.

Contents

Introduction

Sarah Ruth van Gelder

Making peace happens so often in so many ways, we barely notice it. Rarely do you find it on television or in the newspaper. It happens when a mother tucks her children into bed for the night, when a teacher helps young people to put their emotions into words, or a neighbor seeks out a neighbor to talk through a disagreement. Making peace is so common that it is nearly invisible.

What does make headlines is violence. It is not surprising that this is so. Violence is shocking, and people want to understand it. But with so much violence on television, in movies, and in video games, many of us succumb to what communications scholar George Gerbner calls "the mean world syndrome." This syndrome results from being bombarded with stories about selfishness, violence, and dishonesty. Our fears and distrust grow stronger while our esteem for others weakens, and the world seems predominantly a mean and violent place.

The mean world syndrome is, of course, self-fulfilling. The meaner the world, the more you have to keep yourself and your family protected from it, and the less you'll get to know neighbors, especially those who look, talk, or act differently than you. The more you fear violence, the more attention you focus on defending yourself or even taking pre-emptive action.

This mean world syndrome extends to our perception of places like the Middle East. We learn much about war-hardened fighters, but little of ordinary people and their hopes and dreams. We hear of terrorists hiding

in caves, but not of the Afghan civilians hurt or killed in the war. When we discuss the bombing of Iraq, we picture the face of Saddam Hussein, not the children who lack the means to get out of harm's way.

The attack of September 11 strengthened the mean world syndrome. It made our massive expenditures on weaponry and standing armed forces seem necessary. Risking nuclear war, doing whatever it takes to subdue "evil" nations or people appears rational when we are overwhelmed with fear. A massive, space-based weapons systems seems like a good idea in such an angry world. And we even stand silently by as we lose the crown jewels of democracy, our civil liberties, so the government can seek out the "enemies" among us.

Like many people, we at *YES!* magazine and the Positive Futures Network have been struggling with how to respond to these times of fear and violence. This book contains articles from back issues of *YES!* suggesting creative and compassionate alternatives. Making peace is far too important to be left to political leaders. These articles come from a prison inmate; Buddhist, Christian, and Muslim scholars; a diplomat; a seasoned activist; a farmer. Here you'll find news of peace breaking out in Sri Lanka, why ethnic violence *didn't* take off in Macedonia, the Americans who broke the embargo to bring life-saving water purification equipment to Iraq, and other stories of courageous people making peace. It is also a collection of visionary ideas about the nature of this moment in the evolution of human society—ways the United States can move beyond acting as the world's empire, ways to express our longings for peace and make those longings into a practical reality.

Holding out for peace is not naïve. There are real reasons to be fearful. The stories in this volume show, however, that the arts and sciences of peacemaking already exist and are available to be used and developed. They have the audacity to suggest that, not only can we make the world a bit less mean, we can actually create a world that looks to peace making, not violence, as the way to a future.

Sarah Ruth van Gelder
YES! Magazine, Executive Editor
Bainbridge Island, Washington
December 2002

Compassion:
The Radicalism of this Age

Michael Nagler

Nonviolence is not meant to be a tidy compartment, the habit of an occasional activist, a musing on the margins of "the real world." Nonviolence is and must become a science, a way of life, a worldview finally, a culture.

Because nonviolence in this larger sense has received so little systematic study, and precisely because it is so universal, one tends to find the events and people who make up its as-yet untold narrative tucked away in apparently unrelated corners. As with anything this new (and this enormous), you must somehow run across these events and people and hold their story together with the glue of your own insight. This is what I will try to illustrate, weaving the emotional and intellectual dimensions of the nonviolence story from some seemingly unrelated leads.

The German occupation of Denmark was an uneasy business. The underground was well organized, bold, and extremely vexatious to the occupation with their occasional executions of collaborators. Among other things, the Danes did not at all like the Nazi plan for their Jewish population. That plan edged to its climax one fall day in 1943, when a fleet of German ships stood by in Copenhagen harbor to take the Danish Jews away. Their time had come—or so it seemed.

What the Germans did not know was that someone had tipped off the underground. During the night, 7,200 people—virtually the entire Jewish-Danish population—were smuggled out under the noses of the waiting ships to make for safety in neutral Sweden. The motley flotilla, made up of fishing vessels and everything scroungable, pitched and tossed in the rough sea, but it made Sweden with its huddled, seasick cargo by morning.

Then it suddenly looked as if all had been in vain; the king of Sweden wanted to grant asylum to the Jews, but he was frightened of the Nazi presence. Perhaps he feared jeopardizing Sweden's neutrality.

As it happened, however, a famous Danish physicist was just then hiding out in Uppsala. When he heard about the dilemma, he calmly sent word to the king that if the Jews were not given asylum he would turn himself in to the Nazis. The famous physicist was Niels Bohr, and the king immediately accepted the refugees.

I am drawn to this story about Bohr because I sense a connection between his science and his courage. Bohr was the genius behind the "Copenhagen Interpretation" of quantum physics, the interpretation that even Einstein could not accept, namely that the new physical results were telling us something of the nature of reality, and that reality is surpassingly strange. There are suggestive, intriguing parallels between the universe of the new physics and the universe of the timeless mystics. The deep sense of interconnectedness and privileging of consciousness over matter supports—indirectly—the worldview of the nonviolent.

In contrast, the universe opened up by Newton's world of "solid, massy, hard, impenetrable, movable Particles" exhibits depressing and somehow inevitable parallels to the world of violence against nature and creature that we are now struggling to escape. That world of material mechanics, which still holds sway over most minds and is the official science 'story' of the mass media, is a world of scarcity (because matter is finite, because it has a limited capacity to fulfill us). It spawns violence by telling us that we are separate: "I can hurt you without hurting the larger whole that includes myself—and since there isn't enough for both of us, we have a reason to fight each other."

The painting *An Experiment with a Bird in an Air Pump* captures beautifully the central contradiction of the world in which it was created. It was done by Joseph Wright of Derby in 1768, near the beginning of the industrial age, at a time of a decisive break with the West's millennia-old tradition of human connection with the Earth.

The man facing the viewer is a travelling science lecturer, and he is demonstrating a vacuum pump to his rapt onlookers. He is pumping the air out of a glass cage, and to make that visible, there is a bird inside the cage. By watching the bird gasp for breath, in other words, you could see that there's no more air in the cage and be impressed with what technology can do.

But what other impression are we, the painting's audience, to receive? Where is the real dramatic interest in the picture; what takes and holds our eyes? It's the children. They do not follow the explanation of the pump and the air; they see a man killing a little bird. The real story of the painting is in the contrast between the scientist holding the audience spellbound and the distress of the children—and the fact that they are 'just children' and that the adults ignore them. When we hurt nature, it is not that we lack warnings. Not everyone loses sensitivity all at once. The real tragedy is when we ignore those who—like the children in Wright's painting—are aware of what we're doing with their hearts.

We now stand at the other end of the arc that began when Wright painted his high priest of technology demonstrating the vacuum pump and the rights of man over nature. Technology—technologism, shall we say—rose in triumph, and now at least some of us stand aghast at the results. What we have done to the environment could not have been imagined in 1768, or 1968. We desperately need to look at life with the sensitivity of children and protect it with the sophistication of very well informed adults.

Science has for almost 100 years now bolted from Newton's world of "primitive particles." The physics that came from the astounding breakthroughs of Einstein, Heisenberg, and Bohr views things not as matter at all, but energy-changes, fundamentally involving consciousness. Nothing and no one is separate from "us"; all are co-involved with our being.

I wish that we were closer to understanding how this view of interconnection, which ties back so unexpectedly to the earliest myths of our culture, is to be aligned with the ethic of interconnection behind nonviolence and ecology. We cannot follow that intuition with our rational minds as yet—but I feel that it is there, that Bohr the scientist cannot be separated from Bohr the human being who refused to be safe while his people were in danger.

Here is perhaps a trace of that connection. Just before his flight to Sweden, in the summer of 1938, Bohr addressed an international gathering of physicists in Copenhagen. The "grandfather of quantum theory" was best known to the general public for his famous doctrine of "complementarity." This doctrine holds that there is a built-in limit to human understanding of the outside world such that to describe anything "out there" completely we always need at least two mutually exclusive models. A common example is that a photon of light or any other quantum entity is neither particle nor

wave, but will appear as either depending on how we look at it. On the occasion of this distinguished international gathering, he applied his famous idea to things a bit bigger than the electron:

"We may truly say that different human cultures are complementary to each other. Indeed, each such culture represents a harmonious balance of traditional conventions by means of which latent possibilities of human life can unfold themselves in a way which reveals to us new aspects of its unlimited richness and variety."

At this shocking suggestion, the German delegation walked out. They were, after all, Nazis first, and "scientists" second. This was a worldview utterly inimical to Nazi values, a challenge to their whole doctrine of intolerance. That human differences are part of a natural scheme to be cherished, that every race and community and even every individual has his or her role in the scheme of things, and that we need one another if any of us is to be fulfilled as a whole family—all this is gall and wormwood to fascists. If you believe that every sentient being has its own invaluable meaning and purpose, you cannot be a fascist.

The Nazi attempt on Europe implied several unsavory things that go along with the will to use brute force to get what you want. The first is its image of the human being. Hitler was blunt about this. Explaining his success over lunch one day to William Shirer (one of the few people who knew both Hitler and Gandhi first hand) he said, "You know, every man has his price—and you'd be surprised in most cases how low that price is."

Violence is keyed to the lowest image of the human being, nonviolence to the most exalted. Violence drives us apart; nonviolence appeals directly to the mysterious unity among all of us, which is the hidden glory of each of us.

Bohr's Nazi-scattering words were ahead of his time in 1938. He saw that the fascist worldview rested on a concept of order that might be called "disunity through uniformity." They held that only one race, political order—really only one person—was valued, real, clean, while everyone and everything else was inferior and threatening, to be dominated or eliminated if not subordinated to the One Right Way.

A direct antidote to fascism, therefore, was the idea that Hegel had called unity in diversity. Note Bohr's expression, "the latent possibilities of human life can unfold themselves." This was to be echoed by a fellow Northman, Johan Galtung, some years later as a now-famous definition of nonviolence:

"the fulfillment of the latent potential of each individual," while violence is any "avoidable compromise of human needs" which inhibits that fulfillment.

In this spirit, the Dalai Lama, speaking from the margins of the UN Non-governmental Organizations Human Rights Convention in 1993, said, "If we are prevented from using our creative potential, we are deprived of one of the basic characteristics of a human being." And he added, "It is very often the most gifted, dedicated, and creative members of our society who become victims of human rights abuses. Thus the political, social, cultural, and economic developments of a society are obstructed by the violations of human rights."

I am trying to draw a connection between a feeling and a concept, between compassion—which is really the deep wellspring of spiritual awareness that has held the family, society, and the planet together since the beginning of time—and the concept that all life has to be accepted in its diversity. I am trying to trace out the legitimate extension of biodiversity, which we understand, to cultural and individual diversity, which we do not. I am trying to do this because this two-sided and apparently contradictory concept—unity in diversity—goes hand-in-glove with nonviolence. If you will, it is the theology of compassion.

"The more clearly one studies the character of individual human souls, the more baffled one becomes over the great differences between personalities. ... It is, however, precisely through their differentiations that they are all united toward one objective, to contribute toward the perfection of the world, each person according to his special talent," says Rabbi Abraham Isaac Kook.

The human family is growing past six billion individuals. Each of them is invaluable. That foundational, civilizing insight is growing dimmer today; the reinstatement of the death penalty, the countenancing of grotesque human rights violations, even the decline of the family and the support systems that nurture a child—these are all ways we are compromising the sanctity of individual life because we evidently see no choice but to keep redeploying various forms of violence.

For Gandhi, as for every nonviolence advocate from all time, it has been axiomatic that life is sacred, i.e. invaluable; and while the sum total of all life is in a way more precious than that of a given individual, in a way it is not: infinity = infinity. As Augustine said, "because all things are not made equal, they have a goodness [above and beyond their individuality]; each is good, and all together are very good."

As a traditional Hindu, Gandhi had a solid metaphysical basis for this, and he liked to quote a traditional proverb: "As with the fragment, so with the universe." Otherwise put, the macrocosm is in the microcosm. Everything that exists "out there," exists "in here," as philosophers say, *in potentia*. Quantum physicists, mystics, the world's faith traditions, and a lurking suspicion in all of us in our more reflective moments keep returning to this vision again and again.

But this belief is much more than an injunction against killing: its real value lies in the entirely positive reason for that injunction—namely that within the microcosm that is each one of us are the seeds of the whole world order. Just as we build our bodies on a ridiculously small fraction of our DNA (and use a similarly ridiculous fraction of our brain), somehow, in the depths of our consciousness, each of us contains enough 'information'—faith, insight—to regenerate a world.

Today, as the world is torn at by ethnic and pseudo-ethnic hatreds, it seems necessary to go over these truths, however obvious they may sound. It is obvious that people caught up in such ferocious hatreds as are found in what was once Yugoslavia cannot remotely remember that they might share an underlying unity with those they hate. They see only differences, which then take on monstrous proportions and finally bring about the belief that those "others" aren't human. Today it is terrorists, yesterday communists who were beyond the pale of rights and the "discourse of reason." Who knows who it may be next.

Early in May of 1998, several members of the Iraq Sanctions Challenge stood at the bedside of Mustafa, one of at least a dozen dying children in a crowded ward of the main hospital in Basra, Iraq's southern port city. My friend Kathy Kelly was on that mission. She writes:

"His mother, tall, thin, and quite beautiful, sat cross legged on the mattress beside him, waving away flies, as the doctor explained to us that the child, hospitalized for the past 20 days, now suffered from dehydration, diarrhea, acute renal failure, and extensive brain atrophy. Lacking equipment and medicine to diagnose and treat Mustafa, the doctors could only stand by, helpless and frustrated, while the child's condition worsened over three weeks' time. If Mustafa survives, he will be severely crippled.

"Ima Nouri, his mother, is 35 years old. Her serious eyes followed us as we paused before each bedside. She seemed surprised when we asked her to tell us about herself. We learned that she lives in a rural area north of Basra and has two children at home whom she misses very much.

"We mentioned that people in the United States were celebrating Mother's Day on this day and asked if she had a message for mothers in our country.

"Ima suddenly became animated. 'Yes,' she said, 'I have two messages. First, tell them from Iraqi women that these are our children and we love them so much.' Stroking Mustafa's face, she continued, 'Ask them to please try to help us protect them and take care of them. And, for American women, I want them to feel what I am feeling.'"

The word compassion means literally suffering with others, feeling what they are feeling. Of course it hurts, but isn't it better to suffer with others and expand, than to wall off our humanity from them and die within?

In Hebrew, the word for compassion is the plural of the word "womb." To have compassion is to be towards someone a little bit like every mother is to her own child.

Nonviolence is a way to restore the capacity to, as a student of mine said recently, "humanize your enemy and let your 'enemy' humanize you." You can do this in action, where often the fact that you are being nonviolent—i.e. responding with courage and respect under duress—raises your image in the opponents' eyes. Or we can all do it culturally, by raising the 'background' sense of humanity that surrounds all conflicts and all relationships.

The kind of hate we see in the Mideast, in Serbia, in Rwanda, Cambodia, and so many arenas would not arise so easily if the worldview in which all these arenas are situated were more human-centered and humanizing. There would still be problems like water rights and social advantages; but they would be just that—problems to solve, not people to fear and hate.

We need mind and heart together to get over this. "Compassion," says the Dalai Lama, "is the radicalism of this age." And I would add, nonviolence is its science.

Michael Nagler is professor emeritus of classics and comparative literature at the University of California, Berkeley, and co-founder of its Peace and Conflict Studies Program. He is the author of *Is There No Other Way? The Search for a Nonviolent Future* (Berkeley Hills Books, 2001), which won an American Book Award and from which this article was adapted. This article appeared in the Fall 1998 issue of *YES!*

Keeping the Peace

Eran Fraenkel & John Marks

In the spring of 1999, for a few brief months, the world focused on Macedonia. Thousands of international journalists poured into this tiny, ethnically divided country, because of events that spilled over from neighboring Kosovo.

The story was Kosovar refugees, 350,000 of them, fleeing violent ethnic cleansing. Reporters had little interest in Macedonia, a country that, despite many of the same problems as its neighbors, remained relatively calm.

But in the long run, for all our sakes, the story of Macedonia and how it avoided violence is the story that must be told.

Macedonia suffers from many of the same ethnic, social, and political problems as other war-torn Balkan nations. With a population of only 2.2 million, the country is divided into ethnic Macedonians (66 percent), Albanians (23 percent), Turks (4 percent), Roma, or Gypsies (under 2 percent), Serbs (under 2 percent), and Vlachs (under 2 percent). Few people in these segregated communities interact with members of other groups. Schools, the media, and everyday life are defined by one's ethno-linguistic group.

How, given this enormous potential for ethnic conflict, has Macedonia avoided all but sporadic violence? For a country to deal successfully with its differences, it must establish a system in which negotiated settlements predominate and disputing parties recognize that their interests are better served through collaboration than through violence. Ultimately, the idea is to transform an adversarial culture into a culture of peace.

In Macedonia, both the international community and the Macedonians themselves have made some progress in establishing such a system. Though

more could have been done, preventive measures have included a full range of official and unofficial initiatives from the diplomatic, economic, social, military, psychological, and conflict-resolution domains.

There have been three key elements of conflict prevention in Macedonia.

First was domestic political will. Macedonia is governed by a coalition of two seemingly irreconcilable parties: one ultra-nationalist and Macedonian, the other Albanian. Although this coalition government has done little to resolve the primary grievances, it has managed to avoid provoking violence— a boast that neighboring governments cannot make. It has shown its greatest restraint in response to the horrible violence and destruction in nearby Bosnia and then in Kosovo. Macedonians of all ethnic groups, regardless of their mutual mistrust, recognize that everyone will suffer if their country follows the same path as their neighbors.

Second was international presence. In 1993, 1,000 United Nations soldiers, including an American battalion, began patrolling Macedonia's borders with Kosovo and Albania. These blue-helmeted troops had no real military role, but their presence indicated a commitment from the international community and helped keep things calm.

Then in 1999, a new Macedonian government recognized Taiwan in return for promises of a billion dollars in aid. Beijing reacted by vetoing a UN Security Council resolution to continue the presence of UN forces. The UN troops left, and were immediately replaced by NATO soldiers who used the country as a base for peacekeeping efforts in Kosovo. Once the air war began, many ethnic Macedonians, who have close family and other ties with Serbia, felt powerless and abused. Adding economic insult to political injury, the NATO powers wrecked the economy by imposing a trade embargo on Serbia, Macedonia's principal trading partner. Though the US and the European Union promised massive amounts of compensating aid, little has yet been provided. Resentment runs high, but there is little Macedonia can do about it.

Third was NGOs. Western nongovernmental organizations (NGOs) have provided a wide array of technical, humanitarian, and development assistance, and this is where our organization fits into the story.

We at the Search for Common Ground specialize in conflict prevention and resolution. With funding from the Swiss, US, Dutch, and British governments and UNESCO, we work to strengthen Macedonia's immune system against potential violence. Our basic strategy, as articulated at one of

our workshops by Andrew Masondo, a South African military leader, is "Understand the differences; act on the commonalities."

Although the tools of conflict prevention can be applied unilaterally by NGOs, international organizations, and governments, our experience shows that prevention is most effective when all work in concert. Some mechanisms for conflict prevention—for example, those that include benign involvement in a country's internal affairs or result in back-channel talks—are often best left to NGOs. At the same time, only governments can make peace. We are also convinced that applying several tools at the same time increases their overall effectiveness.

In Macedonia, each ethnic group has its own media in its own language. As a result, communities live in virtual information ghettos. Since 1994, we have worked to close this ethno-linguistic chasm. We organized cross-ethnic team reporting that produced more than 60 newspaper articles published simultaneously in the Macedonian, Albanian, Turkish, and Roma press. Our aim is to prevent the media from being used as a tool of social and political fragmentation; instead, it can be a forum in which people of all ethnicities explore their common interests.

We have designed and co-produced four television series, including a documentary series on indigenous traditions of conflict resolution. In 1999, we collaborated with Children's Television Workshop (producer of Sesame Street) on an eight-part series for children ages 7–12. Called *Nashe Maalo* (Our Neighborhood), the series stars Macedonian, Albanian, Turkish, and Roma children who live in a talking apartment building named Karmen. The kids find themselves in conflicts that arise from cultural, gender, and language differences. With Karmen's help, they solve their problems. The series airs on Albanian- and Macedonian-language TV stations, and viewers of all ethnicities and ages have responded with enthusiasm. We also created an accompanying curriculum for use in schools and local communities. *Nashe Maalo* counters the idea contained in most TV fare that disagreement leads inevitably to violence. This is an extraordinarily destructive idea in any country, but particularly in multi-ethnic societies like Macedonia. *Nashe Maalo* aired for a second and third season in 2000 and 2001. We hope it will become a model for programming in other strife-torn countries.

Through these television and newspaper series and a series of training programs for journalists, we have worked closely with nearly every news-

paper and TV station in the country—a relationship made possible by the reservoir of trust built up during our six-year engagement in the country. The strategy paid off when the war in Kosovo threatened Macedonia's delicate ethnic balance. Rather than escalating the conflict, as the press has so often done in other Balkan states, Macedonia's journalists, for the most part, avoided inflammatory reporting.

Indeed, in the middle of the crisis, the Macedonian media participated in our initiative that brought together Macedonians, Albanians from Macedonia, and Kosovar refugees—who are both Albanians and Serbs. This group produced three magazines that were inserted into Macedonian and Albanian daily papers and distributed free of charge throughout the country, to the refugee camps, and eventually into Kosovo. At its height, this project produced nearly 100,000 copies in two languages. Each magazine treated an aspect of the war and its impact on Macedonia from the ethnic Macedonian, Albanian, and Kosovar perspectives. These supplements were regarded by all communities as the one source of non-inflammatory, comprehensive information on the war and its aftermath.

Young children are not born acculturated with the prejudices and stereotypes of their elders, but they easily learn adversarial, exclusionary relationships. In Macedonia, where most schools are segregated by ethnic group and language, we opened three multi-ethnic kindergartens, called Mozaik (mosaic). Each class has four teachers, two Albanians and two Macedonians. All activities are conducted in both languages, and the teachers all speak their own languages. The primary goal of Mozaik is to create an environment in which all languages and cultures—and all children—are valued. Promoting bilingualism is a secondary goal; when it happens, it is not because kids are told they must learn the other language, but simply because they want to talk to each other.

During the first days of the war in Kosovo, most parents in our kindergartens were wary of rising ethnic tensions and kept their children home from school. However, the parents soon relented, despite the social stigma involved in inter-ethnic mixing. While the war was in full swing, we held an evaluation meeting for parents, teachers, and administrators. Not only did they give the kindergartens overwhelming approval, they also went public with a press release that stated: "Mozaik is indispensable for promoting mutual respect and understanding among all people in Macedonia. We urge other parents to join us and to send their children to Mozaik."

Mozaik reaches only a small fraction of Macedonia's children—and only for a year. However, we reach many more children in other ways. We help train Macedonian educators, resulting in conflict resolution programs in about 100 of the country's middle schools. Through conflict resolution games, kids are taught to develop self-respect as a basis for respecting others, to take responsibility for their own actions, and to see another's point of view. Though the games do not concentrate on ethnic issues, the lessons learned are easily applied to ethnic conflict.

Search for Common Ground teaches that relationships between conflicting parties can be improved when the parties work together to identify and address shared problems and to set goals that transcend immediate conflicts. Thus, we sponsor Eko-Patrols in 23 schools with the twin aims of contributing to a cleaner environment and providing a positive experience of inter-ethnic cooperation. Each school adopts a public place, preferably one with historical or cultural significance. Once a week an Eko-Patrol of five kids monitors the site. Once a month, the schools send out bigger, ethnically mixed groups of 30–40 kids to pick up litter. Several times a year, participants from all the schools come together for joint activities.

The kids, aged 12–14, have taken to this project and added their own variations. One group launched a weekly TV show on environmental issues for kids. Another group decided to rate local businesses on environmentally responsible behavior.

Some might argue that little can be done to help resolve seemingly intractable, deeply rooted clashes such as those in the Balkans. But compared to the tremendous loss of life and resources that occurs when prevention fails, the cost of building peace has been small. In Macedonia it has proved possible to prevent ethnic differences from turning deadly.

Since 1994, Dr. Eran Fraenkel has lived in Skopje as director of Search for Common Ground (SFCG) in Macedonia. John Marks is founder and president of SFCG in Washington, DC, and the European Centre for Common Ground in Brussels. They can be reached at jmarks@sfcg.org and sfcg@unet.com.mk or at SFCG, Suite 200, 1601 Connecticut Ave. NW, Washington, DC 20009. This article appeared in the Spring 2000 issue of YES!

Parenting Partnerships

Tera Abelson & Greta Cowan

My work on the book *Family: New Choices, New Voices* began about six years ago as my husband, Mark, and I (Tera) were coming to realize that the romantic aspect of our marriage was over. Though we were ending our marriage, we remained deeply committed to our parenting partnership and friendship. I was struck by the lack of positive role models, especially for divorced parents, and by the power of the institutional model of family. Even our most open-minded friends doubted our ability to harmoniously redesign our family structure. It was as if people were programmed to mistrust partnership inclinations, requiring animosity and alienation between divorcing spouses.

Reading *The Chalice and the Blade* during this time gave language to my observations. In this book, Riane Eisler presents her cultural transformation theory illustrating that the 5,000-year-old "dominator model," based on hierarchy, was preceded by a "partnership model," based on alliance, which thrived for centuries in highly civilized, peaceful, prehistoric cultures. She suggests that we are now in the process of reviving partnership models of social organization. This new language helped me recognize that the resistance to the changes in our family indeed stemmed from dominator programming. I was encouraged by the thought that Mark's and my commitment to family could be part of a global movement toward a partnership world—an active participation in cultural transformation.

The following excerpt is from a photo-essay book that Greta and I are writing. We are collecting stories of inspirational partnership families: partnership marriages, partnership divorces, and parenting partnerships that simply

defy definition. Our hope is that *The Good News About Family* will support creative conflict resolution and innovative family building while serving as an affirmation for those who have already chosen the path of partnership.

Ann and Bill met in a taxicab in 1981. "I was at the bank doing some business for my office," Ann recalls. "I called a Yellow Cab, and Bill was the driver. It was the week the NFL went on strike. It was a Monday."

"It was going to be the last Monday night football game for a while," Bill picks up on the story, "and she started talking about that. ..."

"And he said, 'Why don't you meet me for a drink, and we can watch the last game together?' That was in September. We eloped the following June in Cleveland, where I grew up. We went to an Indians' baseball game for our honeymoon!"

After the celebration, Ann moved into Bill's house in San Francisco. They had been married for about five years when their first child, Danielle, was born in 1986.

"It was the greatest moment of my life, just miraculous!" Bill is emphatic. "And the second greatest moment was when our son, Jesse, was born two years later."

"Bill's the best diaper changer in the world and he loved doing it."

Bill nods in agreement. "I did love it."

"We had waited a long time," Ann says. "I was 35, and he was 42. We had done everything we wanted to do; we had traveled and lived other places. We were ready—so it was really wonderful. We loved being parents. We still do."

When Danielle was five and Jesse was three and a half, Ann initiated a separation from Bill.

"Most people were totally shocked," says Ann. "We were best friends. We did everything together. Maybe we were too close. We didn't have separate lives."

"I think it started to fall apart when we had the kids, because we could never come to an agreement about how to raise them," Bill hypothesizes. "I think we were both insecure about our own abilities to raise children and that insecurity manifested itself in arguments."

Ann shakes her head. "I never felt insecure about having the children or raising them. There were other factors that entered into why I initiated the separation, but I do agree that we could not come to terms about very many things regarding raising the children."

"There is something that Ann hasn't mentioned that's the reason for our divorce." Bill is suddenly solemn. "I was violent with Ann, and I was violent with the kids. I first realized this when Ann was pregnant with Danielle. I was throwing things and pushing her.

"She left me and went to live with my sister for a while. Thank God she had the guts to leave me and make me get some help. If that had never happened, I'd still be the biggest jerk in the world. I went to two separate organizations for about five years. They helped me understand that it was wrong, and I accepted the help. I wasn't trying to say 'No, it's not my fault.' I was open enough to say, 'I need to change. It's not her fault. It's on me.'"

Convinced that Bill was serious about getting help, Ann moved back in just before Danielle was born.

"For a couple of years," she says, "I went to a group for women in abusive relationships and I went to private therapy. Bill and I went to marriage counseling and therapy together. We tried to get it to work."

For about five years they struggled to salvage their marriage but, in 1991, Bill and Ann separated. Ann and the kids left their city life in San Francisco and moved north to Mill Valley. Bill moved about an hour's drive south.

"When Ann finally kicked me out for good, it was the worst day of my life. We were having a tremendous fight, and she told me to leave. She used to tell me that all the time, but finally I said, 'Okay, I'm going.' I realized that I had to. I couldn't live like that anymore. We were screaming at each other day and night.

"I was trying to heal myself, but I was lost. I didn't know how to do anything. ... I didn't know how to raise my kids. ... I didn't know how to be nice to them," Bill says.

The local Children's Protective Services agency allowed Bill to see his children only under direct supervision. However, Bill and Ann could choose friends to supervise instead of CPS personnel.

"I didn't get to see the kids that often," Bill says. "Then, when I was with them, I didn't know how to be with them. But I kept trying. I went to parenting groups; I read books; I tried everything. I realized I didn't know how to discipline the kids. There were no boundaries for me when I was growing up, just a lot of yelling and hitting.

"But eventually things started coming together—all the books I'd read and the groups—and I finally figured out how to set boundaries. I'll never forget the first time.

"It was on Halloween. I was with my friend, Jamie, who was one of the people who supervised my visits with the kids. We went to a shopping center, and before we got out of the car to go trick-or-treating I said, "Okay, kids, here's what we're going to do. ...'"

Bill stops as tears overtake him. Ann gently offers him some tissues. "I'm so glad you got to this." Her voice is calm and reassuring.

Bill picks up the thread of his story and continues, "I said, 'Here are the rules and I want you to follow them. I want you to walk beside me, and don't run. I want you to ask me if you can leave my side. I don't want you touching anything in a store unless you ask me.' Then we got out of the car and went into the shopping center, and they did exactly what I wanted them to do.

"I'll never forget this specific moment: Jesse got so excited that he started to run. He took about one step, stopped, and asked, 'Dad, could I go over there?' I was the happiest person in the world! It was a big turning point in my life.

"I'm still working on setting boundaries, but the violence is under control. I do yell at them sometimes but I'm working on that now and trying not to raise my voice."

After almost two years of Bill having limited contact with Danielle and Jesse, Ann ended the supervised visits.

"I could see that Bill had made some big changes," says Ann. "The biggest thing that motivated me was that he is Dani and Jesse's dad, and it is important that they have both their parents helping them grow up and go out into the world. He's a great dad; he's got a lot of good stuff to give them.

"For a long time after Bill and I were apart, I used to say to myself, 'Well, if it wasn't for Bill's violence, we'd still be together.' After all, we were best friends—we loved each other. But it takes two people to make a marriage and two people to end a marriage. It's amazing to me that people fall in love, get married, choose to have children, get divorced—then hate each other's guts and never speak to each other again. I could never do that in my life. I don't speak negatively about Bill in front of the children. To this day, Bill and I still argue, sometimes we get angry and hang up on one another, but we always come through."

In May of 1993, Bill responded to an intriguing ad in the personals section of the local paper. Carol remembers that the most striking thing about Bill's voice-mail message was the warmth he conveyed when talking about his children. It was this sincerity that motivated her to call him and arrange a first date. Soon after their initial meeting, they were seeing each other on a fairly regular

basis. Within a few weeks, Bill felt close enough to Carol to tell her about his history of violence, the supervised visits, and his determination to heal himself.

Carol appreciated Bill's honesty, was impressed with his commitment to the men's groups, and clearly recognized his ability to evolve. She offered to accompany him on some of his visits with the children and, with her background in psychology, was able to give him helpful feedback. By September of 1993, Bill and Carol were deeply in love and had decided to live together. They found a house in Marin County only 10 minutes away from Ann and the kids.

"I knew that Bill and Carol were in a serious relationship and that they were moving to Marin together," Ann recalls. "The first time I met Carol, I cried through the entire meeting! It wasn't so much about losing Bill. It just made me very sad. It took me a long time to get to know Carol, but now I consider her one of my friends. Bill has somebody to talk to, and I talk to her, too. She's a good mediator and the three of us are a team.

"Carol is a big part of our lives and I don't know what I would do without her. She's also a big part of my children's lives; I call her their "other mother," and I know her whole family—Paul [Carol's former husband], her parents, her children. They are my family now."

Ann adds, "You know, last year we were doing some work on the PTA book fair—it's one of the projects the three of us work on. I was behind the counter working with two other women when Carol walked by. One of the women asked, 'Who's that?' And I said, 'That's Bill's fiancée.'

"She was amazed, 'Fiancée! You're divorced? Everybody thinks you and Bill are married!'

"That's what they thought because we do things together, and I guess we don't speak to each other like some divorced couples do. That's kind of a cute story, isn't it?"

"Carol is a terrific influence," Bill adds. "She's so non-judgmental, and she finds the good in everything. When Ann and I are working something out and need guidance, we usually bring it to Carol. She hasn't let us down yet."

Tera Abelson is a therapist and healer working with the transformation of barriers both personal and cultural. Greta Cowan is a writer, executive coach, corporate facilitator, and faculty member of Columbia Business School. This article appeared in the Fall 1998 issue of *YES!*

The Language of Nonviolence

AN INTERVIEW WITH MARSHALL ROSENBERG

Traveling the globe, Marshall B. Rosenberg teaches Nonviolent Communication to diplomats, educators, corporate managers, parents, military personnel, peace activists, and others in over 20 countries. He has conducted mediation sessions in the Middle East, Sierra Leone, Croatia, and Rwanda. Sarah Ruth van Gelder interviewed Marshall when he was on Bainbridge Island to help mediate a dispute between developers and local activists.

SARAH: What was it that first got you interested in nonviolent communication?

MARSHALL: I got interested in this type of communication through pondering two kinds of smiles. My family was the only Jewish family in our Detroit neighborhood, and I was exposed to a considerable amount of violence. The beatings every day on my way home were not pleasant, of course, but what bothered me most was that the onlookers would smile and enjoy it.

During each day of my childhood, I also saw another kind of smile. My grandmother was totally paralyzed with Lou Gehrig's disease, and my uncle came over to help care for her every day after he finished working. My grandmother was incontinent at that time, so it required cleaning her up. As a boy of eight or nine, I thought it was a horrible job! But I couldn't wait for the uncle to come, because he smiled as though he were getting the greatest pleasure a person could get just by serving my grandmother.

I grew up wondering why it is that some people smile when others are

being beaten and other people smile when they're giving pleasure, even though it may mean doing dirty work.

SARAH: Where did you go to look for the answer to that question?

MARSHALL: I got a doctoral degree in psychology, but I was very dissatisfied with its focus on pathology. The training didn't help me understand very compassionate people like my uncle.

So, for about a year, I studied comparative theology on my own. I saw the commonality that existed in many religions, especially around this word "love." I soon saw that the words "compassion" and "love" were not so much feelings as they were actions. They are a way of serving people with pleasure and getting joy from that service. I think that is part of our nature.

When I say that, people sometimes think I'm rather Pollyanna-ish to talk this way with the enormity of violence in the world. I see an awful lot of violence in my work, but I've become even more convinced that violence is not our nature.

I was in a refugee camp in Sierra Leone, Africa, and there were hundreds of frightened kids just sitting around who had lost their parents. One of the men I worked with went over and told these kids that I liked one of their hymns. Then he called me over as a surprise and said, "These kids have something they want to give you."

Now, I had just seen them a few minutes before—pathetic, frightened, scared. But when he told them that this would be a real gift to me, they started to sing me this hymn, and I couldn't believe the looks of pure joy and happiness on their faces. It's amazing. People, no matter what conditions they're under, can give.

SARAH: How does your approach to communication get people in touch with love and compassion?

MARSHALL: The purpose of the model we use is to enable us to respond compassionately to ourselves and others, and to strengthen our ability to inspire compassion from others.

We call the language that we teach "giraffe language," though its official name is "Nonviolent Communication." I use the image of a giraffe because it's a language of the heart, and a giraffe has the largest heart of any land animal.

Unfortunately for myself, I was taught to speak "jackal language." You see, a jackal is closer to the ground. They get so preoccupied with getting their needs met that they just can't see into the future like the tall giraffe. Jackals

speak in ways that block compassionate communication, because they're motivated by fear, shame, and guilt.

SARAH: Can you talk about jackal language first? I was particularly struck by your idea of how we always have choices in how we act.

MARSHALL: I first got the idea that we always have choices from the psychologist who examined the top Nazi war criminals. What he found was that they were pretty normal, nice people. But I noticed as I was reading through the interviews how often a language was used by these people that denied choice: "should," "one must," "have to."

In Hannah Arendt's book, *Eichmann in Jerusalem*, Eichmann was asked, "Was it difficult for you to send these tens of thousands of people to their death?" And Eichmann answered very candidly, "To tell you the truth, it was easy. Our language made it easy."

His interviewer asked what that language was, and Eichmann said, "My fellow officers and I coined our own name for our language. We called it *amtssprache*—'office talk.'" When asked for examples, Eichmann said, "It's basically a language in which you deny responsibility for your actions. So if anybody says, 'Why did you do it?' you say, 'I had to.' 'Why did you have to?' 'Superiors' orders. Company policy. It's the law.'"

There's no force on Earth that can make us do anything that we don't choose to do, though we may not always like the choices that we're aware of.

SARAH: You've mentioned two other types of language that block compassion—evaluations and demands.

MARSHALL: The Nazis and others who persecute people, in addition to denying responsibility for their actions, evaluate themselves and others through the use of dehumanizing labels, diagnoses, and interpretations. That involves using such words as "kikes," "niggers," or "gooks," etc.

I'm equally concerned about positive diagnoses, by the way. Whether I say you are a nice person or a selfish person, I'm still claiming to know what you are and thereby alienating myself from the truth about you. I believe that diagnosing and interpreting other people disconnects us from their vulnerability and encourages us to punish them.

A third type of jackal language is a demand. As I use the term, demands carry a threat of punitive action if not acted upon. For example, let's say I just asked you to get me some water, and you reply that you are tired and would appreciate it if I asked someone else to get me some water. Then I say, "You're

just lazy. I've done more work than you have today." We would realize that I was making a demand because of my attempt to punish you through shame for not acting in harmony with my desires.

I learned about the self-defeating nature of demands when I was a practicing psychologist. I spent many hours talking with children who weren't doing what their parents were requesting. I learned that the kids were receiving those requests as demands. The children would tell me things like, "I don't feel like studying when my parents threaten to take away my allowance." Or, "Would you feel like taking the garbage out if your parents said that you were lazy and irresponsible?"

SARAH: OK, let's talk about giraffe language. How do you foster compassionate communication?

MARSHALL: We basically ask people to answer the question that we ask all over the world: "How are you?"

Of course, "How are you?" has become ritualized in many cultures, but it's a profoundly important question, because living in harmony with our nature—which I think is compassion—requires being able to stay connected to one another. So, our training involves nakedly and vulnerably revealing at any given moment how you are.

The next step is to talk about what could be done to make life even more wonderful. In my work, I find that if people would just keep their communication focused at that level—"How are you? What would make your life more wonderful?"—this natural compassion flows even when the people have an enormously painful history.

For example, I was asked to work in a village in Nigeria where a quarter of the population had been killed in conflicts between Muslims and Christians that year. I'm in a room with the chiefs of both tribes; my friend had told me earlier there would be at least three people in that room who knew that somebody who killed their child was there with them.

So, what do I do? I try to get people's attention focused on those two areas: "How are you? What would make life more wonderful for you?"

One of the key ingredients is to find out what unmet needs they have. So I asked both sides, "What are your needs?" And a chief from one of the tribes looks at the other and says, "You people are murderers!" And the other side immediately jumps up and says, "You people have been trying to dominate us for years!"

I believe that this analysis implying wrongness creates violence. In a case like this one, I try to hear how the person is behind their talk. I hear the need

that's being expressed, and then I help the other side hear that. Then I keep that flow going back and forth. No matter how they communicate, I translate it into how they are and help each side connect compassionately at that level. Within about two hours, one of the chiefs said, "If we knew how to do this ourselves, we wouldn't have to kill each other."

If I can keep people focused, I have yet to see any conflict that can't be resolved. Now, it's not easy to keep people at that level.

SARAH: Because it's asking people to be vulnerable?

MARSHALL: Well, that's a part of it. Instead of teaching us how to communicate in this vulnerable way, our cultural programming has taught us to imply wrongness in people who behave in ways that you don't like. If you live within such a culture, then yes, it's very scary to be vulnerable.

I get into a lot of settings, especially in businesses, where people are not used to being vulnerable. They're all in a competitive game.

During one session, I got very emotional. Tears came to my eyes. The boss of this organization just looked really disgusted and turned away from me. It was horrible for a few seconds, because I allowed the look on his face to stimulate old jackal programming in me. I thought, "Oh, my God, I've behaved inappropriately. He must think I'm a real mess."

But, when I remembered to direct my attention to how he was feeling and what he was needing, I said to him, "Are you feeling disgusted and needing whoever's running a meeting like this to have his emotions more in control?" At that moment, it wasn't painful for me to be vulnerable, because I was seeing *his* vulnerability.

I really thought I was accurate, but I was surprised with his response, because he said, "No, no. I was just thinking of how my wife wishes I could cry. I'm getting a divorce right now. She says that living with me is like living with a stone."

SARAH: Does your approach require that all involved are willing to play by certain rules?

MARSHALL: No, you can keep this process going with anybody regardless of how they're communicating. The important thing is to teach people how to listen for how the other person *is*, even when that other person doesn't know how to communicate very clearly.

SARAH: I was interested in an example you shared in one of your workshops about a group of teachers who were having a conversation that wasn't

feeding you spiritually.

MARSHALL: Well, I was sitting around with a group of teachers who were all talking about what they did on vacation. Within ten minutes, my energy had dropped very low; I had no idea what people were feeling or wanting.

In giraffe, we know it's not being kind to the other person to smile and open your eyes wide to hide the fact that your head has gone dead. The person in front of you wants their words to enrich you, so when they don't, it's helpful to be kind and stop them. Of course, in the jackal culture, this isn't done.

After listening awhile to the teachers, I screwed up my courage and said, "Excuse me, I'm impatient with the conversation because I'm not feeling as connected with you as I'd like to be. It would help me to know if you're enjoying the conversation." All nine people stopped talking and looked at me as if I had thrown a rat in the punch bowl.

For about two minutes, I thought I'd die, but then I remembered to look at the feelings and needs being expressed through the silence. I said, "I guess you're all angry with me, and you would have liked for me to have kept out of the conversation."

The moment I turned my attention to what they were feeling and needing, I removed their power to demoralize me.

However, the first person who spoke told me, "No, I'm not angry. I was just thinking about what you were saying. I was bored with this conversation." And he had been doing most of the talking! But this doesn't surprise me. I have found that if I am bored, the person doing the talking is probably equally bored, which usually means we're not talking from life; we're acting out some socially-learned habits.

Each one of the nine people then expressed the same feelings I had—impatience, discouragement, lifelessness, inertia. Then one of the women asked, "Marshall, why do we do this? Why do we sit around and bore each other? We get together every week and do this!"

I said, "Because we probably haven't learned to take the risk that I just did, which is to pay attention to our vitality. Are we really getting what we want from life? Each moment is precious, so when our vitality is down, let's do something about it and wake up."

SARAH: How does somebody who feels very strongly about making a change in political or economic institutions use the techniques you teach?

MARSHALL: Well, once you realize that you have choices, you can learn

to live this process in contexts that are very hard. This Kung Fu giraffe, as I call it, involves staying with Nonviolent Communication even in a group situation in which you're in a minority and everybody else is using jackal language.

For example, I see that the product our company is making pollutes the environment. I'm working within an authoritarian institution, so how do I effectively communicate my concerns within that structure even though the group I'm dealing with speaks jackal, and some people have the power to punish me if I don't buy the party line?

The first thing is to get access to the people on the other side. For this process to work, there needs to be a flow of communication and compassion between parties. If we can have enough time to get that flow going, we can resolve any differences.

But let's say these people are not willing to give me access, and I feel that their behavior in the meantime is harmful. Then I might have to use what we call "the protective use of force." You use this kind of force to protect, not punish, the other people. That might involve things like organizing an employee strike, a boycott of the product, or other nonviolent techniques needed to protect the environment. They may not solve the conflict, but they may get the other side to agree to negotiate.

SARAH: There may be cases where one party feels that certain considerations, such as financial ones, are more important than the needs of the other group. I can imagine situations in which there could be a very open conversation and still no resolution at the end of it.

MARSHALL: When we keep this flow going, I have not seen that happen. But let's go back to that situation. Again, suppose I'm concerned that the product a company is making pollutes the environment. I may start by stereotyping the other person: "He's only interested in money. He has no regard for the environment." If I think that way about that person, I become part of the problem, because I've dehumanized that person in my mind. Labels are static, and life is a process. We're missing what's going on when we label, and it leads us to act toward them in a certain way that usually provokes the very thing that we're labeling.

If I'm in conflict with people, I try to hear what needs they have. Now, "needs," as we define the term, are universal; all human beings have the same needs. So if I connect to what people are needing, I'm one with them. I care

about their needs. At the moment that they sense that I am as interested in their needs as my own, we can find a way to get everybody's needs met.

So more concretely, what would that look like? This man might say, "Our work is not going to harm the environment. Our tests have demonstrated that this is not going to harm the environment." So, this person shares the same needs that I have. I want to protect the environment. Apparently, he's concerned about the environment also.

Now, where we might differ is in our ways of measuring whether something is harmful to the environment. But notice our needs are not in conflict. This person doesn't want to destroy someone's habitat, and he doesn't want to be a menace. You see?

SARAH: There may be a tremendous amount of money to be made from the product.

MARSHALL: Well, that's the other side of it. Now, we don't have a need for money, but money can be instrumental in meeting certain needs. This man wants respect. He wants the material security that money can contribute to. I have those same needs. So, this man's needs connect with mine. I'd like to find a way to get security and respect for him in a way that meets my needs as well. I'm confident that if this man trusted that I'm equally concerned with his needs as my own, we can find a way to meet everybody's needs.

SARAH: What do you see going on in the world right now that gives you the most hope?

MARSHALL: I've seen a rapid change in the last 30 years toward a kind of consciousness that gives me hope.

I'm also optimistic because, everywhere in the world, people are hungry to learn new ways of communication. For example, people have heard about our training, and we can't get to them fast enough!

For more information, contact the Center for Nonviolent Communication, PO Box 2662, Sherman, Texas 75091; 903/893-3886; Fax: 903/893-2935; E-mail: cnvc@compuserve.com; www.cnvc.org. Marshall Rosenberg is the author of a number of books, including *Nonviolent Communication* (Puddledancer Press, 1999). This interview appeared in the Summer 1998 issue of *YES!*

Through My Enemy's Eyes

Troy Chapman

Sentenced to die in prison 16 years ago, I set out on a path to find and live within the truth. Having just turned 21, I had spent the previous nine years on an insane roller coaster of addiction, violence, and despair. The death of another human being in a bar fight and my sentence of 60–90 years were the tragic and too predictable end of the road I'd been traveling. In passing this sentence the judge said, "There's no hope that you can ever be rehabilitated."

No hope. If he was right, there was no point in going on, and I quite logically considered taking my own life. But in the end I determined that the judge could not be right and I would live. I don't mean I decided merely not to die, but to really be *alive* from that point on, to embrace life and find some meaning and truth I could live by and for. That was the beginning of a journey that would take me to a place I think of as the "third side."

It began with me. I had to honestly confront and condemn what I'd become, what I'd done, and my whole perception of reality. I became obsessed with the question of what went wrong and how to set it right.

Over the next few years I began to read—the Bible, Dostoyevsky, Gandhi, Camus, Dickens, Steinbeck—anything I could get my hands on. I took up meditation, began observing myself and others and writing down anything that seemed important.

I was being pulled by the future but also pushed by the past. My crime, and later my sentence, stood at the center of all my examinations. Slowly I came to understand my need for redemption and true atonement. I realized

that nothing could atone for what I'd become better than simply turning away from it with my whole being, and this is what I did. I repented in action. I changed. This decision opened up a new turn in my search for truth. I began to look outward again, to re-examine the world around me, but now I looked from this new place within myself.

It sounds as if these are two different pursuits—looking in and looking out—but really they're not. Understanding community and my role in it was simply the next step in my own healing.

I wanted to know if the origins of my insanity were completely within myself or was I, at least in part, a product of a sick culture. Having confronted myself thoroughly I could now ask that question objectively, not looking for excuses or trying to diminish my own accountability, but simply and sincerely, loking for the truth.

I looked at my fellow prisoners, the insane things they'd done to get here. I looked at the prison itself, our "solution" to violence, and saw it to be just more of the same thing it was designed to respond to. I looked at the growing insanity *outside* prison, the despair, rage, addiction, denial, lies, and deceit.

And I knew that I couldn't maintain the integrity of my search without admitting that while something had definitely gone wrong *in me,* something was also very wrong in our culture. To deny or overlook this would be like finding hundreds of three-eyed toads in a pond and never thinking to check the pond for its contribution to the phenomenon. The individuals who are going spiritually insane in droves in our culture are not coming out of a void. As I began to wake up I found myself concerned for these individuals and for us as a whole. I was developing social consciousness, which soon turned into social activism.

My activism was an extension of my spirituality. When I stood up for some cause, such as prisoners' rights, I felt it was an expression of morality. I "fought the system" by writing grievances, filing things in court, and writing the media. When my jailers retaliated by tearing up my cell, destroying my work, or transferring me to another prison, it wasn't something I liked, but I considered it a mark of my success and evidence of *why* I was fighting. I was a warrior on the "right" side of the matter.

This view served me for a while, giving me a sense of moral order. But my continuing inward growth demanded a corresponding outward growth—a change in my view of the world. It started with the recognition that my activ-

ism wasn't very different from my earlier anger. In fact, my anger had crept back in, only now it was wrapped up in the sense that I was doing good and fighting evil. I hadn't gotten rid of my anger at all, only justified it. I still had enemies, was still locked in opposition to them, and I still wanted to win, to destroy them. I'd moved from seeking my enemies' physical destruction to seeking political, intellectual, social, and philosophic destruction, but it was still about enemies. My activism, like my previous thinking, was very dualistic.

Over time this dualism gave way to my hunger for simple goodness. The catalyst for this change was nothing more noble than exhaustion. I was simply tired of being angry all the time, tired of waking up every morning to a battle. I needed some rest. This need led me away from easy moral certitude. I developed the ability to see things through the eyes of my enemies. I saw in them the same fear that had so long governed me. The same confusion, the same grasping for security, the same hunger for love. I saw their humanity, and this ruined me as a warrior.

When a warrior begins to see the enemy as a human being, he begins to hesitate, to wonder if there's another way than war. He is no longer fit for battle and if he doesn't leave the field he will be taken from it by the very people he sympathizes with.

But is this the end of activism? For a while I thought it was, for who can be an activist without decisively taking sides? How could I fight against prisons when I empathized with the jailers?

I knew that if I'd been in their circumstance I would probably have done the same thing. If things had been different and I'd ended up being Joe Citizen instead of Joe Criminal, I would not have exhibited any more wisdom, foresight, or sense of the big picture than these prison builders. I knew that in some sense, they *were* me.

I had arrived at the third side.

I had spent most of my life splitting the world up into two sides, then fighting to defend one against the other. It was a game in which there were strategies, a clear objective, a field of play, and an opponent. The game has rules and no matter which side we're on, we're bound by the rules. The poet Rumi pointed to something beyond this game when he said, "Out beyond ideas of wrong-doing and right-doing there is a field. I'll meet you there."

When I began to see myself in others—even in my enemies—I found

myself heading for Rumi's field. Here the game is not a game. No one wins unless and until everyone wins. The line between victim and perpetrator no longer runs between "I" and "Other." It now runs right through the center of my soul. I am both, as we are all both.

What then is left to fight for? Where does an out-of-work activist go? Well ... God is hiring and God is on the third side. Not the prisoner's or the jailer's side. Not the pro-choice or the pro-life side. Not the Left or the Right.

The third side is that little-represented side of healing. It's the side that cares as much about the enemy as the friend, that says love is the only justice, the only victory there is. It does not want anyone destroyed. It does not want to win if someone else must lose. It wants something much larger than winning and losing.

But what's larger than winning? Especially when we're fighting for the "right" cause? Well, I've watched the game of winning and losing from both the inside and the outside. From inside each win seems like a step forward, but when we get outside the game we see that it's circular. People have been playing this game forever, yet good isn't any more pervasive in our world than it was a thousand years ago. "Activists" back then certainly thought the "big win" was just around the bend. They believed they were moving forward, just as we believe we're moving forward, just as a hamster inside a wire wheel believes *he* is moving forward.

But where is the evidence? Do our Right/Left debates ever produce anything useful to humanity? Is it really the "enemy's" fault that the world's in the shape it's in, or is it partly *our* fault? What's the motive behind our activism? Is it truly a love of goodness or do we engage in battle in order to distract ourselves from the hard work of love, from the bitter pill of looking at ourselves?

Asking myself these questions I realized that enemies always serve a purpose. The war relationship is a symbiotic one in which the enemy on one side serves some need within the enemy on the other side, even while both protest this fact and claim they only fight because they have no choice.

I realized I do have a choice. Indeed, the freedom to choose how to respond may be the only total freedom we have. The world outside isn't within our control, but this freedom always is.

One of the first times I exercised this control a man was trying to walk me off the sidewalk. This is common in prison as scared and angry young men

try to show how tough they are. Having dealt with similar situations for years, I'd always seen them in terms of two choices: back down or go on the offensive. This time another option suddenly occurred to me.

I still remember the confusion in the man's eyes as I stepped off the sidewalk, touched his elbow, and said, "How's it going?" I stepped aside, but I didn't back off. I engaged him, but on a different playing field. He was at a loss and simply mumbled some reply and kept walking.

But I had told him in a language we both understood, "I have no need of an enemy," and I've been telling the world that ever since. Whenever I catch myself thinking of someone as an enemy I ask, "What in me am I trying to avoid or distract myself from?" Inevitably I find my own impotence, my own frustrations, my insignificance, my sense that nothing I do will ever really matter. Ultimately I find my own mortality and the seeming futility of most human endeavor. I find my own self-absorption, my resistance to setting myself aside and truly caring about the other.

Does this mean that I have no work to do but inner work? Not at all, but it does mean that I must face myself. Part of facing myself is responding to the injustice and destruction of our world. Why? Because it's *mine,* and that is really the essence of third-side thinking.

Denying ownership of the insanity "out there" is the root of all violence. Dualistic activism isn't really a step away from this denial, only a more sophisticated expression of it. To step to the third side we must truly own those aspects of our world that we hate most.

Will war, violence, injustice, greed, and all the rest magically disappear if we own them and embrace this kind of activism? I can say only this: they will end *in me.* I will continue to step off the sidewalk, but I won't avert my eyes. Quite the contrary. I will confront you with a bigger vision of your own humanity. I will throw hope in the face of the enemy, and I will subvert anger with sanity and humor.

I have no delusions that pie-in-the-sky "love" will change our world. If I know anything from my years in prison, it's that evil is a real thing. However we explain it theologically or philosophically, there is behavior that is toxic to the planet and to other human beings, and it must be dealt with. I'm not talking about giving those who act out this behavior a hug, then calling it good. That's old-style "liberalism," and it's been as destructive to our world as its now popular counterpart, so-called conservatism. These two represent a

false choice between ineffective permissiveness and arrogant intolerance.

We can and must move beyond such false choices to a place where love and justice not only balance one another, but are, in fact, *one thing*. A place where confrontation and good will—even good *humor*—sit together comfortably; where holding people accountable is considered a complement, not an opposite, to helping them. The only conflict between these many "opposites" is within our own minds, and that is where reconciliation must occur.

With each inner reconciliation we create a new option, a *third* option where before there were only two, locked in eternal conflict. We create, then are able to stand, on the third side.

Troy Chapman, a writer, artist, and songwriter, is currently incarcerated at Kinross Correction Facility in Michigan. He is also cofounder of *Inspirit* newsletter, PO Box 731, Narberth Pennsylvania 19072. Email: Inspirit01@earthlink.net. This article appeared in the Winter 2002 issue of *YES!*

Restorative Justice

TAG EVERS

Burying her son and walking away from his grave were the hardest things Thomas Ann Hines had ever done. Meeting her son's killer 13 years later was the second hardest.

In 1985, Paul Hines, Thomas Ann's only child, was a student at University of Texas in Austin when he was murdered three months before his graduation. He was 21 years old. A 17-year-old stranger had approached Paul in a video arcade and asked him for ride.

Once inside Paul's Camaro, the young man demanded the keys to the car. When Paul refused, the would-be thief shot him once in the chest and fled. Paul was found dead later that evening, slumped over in his Camaro, the car still running.

Thomas Ann was devastated. She wanted the death penalty, but due to the offender's age, he was given a 40-year sentence instead.

"I was filled with rage, anger, fear, and pain," says Thomas Ann, who lives just north of Dallas, Texas. "Every six months, without fail, I went to the parole board and asked, 'Is he dead yet? Does he have AIDS? Has someone killed him?' I was so angry at the system. My son was executed without warning. Yet this person could sit in prison and watch television or play basketball, things my son enjoyed."

She vented her grief through letter-writing. Mother's Day, her son's birthday, her own birthday, and the anniversary of Paul's death all became opportunities to express her anger and loss. The letters fattened the offender's file, adding testimony upon testimony against the occasion of his possible parole.

"Everyone says 'seek closure,' as if you're supposed to fix it," says Hines. "But it never goes away. You close the coffin, and it never goes away."

Yet 13 years later, in June of 1998, at the Alfred D. Hughes Correctional Institute in Gatesville, Texas, Thomas Ann sat across from "Charles," her son's murderer, now a 30-year-old man. "I wanted him to look in the eyes of the mother of the boy he had killed," says Hines. "I wanted him to know there is love in the world."

Hines met with Charles under the auspices of the Victim Offender Mediation/Dialogue program operated by the Texas Department of Victims' Services. She had decided to participate in the program in 1995, and it took Hines three years of mental and emotional preparation, both on her own and in consultation with people from the Mediation/Dialogue program, before she felt ready to meet Charles. The result, for both parties, was profound.

"The intensity and depth of emotion ran the whole gamut—from hopelessness and sheer despair to hope and a sense of faith," says Dave Doerfler, who mediated the session. "Charles was locked in his pain, saying there was nothing he could do to bring back Paul's life. But Thomas Ann was relentless—she broke through—and insisted that while Charles couldn't do anything about her son's life, he could do something about his own."

At the close of their emotional six-hour session, Thomas Ann and Charles reached an agreement whereby Charles would indeed do something about his life. He agreed to work on his GED and pursue vocational training. Additionally, with Thomas Ann's support, Charles listed personal and spiritual goals that might strengthen him as he prepared for his eventual release from prison.

Up to that point, Charles had amassed 148 disciplinary violations, losing up to 10 years of possible "good time." But he now had something he did not have before: hope and the knowledge that someone loved him.

"You can't take away the sense of hope," says Doerfler, who manages the Mediation/Dialogue program, which currently has a waiting list of 250 victims and survivors who wish to meet their offenders. "It's not just one thing, but a combination that makes the difference in these dialogues. They provide a real release for the victim from the bondage and obsession of the past. And the offender gains a sense of emotional and personal accountability, a sense of empathy that is often lacking in the repeat offender.

"Additionally, a ripple effect is created that starts with the personal and extends to an examination of the social, political, and economic realities that

undergird our violent society," continues Doerfler. "In other words, these dialogues are about peacebuilding in the most fundamental of ways."

The Victim Offender Mediation/Dialogue program in Texas is one of 300 such projects in the United States, according to the Center for Restorative Justice and Mediation at the University of Minnesota. Additionally, there are over 700 victim-offender mediation programs operating in Europe, Australia, and New Zealand.

Victim-offender mediation was pioneered in Ontario, Canada, in the mid-1970s by Mennonites influenced by biblical concepts of justice. The model is part of the growing "restorative justice" movement which defines criminal offenses in terms of the harm done to victims and victimized communities and not merely as crimes against the state.

Interest in restorative justice in the United States has grown considerably since the early 1990s. The American Bar Association endorsed the practice of victim-offender mediation in 1994, and in 1996, the US Department of Justice convened its first national conference on restorative justice.

Historically, rehabilitating prisoners was central to the philosophy of the "corrections" system. Such ideals have suffered mightily as politicians and judges have ratcheted up the level of get-tough-on-crime rhetoric with every election cycle.

The result is massive overcrowding of prison facilities and the punitive warehousing of America's inmate population. Nationwide, an estimated 1.73 million people are now behind bars. Typically, expenditures on corrections are the fastest growing components of state budgets, and in several states, including California, total expenditures on corrections eclipses those spent on higher education.

In the prevailing "retributive" model of criminal justice, the role of the state is to prosecute offenders on behalf of injured parties. The injured parties, the actual victims, and their communities are typically relegated to a passive role. Lost in the adversarial process is the notion that crime constitutes a violation of one person by another, resulting in harm that cannot be healed by the mere imposition of punishment.

Restorative justice recognizes the need for a three-dimensional response that includes victims, offenders, and communities. The victim in the restorative justice framework becomes an active participant in defining the

harm caused by the crime. This often involves a face-to-face encounter—a mediated dialogue between the victim and the offender.

It's not an easy process for offenders to go through. When Charles walked into the room with Hines, she saw "the pain in his eyes." After explaining how difficult it was to finally meet the man who killed her son, she said, "But I will not be unkind to you in any way."

Charles began crying, a flow of tears that continued for nearly the entire session. Victims often have questions for which they need answers. "Why did you pick me?" is a common line of inquiry. Hines, as a victim survivor, wanted to know how her son died.

"Charles," she said, "you were last person to see my son alive. Tell me what happened that night." At that point, Hines relates, "It wasn't about me anymore, it was about Charles."

Charles recounted the details of the fateful evening as they both cried and took turns wiping away each other's tears. "I thought you'd holler and scream at me," said Charles. "I thought you'd want me dead."

"Yes, I did. I once wanted you dead," said Hines. "But you never had a chance, Charles." In her preparation for the dialogue, Hines learned how Charles had been put out on the streets at the age of 13, how he had taken up a life of crime and drug-dealing to survive. "My little boy went to bed every night," said Hines, "tucked in by a mother who adored him. You never had that, Charles."

There were two major turning points in Hines' long, painful journey leading up to her meeting with Charles. The first, she relates, occurred four years after Paul's murder, when she began to reach out to other parents of murdered children.

"When you're talking about restorative justice," she says, "it began for me when I started reaching out to others and helping them through their pain, because I didn't have anyone to help me when I was there."

The second turning point took place in 1994, when Raven Kazen, director of the Texas Department of Victims Services, asked Hines to participate in a victims' panel at a maximum security prison in Huntsville.

"Oh my gosh, I went with the intention of giving them a piece of my mind," says Hines. Instead, when she took her place on the panel, before an audience of 200 prisoners, all she could see "was a sea of broken pieces of humanity." It overwhelmed her, she claims: "I looked at them, and all of a sudden, I became a mother again."

After her presentation, one inmate stood up and asked her why she bothered to come to the prison. "The question hit me right smack between the eyes," recalls Hines. "I looked at him and said: 'If my son was sitting in this room, I'd want someone to reach out a hand and lift him up.'"

Hines says the experience helped her take her anger and transform it into something positive, both within her and in the lives of prisoners. She has become somewhat of a prisoner's advocate and speaks several times a week at prisons all over the state of Texas. Each time she goes with a mother's love.

"The criminal justice system operates on the principle that if someone is down, you kick 'em," says Hines. "Until we start looking at the roots of crime instead of the results, it's not going to change."

Restorative justice offers a powerful critique of our flawed criminal justice system. More severe penalties and longer sentences associated with high-cost prison-building sprees are diverting much-needed funds from programs that could prevent crime from occurring in the first place.

By addressing the harm done to victims and developing accountability and competency in the offender, restorative justice efforts such as Texas' Mediation/Dialogue program are on the cutting edge of the growing peacebuilding ethos taking root in contemporary society.

Already, new restorative-justice models that incorporate greater community involvement, such as the sentencing circles used by the First Nations in Canada, are being explored. In New Zealand, for example, a family-group conferencing model based on native Maori traditions has helped produce an 80 percent reduction in that country's juvenile caseload. These approaches welcome input from family members of both victim and offender, as well as community residents, as their respective needs are addressed in a holistic context with the aim of reintegrating the offender into the community.

"Hope is the foundation," reiterates Doerfler, "but it's just the foundation. We can't expect too much of the process, nor can we be overly simplistic, but if we build on hope, emphasizing education, self-esteem, and a social and spiritual support system for both the offender and the victim, good things can happen."

Just ask Thomas Ann Hines. "At the close of our session, I said to Charles: 'I had a choice—I could spend the rest of my life hating you. But I don't hate you. I just want you to move forward with your life.'

"As we parted, Charles reached out and wrapped his arms around me. I've had lots of hugs in my life, but besides Paul, I can't think of a person in the world I'd rather have hug me."

It is time to examine our choices. According to the Minnesota Office of Drug Policy, failure in school is statistically more closely linked with criminal activity than smoking is with cancer. We can live in a society that spends more on managing its criminal population than it does on educating its citizens— a society that has little to invest in low-income youth but plenty to spend on punishing them.

Or we can choose the opposite, funding prevention programs such as family education and support initiatives that deal with child abuse and neglect. Prison building or peace building: the choice is simple.

Tag Evers is a freelance writer from Madison, Wisconsin. This article appeared in the Fall 1998 issue of *YES!*

Can Love Save the World?

WALTER WINK

Michael Kelly thinks he has killed pacifism. In an editorial in the Washington Post of September 26, 2001, he cites George Orwell's 1944 description of pacifism as "objectively pro-Fascist." "If you hamper the war effort on one side you automatically help out that of the other," Orwell reasoned.

Applied to "America's New War," Kelly finds the logic irrefutable. "Organized terrorist groups have attacked America. These groups wish the Americans to not fight. The American pacifists wish the Americans to not fight. If the Americans do not fight, the terrorists will attack America again. And now we know such attacks can kill many thousands of Americans. The American pacifists, therefore, are on the side of future mass murders of Americans. They are objectively pro-terrorist." Hence the pacifist position is "evil."

Would that life were so logical! For what Mr. Kelly overlooks is a third way, neither passive nor aggressive. For millions of years his error has been endlessly repeated. It is the fight/flight response. But that third way has occasionally been tried, and, wonder of wonders, it has frequently succeeded. Religions pioneered the third way as a nonviolent protest against those two invidious alternatives. Starting with the Hebrew midwives, nonviolence was elaborated by Jainism and Buddhism, given political bite by Jews like the prophets and Jesus, articulated by Christians like St. Francis and Martin Luther King, Jr., and made programmatic and practical by the Hindu Gandhi and the Muslim Badshah Khan.

Nevertheless, I agree with Mr. Kelly that pacifism must go. It is endlessly confused with passivity. In the nations in which Christianity has predominated, Jesus' teaching on nonviolence has been perverted into injunctions to

passive nonresistance, which, as we shall see, is the very opposite of active nonviolence. Jesus had said, "You have heard that it was said, 'An eye for an eye and a tooth for a tooth.' But I say to you, do not resist an evildoer. But if anyone strikes you on the right cheek, turn the other also; and if anyone wants to sue you and take your outer garment, give your undergarment as well; and if one of the occupation troops forces you to carry his pack one mile, go two" (Matthew 5:38-41). As it stands, this saying seems to counsel supine surrender. If you are a woman and you are struck by your spouse on one cheek, turn the other; let him pulverize you. If you are sued for a piece of clothing, give all your clothes voluntarily, as an act of pious renunciation. And if a Roman soldier forces you to carry his pack one mile, be a chump: carry it two. And the crowning blow: don't resist evil at all.

For centuries, readers of this advice have instinctively known something was wrong with this picture. Jesus always resisted evil. Why would he tell us to behave in ways he himself refused? And that's where the trouble starts. The Greek word translated as "resist" (antistenai), is literally "to stand (stenai) against (anti)." The term is taken from warfare. When two armies collide, they were said to "stand against" each other. The correct translation is given in the new Scholars Bible: "Don't react violently against the one who is evil." The meaning is clear: don't react in kind, don't mirror your enemy, don't turn into the very thing you hate. Jesus is not telling us not to resist evil, but only not to resist it violently.

Jesus gives three examples to explain his point. The first is: "If anyone strikes you on the right cheek, turn the other also." Most people picture a blow with the right fist. But that would land on the left cheek, and Jesus specifies the right cheek. A left hook wouldn't fit the bill either, since the left hand was used only for unclean tasks, and even to gesture with it brought shame on the one gesturing. Jesus is speaking about striking the right cheek with the back of the right hand. This was not a blow to injure. It was symbolic. It was intended to humiliate, to put an inferior in his or her place. It was given by a master to a slave, a husband to a wife, a parent to a child, or a Roman to a Jew. The message of the powerful to their subjects was clear: You are a nobody, get back down where you belong.

It is to those accustomed to being struck thus that Jesus speaks ("if anyone strikes you"). By turning the other cheek, the person struck puts the striker in an untenable spot. He cannot repeat the backhand, because the other's nose is now in the way. The left cheek makes a fine target, but only persons who are

equals fight with fists, and the last thing the master wants is for the slave to assert equality. This is, of course, no way to avoid trouble; the master might have the slave flogged to within an inch of her life. But the point has been irrevocably made: the "inferior" is saying, in no uncertain terms, "I won't take such treatment anymore. I am your equal. I am a child of God." By turning the other cheek, the oppressed person is saying that she refuses to submit to further humiliation. This is not submission, as the churches have insisted. It is defiance. That may sound a bit idealistic, but people all over the globe of late have been taking their courage in their hands this way and resisting, nonviolently, those who have treated them thus.

Jesus' second example deals with indebtedness, the most onerous social problem in first century Palestine. The wealthy of the Empire sought ways to avoid taxes. The best way was to buy land on the fringes of the Empire. But the poor didn't want to sell. So the rich jacked up interest rates—25 to 250 percent. When the poor couldn't repay, first their moveable property was seized, then their lands, and finally the very clothes on their backs. Scripture allowed the destitute to sleep in their long robes, but they had to surrender them by day (Deuteronomy 24:10-13).

It is to that situation that Jesus speaks. Look, he says, you can't win when they take you to court. But here is something you can do: when they demand your outer garment, give your undergarment as well. That was all they wore. The poor man is stark naked! And in Israel, nakedness brought shame, not on the naked party, but on the one viewing his nakedness. (See the story of Noah, Genesis 9.) Jesus is not asking those already defrauded of their possessions to submit to further indignity. He is enjoining them to guerrilla theater.

Imagine the debtor walking out of the court in his altogethers. To the question what happened, he responds: That creditor got all my clothes. People come pouring out of the streets and alleys and join the little procession to his home. It will be a while before creditors in that village take a poor man to court!

But, of course, the Powers That Be are shrewd, and within weeks new laws will be in place making nakedness in court punishable by fines or incarceration. So the poor need to keep inventing new forms of resistance. Jesus is advocating a kind of Aikido, where the momentum of the oppressor is used to throw the oppressor and make him the laughing stock of the community. Jesus is not averse to using shame to kindle a moral sense in the creditor.

Jesus' third example refers to the angeria, the law that permitted a Roman soldier to force a civilian to carry his 65- to 85-pound pack. But the law stipulated one mile only. At the second marker the soldier was required to

retrieve his pack. By carrying the pack more than a mile, the peasant makes the soldier culpable for violation of military law. Again, Jesus is not just "extending himself" by going the second mile, as the popular platitude puts it. He is putting the soldier in jeopardy of punishment.

So you can see why I agree with Mr. Kelly. The examples Jesus gives are something more than nonresistance. They are gutsy, courageous, and aggressive. So I don't regard myself as a pacifist. I see myself rather as a violent person trying to become nonviolent. Mr. Kelly and I concur that the "flight" option is cowardly, irresponsible, and ineffective. But where he is still mired in the "fight" option, I am prepared to risk active, even militant, nonviolence—a third way. Far from proving impractical, nonviolence has been about the only thing that has been working of late. In 1989-90 alone, 14 nations involving 1.7 billion people underwent nonviolent revolutions, all but one successfully (China). During the 20th century, 3.4 billion people were thus involved. Yet the churches have, since the time of St. Augustine, embraced the Roman "just war theory," convinced that nonviolence won't work, that only violence can save or redeem us. (I call this "the myth of redemptive violence.")

The current crisis challenges both Mr. Kelly and me. Mr. Kelly, because he is unable to point to many successes for the "fight" option in the last two decades. And he is impaled on the spiritual law that says, "If I win, I lose." If we destroy the Taliban and Osama bin Laden, tens of thousands will stand in their places. All-out war with Arab Muslims could lead straight to World War III, complete with biological and nuclear weapons. At the very least, we can expect a world unsafe for Americans, even in our homeland. Civil liberties will be lost, and we may find ourselves in a situation "objectively pro-Fascist." If we win, we lose. Our very lust for retaliation is proving the truth of the adage that violence can lead only to more violence.

There are causes for this war, and most of them should have been taken care of years ago. Most of what Osama bin Laden claims to be fighting for should have been the basis of America's Middle Eastern policy. We should have lifted the sanctions in Iraq, which have killed upwards of a million people, over half of them children under five—a war crime of which we are guilty. We could easily have withdrawn our troops from Saudi Arabia, since it is offensive to pious Muslims to have non-Muslim troops in their holy land. After all, it was Kuwait we fought to save; let Kuwait harbor our troops. We should have used our enormous influence to stop Israelis from settling in the West Bank, and secured for Palestinians a state.

And we should quit propping up anti-democratic dictatorships in the region, many of which would collapse without our support.

Not that these unjust situations adequately account for Osama bin Laden's vendetta against America. The rationale of terrorists is terror, and reasons given today may shift tomorrow. The terrorist who regretted being caught before he could kill 250,000 Americans betrayed the game. It is simply to kill Americans. No pretext can ever excuse the slaughter of innocents, whether Americans in the Twin Towers or Afghan civilians in the Middle East.

But the current crisis also challenges me. I distinguish between force and violence, arguing that force, rightly exercised, is the legitimate use of restraint to prevent some from doing harm to others. Violence, by contrast, is injurious or lethal harm deliberately intended, and can never be justified. I am struggling with that distinction today. Is there a continuum from force to violence, or from police action to war? How, then, do we know how much force we can use before it becomes violence? Could we have sent in special forces to seize Mr. bin Laden and bring him to trial at the World Court? But we didn't know where to look! (But neither do our soldiers.) Didn't the "restrained" use of force already escalate to violence the moment President Bush declared war? Can these distinctions be anything but rationalizations unless we have committed ourselves to nonviolence from the outset?

It's easy to see why Bush declared war. It was in response to the killing of our civilians. But when we kill innocents—inevitable in a war where innocents are mingled among combatants—we write them off as "collateral damage"—as if real people weren't involved. We watch as the full resources of the world's most commanding military are devoted to destroying an entire sector of the Afghanistan population. I cannot see how we can regard this war as anything but immoral.

Doing justice in the Middle East will not mollify true terrorists. But it could remove the source of much outrage, and thus dry up the reservoir of recruits for holy war. To that end, we must act with vulnerability and compassion to remove the causes of anger, even as we ferret out those whose terrorist violence led to the tragedy of September 11, 2001.

Walter Wink is author of *The Human Being: Jesus and the Enigma of the Son of the Man* (Fortress, 2001), www.walterwink.com. This article appeared in the Winter 2002 issue of *YES!*

The Heart of a Muslim

JAMAL RAHMAN

The deaths of thousands of innocent people on September 11 are soul wrenching. I ask myself, as we all do, how a loving Creator could allow this horrific event to occur. The answer is wrapped in mystery. As the Quran says, "We have shown you the dust but concealed the wind."

The perpetrators of the devastating attack, all of them Islamic extremists, claim to be martyrs. The real martyrs, of course, are the innocent people whose lives were tragically snuffed out.

How do I, as a Muslim, honor them? I honor the dead by honoring the truth.

Islam is a religion of peace. Force is permitted only in self-defense. The Quran says that if anyone takes one innocent life, it is as if "he killed all of mankind." It advises a Muslim to "show forgiveness, enjoin kindness, and stay away from the ignorant." Repeatedly, the Quran tell us not to "sow corruption on earth" and to "stand firmly for justice, as witnesses to God even as against yourself or your parents or your kin, and whether it be against rich or poor."

But if Islam espouses peace and moderation, how do we explain the growth of radicalism bent on violence?

Again, there are no easy answers. Like other religions, Islam has its share of zealots who clamor for attention. The mystic Rumi cautioned us about them, describing them as "All fireworks and no light, all husk and no kernel."

What makes these times volatile is the vast pool of poor, illiterate Muslims around the world who lead lives of despair and defeat. Not only do they suffer at the hands of their own governments, they feel authentic anger and anguish

at the policies of the United States: its blind support of Israel, its devastation of the lives of generations of Iraqi Muslims, and its practice of preaching democracy while propping up a corrupt, feudal monarchy in Saudi Arabia. Islamic radicals easily find supporters among the disaffected. In the hands of angry men with untamed egos, religious verses misinterpreted and taken out of context become weapons of destruction. Perpetrators of murder become "martyrs." Acts of violence become "Jihad." And suicide becomes a passageway to the sensual pleasures of heaven.

The truth of Islam is quite different. A martyr is one who witnesses the truth and gives his life for it. The greater meaning of Jihad is about battling and taming the imperious fragments of one's ego; the lesser Jihad is about defending one's religion when it is attacked. Suicide is expressly forbidden in Islam. The vivid imagery of paradise is metaphorical, meant to incline the heart of the believer to engage in "deeds which are pleasing in the eyes of the Lord."

At a recent retreat, I was touched by a story of an African American peace activist. As a child of seven, he slapped a white child who called him "nigger." At home his father congratulated him, but his mother tenderly chided him, saying, "What good did that do?" Later she said, "Son, there has to be a better way." Her words resonated deeply in the child's soul. Today, an adult, he dedicates his life to finding a better way.

We owe it to the brave, innocent people who have been sacrificed all over the world to find a better way.

In Islam, finding a better way is not about rushing out to change governments and institutions. Our actions must be rooted in higher consciousness. Otherwise, we are like the sincere, action-oriented monkey my beloved parents told me about. With great zeal, the monkey plucked fish out of ponds to save them from a watery grave.

Does this mean we should work only on ourselves? No. Work equally in the visible and invisible world, advise Islamic mystics. Participate fully in the bazaar of life—buying, selling, marrying, raising children, and doing "abiding good deeds." But complement this outer work daily with an inner practice that nurtures and nourishes the soul—prayers, silence, music, nature, play. Everything in the visible world, reveals the Quran, has its roots in the invisible world. Water those roots regularly.

Can we do this work in both realms with compassion for ourselves? The inner meaning of the most repeated verse in the Quran (Allah is Infinitely

Compassionate, Merciful, and Beneficent) is that God wants us to be compassionate with ourselves. Little do we know who we are, where we come from, or where we are going. Have mercy on yourself, the Quran teaches, for you are precious in God's eyes. Compassion for yourself allows your divine identity to step forward; compassionate towards yourself, you are able to hold compassion for the whole world.

One way to do our spiritual work is to cultivate the art of listening. The ultimate listening is, of course, hearing the inner voice of the soul in us. But we must listen to other voices as well. We begin by making an effort to truly listen to others: family, friends, colleagues at work, voices in the community we disagree with.

A Christian minister I know well practices compassionate listening with renewed enthusiasm these days. He listens not only to family and friends but also to voices he previously ignored, and he is excited about a startling realization: "Maybe the anguish I feel now is what others have been feeling for a long time." My friend is not talking about Islamic extremists. He is talking of Native Americans, African Americans, and Chicanos. He admits that there's nothing novel about this insight except that, for the first time, he *feels* it in his gut. As a result, he makes an important distinction when he talks about the Islamic terrorists—their actions are evil, but their beings are not.

The 15th-century Sufi mystic Kabir offers similar advice: "Do what is right but never leave the person out of your heart." Protect yourself. Don't allow yourself to be abused. Do what is right. But if you're angry, know that you are fighting the antagonism, not the antagonist. This knowledge alone, Kabir insists, has the power to shift heaven and earth.

If this is so, can we extend this listening to Osama bin Laden? After all, he is using grievances that we are reluctant to hear to recruit thousands of Muslims. We don't have to agree with Osama bin Laden or condone his actions. But if we care to listen, we might hear the cry of authentic pain and despair that many Muslims feel because of US policies.

Another aspect of compassionate listening was one of Gandhi's central messages: "It is a sacred duty of every individual to have an appreciative understanding of other religions." We are asked to remain rooted in our own tradition but to ennoble and enrich something in us by being open to the beauty of other traditions. A Christian bishop calls this "grounded openness;" a rabbi calls this process "developing our inner faith;" a Muslim scholar says that interfaith appreciation is about completion, not conversion.

If there's one lesson driven home by the September 11 events, it is that we are all truly interconnected. This is not a new lesson. What *is* new is that we are experiencing this interwovenness in our hearts. Victim and victimizer, liberal and fundamentalist, rich and poor, empowered and disempowered, distant and near—all are unimaginably connected. The gentle Buddhist monk Thich Nhat Hanh expressed this eloquently in a poem:

I am the twelve-year-old girl
refugee on a small boat
who throws herself into the ocean
after having been raped by a sea pirate
and I am the pirate,
my heart not yet capable of seeing and loving.
Please call me by my true name
so I can wake up
and the door of my heart
could be left open,
the door of compassion.

Integral to this insight of interconnection is the realization that we need to double and redouble our efforts to empower women. Extremists of every stripe are mostly men. (Note that the practice of veiling women's faces has its roots not in the Quran but in male-dominated cultures.) Desperately and urgently we need to balance male ego-driven fanaticism with the gentler, kinder, spirit-filled voices and energies of women. The sharp edges of male extremism require smoothing and healing.

Once a group of self-absorbed men boasted to Rabia, a beloved female saint: "The crown of prophethood has been placed on men's heads. The belt of nobility has been fastened around men's waists. No woman has ever been a prophet." Rabia politely but firmly replied, "But egoism and self worship and 'I am your Lord, the most high' have never sprung from a woman's breast. All these things have been the specialty of men."

In the 7th-century age of *jahilya* (savagery), Prophet Muhammad revolutionized the rights of women. For the first time women were given the rights of inheritance, property ownership, and divorce. Sexual relations were permitted only within the locus of marriage. Today, 14 centuries later,

Muslim men must recognize that women in Islamic societies are still treated like second-class citizens. Sporadic progress has been made here and there, but in the spirit of the Quran and the Prophet's example, we have to work especially hard to give women their rightful voice and place in society. This is the best antidote to extremism of every kind.

The Quran asks, "Do you love your Creator? Then, love your fellow beings first." The people who died September 11 came from all major faiths of the world. Certainly they would want us to double and redouble our efforts to engage in what spiritual leaders call "a dialogue of the head, heart, and hands" between religions. This is to be conducted at all levels—governmental, institutional, and particularly at the community and personal level. Dialogue of the head between religions is about focusing on commonalities and considering the differences as facts that distinguish them. The next step of dialogue is about personal bonding and experiencing practices of other religions. Dialogue of hands, which usually grows out of the above two, is about participating in collaborative projects, often sharing the struggle for peace, justice, and earth care.

September 11 is not just about Islamic extremists who must be found and destroyed. It is far more important than that. It is a tragedy that has become a turning point—an amazing opportunity for awareness, compassion, community, and the end of politics-as-usual. On that grim day we were catapulted, against our will, across a new threshold of consciousness. Now we must make a bold leap forward, adopting new ways of thinking and being, or risk falling back into old, lethal patterns.

I am confident we shall make the leap, led by courageous, creative, and compassionate individuals and communities in America. This is still a place where there is, relatively speaking, freedom of expression and freedom of worship. People here carry lighter cultural baggage than elsewhere. There is naïveté and apathy here, but also freshness of spirit.

Enormous was the tragedy of September 11, but enormous are the opportunities. Enormous is my faith, believing in the Infinite Compassion, Mercy and Beneficence of God.

Jamal Rahman, an author and teacher, is a Sufi minister at Interfaith Community Church in Seattle, Washington. This article appeared in the Winter 2002 issue of *YES!*

The Great Community of Earth

Thomas Berry

At a special event held during the UN Summit for Religious and Spiritual Leaders in August 2000, Thomas Berry told these stories of our common dreams for the Earth.

During these past two days much has been accomplished to advance the cause of peace by our discussions and simply by our being with each other. We have learned to trust and admire each other and to share with each other the traditions we represent.

This evening I suggest that we continue this presence to each other by looking beyond ourselves to the larger universe we live in. If it were convenient, I would suggest that we go outside this building, that we go beyond all the light and noise of the city and look up at the sky overarching the Earth. At this time in the evening we would see the stars begin to appear as the sun disappears over the horizon. The light of day gives way to the darkness of night. A stillness, a healing quiet comes over the landscape.

It's a moment when some other world makes itself known, a numinous presence beyond human understanding. We experience the wonder of things as the vast realms of space overwhelm the limitations of our human minds. As the sky turns golden and the clouds reflect the blazing colors of evening, we participate for a moment in the forgiveness, the peace, the intimacy of all things with each other.

Parents hold their children more closely and tell them stories as they go off into dreamland, wonderful stories of times gone by, stories of the animals, of the good fairies, adventure stories of heroic wanderings through the

wilderness, stories of dragons threatening to devour the people and of courageous persons who saved our world in perilous times.

These final thoughts of the day are continued in the minds of children as even in their sleep they begin to dream of their own future, dreams of the noble deeds that would give meaning to their lives. Whether awake or asleep, the world of wonder fills their minds, the world of beauty fills their imaginations, the world of intimacy fills their emotions.

When we look back over our own lives, we realize that whatever of significance we have achieved in our own personal lives and in the larger cultural domain has been the fulfillment of thoughts and dreams that we had early in our lives, dreams that sustained us when we encountered difficulties through the years.

Beyond the dreams of our personal future, there are the shared dreams that give shape and form to each of our cultural traditions. Because this other world cannot be explained by any technical or scientific language, we present it by analogy and myth and story. Even beyond childhood, this is the world of the human mind.

So tonight, as we look up at the evening sky with the stars emerging faintly against the fading background of the sunset, we think of the mythic foundations of our future. We need to engage in a shared dream experience.

The experiences that we have spoken of as we look up at the starry sky at night and in the morning see the landscape revealed as the sun dawns over the Earth—these reveal a physical world but also a more profound world that cannot be bought with money, cannot be manufactured with technology, cannot be listed on the stock market, cannot be made in the chemical laboratory, cannot be reproduced with all our genetic engineering, cannot be sent by e-mail. These experiences require only that we follow the deepest feelings of the human soul.

What we look for is no longer the Pax Romana, the peace of imperial Rome, nor is it simply the Pax Humana, the peace among humans, but the Pax Gaia, the peace of earth and every being on the Earth. This is the original and the final peace, the peace granted by whatever power it is that brings our world into being. Within the universe, the planet Earth with all its wonder is the place for the meeting of the divine and the human.

As humans we are born of the Earth, nourished by the Earth, healed by the Earth. The natural world tells us: I will feed you, I will clothe you, I will shelter you, I will heal you. Only do not so devour me or use me that you destroy my capacity to mediate the divine and the human. For I offer you a

communion with the divine. I offer you gifts that you can exchange with each other. I offer you flowers whereby you may express your reverence for the divine and your love for each other. In the vastness of the sea, in the snow-covered mountains, in the rivers flowing through the valleys, in the serenity of the landscape, and in the foreboding of the great storms that sweep over the land, in all these experiences I offer you inspiration for your music, for your art, your dance.

All these benefits the Earth gives to us, individually, in our communities, and throughout the entire Earth. Yet we cannot be fully nourished in the depths of our being if we try to isolate ourselves individually or if we seek to deprive others of their share by increasing our own, for the food that we eat nourishes us in both our souls and our bodies. To eat alone is to be starved in some part of our being.

We need to reflect that our individual delight in the song of the birds and the sound of the crickets and cicadas in the evening is enhanced, not diminished, when we listen together with our families and our friends. We experience an easing of the tensions that develop between us, for the songs that we hear draw us into the intimacy of the same psychic space. So it is with music. Our folk music as well as the symphonies of Mozart or Beethoven draw an unlimited number of persons into the same soulspace.

Perhaps our greatest resource for peace is in an awareness that we enrich ourselves when we share our possessions with others. We discover peace when we learn to esteem those goods whereby we benefit ourselves in proportion as we give them to others. The very structure and functioning of the universe and of the planet Earth reveal an indescribable diversity bound in an all-embracing unity. The heavens themselves are curved over the earth in an encompassing embrace.

Here I would recall the experience of Henry Thoreau, an American naturalist of the mid-19th century who lived a very simple life with few personal possessions. At one time he was attracted to purchase an especially beautiful bit of land with a pasture and a wooded area. He even made a deposit. But then he realized that it was not necessary to purchase the land because, he reasoned, he already possessed the land in its wonder and its beauty as he passed by each day. This intimacy with the land could not be taken away from him, no matter who owned the land in its physical reality. So indeed that same bit of land could be owned in its wonder and beauty by an unlimited number of persons, even though in its physical reality it might be owned by a single person.

Such was the argument of Mencius, the Chinese writer. He taught the emperor that he should open up the royal park for others, since it would be an even greater joy to have others present with him, just as at a musical concert each of us enjoys the music, not diminishing but increasing our own joy as we share it with others. So, too, in the Bodhisattva tradition of India there were those such as Shantideva, in the fifth century of our era, who took a vow to refuse beatitude itself until all living creatures were saved. For only when they participated in his joy could he be fully caught up in the delight of paradise.

It has taken these many centuries for us to meet with each other in the comprehensive manner that is now possible. While for the many long centuries we had fragments of information concerning each other, we can now come together, speak with each other, dine with each other. Above all we can tell our stories to each other.

Tonight we might recall the ancient law of hospitality whereby the wanderer was welcomed. So it was with Ulysses in his long voyage home after the Trojan war. When exhausted and driven ashore on occasion and surrounded by a people that he had never met before, he was consistently rested, invited to dine with the people of the place, and then in the quiet moment afterward was invited to tell his story. So it has been, I trust, with each of us in these past few days. To some extent we have been able to tell our stories to each other. Now a new phase in all our stories has begun, as we begin to shape the Great Story of all peoples.

I would suggest that we see these early years of the 21st century as the period when we discover the great community of the Earth, a comprehensive community of all the living and non-living components of the planet. We are just discovering that the human project is itself a component of the Earth project, that our intimacy with the Earth is our way to intimacy with each other. Such are the foundations of our journey into the future.

From remarks made at the August 30, 2000, Thomas Berry Award and Lecture, sponsored by the Center for Respect of Life and Environment and the Forum on Religion and Ecology at the UN Millennium World Peace Summit for Religious and Spiritual Leaders. Thomas Berry is a cultural historian, author, and teacher of religion now living in the southern Appalachians. This article appeared in the Winter 2001 issue of *YES!*

The Failure of War

WENDELL BERRY

If you know even as little history as I do, it is hard not to doubt the efficacy of modern war as a solution to any problem except that of retribution—the "justice" of exchanging one damage for another.

Apologists for war will insist that war answers the problem of national self-defense. But the doubter, in reply, will ask to what extent the cost even of a successful war of national defense—in life, money, material, foods, health, and (inevitably) freedom—may amount to a national defeat. National defense through war always involves some degree of national defeat. This paradox has been with us from the very beginning of our republic. Militarization in defense of freedom reduces the freedom of the defenders. There is a fundamental inconsistency between war and freedom.

In a modern war, fought with modern weapons and on the modern scale, neither side can limit to "the enemy" the damage that it does. These wars damage the world. We know enough by now to know that you cannot damage a part of the world without damaging all of it. Modern war has not only made it impossible to kill "combatants" without killing "noncombatants," it has made it impossible to damage your enemy without damaging yourself.

That many have considered the increasing unacceptability of modern warfare is shown by the language of the propaganda surrounding it. Modern wars have characteristically been fought to end war; they have been fought in the name of peace. Our most terrible weapons have been made, ostensibly, to preserve and assure the peace of the world. "All we want is peace," we say as we increase relentlessly our capacity to make war.

Yet at the end of a century in which we have fought two wars to end war and several more to prevent war and preserve peace, and in which scientific and technological progress has made war ever more terrible and less controllable, we still, by policy, give no consideration to nonviolent means of national defense. We do indeed make much of diplomacy and diplomatic relations, but by diplomacy we mean invariably ultimatums for peace backed by the threat of war. It is always understood that we stand ready to kill those with whom we are "peacefully negotiating."

Our century of war, militarism, and political terror has produced great—and successful—advocates of true peace, among whom Mohandas Gandhi and Martin Luther King, Jr., are the paramount examples. The considerable success that they achieved testifies to the presence, in the midst of violence, of an authentic and powerful desire for peace and, more important, of the proven will to make the necessary sacrifices. But so far as our government is concerned, these men and their great and authenticating accomplishments might as well never have existed. To achieve peace by peaceable means is not yet our goal. We cling to the hopeless paradox of making peace by making war.

The most dangerous superstition of the parties of violence is the idea that sanctioned violence can prevent or control unsanctioned violence. But if violence is "just" in one instance as determined by the state, why might it not also be "just" in another instance, as determined by an individual? How can a society that justifies capital punishment and warfare prevent its justifications from being extended to assassination and terrorism? If a government perceives that some causes are so important as to justify the killing of children, how can it hope to prevent the contagion of its logic spreading to its citizens—or to its citizens' children?

If we give to these small absurdities the magnitude of international relations, we produce, unsurprisingly, some much larger absurdities. What could be more absurd, to begin with, than our attitude of high moral outrage against other nations for manufacturing the selfsame weapons that we manufacture? The difference, as our leaders say, is that we will use these weapons virtuously, whereas our enemies will use them maliciously—a proposition that too readily conforms to a proposition of much less dignity: we will use them in our interest, whereas our enemies will use them in theirs.

Or we must say, at least, that the issue of virtue in war is as obscure, ambiguous, and troubling as Abraham Lincoln found to be the issue of prayer in

war: "Both [the North and the South] read the same bible, and pray to the same God, and each invokes his aid against the other... The prayers of both could not be answered—that of neither could be answered fully."

Recent American wars, having been both "foreign" and "limited," have been fought under the assumption that little or no personal sacrifice is required. In "foreign" wars, we do not directly experience the damage that we inflict upon the enemy. We hear and see this damage reported in the news, but we are not affected. These limited, "foreign" wars require that some of our young people should be killed or crippled, and that some families should grieve, but these "casualties" are so widely distributed among our population as hardly to be noticed.

Otherwise, we do not feel ourselves to be involved. We pay taxes to support the war, but that is nothing new, for we pay war taxes also in time of "peace." We experience no shortages, we suffer no rationing, we endure no limitations. We earn, borrow, spend, and consume in wartime as in peacetime.

And of course no sacrifice is required of those large economic interests that now principally constitute our economy. No corporation will be required to submit to any limitation or to sacrifice a dollar. On the contrary, war is the great cure-all and opportunity of our corporate economy, which subsists and thrives upon war. War ended the Great Depression of the 1930s, and we have maintained a war economy—an economy, one might justly say, of general violence—ever since, sacrificing to it an enormous economic and ecological wealth, including, as designated victims, the farmers and the industrial working class.

And so great costs are involved in our fixation on war, but the costs are "externalized" as "acceptable losses." And here we see how progress in war, progress in technology, and progress in the industrial economy are parallel to one another—or, very often, are merely identical.

Romantic nationalists, which is to say most apologists for war, always imply in their public speeches a mathematics or an accounting of war. Thus by its suffering in the Civil War, the North is said to have "paid for" the emancipation of the slaves and the preservation of the Union. Thus we may speak of our liberty as having been "bought" by the bloodshed of patriots. I am fully aware of the truth in such statements. I know that I am one of many who have benefited from painful sacrifices made by other people, and I would not like to be ungrateful. Moreover, I am a patriot myself and I know that the time

may come for any of us when we must make extreme sacrifices for the sake of liberty—a fact confirmed by the fates of Gandhi and King.

But still I am suspicious of this kind of accounting. For one reason, it is necessarily done by the living on behalf of the dead. And I think we must be careful about too easily accepting, or being too easily grateful for, sacrifices made by others, especially if we have made none ourselves. For another reason, though our leaders in war always assume that there is an acceptable price, there is never a previously stated level of acceptability. The acceptable price, finally, is whatever is paid.

It is easy to see the similarity between this accounting of the price of war and our usual accounting of "the price of progress." We seem to have agreed that whatever has been (or will be) paid for so-called progress is an acceptable price. If that price includes the diminishment of privacy and the increase of government secrecy, so be it. If it means a radical reduction in the number of small businesses and the virtual destruction of the farm population, so be it. If it means the devastation of whole regions by extractive industries, so be it. If it means that a mere handful of people should own more billions of wealth than is owned by all of the world's poor, so be it.

But let us have the candor to acknowledge that what we call "the economy" or "the free market" is less and less distinguishable from warfare. For about half of the last century, we worried about world conquest by international communism. Now with less worry (so far) we are witnessing world conquest by international capitalism. Though its political means are milder (so far) than those of communism, this newly internationalized capitalism may prove even more destructive of human cultures and communities, of freedom, and of nature. Its tendency is just as much toward total dominance and control. Confronting this conquest, ratified and licensed by the new international trade agreements, no place and no community in the world may consider itself safe from some form of plunder. More and more people all over the world are recognizing that this is so, and they are saying that world conquest of any kind is wrong, period.

They are doing more than that. They are saying that local conquest also is wrong, and wherever it is taking place local people are joining together to oppose it. All over my own state of Kentucky this opposition is growing—from the west, where the exiled people of the Land Between the Lakes are struggling to save their homeland from bureaucratic depredation, and to the

east, where the native people of the mountains are still struggling to preserve their land from destruction by absentee corporations.

To have an economy that is warlike, that aims at conquest and that destroys virtually everything that it is dependent on, placing no value on the health of nature or of human communities, is absurd enough. It is even more absurd that this economy, that in some respects is so much at one with our military industries and programs, is in other respects directly in conflict with our professed aim of national defense.

It seems only reasonable, only sane, to suppose that a gigantic program of preparedness for national defense should be founded first of all upon a principle of national and even regional economic independence. A nation determined to defend itself and its freedoms should be prepared, and always preparing, to live from its own resources and from the work and the skills of its own people. But that is not what we are doing in the United States today. What we are doing is squandering in the most prodigal manner the natural and human resources of the nation.

At present, in the face of declining finite sources of fossil fuel energies, we have virtually no energy policy, either for conservation or for the development of safe and clean alternative sources. At present, our energy policy simply is to use all that we have. Moreover, in the face of a growing population needing to be fed, we have virtually no policy for land conservation and no policy of just compensation to the primary producers of food. Our agricultural policy is to use up everything that we have, while depending increasingly on imported food, energy, technology, and labor.

Those are just two examples of our general indifference to our own needs. We thus are elaborating a surely dangerous contradiction between our militant nationalism and our espousal of the international "free market" ideology. How do we escape from this absurdity?

I don't think there is an easy answer. Obviously, we would be less absurd if we took better care of things. We would be less absurd if we founded our public policies upon an honest description of our needs and our predicament, rather than upon fantastical descriptions of our wishes. We would be less absurd if our leaders would consider in good faith the proven alternatives to violence.

Such things are easy to say, but we are disposed, somewhat by culture and somewhat by nature, to solve our problems by violence, and even to enjoy

doing so. And yet by now all of us must at least have suspected that our right to live, to be free, and to be at peace is not guaranteed by any act of violence. It can be guaranteed only by our willingness that all other persons should live, be free, and be at peace—and by our willingness to use or give our own lives to make that possible. To be incapable of such willingness is merely to resign ourselves to the absurdity we are in; and yet, if you are like me, you are unsure to what extent you are capable of it.

Here is the other question that I have been leading toward, one that the predicament of modern warfare forces upon us: How many deaths of other people's children by bombing or starvation are we willing to accept in order that we may be free, affluent, and (supposedly) at peace? To that question I answer: None. Please, no children. Don't kill any children for my benefit.

If that is your answer too, then you must know that we have not come to rest, far from it. For surely we must feel ourselves swarmed about with more questions that are urgent, personal, and intimidating. But perhaps also we feel ourselves beginning to be free, facing at last in our own selves the greatest challenge ever laid before us, the most comprehensive vision of human progress, the best advice, and the least obeyed:

"Love your enemies, bless them that curse you, do good to them that hate you, and pray for them which despitefully use you and persecute you; That ye may be the children of your Father which is in heaven: for he maketh his sun to rise on the evil and the good, and sendeth rain on the just and on the unjust."

Wendell Berry, poet, philosopher, and conservationist, farms in Kentucky. ©Wendell Berry. This article appeared in the Winter 2002 issue of *YES!*

In the Eyes of the World

WALDEN BELLO

The assault on the World Trade Center was unpardonable, but it is important not to lose perspective, especially a historical one. For a response dictated by fury such as that now displayed by some American politicians, while understandable, is likely to serve simply as one more proof for Santayana's dictum that those who do not remember history are bound to repeat it.

The scale and consequences of the September 11 attack are massive indeed, but this was not the worst act of mass terrorism in US history, as some US media are wont to claim. The over 3,000 lives lost are irreplaceable, but one must not forget that the atomic raids on Hiroshima and Nagasaki killed 210,000 people, most of them civilians, most perishing instantaneously. One may object that you can't compare the September 11 attack to the nuclear bombings since, after all, Hiroshima and Nagasaki were targets in a war. But why not, since the purpose of the nuclear bombings was not mainly to destroy military or infrastructure targets, but to terrorize and destroy the civilian population? Indeed, the whole allied air campaign against Germany and Japan in 1944–45, which produced the firestorms in Dresden, Hamburg, and Tokyo that killed tens of thousands, had as its central aim to kill and maim as many civilians as possible.

Similarly, during the Korean War, terror bombing of civilians was the policy of the US Air Force's Far Eastern Bombing Command, which was instructed to pulverize anything that moved in enemy territory. After indiscriminately dropping 1,400 tons of bombs and 23,000 gallons of napalm, the unit commander, General O'Donnell, uttered his famous lines: "Every-

thing is destroyed. There is nothing standing worthy of the name. Just before the Chinese came we were grounded. There were no more targets in Korea."

During the Cold War, mass elimination of the enemy's civilian population, alongside the destruction of his armed forces or industry, was institutionalized in the strategy of massive nuclear retaliation that lay at the center of the doctrine of deterrence. In Indochina, where the US was frustrated by the fact that combatants and civilians seemed indistinguishable, indiscriminate killing of civilians was a central component of the American war. In the air war, US forces detonated 13 million tons of high explosive from 1965 to 1971, or the energy equivalent of 450 Hiroshima nuclear bombs. In the "counterinsurgency war" on the ground, 20,000 civilians were systematically assassinated under the CIA's Operation Phoenix program in the Mekong Delta.

But must not such actions against civilians be judged in the context of a broader strategic objective of sapping the enemy's will to fight and thus bringing the war to a conclusion? Then how different is this justification from the terrorists' aim to change the foreign policy of the US government by eroding the support of the country's civilian population?

The point is not to engage in a "maleficent calculus," as the 19th-century English philosopher Jeremy Bentham would have called this exercise, but to point out that the US government hardly possesses the high ground in the current moral equation. Indeed, one can say that terrorists like Osama bin Laden, an ex-CIA protégé, have learned their lessons on the strategic targeting of the civilian population from Washington's traditional strategy of total warfare, where damage to the civilian population is not seen simply as collateral but as essential to achieving the ends of war.

In the aftermath of the World Trade Center assault, the perpetrators of the horrible deed have been called "irrational" or "madmen" or people who embody evil. This is understandable as an emotional reaction but dangerous as a basis for policy. The truth is the perpetrators of the deed were very rational. If they were indeed people connected with Osama bin Laden, their goal was most likely to raise the costs to the United States of maintaining its current policies in the Middle East, which they consider unjust and inequitable, and this was their way of doing it. They very rationally picked the targets and weapons to be used, paying attention not only to maximum destruction but also to maximum symbolism. The choice of the World Trade Center towers and the Pentagon as the targets, and American and United

Airlines planes as the delivery vehicles doubling as warheads, was the product of cold-blooded thinking and planning. The loss of their own lives was factored into the calculation. What we saw was a rational calculus of means to achieve a desired end. In the view of these people, terrorism, like war, is the extension of politics by other means. These are Clausewitzian minds, and the worst mistake one can make is to regard them as madmen.

One metaphor that the Washington establishment has used to capture the essence of recent events is that of a second Pearl Harbor, with the implication that like the first, the September 11 tragedy will galvanize the American people to an unprecedented level of unity to win the war against still unidentified enemies. The other side, one suspects, operates with a different metaphor, that of the Tet Offensive of 1968. The objective of the Vietnamese was to launch massive simultaneous uprisings that, even if defeated separately, would nevertheless add up to a strategic victory by convincing the other side, especially its civilian base, that the war was unwinnable. The aim was to rob the US of the will to win the war, and here the Vietnamese succeeded.

The perpetrators of the September 11 assault are operating with a similar calculus and, despite the current jingoistic talk in Washington, it is not certain that they are wrong. Will the American people really bear any burden and pay any price in a struggle that will persist long into the future, with no assurance of victory—indeed, with no clear sense of who the enemies are and of what "victory" will consist of?

The media are full of news about an alliance against terrorism, conveying the impression that coordination among key states combined with the outrage of citizens everywhere will give a Washington-led coalition an unbeatable edge. Perhaps it will in the short run, although even this is not certain. For the problem is that, as in guerrilla wars, this is not a war that will be won strictly or mainly by military means.

If it was bin Laden's network that was responsible for the World Trade Center attack, then the underlying issues are the twin pillars of US policy in the Middle East. One is subordination of the interests of the peoples of the region to the untrammeled access by the US to Middle East oil in order to maintain its high-consumption, petroleum-based civilization. To this end, the US overthrew the nationalist government of Mossadegh in Iran in 1953, cultivated the repressive Shah of Iran as the gendarme of the Persian Gulf,

supported antidemocratic feudal regimes in the Arabian peninsula, and introduced a massive permanent military presence in Saudi Arabia, which contains some of Islam's most sacred shrines and cities. The war against Saddam Hussein was justified as a war to beat back aggression, but everybody knew that Washington's key motivation was to ensure that the region's most massive oil reserves would remain under the control of pro-Western elites.

The other pillar is unstinting support for Israel. That Arab feelings about Israel are so elemental is not difficult to comprehend. It is hard to argue against the fact that the state of Israel was born on the basis of the massive dispossession of the Palestinian people of their country and their lands. It is impossible to deny that Israel is a European settler-state, one whose establishment was essentially a displacement from European territory of the ethnocultural contradictions of European society. The Holocaust was an unspeakable crime against humanity, but it was utterly wrong to impose its political consequences—chief of which was the creation of Israel—on a people who had nothing to do with it. It is hard to contradict Arab claims that it was essentially support from the United States that created the state of Israel; that it has been massive US military aid and backing that has maintained it in the last half century; and that it is deep confidence in perpetual US military and political support that enables Israel to sabotage in practice the emergence of a viable Palestinian state.

Unless the US abandons these two pillars of its policies, there will always be thousands of recruits for acts of terrorism such as that which occurred on September 11. And while we may condemn terrorist acts—as we must, strongly—it is another thing to expect desperate people not to adopt them, especially when they can point to the fact that it was such methods that targeted civilians as well as military personnel, combined with the Intifada, that forced Israel to agree to the 1993 Oslo Accord that led to the creation of the Palestinian entity.

Another reason why the strategic equation does not favor the US is that there are a great many people in the world who are ambivalent about terrorism. In contrast to the European reaction, the response to the September 11 event in the South has been muted. A survey would probably reveal that while many people in the Third World are appalled by the hijackers' methods, they are not unsympathetic to their political objectives. As one Chinese-Filipino entrepreneur said, "It's horrible, but on the other hand, the US had it

coming." If this reaction is common among middle-class people, it would not be surprising if such ambivalence towards terrorism is widespread among the 80 percent of the world's population marginalized by current global political and economic arrangements.

There is simply too much distrust, dislike, or just plain hatred of a country that has become so callous in its pursuit of economic power, so arrogant in its political and military relations with the rest of the world, and so brazen in declaring its cultural superiority over the rest of us. As in the equation of guerrilla war, civilian ambivalence in the theater of battle translates strategically to a minus when it comes to the staying power of the authorities and a plus when it comes to that of the terrorists.

In sum, if there is one thing we can be certain of, it is that massive retaliation on the part of the US will not put an end to terrorism. It will simply amplify the upward spiral of violence, as the other side will resort to even more spectacular deeds, fed by unending waves of recruits. The September 11 tragedy is the clearest evidence of the bankruptcy of the 30-year-old policy of mailed-fist, massive retaliation response to terrorism. This policy has simply resulted in the extreme professionalization of terrorism.

The only response that will really contribute to global security and peace is for Washington to address not the symptoms but the roots of terrorism. It is for the United States to reexamine and substantially change its policies in the Middle East and the Third World, supporting arrangements that will promote equity, justice, and genuine national sovereignty for currently marginalized peoples.

Any other way leads to endless war.

Walden Bello is executive director of Focus on the Global South and professor at the University of the Philippines. This article appeared in the Winter 2002 issue of YES!

Instead of Empire: What Future for the United States?

A ROUNDTABLE DISCUSSION

To explore possibilities for a post-empire America, in October 2002 *YES!* editors invited five people to shed the light of their experience, spiritual leadership, and knowledge of world affairs. This is not a debate on whether we should go to war but an exploration of what might happen if the US chose a path that is neither the Clinton-promoted future founded in globalizing corporations, nor the Bush Doctrine of endless war. Each of them responded to questions sent them by *YES!*

RABBI MICHAEL LERNER
is founding editor of *Tikkun* and author
of *Politics of Meaning* and *Spirit Matters*

THE MOST REV. FRANK T. GRISWOLD
is presiding bishop and primate of the
Episcopal Church, USA

PHYLLIS BENNIS
is a fellow with the Institute for Policy
Studies & the Transnational Institute,
Amsterdam

MARC LUYCKX
is a futurist, formerly with the European
Union, and a Brussels-based consultant

HARLAN CLEVELAND
is a former NATO ambassador and president of
the World Academy of Arts and Sciences

The primary concern that seems to drive the willingness of Americans to go to war is the sense that we are not safe, especially since 9/11. What are the sources of threats to the US, and what could we do to increase our security?

HARLAN CLEVELAND: I have to start by quarrelling with the question. "The willingness of Americans to go to war" is not at all clear to me. If it's easy (as it won't be); if it's short on American casualties (a dubious assumption); if we have plenty of help and don't have to go it alone (the Bush team may have blown the potential of a real coalition, in the UN or outside its purview), then there might well be an American majority for a "military solution" in Iraq. But none of these conditions exists, and the common sense of the American people still has a chance to prevail.

As to the essence of your question, the threats are palpable, but they have been enormously enhanced by the behavior of the US government. To the extent our government uses overwhelming power to bypass and belittle people who might otherwise be our friends and supporters, we'll engender reluctance and sabotage. Our government is alienating these potential members of the Club of Democracies with a fatal mixture of arrogance and neglect. In the past few months I have come to believe that the objective threats to US security pale by comparison to what our government is doing to arm our enemies and disarm our friends.

FRANK T. GRISWOLD: I think the real threat to the US is fear itself. We seem to be developing a paranoia that ultimately will poison the spirit of the nation, making us all suspicious and overly defensive.

The truth is, there is no such thing as absolute security. Life by its very nature puts us in a stance of vulnerability. You cannot protect yourself against everything, and no amount of government surveillance or police security or training people to be on the watch for suspicious people will ultimately protect us. The myth of security is itself dangerous. Having said that, obviously there are steps that nations take to ensure the security of the populace.

With respect to the real sources of threats, I think our deportment in the world creates the greatest exposure to anger and terrorist attack. We need to examine our relationships with other nations, particularly those parts of the

world suffering from hunger, poverty, and violence. How do our policies, ordered to our own interests, affect other nations? How does the export of our culture, often at its worst, undermine the identity and values of other societies? By addressing these and other questions, and not simply arming ourselves, we can protect ourselves most effectively and most authentically.

MICHAEL LERNER: There are two basic theories about how to get security in the world. One says you get security by having enough physical strength and power to scare off or dominate everyone else who might threaten you. The other says that security comes from loving connection and mutual recognition with others. Both have strong historical bases, and it usually makes sense to have some kind of balance between the two. Unfortunately, the US is out of balance, and in our case we've tilted way too far toward domination and way too little toward loving connection with others.

PHYLLIS BENNIS: Threats to the US have to be defined to clarify if we are speaking of threats to the traditionally defined "national interest"— usually meaning corporate wealth, military strength, and diplomatic power— or threats to the *people* of the US. Americans are threatened by virtue of living in the center of the most powerful empire that has ever existed. There is no reason to think that the contemporary US empire will engender less antagonism or last longer than earlier empires.

The single biggest threat to Americans' safety lies in US foreign policy, which has caused impoverishment and political disempowerment of nations and peoples across the world. There is an understandable tendency to blame Americans for the actions of their government or their military. While American citizens have not been routinely singled out for attack by international terrorism, that could soon change as our foreign policy becomes more aggressively committed to the extension of US military power around the world.

Protecting American lives can best be accomplished by creating a new internationalist movement in which Americans participate with (some) governments and (many) civil society organizations from around the world to counter the power-driven blandishments of empire that currently define the US global superpower.

The US spends about the same amount on the military as the next 20 military powers combined, including our allies. Does the world need

the US to act as an empire in order to keep the peace? What might a world without empire look like?

MARK LUYCKX: When astronauts came back from space and showed us that this blue planet is such a fragile gift, we collectively entered a new era.

We have to recognize that the industrial, hyperrational, patriarchal, top-down values, which were successful for getting the US to the moon, can't provide satisfactory answers to the urgent global question of our collective survival.

We need a new set of values: more feminine values, more inclusive values of connectedness with nature and the cosmos. We need to give priority to the common good of humanity over national or particular interest.

In defense matters the same paradigm shift is underway. The latest treaty on Conventional Forces in Europe, signed by the US, puts forward a brand new concept. Instead of being based on the classical concept of "balance of forces," it is based on "mutual vulnerability." Rather than relying on secrecy, this new treaty relies on transparency. Indeed, as Harlan Cleveland has been warning us since 1984, in the knowledge society, information always leaks. It is impossible to base future strategies on secrecy.

What to do with the terrorist? Should we employ the same violent strategies as the terrorists themselves? This is what Bush's strategies propose. Or should we seek the common good for the whole of the planet? The most urgent need may be to invent a new Marshall Plan for the whole world.

BENNIS: What the world needs to keep the peace is not an empire lording over the rest of the world, but a democratic international system based on law, global institutions, and the UN Charter. The vast disparities of incomes within countries and between North and South, the disempowerment of peoples around the world whose repressive governments rely on US financial, political, and military backing—these are the real threats to the peace, and a US empire does not make any of us safer.

A world without an empire would not be a utopia; it would simply allow nations around the world a chance to build better lives for their people and allow people around the world a chance at gaining human rights.

Empires are an old story, really—the story of a strategically unchallenged dominion, at the apogee of its power and influence, rewriting global rules.

Two thousand years ago, Thucydides described the conquering of the island of Mylos by the Greeks in order to ensure stability for the Greek Empire's "democratic" golden age. The Melians asked, "What about democracy?" And the Athenians responded, "For *us* there is democracy; for *you* there is the law of empire."

The Roman empire did the same, creating one set of laws for Rome's own citizens, imposing another on its far-flung possessions. The sun-never-sets-on-us British empire did much the same thing. And then, at the end of the 20th century, having achieved once unimaginable heights of military, economic, and political power, it was Washington's turn. It remains for us, in this country, to bring an end to empire and a beginning of a search for real democracy in its stead.

CLEVELAND: If military power is used to dominate, the result won't be peace; too many people will express their resentment and their desire to be free in ways that make military force as we have known it irrelevant. Imperial ambitions would produce a widespread messiness that wouldn't resemble peace, but also wouldn't resemble war as we have known it. It would resemble in the international arena something like we have already seen in the so-called "failed states"—anarchy, warlordism, constantly changing loyalties—opposition to the empire-builders being the primary glue that holds disparate groups together.

As an alumnus of both the Marshall Plan and NATO, I am convinced that there is a different, and more effective, way to wield great power. That's to use it to help build societies that share our historic beliefs in pluralism (being different together), tolerance (of others' beliefs, race, and cultural histories), and authority (derived from the governed). Working in this direction speaks to the most basic feelings of almost everyone. The US still has a chance to be a "city on a hill"—just so the hill is defined not as megatonnage of weaponry but as an aspiration for progress and equality in which, sooner or later, all people can share if they work at it.

A number of people have made a link between Iraq having the world's second largest oil reserves and the US interest in invading the country. US dependence on imported oil is increasing. What options does the US have apart from using military might to ensure access to oil?

BENNIS: US interest in Middle East oil is not primarily about making sure we can get the oil we need. The US doesn't import that much from the region (although the amount is indeed rising)—we have a wide range of alternative sources.

The oil issue during the 1990-91 Gulf crisis and today is far more subtle and far more linked to US imperial design. The key aspect of oil policy has to do not only with direct control of the oil fields, but in continuing to act as guarantor of oil access for US allies in Europe and Japan who are far more dependent on Middle East oil. Playing that role insures not only a means to satisfy the US corporate-bloated appetite for oil, but gains the US power vis-à-vis our allies, preserving the US role as a "hyper-power" with global reach.

Our key option is to diminish our dependence on imported oil by decreasing our dependence on *all* oil—meaning we should reinvest money and research into serious alternative fuels. We must reject the view first put forward by President Jimmy Carter who called the Persian Gulf's petroleum, half a world away from us, "our oil," and recognize instead that we have no more right to other countries' oil than anyone else. And we must diminish the power of US-based oil companies in domestic US politics—which means that we must undermine the influence of this petro-administration in the White House. We need regime change in Washington!

LUYCKX: Is this policy the right one in a pre-hydrogen era? If you listen to the Rocky Mountain Institute, soon we will have hydrogen fuel cars, with zero pollution.

Perhaps many in the US find war attractive partly because it provides a sense of being part of a powerful effort with a transcendent purpose. Apart from war, where do you think America could find a sense of national purpose?

GRISWOLD: In the gospel it is reported that when Jesus was arrested, the enmity that had existed between Pilate and Herod was overcome, and on that day they became friends. This story has repeated itself over the ages as a sense of common purpose has been achieved through the identification of a common enemy. In our own day, the disparate elements of our nation have

been gathered up and given a sense of national unity through the use of demonizing rhetoric, the language of paranoia, and a personally focused object of evil, namely Saddam Hussein.

One of the most disconcerting elements of our present national ethos is the sense—sometimes spoken and sometimes not—that God holds the United States in special favor and blesses our policies. Indeed some unthinking patriotism is rooted in that perspective. As God's blessing is claimed for our national purposes, we would do well to remember that being in relationship with God means yielding one's perspectives to the larger perspective of God rather than seeking to enlist God's approval for one's own points of view. Praying is not simply about putting forth our petitions but about having our own attitudes and opinions enlarged by those of God, who embraces the whole world, seeks the well being of all persons, and looks upon the people of all nations with compassion and love.

I believe our national leaders are bound to call us to live out of our better natures, our deepest aspirations to make meaning, live in peace, and be mindful of the suffering and injustice both here and around the world—rather than out of fear and the ensuing clutch on what serves our self-interest. Since we declare ourselves as one nation "under God," might we not look for a new sense of national unity based on a larger vision of the common good: one that takes us beyond our borders and unites us with the struggles, sufferings, and aspirations of the world?

CLEVELAND: Not all wars have "the power of creating a sense of unity and national purpose." The war in Vietnam was, in the end, so divisive that it eroded the American sense of unity and induced millions of Americans to question our national purpose. France's war in Algeria had a similar effect. I predict that a unilateral, "preemptive" attack on Iraq will not be widely regarded as serving a "transcendent" purpose. Even if it's instantly successful, its long-running aftermath will likely become a quagmire.

Apart from World War II, America in my lifetime has found a transcendent sense of purpose in four sustained government initiatives. One was FDR's New Deal, focused on poverty, unemployment, and public works. Another was the Marshall Plan (1948), soon followed (and bracketed in the public mind with) the North Atlantic Alliance (1949). Yet another was the civil rights movement, culminating in the legislation of the 1960s. And another,

also in the 1960s, was the early phase of the space program, driven by JFK's 1961 promise to put a man on the Moon. There is an opportunity now for a different kind of "Marshall Plan" for the Middle East.

LERNER: First, let the US become the major force in the world committed to eliminating hunger, homelessness, disease, inadequate health care and inadequate schooling. Let it do so by becoming the major force in the world committing its resources to redistributing wealth globally so that everyone can live at a level of material well-being comparable to that of the American middle class today, and let this be accomplished in a way that is ecologically sustainable.

Second, let the US become the major force rectifying the damage done to the Earth by 150 years of ecological irresponsibility, instead of being perceived as the major force limiting serious ecological reform.

Third, let the US become the world champion of a new definition of productivity, efficiency, and rationality, so that they become measured not only by the extent to which any given institution or social practice maximizes money and power, but also to the extent that that institution or social practice tends to produce loving and caring human beings who are morally, ecologically, and spiritually responsible, and who respond to the universe with awe and wonder at the grandeur of creation.

To help fund these steps, let the US take the entire $1.5 trillion that George Bush allocated for tax cuts and let that be dedicated to financing these three directions.

This article appeared in the Winter 2003 issue of YES!

What Happens to Your Heart

David Morse

They journey to Iraq from every quarter of the United States and from around the globe, traveling mostly in small groups. They include extraordinary individuals from more than a dozen organizations whose concern for the children of Iraq has propelled them into action. Most are not famous, although they include two Nobel Peace laureates. Their lives are living testimony to the power of spirit in action.

But their pilgrimage goes unreported in the US media—for a reason: this is not the kind of story most readers will want to read about over coffee. The brutal fact is that the US continues to wage the Gulf War in Iraq today, in the form of economic sanctions that claim the lives of 5,000 Iraqi children per month, mostly as a result of still unrepaired water purification and sewage treatment plants that have left much of Iraq's fragile water supply contaminated. Most readers prefer not to know that these deaths are occurring and that they are the direct consequence of US policies.

"Those children die quietly," says Doug Hostetter, who has traveled to Iraq three times. "No media. No outrage."

Hostetter, who is 55, with a thick salt-and-pepper beard and steady clear voice, is former International/Interfaith Secretary of the Fellowship of Reconciliation, based in Nyack, New York. He is a Mennonite, but says he has found his own spirituality deepened and enriched through cooperative work with people of various faiths. He married into a Jewish family, took in two Bosnian Muslim students during the war in Bosnia, and has worked with Methodist and Quaker organizations. He is typical of those leading the

delegations into Iraq, whose compassion transcends the bounds of any particular religious faith.

Much of Hostetter's time has been devoted to the Campaign of Conscience, a gutsy project undertaken jointly by Fellowship of Reconciliation (FOR) and the American Friends Service Committee (AFSC), that attempted to install four small water purifiers to provide clean water for a few hundred Iraqis. Because the purifiers use chlorine, they violate UN sanctions and US law against "dual use" chemicals that could conceivably be used by the Iraqi military. By signing on to the Campaign of Conscience, some 90 Quaker meetings in the US have joined in this act of collective civil disobedience. By publicly breaking the law and risking US government fines up to $1 million, they are challenging the inhumanity of the sanctions.

From his first visit in 1990, just before the Gulf War, Hostetter recalls a highly industrialized Iraq with "the best education and medical systems in the Arab world, a large middle class, beautiful cities." He shakes his head in wonder. "We have destroyed it, and we have kept it destroyed."

The 10 years of sanctions that followed the bombing of civilian infrastructure targets—electric generating plants and water-treatment facilities—have been condemned by most international observers.

A 1998 UNICEF report estimates that half a million Iraqi children have died as a consequence of the sanctions, which inflict suffering mostly on the poor and the physically vulnerable. Children succumb to water-borne diseases such as cholera, typhoid, and dysentery. And they die due to the lack of medical facilities for treating birth defects—which are on the rise in areas contaminated by spent uranium and chemical pollutants.

Hostetter repeats Nobel Peace laureate Mairead Corrigan Maguire's burning question, "In 50 years, the next generation will ask: 'What were you doing when the children of Iraq were dying?'"

Jim Jennings, founder of a group called Conscience International, was similarly drawn to Iraq. Asked what was his most moving experience during the dozen visits he had made, he said it was "putting my hand on a dying baby, whose body was just starting to chill." For Jennings, a 63-year-old professor of archaeology and Middle Eastern history, the relief effort is "a must-do kind of thing—not something I can shrink from. The children of Iraq are on the conscience of America."

Although it is the suffering that has brought Jennings and others to Iraq, the relief work has rich rewards—as Michael Carley discovered during a trip

last March to the southeastern corner of Iraq, the area hit hardest by the Gulf War. Carley describes his elation when the bus pulled up to Labanni and he saw the water purification plant that his organization, Veterans for Peace, had rebuilt in partnership with a Michigan-based group, LIFE for Relief and Development. Seeing the fresh paint and realizing that the Labanni plant was fully operational, Carley broke into tears. "It just wallops you—the fact that it's working and is saving thousands of children's lives!"

Unlike the AFSC-FOR water chlorinators, which will deliver clean water to only a few hundred people, the rebuilding of the Labanni water plant restored water to tens of thousands of people. (AFSC-FOR has recently followed suit, shifting its focus from the chlorinators to restoring a water system that would serve 9,000 people in northeastern Iraq. "If I never do anything for the rest of my life," Carley says, "I will always know I had this project." Carley, at 41, does not consider himself a religious person. But he does consider himself blessed. "I am surrounded by deeply motivated people who are powerfully led by their spiritual beliefs."

Among the members of Carley's delegation was a Gulf War veteran, Candy Lovett, who at 40 suffers from Gulf War Syndrome and is confined to a wheelchair. She chose to participate symbolically in the project but Lovett was looking for something else, as she told me before the trip. The moment came for her in the nearby city of Basrah, when the delegation was meeting in the home of a mother who had lost a child to an American bomb in 1999. Lovett asked her for forgiveness. The mother, Fartous Iqbal, knelt by Lovett's wheelchair and said in English, "Of course you are forgiven." Lovett says, "I felt a big weight come off my shoulders."

One of the most articulate voices in the movement is Kathy Kelly, founder of the organization Voices in the Wilderness. Kelly, who has a bright smile and an astonishing array of facts at her fingertips, has led some 35 delegations into Iraq. She was in Iraq when American bombs started falling at the onset of the Gulf War. More recently she lived for seven months in Basra, a city that suffers from both the sanctions and the ongoing bombardment used to enforce the so-called "no-fly zone" declared without UN approval by the United States and Britain.

"Every morning," she says, "usually around 2:30, the planes would come, and we would wonder whether civilians had been hit. Little girls would make a sound—la-la-la-la—and hold their ears, trying to drown out the sound that

terrified them. For the current bombings they're using National Guard re-servists. They're up there at 30,000 feet and have little sense of consequences. That's why we think it's so important to have these people-to-people encounters with Iraq."

The media's unwillingness to focus on Iraq is a source of anguish for Kelly. "If people in the US knew the plight of these parents, if they could see the faces of those children—gorgeous children—then they would stop seeing Iraq as the personification of one demonized person, Saddam Hussein; they'd be seeing people just like you and me. Then I don't think the sanctions could stand the light of another day."

She cites a 1991 report by the Defense Intelligence Agency, only recently declassified, that pinpoints the vulnerability of the Iraqi water system and predicts the consequences in civilian suffering. She thinks Americans would be furious if they knew how cold-bloodedly the impact of the bombing was calculated.

Although Kathy Kelly's own spiritual roots are in Catholicism, she embodies the same values of nonviolence and simplicity espoused by Quakers and Mennonites. She pays no taxes. "I won't pay for weapons, for prisons." She operates Voices in the Wilderness out of her elderly father's home in Chicago. She tells of the IRS agent who showed up to assess what could be seized for taxes; he looked around and said, "You don't really have anything, do you? I'm going to put you down as uncollectible." Kelly chuckles. "Janis Joplin had it right. 'Freedom's just another word for nothing left to lose.'" Her voluntary poverty is part of a larger vision. Kelly, 49, believes we have to "unhinge ourselves from a consumptive lifestyle. We need to move away from the assumption that it's okay to take other people's precious commodities—their oil—at cut-rate prices."

Kelly's words touch on the broader spirit that animates this movement. Everyone I spoke with communicated a dedication to social justice based on nonviolence and an assumption that their spiritual lives were inseparable from their political lives. All expressed anger, but it was subordinated to hope.

This was certainly true of a Canadian couple, Rick McCutcheon and Tamara Fleming. I interviewed them shortly after they returned from seven and a half months overseeing several projects in Iraq. The projects ranged from distributing 2,000 metric tons of beans and lentils donated by

Canadian farmers, to rehabilitating nine schools in the Baghdad area, to teaching Iraqi farmers modern methods of propagating tomato seedlings.

I asked Fleming, 28, what she had gotten from the experience spiritually. "What happens to your heart?" I asked her. "For me," she says, "it was seeing the darkness of the situation. The malnutrition, the unemployment, the suffering. And then seeing the light. Driving around Baghdad in some rickety old taxi, you come across a wedding and see people celebrating, clapping hands, playing drums. They keep going. You see the survival mechanisms at work, and it fuels my desire to keep going, to keep talking about the issues."

After listening thoughtfully to his wife's response, McCutcheon returned to the question. "How does it affect your heart?" he mused. "As I was listening to Tam, I was thinking, it breaks it open. There's this Buddhist idea of the heart of compassion just breaking open." He talked of the political burnout he had experienced in Toronto before they left for Iraq, his sense of futility. His voice was gentle. "My heart had just filled with that darkness for many years. And then it just breaks open. And there in the midst of this suffering, is light."

David Morse's essays and stories have appeared in such publications as *Dissent* and *Friends' Journal*. He can be contacted at his Web site: www.david-morse.com. For more information, or to find out how to oppose further military action against Iraq, see: www.peaceresponse.org/ iraq.shtml. This article appeared in the Spring 2002 issue of *YES!*

The Sound of Bombs
Not Exploding

JOANNA MACY

Sitting on the grass as far as I could see, 650,000 people made the biggest silence I ever heard. As the silence deepened, I thought: This is the sound of bombs and landmines not exploding, of rockets not launched, and machine guns laid aside. It is possible for us all.

In war-torn Sri Lanka, this was Peace Samadhi Day, March 15, 2002, perhaps the largest meditation for peace in the history of the world. Organized by the nongovernmental Sarvodaya movement, the meditation both supported the cease-fire recently negotiated with Norwegian help between the Sinhalese-identified Sri Lankan government and the Tamil Tiger secessionist party, and celebrated the launching of Sarvodaya's "village-to-village, heart-to-heart" Link-Up program.

As I walked among the white-clad people who filled the paths to the great stupas and the grounds of the ancient, sacred city of Anuradhapura, I could not tell from which side of Sri Lanka's civil war these pilgrims came. No placards or shouted slogans proclaimed their identities. Only place names on the parked buses gave a clue. They came from Hindu Tamil and Buddhist Sinhalese areas that had been pitted against each other for the last 19 years.

Power struggles between the Sinhalese and Tamils are rooted in historic waves of invasion and foreign occupation on this island nation (formerly called Ceylon) off the tip of India. Since Independence in 1948, the Sinhalese majority has controlled the government and promoted policies favoring Sinhalese such as making Sinhala the only official language and giving state support to Buddhism. Hindu Tamils have grown increasingly resentful, and

in 1983 Tamil Tigers ambushed and killed 13 Sinhalese soldiers, setting off full-scale riots in which hundreds of Tamils died and more than 100,000 fled the country. Ever since then, violence and retaliation have fed each other. By 2001, more than 65,000 people had died in this war. Over 700,000 more had been forced from their homes. The economy is wrecked and a generation of Sri Lankans has been traumatized.

Late in 2001, Sri Lanka's Prime Minister, Ranil Wickremesinghe was elected on a pro-peace mandate. In February, with Norwegian assistance, he signed a cease-fire agreement with Tamil leaders. Previous peace negotiations failed in 1987, 1989, and 1995, and today, Sri Lanka's president is leery of recognizing the Tamil separatists. Nevertheless, in September 2002, the government and Tamil Tiger leaders began negotiations in Thailand.

What role has Sarvodaya played in this outbreak of peace? It is difficult to prove a direct link, but a report prepared in collaboration with the Norwegian Agency for Overseas Development by Professor K. T. Silva provides a clue. "When ethnic violence spread in several areas ... some of the local Sarvodaya leaders appealed to the residents not to join demonstrations or street riots. ... In some instances, they gave protection to estate [plantation] residents who were Sinhalese and were vulnerable to attack by agitated mobs. As a result, only a few incidents were reported in estates covered by the project while law and order rapidly deteriorated in the surrounding areas." Perhaps the Sarvodaya movement's 44 years of bringing conflict-resolution skills and economic development to more than half of Sri Lanka's villages have indeed helped to shift the balance in favor of peace.

On Peace Samadhi Day (*samadhi* means "conscious awareness"), Sarvodaya followers are ceremonially inaugurating the Link-Up program near an ancient bodhi tree. A thousand villages in the more devastated Tamil areas are paired with a thousand in the Sinhalese areas. The latter will bring materials and skilled and unskilled labor so that both parties can work together to rebuild homes, schools, wells, toilets, and places of worship destroyed in the fighting.

To symbolize this partnership, a village from each side has been selected, and after the temple bell is rung—at the precise moment when bells rang out across Sri Lanka—young people from each of these two villages come forward. They bear round trays of special festive food that they have prepared, and they feed each other. Then the plates are passed among the rest of us gathered here. Even if the cease-fire is sabotaged or the peace talks fail, I want

to remember that taste of sweet rice and coconut. It tells me that this is what we really want most of all: to stop the fighting and feed each other.

Over the last year and a half, Dr. A. T. Ariyaratne, Sarvodaya's founder, has convened public peace meditations to change the "psychosphere." These gatherings let ordinary people demonstrate and deepen their desire to end the war. Sarvodaya—the name means "everybody wakes up"—is a Buddhist-inspired community development movement active in over 12,000 villages in all parts of this island republic. Its campaign for peace, moving into high gear with the fragile but promising cease-fire, aims to restore not only inter-ethnic harmony, but also the basic necessities for economic well-being. These two are inseparable in Sarvodayan eyes.

Along with respect for the land and for the human spirit, Sarvodaya's peace plan includes development strategies for the dry zones, the most economically hard-pressed areas of Sri Lanka. It features locally generated energy as well as sustainable irrigation, soil renewal, and the community-controlled microcredit schemes that the movement has pioneered in the last decade. The aim of the movement is a "no poverty, no affluence" society, reducing the disparity between rich and poor brought about by late capitalism and corporate globalization. The priority placed on care for the land reminds me that "a safe and beautiful environment" is the very first of Sarvodaya's Basic Human Needs.

Peace does not happen with the signing of documents; the effects of war continue to fester far into the future, often to erupt again in violence. Sarvodayans point out that the seeds of Sri Lanka's civil war were planted 500 years ago with European colonization, and estimates that healing will require an equal amount of time. So the peace plan extends over the next 500 years: five years to put dry-zone development measures in place; ten years to resettle all the refugees; 50 years to achieve the lowest poverty rate in the world and abolish Sri Lanka's standing army. The vision continues beyond that. By 2100, Sri Lanka becomes "the first country to eliminate poverty, both economic and spiritual." By the year 2500, "Global climate warming may cause changes to Sri Lankan environment; but because of the history of working together over hundreds of years, these changes will not be disasters. In 500 years, people might be living on other planets; however, Sri Lanka will remain their image of Paradise on Earth."

I think of the tightrope walker who, to maintain her balance and move steadily forward, must raise her eyes and keep looking ahead. When we raise our eyes to look forward in our work for peace and justice, when we feel our

connections to future generations, we can remain steady and determined despite the immediate challenges we face. My friends in the Sarvodaya movement have shown that we ordinary humans are capable of that.

Joanna Macy is a scholar of Buddhism and author of several books, including *Coming Back to Life* (New Society, 1998) and a memoir, *Widening Circles* (New Society, 2000). This article appeared in the Summer 2002 issue of *YES!* and was adapted with permission from an article appearing in *EarthLight*, Spring 2002.

Building a New Force

MICHAEL NAGLER

When Israeli tanks rolled into Ramallah during "Operation Defensive Shield" last April, they met with a surprise: international volunteers had somehow gotten into the city and walked blithely past them, ignoring threats backed by gunshots fired over their heads, to enter the building where besieged Palestinian leader Yasser Arafat was trapped, thus discouraging further military action against him. This was an unusual event in the history of modern warfare. The press noticed. For a while, "human shields" made daily headlines: "Both television and newspapers [gave] a heroine's welcome to Sophia Deeg, a 50-year-old Munich teacher who acted as a human shield for Arafat at his Ramallah compound," reported the San Francisco *Chronicle* on May 2.

For a moment, the media gave a glimpse of a radical possibility: a different kind of force, a nonviolent army that could constitute an entirely new and creative response to conflict. Such a force is not a dream; an actual Nonviolent Peaceforce (NP) is being born. Nonviolent intervention has been going on—without benefit of media coverage—for some time. This new organization is poised to take it to a new stage by creating a 2,000-member professional corps, along with 4,000 reservists, 5,000 volunteers, and a research division, ready to respond wherever there is conflict around the globe.

NP's mission is not merely to end violence after it has already begun, but to prevent or dampen outbreaks of violent conflict before they escalate. The

Peaceforce would enter a conflict only after being invited, with the aim of creating the space for local groups to resolve their own disputes peacefully.

NP would draw its membership from throughout the globe, so that it could circumvent political divisions and visa problems. Its 2,000 professional peacekeepers would be paid, trained, and signed on for two-year contracts.

The Nonviolent Peaceforce began to take shape in 1999 when San Francisco-based civil rights and peace activist David Hartsough and veteran St. Paul community organizer Mel Duncan discovered each other at the Hague Peace Conference.

In three years the project, operating from offices in St. Paul and San Francisco, has garnered endorsements from seven Nobel Peace laureates, established bases in Europe and Asia, and built up a network of participants and potential volunteers from around the world, emphasizing the global South, in part to avoid the problem of 'peace imperialism'.

An international convening event took place in Delhi, India, November 28 through December 2, 2002. At this event, delegates elected an international governing committee to carry the dream further, and selected Sri Lanka as a pilot area for its first field effort, based on an in-depth study completed the year before.

Knowing that success depended on careful planning, Hartsough and Duncan decided that before the Peaceforce coalesced, they should conduct a feasibility study to document and glean strategy from the many small peace-team projects already working around the globe. What the study found was a 100-year history of nonviolent intervention that has intensified in the last 20 years, yielding a growing body of evidence that nonviolent intervention does work.

Nonviolent intervention is a recurrent vision among people who refuse to believe that humankind is condemned either to fight or stand by helplessly when violence rages. Though people no doubt have stepped in to break up fights as long as there have been fights (the Buddha is said to have defused a war over water this way, and Chinese philosopher Mo Tzu made a name for himself by doing this in the fifth century BCE) what is now called nonviolent intervention arose 100 years ago, in Mahatma Gandhi's great campaigns for Indian rights in South Africa. When Gandhi was not calling his Satyagraha volunteers "pilgrims," he often referred to them as nonviolent "soldiers."

Gandhi (who had served in two wars) realized that, while war itself is an unnecessary evil, there are some qualities of war that are not only positive but indispensable. Soldiers need courage, discipline, training, loyalty, and restraint. But nonviolent activists need these qualities even more. Why not turn the restless energies of men (and women) into different channels, creating a disciplined "army of peace"? They would use the same courage and sacrifice, but for the opposite purpose: instead of violence they would harness these qualities for nonviolence; instead of mobilizing what peace theorist Kenneth Boulding would later call "threat power," they would use it for "integrative power."

Since Gandhi's time and especially in the last two decades, various forms of nonviolent third-party intervention across borders have had dramatic successes in protecting life and reducing human rights abuses and destructive conflict all over the world. These interventions have taken a number of different forms.

One element is witnessing—being present as an observer, sharing information with the outside world, and demonstrating to all the parties involved that the world is watching. "My heart breaks," a Quaker volunteer in Hebron writes in *Peace Team News*, "as I recall the kindness we received from these gentle people, the smiles and the thanks that greeted us, the words of hope ... that we might let the world know of their suffering and despair."

The protected are not the only ones moved by this courageous kind of intervention. This story is told by volunteers who found their way into Jenin blocked by a large group of soldiers, according to the *Catholic Radical*: After some discussion back and forth, the commanding officer said to them, "You people have a lot of faith." One of them answered, "When the people of Israel fled to the Red Sea, they didn't even bring a boat, but God got them through." The officer paused awhile. Then he said, "Go back 100 meters and cut through the fields."

The mere presence of internationals changes the atmosphere of conflict, often defusing hatred. When they 'short-circuit' entrenched hostility in the way we've just seen, third parties can actually reawaken the humanity in people under arms. These people are voluntarily risking their own lives and safety to reflect, through their concern, the humanity of those who have become mere victims.

Elana Wesley, part of a team of internationals in the Balata refugee camp

in Palestine in June, describes her team's efforts: "As the Israeli forces made their way from house to house, knocking down joint walls between families, the internationals tried to explain to soldiers that the doors were open to adjoining rooms and apartments and there was no need to make holes in walls to gain access...The internationals *offered to walk in front of the soldiers* so they could enter through doors rather than destroying walls."

The phrase that I've emphasized illustrates one of the key principles of nonviolent intervention: non-partisanship. You are not there to protect one group from another, even when your actions do have that effect. You are trying not to be part of the political mix at all. You are there to protect peace, for everyone, and that means getting in the way of violence against anyone— as did the African-American woman from Michigan Peace Teams who covered a fallen Klansman with her own body when he was attacked by an anti-racist mob.

Another kind of nonviolent intervention is accompaniment. Peace Brigades International volunteers have successfully accompanied threatened human rights workers for 20 years now all over Central America, East Timor, Sri Lanka, and elsewhere. They monitor, and thus moderate or prevent, human rights abuses—and in the extreme they can even stand between armed groups to stop violence.

The latter kind of action—the real 'war stopper'— has captured the imagination of visionaries since Anglican minister Maude Roydon tried to raise an "army" of peacemakers to get between Chinese and invading Japanese forces in 1932. Unarmed groups within a society— the civilians who interposed themselves between government forces and the Polisario guerrillas in the Western Sahara in the 1970s, for example—have put themselves between hostile forces and stopped potentially disastrous conflicts. But the method has yet to be tested by third parties intervening on a large scale.

The largest peace teams right now are active in one of the places where the violence is worst—in Colombia. "Large," of course, means ridiculously small when compared to the kind of force needed for armed operations. Peace Brigades International's team in that country is all of 36 people, yet they are succeeding not only in protecting threatened human rights workers but also the fledgling peace communities in the north of the country.

It is the potency of such tiny efforts that inspires activists to dream of what a larger project might accomplish. If 36 people can shift the terms of conflict,

"What would it mean if there were 100 of us?" asks Donna Howard, who is furnishing protective accompaniment to a woman whose partner was recently assassinated in Guatemala. Howard is part of the team building the Nonviolent Peaceforce, which asks the far more ambitious question: What would it mean if the world had at its disposal thousands of trained nonviolent soldiers?

The new project, if it succeeds, will result in a worldwide peace service capable of intervening in a conflict or incipient conflict more quickly than the UN peacekeeping division and—more importantly—with a different kind of power from that of national militaries. While the US government insists there is no alternative to endless war, the Nonviolent Peaceforce is quietly attempting to institutionalize a proven alternative. If it succeeds, the world will have two kinds of standing army to choose from.

The NP study concludes that nonviolent intervention is humanity's greatest chance to mobilize civil society against the war system, and finally to bring it to an end. As long as the international community can think of nothing else to do but bomb someone to stop some conflict it deems intolerable, as long as societies know of no other way to defend themselves but to take up arms, war will be with us. But when they do come to know that there is actually an alternative, more and more people will demand that their governments choose it.

Recently, Kathy Kern, a long-term nonviolent volunteer with Christian Peacemaker Teams in Hebron, found herself shouting to an Israeli soldier who warned her (in an unmistakable American accent) not to try to rescue a woman and child trapped in a house that they had encircled with armored vehicles. "You are putting yourself in danger," the soldier warned. Kathy yelled back, "Everyone here is in danger." That gave him pause. Then he added, "Kathy, you are making a fool of yourself. You are turning this into a circus."

Hmm. This could be the best thing that ever happened to the war system.

Michael Nagler is professor emeritus of classics and comparative literature at the University of California, Berkeley, and co-founder of its Peace and Conflict Studies Program. He is the author of *Is There No Other Way? The Search for a Nonviolent Future,* which won an American Book Award. This article appeared in the Fall 2002 issue of *YES!*

Resources

Fellowship of Reconciliation, an interfaith peace group, promotes living in harmony with the Earth, diversity, and nonviolent conflict resolution.
PO Box 271, Nyack, NY 10960, 845/358-4601, www.forusa.org

Metta Center for Nonviolent Education promotes nonviolence through study circles, media initiatives and educational materials development.
2398 Bancroft Way, Berkeley, CA 94704, 510/549-3096, www.mettacenter.org

Minnesota Center Against Violence and Abuse offers curricula (grades 7-12 and 1-6) to study peace, conditioning, and ethics.
105 Peters Hall, 1404 Gortner Avenue, St. Paul, Minnesota 55108-6142
612/624-0721, www.mincava.umn.edu/papers/Book/

Nonviolence.Org provides news, commentary, and links to organizations for peace and nonviolence.
P.O. Box 38504, Philadelphia, Pennsylvania 19104
215/681-0783, www.nonviolence.org

Nonviolent PeaceForce is an international, intergenerational force trained in nonviolent intervention to be deployed in conflict situations.
801 Front Ave. St. Paul, MN 55103, www.nonviolentpeaceforce.org

Peace-Action works to abolish nuclear weapons and international weapons trade and promotes non-military solutions to international conflicts.
1819 H Street NW Suite 420, Washington, DC 20006
202/862-9740, www.peace-action.org

Peace Brigades International sends trained volunteers to accompany activists threatened by political violence.
428 8th St. SE, 2nd floor, Washington, DC 20003
202/544-3765, www.peacebrigades.org

The United Nations Educational, Scientific, and Cultural Organization (UNESCO) offers educational resources on The International Decade for a Culture of Peace and Nonviolence for the Children of the World (2001-2010, established by UN Resolution A/RES/53/25).
UN DCII Building, 2 UN Plaza, Office 900, New York, NY 10017
212/963-5978, www.unesco.org/iycp/

Books

Bearing Witness: A Zen Master's Lessons in Making Peace, by Bernard Glassman (Random House, 1999), offers teaching stories that illustrate ways of making peace. Each chapter focuses on an event or person and demonstrates how a vow of peace is put into practice.

Engaged Spirituality in an Age of Globalization, by Robert King (Continuum Publication Group, 2001), explores the convergence of the viewpoints of Thomas Merton and Thich Nhat Hanh and their impact on current thinking regarding spirituality and social action.

Is There No Other Way? The Search for a Nonviolent Future, by Michael Nagler (Berkeley Hills Books, 2000), outlines the legacy of nonviolence in the struggles against Nazism, racism, and ethnic conflicts and determines that nonviolence has proven its power against arms and social injustice.

Martin Luther King: The Inconvenient Hero, by Vincent Harding (Crisis Books, 1999), reflects on the forgotten legacy of King and the meaning of his life today, focusing particularly on the years after King's "I Have a Dream" speech, when King widened his message and his tactics.

Nonviolent Soldier of Islam, by Eknath Easwaran (Nilgiri Press, 1999), tells the life-story of Badshah Khan, Gandhi's Muslim coworker.

The Power of Nonviolence, by Howard Zinn (Beacon Press, 2002), a stirring anthology of writings about peace and nonviolence by authors from Buddha to Arundhati Roy, with an introduction by Howard Zinn about September 11 and the US response to the terrorist attacks.

For more titles, see:
www.nonviolentpeaceforce.org/Get_ready/reading_list.htm

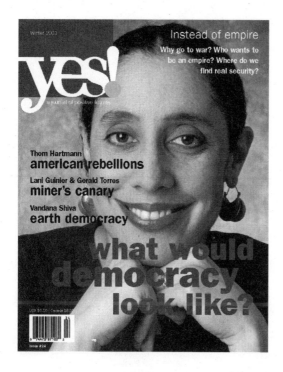

Want to change
the world?

Just say *YES!*

Subscribe to *YES!* magazine

Your independent voice for a just, sustainable, and compassionate world.

You are invited to become a new subscriber to *YES!* magazine. You'll receive four quarterly issues at the introductory price of $19, a $7 savings off the cover price.

Send in the enclosed card today! Already a subscriber? Pass the card along to your friends, or have them contact us at:

YES! A Journal of Positive Futures
PO Box 10818, Bainbridge Island, WA 98110-0818
Phone: 206/842-0216 Fax: 206/842-5208
Toll Free: 800/937-4451 Online: www.yesmagazine.org

Get Inspired.

Get Informed.

Get *YES!*

‖‖‖‖